BLINDED BY THE LIGHT

"Look what I found!" Geogee shouted. He waved over his head a red rod, swinging it around so that light flashed from its surface.

Jony made a grab for it. Their hands met on the surface of the rod. From its tip shot a beam so brilliant that Jony was temporarily blinded. He heard screams from the twins and the clatter of something metallic falling.

"Geogee—" somehow he managed to get out, "leave that thing alone!"

"I—I can't see, Jony..." Geogee's voice approached a scream. "Jony—Maba—"

"It's all right." Maba answered him. "This is me, Geogee. Take my hand. That—that thing. It...Jony," her voice trembled. "Where the light went...there just isn't anything! Jony, what happened?"

He blinked, his eyes were tearing, but he could see, as if through a watery haze. His first horrible fear was dulled. The red rod lay on the floor. He made a careful detour around it to reach the children. Maba had her arms about her twin, was hugging him close, but she was looking beyond him and Jony followed her line of sight.

Where the top row of squares had been piled upon a firm base of th̶ ̶f̶i̶l̶l̶ ̶t̶h̶e̶r̶e̶ ̶w̶a̶s̶—as Maba had reported—nothi̶n̶

What if Mab̶ ̶ ̶ ̶ ̶ ̶ ̶ ̶ ̶ ̶ ̶ ̶eam? Jony shuddered, ̶ ̶ ̶ ̶ ̶ ̶ ̶ ̶ ̶ ̶ ̶ ̶t the answer his imag̶

"We must ge̶t̶ ̶o̶u̶

BAEN BOOKS by ANDRE NORTON

THE IRON BREED

ANDRE NORTON

THE IRON BREED

This is a work of fiction. All the characters and events portrayed in this book are fictional, and any resemblance to real people or incidents is purely coincidental.

Iron Cage copyright © 1974 by Andre Norton. *Breed to Come* copyright © 1972 by Andre Norton.

A Baen Books Original

Baen Publishing Enterprises
P.O. Box 1403
Riverdale, NY 10471
www.baen.com

ISBN: 978-1-4767-3619-8

Cover art by Stephen Hickman

First Baen mass market paperback printing, January 2014

Distributed by Simon & Schuster
1230 Avenue of the Americas
New York, NY 10020

Pages by Joy Freeman (www.pagesbyjoy.com)
Printed in the United States of America

CONTENTS

IRON
CAGE

There was once a time when many animals, including man, needed each other to survive the onslaughts of raging elements in a hostile world. Their affinity must have been very deep, involving senses and abilities long lost.

We have a tendency to patronize animals, to limit their abilities, to compare adversely their physical forms, minds, and lives with our high estate. But animals live in realms of their own, realms totally different and far older than ours. They dwell within the earth, in jungles and desert, in seas and the skies. They possess senses, and extensions of senses, we have lost or never attained. They see sights we shall never see. They hear sounds we shall never hear. They respond to terrestrial and cosmic rhythms and cycles that we have never charted.

If man could remove hate and fear from his heart, then might this fundamental bond of affinity and affection bring beneficent cooperation between all the kingdoms of Life.

—Vincent and Margaret Gaddis
The Strange World of Animals and Pets

> PROLOGUE <

"What are you going to do with the cat?"

"Send her to the Humane Society. We certainly can't take her with us. And she's going to have kittens again."

"But what will Cathy—?"

"We've told her that we have found a good home for Bitsy. After all, they *do* find homes for some of them, don't they?"

"A female—and pregnant?"

"Well, there's nothing else to do. The Hawkins boy has promised to pick her up. There he is in the driveway now. He'll run her over to the Humane Society. Just don't let Cathy know. She gets entirely too emotional about animals. Really, I don't know what I am going to do with that child! I've made up my mind about one thing—no more pets! Luckily we'll be in the new apartment where they aren't allowed."

The black and white cat crouched in the carton into which she had been unceremoniously thrust an hour earlier. Her protesting yowls had brought no escape, any more than her frenzied scratching, which only

3

made the carton rock a little on the porch step. Fear possessed her now, though she could not understand the words muffled by the box, behind the screen door. She had been uneasy all morning, her time for kittening was very near. She must get *out,* find a safe place. Every instinct told her that; yet her utmost efforts had not brought freedom.

At the sound of the car pulling into the drive, she crouched even flatter. Then the box which held her was jerked up roughly, so she was shaken from side to side. Inside—She was inside the car. She yowled once again, despairingly, afraid, seeking the hands, the voice which always meant security and comfort. But there came no answer at all. In her nervous reaction she fouled the box with spray, which made her even more eager for freedom. The car was stopping.

"What's the matter with you, man? How come you're so late?"

"Got an errand to run for the Stansons—they're moving tomorrow. Got to take their old cat to the Humane Society and dump her off."

"The Humane Society? You know where that is? About five miles away from here. And we're late now! Go all that way just to dump a cat—man, you're crazy!"

"So? What do I do then, smart brain?"

"She in that box? Phew, she's stinking up the car, too. You'd better get rid of her fast if you plan to take that Henslow chick out tonight. Cat stink like that stays forever. I'll tell you what to do, dumbhead. You drive out a little way along the highway; there's a woods on the second turn that's a real dump. See, it's going to rain—and you want to make time if you're still planning on going to the game."

"I guess that's all right."

"It sure is. Get rid of that old, stinking cat and get back here, but quick. We've still got to meet those chicks, and they aren't the kind you keep waiting."

The cat whimpered. Those harsh voices were only a noise, meaning nothing. She was gasping now, the evil smell of the box making her sick—if she could only get out! Once more the car stopped, the box again caught up roughly. Thrust through an open window, it hit the ground hard, rolling down a slope to lie with the other illegally dumped trash. The cat, shaken, in pain, cried out again.

There came the sound of the car driving away— then nothing. Except the rain striking on the box. She fought once more for freedom with claws dragging down the carton side. Why was she here? Where was home? The rough handling had started her labor. She writhed and cried sharply in pain. There was no room! The box shook under the pummeling of a rising storm. One kitten had come. The cat nosed it once, but made no effort to lick it into life. It was dead. She fought now with new frenzy at the side of the carton, and, softened by the rain, the heavy cardboard began to give. The chance at freedom made her wild and she worked at the hole until she had torn open a doorway. Rain beat in upon her, soaking her fur, making her cry aloud again.

Instinct ruled her. She must find shelter, a place— before . . . before . . .

Crying still, she pulled out of the box, looked around. There was the massive pile of dumped litter. Not too far away a refrigerator lay on its side, the door ripped off. Toward this small hope of shelter the cat dragged herself. She was inside when the next kitten came, feebly alive. And then there were two more. She had found shelter, but food, drink—she was too tired, too beaten by fear and shock to try to hunt for those. She lay on her side and whimpered a little as she slept.

➤ ONE ◄

"This is the maun female? What will you do with her? She is heavy with young."

"Worthless for our purpose. She is mad, also. When we took her last young for experiments, she turned dangerous. We bred her to the younger male, but she fought him badly. Luckily he was mind-controlled and, so, useful in such cases."

"It is odd, the mind-controls do not work evenly. There are reports—"

"Do not speak of reports! They pile in the reader, and when does one have a chance to really sort through them? Now, with Lllayron ordering this early take-off, a goodly number of the experiments will never be carried through. This female—we cannot space with her—she would never deliver living young. Not that that is of much interest, since she is plainly a reject. To dispose of her is best."

Rutee crouched in the cage, hunched over, her arms protectively around her bulging abdomen. A baby—another baby in this hellish place! She wished she could kill herself and the child before it was born! Only there was no way. If you did not eat they tied you down and force-fed you with their shots. Just as they had made her have—Rutee tried to close her mind to memory.

She was not mind-controlled as were most of the other experimental livestock. Bron had not been either. That was why they had killed him right at the start. That—that *thing* they had used to father what she now carried... No, *that* she must *not* remember.

The aliens were probably discussing her. But not one of her species had ever heard an alien speak. Either they were telepathic or their range of communication was above or below the power of her human ear. She could sense, however, that they were concerned with her. And she was smart enough to know that some event beyond the regular lab procedure was close at hand. They had been doing a lot of packing, putting things in special containers and sealing them. Was what she suspected the truth? Were they preparing to space again? Then—what of the baby?

She curled into a tighter ball, remembering what had happened to Luci who had been caged with her for a while right after they had all been captured. Luci had been pregnant, too. And in space she had died. Rutee tried to think clearly.

Over the months—how long had she been here? There was no way of reckoning time. But it had been long enough for her to learn that somehow she differed from most of the others. When they turned that controller thing on her, she felt only a prickling, not the compulsion which apparently gripped her fellow victims. Jony, he had not either!

She turned her head a little, trying to see down the line of cages.

"Jony!" she called softly. "Are you there, Jony?"

One of her discoveries had been that the aliens did not or could not hear her voice any more than she could theirs. It had given her one little ray of hope.

Perhaps now was the time to make the final effort.

"Jony?" she called again.

"Rutee," he answered her. Then he was still there! Each period of waking time she always feared he would not be.

"Jony," she picked her words carefully. "I think that something is going to happen. Do you remember what I told you—about the locks of the cage?"

"I've already done it, Rutee. When they brought the eating bowl a little while ago, I did it!" There was excited triumph in his reply.

Rutee drew a deep breath. Jony was almost alarmingly bright sometimes; he seemed able to sense things quickly. For a seven-year-old he was unusual. But then, he was Bron's own son. Bron's and hers, born out of their love and belief in each other and a future they had thought they had, when they had been colonists on that planet they had named Ishtar. No, this was no time to remember—it was a time to act.

She studied the aliens searchingly.

Their physical strangeness was so far removed from the norm her people had always considered "human" that she had never been able to think of them as anything but devilish nightmares—even apart from the treatment they accorded their unfortunate "specimens." Towering on their spindly legs far over the tallest man she had ever seen, they had round pouchy bodies and heads which appeared to rest on their narrow shoulders without benefit of neck. Their mouths were gaping slits, their eyes protruded like goggling globes. Their entire greenish-yellow bodies were entirely hairless.

And their minds—Rutee shuddered. She could not deny them mental process superior to her own species. To these monsters her flesh and blood were only animals—to be used as such and discarded.

One was coming now to unfasten the clamps which held her cage in a line with the rest. They—they were taking her away? Jony—no, no!

Rutee wanted to beat on the bars, tear at them. However, better act as if she were cowed. She did not want them to bring a pressure stick, give her jolts of pain.

"Jony, they are moving my cage. I do not know what they are going to do with me." She tried to make her message matter-of-fact.

"They are going to put you in the dump place," Jony's words startled her. "But they will not!"

The dump place—where the dead and the useless disappeared! Rutee wanted to scream aloud her fear, though that would do no good.

"They won't do it!" Jony repeated. Perhaps he did sense all she felt at that time. He had those odd flashes of empathy. "Wait for me, Rutee!"

"Jony!" Now she was suddenly more afraid for him than she was for herself. "Don't try anything—don't let them hurt you."

"They won't. Just wait, Rutee."

The alien had her cage freed and was carrying it beside his giant's body down the aisle. She clung to the bars, trying not to be hurled from side to side. They were close to the dump door now. Rutee hoped death came quickly on the other side.

But, to her amazement, they passed that. After Jony's words she had been so certain of her fate that she was a little dazed as they went out the lab door, down a corridor, only able to understand that death, apparently, had been put off for a little while. She was still puzzled as they came into the open, down the ramp of the ship which towered far above any building she had ever seen.

It was when they were on their way down the ramp she caught sight of Jony. Not in another cage, but slipping along the floor, progressing by quick darts, a few feet forward at a time, and then freezing into immobility before he made another dash. Jony had indeed triggered his lock; he was free. The wonder and hope of that filled her for a long moment with an emotion close to joy.

Jony never understood how he knew things. It was as if answers just came into his head. But while Rutee had sensed that change was coming, he had known it for certain. This place (Rutee said it was a spaceship) was going away, up into the sky. And Rutee—the Big Ones were going to get rid of Rutee. Perhaps he could get free, reach her cage and open it from the outside. He had to!

Moments earlier when he had been sure of what was happening even as Rutee herself, he had balled up, his arms about his crooked knees, his chin resting on those same knees. Some time ago he had made his big discovery. Rutee had told him that he was not like the others, who did just what the Big Ones told them. Sometimes, if he tried very hard, he could make a Big One do just as he thought!

Now—now he must do that with the Big One who was standing in front of Rutee's cage. There was only one of the enemy, so he had a chance. Jony put to work all his power of concentration (which was such as would have astounded Rutee if she had known) into a single thought. Rutee—must—not—go—in—the—dump—place. Rutee—must—NOT—

He was startled out of that concentration by Rutee's call. However, after he had answered, his thoughts once more centered only on the Big One and Rutee's cage.

That was loose now, grasped in a single hand where the six digits were all small, boneless tentacles, yet with a power of grip his own five fingers could never possess. Jony thought—

The door to the dump place, the Big One had passed it! Jony unrolled in an instant, was out of his cage, clambering down the wire of the empty one below, making the last drop to the floor. Then he moved in small rushes from one hiding place he marked out ahead to the next. He reached the ramp to see the Big One with Rutee's cage stamping down ahead of him. Jony drew a deep breath and ran full speed. He flashed past the Big One, heading on into the open world beyond, expecting every moment that one of those great hands would reach from above, wrap its tentacles about him, take him prisoner again.

But, fear-ridden though he was, he turned when he was aware of cover over him. Throwing himself flat, he rolled back into the dim shadow of a towering bush. Once in that shadow, Jony drew several gasping breaths, hardly daring to believe he was still free. Then, resolutely, he wriggled forward to peer back at the only place he had ever known as a shelter.

He could see only a bit of it, the ramp, the hatch from which it sprang, then the rest towering up and up so it was hidden beyond his range of sight. The Big One had paused at the foot of the ramp. Jony sensed his bewilderment.

Once more Jony concentrated. The cage—put it over there.

Fiercely he aimed that thought at the enemy. There was still a feedback of confusion from the alien. However, he *was* moving forward away from the ramp, the cage in his hand.

Then the Big One stiffened, glancing back at the ramp as if he had been called by someone at its head. Jony shivered. There was no way of contacting the other now—he would return to the ship with Rutee and—

Only the alien did not. At least he did not take the cage. Instead he threw it from him, went pounding back up the ramp. Even as he reached the hatch, it began to close and the ramp was jerked in. The Big One was inside as the ship sealed itself.

Rutee—the cage—Jony scrambled from his hiding hole, fought his way through brush which lashed his bare body, leaving long, smarting scratches.

"Rutee!" He cried aloud. Then his voice was swallowed up in a thunderous rumble of sound, so terrible he crouched against the side of a huge tree, his hands flying to his ears to keep out that deafening explosion of noise. There was a wind beating in to follow. Jony tried to make himself even smaller. Could he have dug his way into the root-bound ground beneath him he would have gladly done so.

For moments he only endured; his fear, filling all his mind, sent his body into convulsive shivering. He whimpered.

The wind died and the sound was gone. He took his hands from his ears, gulped in air. Tears streaked his scratched face. Still he shivered. It was cold here. And dark—the gloom in the brush was thick as it had never been in the cage room which was all he could remember.

"Rutee?" her name was a hissed whisper. Somehow he could not force his dry lips to make that any louder. He wanted Rutee! He must find her!

Blundering blindly on, Jony tunneled away through brush, twice coming up against growth which resisted his passage. He staggered along beside it until he could find some way to get through. His head was whirling and he could not think; he only knew that he must find Rutee!

The cage had arched through the air when the alien had thrown it. Rutee had had a moment or two of panic. Then she was shaken and bruised as her prison landed on a wall of brush, its weight bearing down the vegetation that acted as a brake for its descent. The smashing fall she had expected was eased by so much. Perhaps that had saved her life—for now.

She lay on the floor, broken branches spearing at her through the heavy wire mesh, threatening her. Both hands were pressed to her belly. Pain—the child—it must be coming. She was trapped in here...

She had a few moments to endure that fresh terror before the world went mad with sound. Then came a blast of wind. Only because she was lying on her side facing in the right direction did she see the rise of the ship which had been her prison. And that only briefly, for with the fantastic speed of the alien ships it vanished.

Jony—she had seen him run down the ramp; he had reached the outer world. "Jony," she whispered his name feebly, moaning as pain bore down upon her again relentlessly with an agony which filled the whole world for an endless moment.

When the thrust subsided Rutee moved, sat up. She crawled to the door of the cage, working her hands through the mesh to try to reach the latch, though she knew of old such action was useless. She was trapped as securely here as she had been in the lab. Only that stubborn will to live which had possessed her ever since her capture kept her fumbling away as best she could.

At length the pain hit again. She groveled and wept, hating herself for her own weakness. Jony—where was Jony? It was getting much darker; clouds were gathering. Now rain began, and the chill of those pelting drops set her shivering.

Summoning all her strength as the pain ebbed again, Rutee screamed aloud into the storm:

"Jony!"

Her only answer was another gust of cold rain beating in upon her. She was so cold...cold...Never before could she remember being so cold. There should be clothing to put on, heat—protection against this cold. There had been once—when, where? Rutee wept. Her head hurt when she tried to remember. She was cold and she hurt—she needed to get to where it was warm, she must because...because...She could

not remember the reason for that either, as pain came
again to fill every inch of her with torment.

But Jony had heard that scream, even through the
fury of the storm. He began to think again, stopped
just running mindlessly seeking without a guide.
Purposefully he turned, breaking a way to the right,
refusing to accept the brush and the soaking vegetation as a barrier.

Rutee was ahead, somewhere. He must find Rutee.
He concentrated on that one thought with the same
intensity of purpose which had made the Big One do
what *he* wished and not throw Rutee into the dump
place. Mud plastered him almost knee high and his
shivering never stopped. This was the first time in his
life he had ever been Outside. But he did not even
look around him with faint curiosity. All his will was
directed toward one end: finding Rutee. She needed
him. The wave of her need was so strong that it was
like a pain, though he could not have put it into
words; he could only feel it.

Twice he stopped short, his hands flying to his
head, as they had by instinct tried to close his ears to
the blast of the ship's lifting. There were—thoughts—
feelings . . . Only these had nothing to do with Rutee.
They were as strange as those he sometimes touched
when the Big Ones gathered. At first he crept into
the brush again, almost sure that one of the enemy
hunted. But there was a difference . . . No, no Big
One had come after him; the ship was safely gone.

The next time, and the next, that Jony felt the touch
which he could not explain, he doggedly refused to
think about it. He must hold Rutee in his mind, or
he would never find her in this wild place.

Jony staggered, his bruised hand out to a tree trunk in support.

Rutee! She was near and she hurt! She hurt so bad, Jony wanted to double up, as his nerves made instant sympathetic response. He had to wait for what seemed a long time, crying a little, his breath coming in harsh gasps which he felt but could not hear. Her pain had eased; he could go on.

He came to where even through the darkness of the storm he could see the bulk of the cage. It was not quite at ground level, being held up by a mass of crushed foliage and branches. Rutee was only a pale, small huddle within it. Jony knew he could open the lock—if he could reach it. Only that was well above his head, for as he neared the place he realized that the bottom of the cage itself was above him.

Somehow he would have to climb up over all the brush and the wire netting.

Twice he jumped, caught branches, teetered on rain-wet footing, and was spilled painfully, when they gave under his weight, slight as it was. But his determination never faltered; he only tried again. There was a deep, bleeding furrow down his leg where a splintered branch had gouged. And his arms and shoulders ached with the strain he put on them as he strove to pull up higher.

At last he worked his way up until he could catch at the wire. There he clung, speechless, caught in a spasm of the pain which radiated from Rutee, hanging on desperately because he must, until he dared move again. Too, as he climbed toward the locking device, his weight pulled the cage forward. That it might crash forward to crush him beneath it was not in Jony's thoughts now; he had only room for one thing: the belief that he must reach the lock—get Rutee out.

He heard her cries, and then his hand closed on the fastening, which she had been unable to touch. It went this way... One-handed, Jony held to his perch, flattened against the wire as the cage trembled. Yes—now *this* way!

Through the storm's sounds he could not hear the faint click of the released device. However, his weight against the door caused it to swing open and out. Jony dangled by one hand for a heart-thumping instant. Then his toes, his feet found anchorage on the wires; his two arms wrapped in and around it. Only the cage was tipping more and more in his direction.

Fear froze him where he was, aware at last that all might crash down. Rutee was moving, crawling to the very edge of the doorway on her hands and knees.

She had been only half-aware of Jony's coming. But, after her last pain had ebbed, she knew at once his danger. He had paid no attention to her orders to get down and away, perhaps he never even heard them. Now he clung as if plastered to the door, suspended over a dark drop she did not know the extent of. She had now, not only to escape herself, but perhaps save Jony.

Cautiously she lowered her clumsy body half over the edge of the tilting cage, groping with her legs, her feet, for some means of support. Twice she kicked against the branches, but these gave too easily to pressure; she dared not trust her weight to such. A third time her right foot scraped painfully along something horizontal and then thumped home, with a jar that brought an agonized moan from her, on a surface which did not slip away or sway as she dared exert more pressure.

She must move now. The cage was certainly going to slide forward, and, if she remained where she was, it might mean that both she and Jony would be crushed. There was a lull in the rising of the wind, though the rain was still steady. Her first attempt at speech was a hoarse croak, but she tried again.

"Move, Jony, to the left." It was so hard to think. Her mind seemed all fuzzy as it had when the aliens had experimented with her that first time. And she dared not linger where she was to see if Jony heard and obeyed. Her weight and his, both at the forepart of the cage, was pulling it out and down.

Now she had both her feet on that firm support; and she allowed her grasp on the cage itself to loosen, as she dropped one hand and the other to the unseen sturdy point she had found. When her grip on that was sure, she dared to look up.

Jony moved! He had dropped down to the bottom edge of the cage door, was feeling for footholds below. She wondered if she could reach him, but was sure she could not. Not when, as her pains hit once more, she could only cling with a death-tight grip to her own hold.

The cage was going; Jony knew it. He allowed his hold on the wire to loosen and, as he slipped, grabbed desperately. A slime of mashed leaves made the handfuls he grasped slippery and treacherous. Finally he thudded into a mass which swayed but did not spill him over. The cage fell, and Jony had all he could do to keep his small hold from being torn away by the resulting flailing of the broken brush.

He was shaking so hard now, not only from the chill of the beating rain, but also from the narrow margin of his escape, that he dared not move. But he screamed as something closed tightly about his ankle.

Just before he kicked out wildly and disastrously to free himself he heard Rutee: "Jony!"

With a cry he lowered himself, felt her chill flesh against his as she held him tightly to her. They were closer than they had been for a long time. Close—and safe! He said her name over and over, burrowing his head against her shoulder.

But Rutee was not the same—she was hurt. Even as he clung to her, her body jerked and she cried out. He could again feel her pain.

"Rutee!" Fear was so strong in Jony it was as if he could taste it, a bitter taste in his mouth. "Rutee, you are hurt!"

"I—I must find a place, Jony—a safe place." Her voice came in small spurts of words. "Soon—Jony— please—soon . . ."

But it was dark. And where were there any safe places in this *Outside?* Jony knew about the Outside, but only because Rutee had told him before the Big Ones had pulled him away from her long ago and put him in a cage by himself. The strangeness of Outside itself began to impress him as it had not when he had been so intent on finding Rutee.

"Jony—" Rutee's arm about his shoulders was so convulsively tight it hurt, but he did not fight against her hold. "You—you will have to help—help me—"

"Yes. We have to climb down, Rutee. It's hard . . ."

Jony could never remember the details of that descent. That they made it at all, he realized long afterwards, was a wonder. Even when they stood together on the muddy ground they were not safe. It was so dark that any distance away there were only thick shadows. Also they had to go slowly because Rutee hurt so. When those pains came, she was forced to stop and wait. The second time that happened Jony held her hand between his two.

"Rutee—let me go over there. You wait here. Maybe I can find a safe place..."

"No..."

However, Jony broke her attempt to hold him and ran across a small open space to the shadow he had chosen. He did not know just why he had picked that particular direction, but it seemed of utmost importance.

In the dusk he blundered into a dry pocket. Sometime in the far past a very giant among trees had fallen here. Its upended mass of roots towered skyward; and the cavity which held those was a deep hollow over which vines had crawled and intertwined to enmesh some nearby saplings, forming a roof, which, while not entirely waterproof, kept the worst of the wind and rain away. Drifted into the hollow was a mat of leaves, deep with numerous years of accumulation. Jony's feet sank almost ankle deep in their softness, as he explored swiftly with both hand and eye.

Rutee could come here; he would bring her. And... he was already running back to where she stood as a pale figure in the dusk, to catch her hand.

"Come, Rutee—come..." He led, half-supported her with all the wiry strength of his small body, toward the rude nest he had found.

> TWO <

Rutee lay moaning on the leaves. Jony had tried to heap them up over her body, to keep her warmer. But she shoved them off, her swollen body twisting with each new pain. Jony crouched beside her, not knowing what he could do. Rutee—Rutee was hurting! He needed to help her, only he did not know how.

Twice he crawled to the edge of their poor shelter, gazed out into the dusk and the rain. There was no help to be found there. Only Rutee was hurting—bad! He could sense her pain in his own self.

Rutee was caught up in that world of agony. She no longer was aware of Jony, of where she lay, of anything but the pain which filled her tormented body.

Jony began to cry a little. He wanted to strike out—to hurt someone—something—as Rutee hurt. The Big Ones—they had done this! A small, cold seed of hatred lodged deep in him and took root in that moment of despair. Let the Big Ones come hunting them—just let them! Jony's hand closed upon a large stone, his fingers curled about it as he jerked it free from the leaves and the earth. He clutched the crude weapon to him, in his mind seeing the stone fly from his hand, strike full into the ugly face of a Big One—smash—smash—smash!

Yet that trick of mind which had set him apart from the other young, the mind-controlled, also told him that he would fail in any such attempt. A Big One could crush him between wriggling fingers so there was nothing left at all.

"Rutee!" He leaned closer to her, called pleadingly, "Please, Rutee—"

A moan was his only answer. He had to do something—he had to! Jony crawled out into the open, unable to listen any more, his arm crooked over his eyes as if so he could erase the sight of Rutee which was burned into his mind.

He turned his face up into the rain and the wind, knowing in one part of him there was no one there to listen, to help, but saying because he had to: "Please...help Rutee...please!"

Awareness—Jony spun around. In the dark he could not see, but he knew. Knew that someone, something, was back there in the shadows, watching—listening. But the mind he sensed was not that of a Big One. No, Jony scowled in perplexity for he could not understand the thought he had touched. This was as if something had flashed across his sight for a single instant and then was gone. He was certain of only one thing: whatever witnessed his misery did not mean him harm.

Drawing a deep breath, Jony made himself take one step and then two toward that gathering of shadows.

"You—please—can you help?" he spoke his plea

aloud. For a moment or two he thought that the watcher was gone, had melted back into the unknown, for he could no longer pick up the sensation of a presence.

Then there was movement as a shape shambled forward. Though the light was poor Jony could see it was big (not as large as one of the Big Ones but still perhaps twice his own size). He caught his lower lip between his teeth and stood his ground. It—first it had wondered about him, he knew that, and now it was coming because it wanted to...

It wanted to help!

Jony was as sure of that as he was of his own misery or Rutee's pain.

"Please," he said uncertainly—perhaps it could not hear him, nor understand his words if it did. There was a sense of good will which enveloped him as it moved to stand—or hunker—directly before him.

No, this was not a Big One. In no way did the creature resemble those hated enemies. It had a round-ish body covered with thick fur, the color marbled with strange patches of light and dark, so that Jony had to watch very carefully or it simply faded back to become a part of the brush again. The four limbs were thick and sturdy. The stranger squatted on the back two, the front ones dangling over its rounded belly. Those forefeet ended in paws which were oddly handlike in outline, though the hairless skin on them was very dark. A round head crowned wide shoulders, with a short, thick neck between. The face was a muzzle, ending in a button of a nose. But the eyes above that were very large and luminous in the dark as they now regarded Jony.

He ventured to move, reaching out one of his own hands to touch the stranger on the forearm. The fur beneath his fingers was damp but very soft. Jony had no fear now; rather a feeling that help had come. He closed his hold on that limb, though his small hand could not span it. But he could feel the muscles strong and hard under the furred skin.

"Rutee?" he said.

There was a queer whining noise from the other—not words—but the sound did carry a message into Jony's mind. Yes, this was help! He turned back to the hollow. The strange creature arose on its hind legs and shuffled along, towering well above the boy. One of the dark-skinned hands rested on Jony's shoulder. And he found the weight vastly comforting.

But there was so little room within the poor shelter Jony had found he had to edge against the rotting roots at the far end so that the stranger could crowd in. The round head swung low, the muzzle nearly touching Rutee, as the creature moved its nose slowly along the woman's contorted body.

"Jony?" Rutee lay with her eyes wide open, but she did not even try to see the boy. Nor when her gaze met that of the sniffing stranger, did she show any surprise. Her arm flailed out. Jony caught her wrist, held tightly, quivering himself as her pain fed into his own body.

The beast was doing something with its black paw-hands, Jony was not sure what. His faith in its help was blind but continued. Rutee shrieked, the sound she made tearing at his head, his mind. He cried out in turn and closed his eyes. He would have put his hands over his ears, but her hold had turned to meet his and was merciless.

Then came another sound—a weak, wailing cry! Jony, astounded, dared to look again. The black paw-hands held the struggling thing which was making that noise. Round head dropped, the nose sniffed carefully along what the creature held as if it needed scent, more than sight, for this matter of importance. Then it held out to Jony the squirming thing. Rutee's hand had dropped away. She lay breathing in long hard gasps.

Against his will Jony took the baby. The stranger had turned back swiftly to Rutee, was again sniffing. Again Rutee screamed weakly, her body jerking.

For the second time the paw-hands held another baby, and the nose sniffed. But this time a long tongue came out between strong teeth. Jony was jolted—it was going to eat—! Before his protest formed in full, he saw that the tongue was washing the baby, thoroughly, from head to foot. Another sniffing examination followed before the child the stranger held was placed gently down on the leaves beside Rutee.

Jony had hardly been aware of the baby in his own hands though that was still crying, squirming against his briar-scratched skin. The paw-hands reached out and he surrendered the baby, to see it washed in turn and then laid down.

Darkness gathered in the hollow, but not so much that Jony could not see Rutee's eyes were closed. Her head had fallen to one side. Frantically he aimed a thought in the way which had been instinctive for him ever since he could remember. No—there was no blankness there. Rutee was alive!

The babies lay against her body, one on either side as the stranger had so carefully placed them. Now the paw-hands raked through the leaves, drawing up bunches of them to place across both Rutee and the twins. Jony could understand. It was so cold, and some of the rain still sifted in. Rutee, the babies needed protection. He set to work on his side, hunting the driest handfuls to spread over the unconscious woman.

He sensed the approval of the stranger. This was right. When Rutee and the babies were covered, except for their faces, the furred one backed away.

"No!" Jony could not bear to be left alone. What if Rutee were sick—hurt again? And the babies—he did not know what to do for the babies! He was frantic in his need to keep the stranger with them.

Paw-hands fell on his shoulders, holding him very still, while those great luminous eyes stared straight into his. Jony wanted to turn his head, to avoid that level gaze, because in his head there was a swaying feeling as if he could not catch hold of an important thought, but only touch the edge of it fleetingly.

He calmed down. There was a purpose in the creature's going, something important to be done. Jony nodded as quickly as if he had been reassured in words familiar to him. He would not be alone except for a little. He had asked for help, there would be help.

Jony considered the thought of help. He had never asked for it since he had been taken forcibly from Rutee's cage and put by himself. Long before that had been done he had known, and Rutee had made it clear to him, that even those who were of his own kind, or at least looked like him, must never be trusted. They thought only the thoughts the Big Ones allowed them. Rutee was not like them, and he was not. He did not know why, only that the fact was important, Rutee had impressed on him. Never to be one who the Big Ones could use. This had been the main lesson of his childhood.

His world had been the cages and what he could see of the lab beyond their walls. However, Rutee had told of Outside. She had once lived Outside, before the Big Ones had come to put her and the others in cages. Jony now began to think back, as he had so many times, on what Rutee had taught him. When they had put him in a cage by himself, he had made himself remember all he could of what Rutee had said.

They were small and weak, and the Big Ones had ways of hurting and forcing them to be what the Big Ones wanted. But it had not been so with Rutee, or with Bron. Of course he could not remember Bron, though Rutee had talked of him so much that Jony sometimes believed he could.

Rutee, and Bron, and many people (far more than still lingered in the cages of the Big Ones) had lived Outside. Then the Big Ones had come. They puffed the smell-stuff which made people go to sleep, and picked up those they wanted. Rutee never knew what had happened to the rest of her people.

Afterwards the Big Ones had used what Rutee called the controllers on their prisoners. Some—Bron was one of those—fought, and he had been put into the dump place. But most of the others became just what the Big Ones wanted after they were controlled.

Some were taken out of their cages while the Big Ones did horrible things to them. Mostly those ended in the dump place when the Big Ones were finished. But young ones such as Jony, and some of those like Rutee, they kept. To the Big Ones they were not people; they were things, just to use.

Rutee had told him over and over that he must never let them use him, that he was not a *thing*. He was Jony and there was no one else exactly like him, just as there was no one exactly like Rutee. Jony moved now, remembering that, looking more closely at the twins.

Their small, damp, wrinkled faces did not look like Rutee's. And there were two of them. Did that mean they *were* alike? Rutee's head turned restlessly on the leaves and Jony became instantly alert.

"Water—" she said faintly, but she did not open her eyes.

Water? There was plenty falling outside the hollow, but Jony did not see how he was going to bring any in. However, he crept out, noticing as he did so, that it seemed to be lightening, but maybe that was only in contrast to the dusk of the hollow. Water?

He looked about him. Not too far away was a plant with big leaves, each one the width of Jony's hand or more. He twisted one of them loose, holding it with upcurved edges where a trickle of rain poured off a vine stem. When he had all he could gather without spilling, he edged carefully in and raised Rutee's head a little, putting the tip of the leaf to her lips so the scant burden of moisture ran into her mouth. She swallowed desperately, and he made the trip again and again.

The last time he returned her eyes were open and looked at him as if she saw him, Jony.

"Jony?"

"Drink." He held the leaf for her. As she tried to raise her head higher, one of the babies whimpered. Startled, she looked down at its flushed face.

"Baby!" She raised her hand slowly, touched fingertip to the tiny cheek.

Jony jerked back, dropping the leaf. He did not know just why, but he felt lost when he saw the way Rutee looked at the newcomer. Rutee—she was the bigger part of Jony's life, she always had been. Now there were the two babies...

"You got two," he said harshly. "Two babies!"

Rutee looked surprised as her gaze followed his gesture to the other side.

"Two—?" she repeated wonderingly. "But, Jony—how...?"

"It was the—the good thing who came—" he answered in a rush of words, content again that Rutee was now looking straight at him and not at either of those intruders. "It came and—and helped..." He was not sure just *what* the stranger had done, only that it had been there, licked the babies, bedding them down at last beside Rutee.

"The good thing?" she repeated his words again. "What do you mean, Jony?"

He used what words he could to describe the half-seen furred creature who had answered his cry for help.

"I don't understand," Rutee said when he had done. "You are sure, Jony, this isn't just something you thought about? Oh, Jony, what—who—could it have been? And—Jony!" Her eyes were big, frightened. She was no longer looking at Jony, but over his shoulder. A twitch of fear of the unknown arose in him to answer. He screwed his head far enough around to see outside.

The stranger was back, crouched down, peering in at them.

"It's the one, Rutee—the one who came to help!" Jony's fear was gone the moment he sighted those shining eyes.

However, the woman watched the creature warily. Slowly she began to sense the feeling it brought with it: comfort, help. And she, who had learned through terror, horror, and continued fear, to look upon the whole world as a potential enemy, relaxed. Rutee did not know what—who—this being was, but she was sure within her that the creature meant her and the children no harm, quite the reverse. Now she lay back weakly in her nest of leaves and left action to it.

Though its body seemed clumsy, perhaps because of its solid bulk, it moved briskly. But it did not try to insert itself into their refuge this time; instead, it dropped a mass which it had carried looped in one forearm close to its breast, shoving it at Jony.

Obedient to its manifest signal, the boy pulled the offering to him. Branches had been broken, leaving sharp, bark-peeled ends. But still clinging to those boughs were a number of bright green balls. The creature snapped a single one of those from the stem and put it into its gaping mouth. The meaning was plain: this was food.

Food to Jony had always been the squares of dull brown substance which the Big Ones had dropped into the feeding slot of his cage at regular intervals. Now, at the sight of the creature's eating, he was immediately aware that he was hungry. In fact his hunger was an ache which was close to pain. He grabbed at the nearest of the balls for himself.

"No, Jony!" Rutee protested. How could she make him understand that what might be meat or drink to an alien whose world this was, could in turn be deadly poison to someone from another planet? She should have warned him, she should have...

The globe was already in Jony's mouth. He bit down hard. A little juice dribbled from between his lips to glisten on his grimy chin. He swallowed before she could snatch it from him.

"Rutee—" he beamed at her. "Good! Better than cage food. Good!"

He was breaking balls recklessly from the branches, and those in one hand he forced upon her.

"Eat, Rutee!"

The woman looked longingly at the fruit. It had been a long time since she had tasted anything but the dry and flavorless rations which had kept her alive but had no savor in them. Now she resigned herself. There would be no more of those cakes given to the caged ones; the ship had taken off and they were here now. Either they could live on native food or they would starve. And she still had enough desire to live to make her take one of the fruits from Jony and bite into it slowly.

Sweet, and full of moisture which was even better for her dry mouth than the rainwater Jony had brought her. This was like—like what...Her mind summoned up dim memories of that life long ago. No, she could find nothing there to compare this to. The fruit appeared to have no pit or seed, was all edible. She swallowed and reached for more, the need in her very great.

Together she and Jony cleaned the branches of all the fruit. It was only when Rutee was sure that the last globe was gone she remembered the giver. The strange, heavy-looking creature still squatted there watching them. The rain had stopped; there was further lightening of the world without.

Jony straightened out one leg and gave a little gasp. Rutee saw the raw gouge in his skin; blood stood out in new drops when he moved.

"Jony—" She tried to lever herself up on her hands from out of the leaves. As she moved one of the babies wailed loudly. Rutee found the world swinging unsteadily around her dazed head.

She saw a large hand (or was it closer to a paw?) reach within their small shelter. The hand closed firmly about Jony's ankle and drew him away from her side.

The boy did not fight. Even when he lay across the outstretched arm of the creature, Jony had no fear. Nor did he experience the instant revulsion which had always arisen in him when he had been handled by the slimy hands of the Big Ones. He did not struggle as the stranger straightened out his leg, sniffed along the broken flesh as it had along Rutee's body.

But he was surprised as that long tongue came forth and touched the torn skin, rasped over his wound. Jony was held firmly so that his start did not send him rolling away, but kept him just the proper distance from the probing tongue. As the creature had earlier licked the babies from head to foot, so now it washed the gouge. Nor was Jony released at once when the other raised its head, snapped its tongue back between its jaws.

Instead he was held against a broad, furry chest, one massive arm both cradling and restraining him, as the stranger got to its feet, strode away from the tree shelter. Jony squirmed and would have fought then, for his freedom, to return to Rutee. But there was no way he could break the grip which held him prisoner.

They had not gone far before the stranger paused, reaching out with its free hand to tear up from the ground a long-leafed plant. The muzzle above Jony's head opened; teeth worried the top-most leaves free of their parent stem, chomped away.

Jony smelled a queer scent—saw a little dribble of juice at the corners of the full lips. Then the creature spat what it chewed into the palm of its hand as a thick glob of paste.

With the tip of its tongue it prodded what it held, seemed satisfied. Swiftly it applied the mass to the tear on Jony's skin. The boy tried to evade the plastering, for the stuff stung fiercely. But the stranger held him tightly until there was a thick smear covering the whole of the gouge. Now the stinging subsided, and with it vanished the smarting pain of which Jony had been only half-aware during his anxiety over Rutee.

"Jony—Jony—what has that thing done!" Rutee had somehow reached the edge of the shelter, was looking up and out, her face very pale under the leaf dust. "Jony—!"

"It's all right," he roused to reassure her. "The good one just put some chewed leaves on my leg. See." He moved a little so he could show the plastered leg. "It hurt a little, just at first, but it is all right now."

Gently the stranger lowered Jony to the ground. He limped a little when he walked, yes, but the wound no longer smarted. Now he turned around, still favoring his leg, and looked all the way up to the muzzled face above him.

"Thank you . . ." Because words probably did not

mean anything to the stranger, Jony concentrated, as
fiercely as he had when he had saved Rutee from the
dump place, on making his gratitude known.

Once he was sure that thought had touched thought,
if very fleetingly, and that the stranger did understand. Then one of the babies began crying in loud
wails. Rutee drew back into her shelter, took them
both up, one in each arm, and held them close to
her, crooning softly until the crying died down into a
small whimpering. Jony watched. Once more his faint
resentment of Rutee's preoccupation with the little
ones troubled him. Though he did not know why he
wished these two interlopers gone.

There was a warm touch on his shoulder. He looked
around. It seemed to him that the muzzle wore a smile,
if those thick lips could ever move in a way to imitate
his. Jony grinned and reached out to clasp one of the
paw-hands, which closed very tight and protectively
around his own much smaller and weaker fist.

> THREE <

Sunlight struck bright on the surface of the stream which frothed from the edge of the small falls on through the narrow valley. The same steady beams heated the rocks, drying quickly any spatter of spray that had reached this point. Jony lay belly down, his head propped on arms folded before him so he could watch where Maba and Geogee were diving back and forth under the falling water, shrieking at each other worse than a couple of vor birds.

They were not alone. Two of the People cublings splashed around them. But Huuf and Uga were more intent on a little fishing, trying to lever water-dwelling tidbits out from under streambed stones.

In the brilliant sunlight the patchy coloring of the People's fur, which gave them such good concealment in the brush, looked ragged. There was no pattern to the splotches of light and dark which dappled their stocky bodies. The fur of all patches was a green-yellow but in such a diversity of shades as to make their outlines almost indiscernible even here in the open. Only on their round heads was the color laid in an even design of light on the muzzle, dark about their large eyes.

Jony and the twins were not so well provided with body covering, to his resentment and disgust. He did wear a kilt of drab, coarse stuff which was dabbled with berry and vine juice to resemble the People's shading. But, compared to the soft fur of his companions, he considered it highly inadequate, which it was.

Though he lay at ease, his mind was alert on sentry duty. For more seasons than he could now count, for he had never tried to keep track, they had shared the life of the People. Formidable as they were (even a second season cub could best Jony in a friendly strength-match) they had their enemies, also. And Jony had early discovered that that inner sense of his was, in its way, a more accurate warning than any the People possessed.

He tried now to count how many seasons it had been since Rutee had died of the coughing sickness. She had never been strong, Jony realized now, since the birth of the twins. But she had held on to life until they were almost as old as Jony had been when they had escaped from the Big Ones. In this time he had grown taller, taller than Rutee, nearly as tall as Voak who headed this clan of the People. It had been Voak's mate, Yaa, who had found them, saved Rutee and the babies, brought them back to be of the clan. When Rutee left them, Yaa had taken over the raising of Maba and Geogee as if they were her own cublings.

Jony sent out a questing thought. He detected nothing—save that which should be on wing or on paw, going about the normal business of living. He allowed his mind a chance to deal with his own present burning desire: further exploration.

The clan had their established hunting grounds. Mainly the People were vegetarians, with a liking for a water creature now and then, or thumb-thick grubs which could be found in the rotted wood of certain fallen trees. But last season there had been a drought in the section held loosely by Voak's and Yaa's kin. A drying land had forced them to move away into the hills, beyond which rose those mountains that held up the sky bowl.

Grumbling and snorting, they had come. The People were a settled lot who distrusted and disliked change. But Jony had welcomed the move. There was something which ever urged him on, a curiosity which was as much a part of him as the clubbed braid of his dark hair, his sun-browned skin. He wanted always to know what lay a little farther on.

During that journey they had come across a thing which astounded Jony by its very being. It was like the stream below, save it was not formed of water, but stone (or something as hard as the rock about Jony now). However, in the likeness of a stream, it ran as a narrow length from the lowlands up toward the hills. The top of it was uniformly smooth, though in places earth had drifted across its surface, even as sand bars pushed at the water of the stream.

Jony had run along that surface for a space, finding excitement in being able to move so quickly without stone or brush to impede his going. In the sign language of the People (Jony and his kind could not reproduce their grunting speech), he had tried to ask questions about this strange river of rock. He had been with Trush that day. Trush had been Yaa's cubling when she had come to Rutee's aid.

To Jony's vast surprise, Trush had turned away his head, started determinedly walking away from the rock river, refusing to answer any of Jony's questions, acting as if no one must see or speak of such a thing. His displeasure was enough to subdue Jony; and the boy had reluctantly joined in that retreat, though he had been plagued ever since by the memory of the strange thing and the need to know more.

By his People-trained ability of location he was certain that, had the river of rock really penetrated deeply into the hills, it could not lie far now from this present site. As soon as he could persuade Maba and Geogee to leave the water and see them back with the cubs to the clan campsite, he was going to do a little prowling on his own.

However, unless Jony wanted to arouse the only too annoying curiosity of the twins, he must do nothing to make them suspicious. Jony sighed. He considered that he was as cautious and reasonable as Voak, but the twins rushed madly into action without ever thinking. Also, they both lacked his own ability to sense danger, or to use the control he could hold by concentration upon some other minds.

Not that he could so influence the People. Their minds were too different. Jony had never been able to enter, let alone bend, any one of them to his will, as he had that Big One during the crucial moments of escape. Perhaps (he had talked about it with Rutee often), perhaps this was because the Big Ones had used the mind-controller, and so in some way were themselves more vulnerable to such power. But neither of the twins had such a talent. Rutee explained, when Jony had grown older (it was just before she had died, when she had him promise to watch over them), that their father had been wholly mind-controlled. And she thought perhaps that might make them more susceptible to influence.

She had made Jony promise then that he, himself, would never try to control either Maba or Geogee by such a power. To do so was an evil thing. Her distress had been so great when she spoke of this that Jony had promised at once. Though many times his exasperation with the twins' reckless disregard for their own safety—and that of others—made him wish she had not demanded that of him.

So he had to use other methods of persuasion to control them, and, the older they grew, the more they resented his orders. Jony stirred impatiently on the rock, which was now almost too hot to make a comfortable lounging place. He sat up and called down:

"You two—time to come out!"

Maba laughed and jumped back, so the falling curtain of water hid her slim brown body. Geogee bobbed up and down in the stream and made a face.

"Come and make us!" he hooted.

However, if they disregarded Jony's command, they had still to reckon with Huuf and Uga. Huuf moved up behind Geogee, his hands out, to close upon the boy's upper arms. In spite of Geogee's irate yells and kicks, he bore him calmly to the bank, to dump him on the grass not far from where Geogee's kilt lay in a tangle. Uga disappeared under the spray curtain, to return in less than a breath, not carrying the screaming

Maba, but leading her by the long streamers of her hair, on which Uga had a good and unshakable grip.

"Jony—" Maba screamed as soon as she was through the water curtain into the open. "Make her stop! She's hurting me!"

"Do as you're told," he replied with satisfaction, "and you won't get hurt. It's time to head back and you know it."

Though perhaps she did not. None of the three had the built-in sense of time which moved the People calmly and serenely through their days, a time to eat, a time to doze, a time to make nettings, to heap up bedding for the night, to look about them.

The People used some tools. They knotted nets which they employed as loose bags to carry fruit and edible roots with them. Also each treasured a staff such as Jony now reached for. These were carefully made from a well-selected thick branch or sapling.

One end curved in a hook for pulling down fruit-laden branches. The other end was sharpened by much patient rubbing between stones to aid in digging up roots and grubs. It could also be a weapon upon occasion. Voak had slain a vor bird with his staff. Though after he had thrown away the staff, since a kill-thing must not be used again.

The People were equipped with their own armament. The tremendous strength of their thickly muscled arms and their fangs was enough to make them formidable opponents. Only the vor birds, which could attack from aloft, and smaa, a legged reptile with lightning lash speed, were any real danger. Of course there were the Red Heads, too. Jony had only seen them once, and the memory was enough to make him shiver even now.

They had looked (to the unknowing) like tall plants, with huge flaming scarlet balls for flowers, one large ball aloft on each stalk. By day they were root-fixed in the ground—growing. At dusk their life changed. Feet, which were also roots, wriggled out of their chosen pits of sod as they set out to catch and devour any life they could meet.

From the lower parts of their ball heads they discharged a light yellowish powder, the brisk waving of which had seemed like leaves wafted out into the air. Whatever breathed that powder became quickly insensate; the Red Heads would gather up the limp body, enfolding it in thorned leaves which aided in sucking the juices from it. Once this grisly meal was concluded, the shrunken remains were hurled into the open root holes, as if the refuse of their horrible meals would nourish them even longer.

The People knew no way of defeating the Red Heads. One merely avoided them as best one could. Luckily their coloring was such that they could be easily sighted. And they were the first enemy to scout for upon coming into any unfamiliar territory.

Jony watched Maba and Geogee dry themselves off with bunches of grass and belt on their kilts. Rutee had taught them how to weave those, using the same fibers, but thinner and split, which the People processed to construct their nets. In addition all three possessed squares of more closely woven stuff, packed tighter with feathers of vor birds, which they pulled about them in the cold times.

Jony leaped down from his rock perch, crossed the stream with a couple of jumps from rock to rock. The cubs already headed purposefully toward that clump

of trees which marked their present campsite. Both
had full nets; their morning had been spent to better
purpose than just playing in the water.

"You let them pull us out!" Maba's lower lip stuck
out as she scowled at Jony. "You think they know
more than we do!"

Geogee nodded in agreement, his scowl just as heavy.

The twins resembled each other in that their hair
was fair, almost white where the sun had bleached it,
and they had the same general contour of feature. Jony
had never been able to see anything of Rutee in them.
But Rutee had always said that Jony, himself, was like
his father. He often wished that Maba, at least, had had
Rutee's dark hair, her face. Now it sometimes seemed
he could not, in spite of all his concentration, recall
Rutee at all. Except as just a shadowy shape whom he
continued to miss with a dull ache.

"They do know more than you do," he said shortly.
"If you'd copy them a little, it would be better—"

"Why?" Geogee asked. "We aren't them. Why do
we have to act like them at all?"

Jony frowned in return. He had been through this
many times during the past seasons. The older the
twins grew, the more they wanted to question and
argue. At times he had even had to cuff them, as
Voak had cuffed him once or twice in the past when
he had been foolish and thoughtless.

"We act like them because they have learned to
live here. This is their world; they know best how
to use it."

"Then where's our world? And why can't we go
there?" Maba asked a question he had also answered
many times over.

"I don't know where our world is. You know how we came here—the Big Ones had Rutee and me in their sky ship. We got away from them. Rutee saw their ship go back into the sky. We were left here. Which is much better than being in the cages of the Big Ones. Now get going; Yaa is waiting."

"Yaa is always waiting." Maba refused to let his warning silence her. "She wants me to make some more netting. I don't see why I have to. While you get to go off out there." She made a wide circle with her arm to include the hills ahead of them. "I want to go too."

"Yes," Geogee nodded. "Huuf goes, so we can . . ."

"Huuf," Jony tried to put full emphasis on what he said now, "watches all the time. He does not run off and hide, or pretend he is lost in order to have the whole clan out hunting for him."

Maba laughed. "That was fun," she broke out. "Even if Yaa did slap us when we got back. We want to go and see things, Jony, just not always stay around where the People are. They really don't *like* anything different to do."

She was right, of course. But both the twins must learn caution, and they seemed unable to understand, or want to understand, that danger walked with the unknown. For Jony the situation was different. He was much older, bigger, and he had his warning sense to call upon. If the twins only had that, he would not have worried so about their taking off into the unknown. But they had not the least trace of his talent.

"Wait until you're older—" he began when Geogee interrupted.

"You say that every time. We do get older, and still

you keep on saying it. You're just never going to let us go. But you wait, Jony. I'm 'most as tall as you now. Someday I'm just going to walk away to go and see things for myself. And Voak and Yaa, they aren't going to stop me, even, any more than you can then, Jony. You'll see!"

Maba was smiling, and Jony distrusted that smile. He had seen that expression before and it generally meant trouble to come. But he could rely upon Yaa; she would not let either twin out of her sight once they were back in camp.

Oddly enough both Maba and Geogee went the rest of the way uncomplainingly and with no more questions. Jony saw them back under Yaa's kind, all-seeing eyes, then went to the opposite side of the campsite where the unmated males had their own small inner circle. The clan was a small one, closely related by blood ties. If any of these younger males wished a mate, he must wait until one of the clan assemblies, which occurred before the coming of the cold, and try then to urge a female away from another family group to join with him. Three of the older ones were already impatient to reach that satisfactory situation in life. But there were four younger, who with Jony, were not yet interested in such complications.

Jony munched a crumbling cake of ground nuts mixed with sap which was their principal noon eating. The food was flavorsome enough, but he looked forward with more anticipation to the evening meal when the results of the morning's fishing would be shared out as additional tasty tidbits.

Trush had had the misfortune to break his staff two days earlier, and had spent the morning largely in careful search for raw material for its replacement. He had been lucky enough to discover a sapling hooked in just the right proportions, and was now engaged in the patient rubbing of its thicker end into the proper point.

Otik had brought back a collection of stones which he was picking over carefully, trying one and then another for abrasive uses. Gylfi worked on the shell of a giant crawler; he had scooped out all the meat (a delicacy greatly appreciated by all the clan), and set the shell with the body side down over a zat nest last night. By morning these obliging insects had divested the interior of the very last vestige of organic material. Gylfi now had a rock-hard bowl over which he stretched a section of carefully dried and smoked vor bird skin which he had treasured with just this purpose in mind.

He smeared the sap of a vine (a nuisance because of its strong adhesive qualities) around the edge of his bowl and pulled the skin taut across, binding a twist of grass cord about it to make sure of no slippage until the vine sap was thoroughly dry. His work was patient and thorough, and Jony knew what pride he took in it. Once the sap dried, Gylfi would have a handsome drum to thump.

The People did not sing—unless their series of ululating, throaty calls was singing. But they had a strange love of dance. Each full moon overhead brought them to stamp and leap, stamp and leap for hours. Jony usually found such gatherings dull. He would watch for a while and then seek out his sleeping nest. Or else offer, as was more often the case, to go on guard duty so that some clan member could fully enjoy the entertainment.

With all three of his usual companions enwrapped

in their own affairs he felt safe, though a little guilty in seeking out what he wanted to do. Finishing his handful of crumbs, he signaled to Trush that he was on scout. Plainly preoccupied with his own affairs, Trush only hunched a shoulder.

A glance across the campsite assured Jony that Maba and Geogee were both netting, one on either side of Yaa. So he slipped away hurriedly hoping that neither saw him go.

There were times when Jony found a certain pleasure in being alone. Though he lacked the homing ability of the People, he could mark his trail when he reached unfamiliar territory and never feared being lost. The world about him was a constant source of wonder and interest. There was always some life-form to hold one's attention, from a strange insect on the wing or underfoot, to a plant with flowers or leaves which were either odd enough to catch the eye, or beautiful and pleasing. On impulse he plucked now a cluster of orange-red blossoms, none larger than his little fingernail, but with gleaming petals and a heady, sweet scent, and tucked the spray into the hair above his ear, just because the color excited his eyes and pleased him for the moment.

The People did not seem to have much interest in any vegetation, unless it offered them food, or some tool, or was an annoyance and an obstruction. But Jony and the twins often picked flowers and wore them. The colors and the scents satisfied some longing in them which they did not understand.

Now Jony turned, started an upward climb, still angling south. If he could find his stone river, perhaps someday he might even trace it to its source.

Nowhere else had he seen stones so smoothed, set in straight lines on the ground. It was as if they did not lie there naturally at all, but rather had been placed so for some purpose. By whom—for what?

He reached the top of the ridge. From here he would mark his trail and—But, even as he raised the sharpened end of his staff to scrape across a tree trunk, he looked down slope—and what he saw held him quiet in sheer amazement.

There were...what? Jony had no name for those towering things beyond. For one startled moment a thrill of fear ran through him, the dim memory of the ship of the Big Ones. But a second later he knew that what he saw was not the Big Ones, standing silently as a part of the land on which they were based. Yet neither were they piles of rock raised in pinnacles by some chance. The towering fingers of stone were too perfect, too patterned in their arrangement. No, someone—something—had put rocks to use and built, one atop another, straight-edged mounds and heights.

To the edge of that building ran the river of stone, straight and even, only a little covered by the creeping earth in shallow drifts. It was plain, Jony decided, that this was truly the source of that river. So that, too, must have been made. But how—and again why?

He kept under cover, using each bit of brush, each stand of trees, as he advanced. At the same time he alerted that other sense of his, probing, seeking for some trace of thought—thought which was akin to that of the Big Ones. For only some people with the same powers and needs as his ancient enemies would or could devise what lay ahead. It was not in the nature of the People to work so with stone.

But all his mind-search brought not the least suggestion of such life. He could detect only those faint sources which were always about: the native insects, a flying tiling. Not even the in-and-out wavering pattern of the People, or the cold menace of smaa, could he pick up. No, there was no life in the pile ahead. Jony began to be certain of that. So he moved on more confidently with greater excitement and an awakened curiosity he would have to satisfy.

› FOUR ‹

Boldly at last, Jony stepped out on the stone river, to walk confidently toward those piles ahead. They varied in size, some merely his height plus that of his staff, if he held it straight upright. However, there were others so tall he had to tilt back his head to see where their tips touched the sky. Now the stone river led him on between the outermost piles.

Jony hesitated. He wanted so much to explore. Yet he was still cautious. Once more he quested intently for any emanation ahead signaling danger. Did the People know of this place? Trush's odd reaction when they had first come upon the stone river remained vivid in Jony's memory. He had not warned Jony off; he had simply pointedly ignored the strange find. Why?

There were many holes in the stone heaps ahead, some small, some large. Again each was regular, as if it had been formed for a purpose, not just because some stone fell out of place during the course of time. Holding his staff at ready, as if he crept up on a smaa's hunting territory, Jony advanced step by wary step, his glance shooting ever from side to side, his extra sense at full alert.

Those larger holes were on the level where he walked now. They reminded him a little of the entrances to caves, but were still too regular and repeated in pattern to be like those dens where the People sheltered during the time of cold. On impulse Jony entered the nearest, peering at what lay on the inner side of that opening.

A limited amount of light came from the other, smaller holes; enough to see an open space, more door holes. Jony's sense picked up a feeling of emptiness. He grew greatly daring, went farther. Unidentifiable masses lay on the floor. He poked at one gingerly with the sharp end of his staff. The whole mound collapsed in an out-puffing of dust.

Jony sneezed, retreated quickly. He did not care for the faintly sourish odor, unlike any he had sniffed before. But his curiosity still held. Those much larger heaps farther along the stone river, were they all alike?

He sighted some straggles of vine, a few clumps of tough grass which had managed to root in cracks of the stone. There was a cawing. A flight of six foraws took off from an upper ledge, as if propelled by some vast need for instant escape. But that was the way foraws were. Jony, ashamed of his own start at their sudden clamor, pushed on at a bolder pace.

Here were other rivers of stone, smaller ones, which branched away from the one he followed. All of those were also walled with the piles which had openings, but lay silent and deserted. Not all, perhaps; Jony sighted the spoor of several small creatures in the drifted earth. Apparently this was a safe shelter they claimed as their own.

At last the river came into an open space ending at the foot of the largest heap of all. Here the blocks of smoothed stone had been set up like the ledges along the falls, but far more evenly, so that a man might climb them with ease. Jony did that, heading for an opening at the top which was four—five times as wide as any he had seen elsewhere. However, as he neared that, he stopped short. For within the shadowed overhead of that opening someone stood waiting.

Jony crouched, his staff swung up, point ready, as he stared at the other. He was taller than Jony—but—he was not a Big One as Jony's old memories first suggested. No, his face . . .

Her face! Jony made a quick adjustment in terms as he saw the waiting one in greater detail. She was like Rutee, a little, big though she was. But she was—stone!

Jony guessed at the truth. Somehow those who had piled up this place had made one of themselves into stone. Or else had been able to fashion stone as the People working a sapling into a shape they desired. And the marvel of such skill made him gasp.

He had to go directly to the figure, venture to touch its cold surface, before he was assured this explanation was the truth. The stone was not rough, but smooth under his fingertips. Somehow he liked the feel of it as he rubbed along, following one curve and then another as high as he could reach. But he could not, even standing on tiptoe, touch more than the chin of the face above him.

Standing so close he could see that once there had been other colors laid on it besides the gray-white stuff of which it was made. In the folds of the clothing the figure wore, were dim traces of blue. And about her neck was a massive carving of many links which was still yellow.

Her hair did not hang loose as Rutee's and Maba's, but was gathered up into a massing which added to her height. One of her hands was held at a stiff odd angle at the wrist, the tips of her fingers pointing skyward, the palm flattened out toward him. On impulse Jony fitted his hand to that one, palm to palm—

No!

He stumbled back, away from the woman of stone. His mind was confused. What had happened? He had expected to meet cold stone as his touch had already found. But when he had laid his hand right there—the result had been a shock of feeling he could neither understand nor explain.

Warily now, Jony surveyed the figure for every small detail. The other hand lay on the breast, palm inward. The calm, still face in his mind confused with Rutee's, was posed that the eyes might look ever down the river of stone which had led him here. As if they sought someone who had not yet come.

There was certainly nothing alive about the thing. Jony went so far now as to gingerly touch the upheld hand with the very tip of his staff. Nothing happened. He must have been dreaming in some manner. But he decided he had no desire to try the experiment again.

Instead he made as wide a detour as the doorway would allow around the woman, heading on into whatever might lie behind her in this largest stone heap of all.

At first he went very slowly, for the dim light inside seemed almost nonexistent to his unadjusted eyes. Then he began to see that he was edging into a very wide space down which ran rows of tall, round stones set up to resemble the trunks of forest trees. The upper parts of these vanished somewhere in the high dusk over his head.

Jony shivered. This place brought back old memories of fear. By its size it seemed to have been fashioned for Big Ones, not for creatures of his own height. Yet the stone woman, tall as she was, had looked like Rutee, and had not had the horrifying alienness of his old enemy. It was that thought, as well as his ever ready curiosity, which encouraged him on.

Just as the river of stone had led directly to this heap, so did the lines of pillars produce a guide. Now he could see, too, that there was more light ahead. Jony quickened pace, his bare feet shuffling through a soft carpet of dust as he went.

Here, far above, there was another kind of hole, much larger, giving onto the sky. Directly under that another series of ledges supported a single wide block of stone which was not gray-white as all the rest. Instead, it was made up of many colors laid upon a dark, almost black, background.

Jony, studying it as he drew closer, could not make out any pattern, any more than one could see a pattern to the fur coloring of the People. Yet, these vivid colors (not in the least faded as those on the woman) must have some meaning. They were small dots of brilliance, some widely scattered, others loosely clustered here and there. Many shone as if the sunlight were truly caught within them, although no beam reached through that hole so far above.

Such were pictured on all four sides of the stone, Jony saw, as he moved around it. Yet never once was the positioning, the number of dots, or their seem-ingly random settings repeated. He could not see the top of the stone as the ledges raised that well above his eye level. Was it the same on top? And what was its meaning?

Jony was at last emboldened to climb. The last ledge, on which the stone rested, was wide enough that there was good room to circle about the block without touching. Jony was wary of any close contact since his queer experience with the stone woman. But he was well able to see that there were no patterns of brilliant dots here. There was—

He jerked back, astonished, nearly losing his footing and tumbling back down the ledges. Had he seen, very dimly—a face?

If he had, it must be that of another stone person, he reassured himself. And what harm could such do him unless he touched it? Resolutely he thrust aside uneasiness, to again approach the stone.

Dust lay thick upon the surface; a dust which had not obscured the dotted sides. Jony swept it off with his staff as best he could. The wood slid over so smoothly there could not be a figure there.

He neared the block within hand's distance, to look again. There it was! But *inside* the stone, in some queer, unnatural way. As if the whole block were hollow as a dead tree trunk, and with a top as clear as stream water, so that one could look down into what lay within.

Greatly daring, Jony reached out his fingers, gave a swift tap to that covering, jerked away. He had had no strange reaction this time, but that touch had assured him that there *was* a solid, if transparent, covering.

His wariness so eased, he pressed close enough to view what did lie within. There was a figure in the interior of the stone right enough. Jony leaned as closely above the lid as he dared to study it. The body was wrapped—except for the hands and face— around and around with strips of material which gave off a very faint luminescence, a little as did the eyes of the People in the dark.

Save this was not one of the People. The hands were much like his own in shape, though larger, as the whole figure was larger. They rested on the body at breast height, the fingers loosely locked over a staff which was not unlike the one in his own hand, except that it did not possess a crook at one end. And it was a dull red in color. Jony could not make out the features of the sleeper (if sleeper this was), for there was a mask of the same red covering the face smoothly, bearing no hint of eyes, nose, or mouth.

Was this a dead man—left so by his people? Jony glanced around him at the great dusty hall. If so, the stranger must have lain here for a long, long time. The People walled their dead in caves, leaving with them food for the Night Journey and a stout staff made new just for their going. Rutee had been left so.

Jony did not know what waited beyond death. Rutee had always said to die would be like waking in another place, a better place. There one would meet with those one loved. Even as she had died, she called out once:

"Bron!" And her voice had been one of welcome.

He did not know if the People believed the same, but they were careful in their burials. Thus he thought they, too, might judge death a gateway to another place and time. Someone had taken great care to put this stranger in this place. He should not be disturbed.

Jony descended to the floor of the great space. How long had he slept here, that masked man (or perhaps it was even a masked woman, he could not be sure)? Standing there, watching those points of light on the stone, Jony shrank a little. It suddenly seemed to him that many long, long seasons were crowding in upon him all at once, that he could not breathe because they hung about so thick.

He gave a gasp, ran for the door, skimming past the woman of stone without giving her another look. It was better outside. But that feeling of being entrapped in time was still with him. Now he wanted out of this place entirely, back to the open world of the People.

Down the river of stone he pounded as if pursued by one of the Big Ones in person. His side ached as he reached the open, away from all those dead heaps of piled up stone; he skidded off the river, to the familiar, welcoming ground.

He did not halt in his flight until he reached the top of the ridge from which he had first viewed the stone place. Then, gasping, he did turn to look over his shoulder. The time was close to sundown. Shadows had crept out, as if during the light hours they had hiding places within the piles of stone. Jony shivered. He was not sure what had happened to him, only back there a burden had rested and had almost fastened on him. Perhaps Trush had been entirely right: the river, the heaps—they were to be avoided.

Still, as his breathing slowed and he made his way back to the campsite, Jony kept seeing somehow the red-masked sleeper caught in the stone. Curiosity still nagged him. Who *was* that one? Why did he lie there? As if waiting...

Waiting for what?

Jony shook his head vigorously, as if he would shake those disturbing thoughts well out of his mind. He saw ahead a vine heavy with pale green fruit, prepared to jerk it down to hand level with the crook of his staff. At least he would not return empty-handed. He decided not to let anyone know his adventure of the afternoon.

Whether he would ever return to the stone place, he did not know. Perhaps it was enough that he had seen it this one time. Better that way—or was it? But at least he had no intention of making this journey again soon.

He was just reaching for the vine when his extra sense broke through his preoccupation with what he had seen that afternoon. Something was the matter—he was needed urgently!

Jony began to run at the best pace the rough ground allowed, all his speculations and discoveries lost in the rising knowledge that trouble lay somewhere ahead, and that it very definitely involved him. An attack by a smaa on the campsite? He thought of the worst danger he knew. But those enemies were seldom found in this part of the country. There was the possibility, in its way even worse, that the Big Ones' space ships had returned!

Old fears closed in about him. Neither he nor Rutee had ever known what had led to the swift departure of the alien ship after their own escape. It could be that the ship had returned to hunt them down. And no weapon which the People had could successfully stand between them and swift capture if the Big Ones willed it. He had heard too many times over Rutee's description of how the aliens had so easily taken the colony which had been her home.

Jony had not yet reached the camp when Trush materialized in that odd way the People could from their shape-hiding coloring of the vegetation. The clansman had his staff, only half-prepared for real action, in his paw-hand. His other hand signed a message Jony was not expecting.

"Little—light fur—gone!"

Geogee, Maba, or both! Jony had been too ready to believe Yaa could control them. He held up two fingers to signify both twins. To that Trush assented with a quick dip of his muzzle in the affirmative gesture of the People.

Jony, breathing hard, plowed to a stop opposite Trush. The first thought which had flashed into his mind was that in some manner the children must have sneaked away to follow him, perhaps become lost in the territory around the ridges. While the People had excellent night sight, his own was far inferior.

"Which way?" he asked in sign language.

With the end of his unfinished staff Trush pointed over Jony's own shoulder, toward the ridge from which the boy had just come. So the twins *had* followed him! But had they gone all the way—into the place of piled stones? Jony thought of the many hiding sites there and also of what else might lurk in the darkness which was fast falling. Remembering Trush's attitude toward the river of stone, Jony feared that the People would be reluctant, might even completely refuse, to help him search there if he must.

Trush, shouldering his staff, moved ahead, his eyes bent down as if he could read plainly some track. Jony, well realizing how inferior his own ability to trail was when compared to that of his companion, fell in behind. He longed to know how long the twins had been gone, but the People never measured time.

Behind Trush's more massive person Jony once more ascended the ridge. When he gained the crest Trush was standing very still indeed.

"Where . . . ?" Jony signed.

That round head turned a little, and the large eyes regarded him unblinkingly. Jony, not for the first time, wished desperately that he could read the mind behind those eyes, know just a little of the other's thoughts. But all he could sense was a strong disturbance, as if Trush were being forced to face some danger much against his will, struggling to find a way out of such an entrapment.

Very slowly the clansman raised his staff, though he half-averted his face as it pointed with its tip straight at the distant stone piles. Trush did not even make a hand gesture to underline his answer.

Jony drew a deep breath. In the fading light the stone piles had an odd repellent look which he had not seen earlier as the sun had brightened them. As if, with the coming of dark, an old evil awoke. Jony closed his mind resolutely against such fancies, centered his questing thoughts rather on what lay at the end of the stone river.

Yes! He touched one mind—that was Geogee somewhere ahead. Jony leaned upon his staff. If only he had not promised Rutee, sworn to her never to mind compel either of the twins, he could bring them out!

A little alarmed now, Jony quested farther—where was Maba? Her pattern of thought was usually as clear to him as her face was in his sight, but now he could not locate it at all!

Fear came fully alive. Only unconsciousness could prevent mind-touch. Was Maba hurt—or perhaps even dead?

Jony found himself frantically descending before he realized he had even moved. He did not expect Trush to follow. If the twins were in the stone piles he, himself, must find them and bring them back to safety.

His feet thudded dully on the river of stone, and he carried his staff before him at the ready. Though this afternoon curiosity had drawn him to this place, now he was angry and ashamed. The twins must have seen him go, followed in their usual reckless, unthinking fashion. Who could guess what they might meet within those dens now so shadow filled? His own experience with the stone woman—he had no explanation for that. And there could be other traps, or dangers which were totally foreign to everything they knew.

Jony's rush took him past the first of the dens, those which were smaller. He made himself slow down. This was a time to use questing thought, not to rush blindly about accomplishing nothing in the dusk.

At once he was able to pick up Geogee again. With that touch came fear, naked and sharp—Geogee was afraid. If he, Jony, could not compel, surely he could call the other; use mind-linkage as a guide through this place of unknown dangers.

"Geogee!" He built in his mind as strong a picture of the boy as he could hold. "Geogee, where are you?"

Fear built a barrier. Geogee was so torn by terror he was not thinking in any clear pattern Jony could pick up and analyze. Communication came as distorted jolts like blows, aimed out wildly in every direction.

Jony could not maintain rational contact, but he could use that center of disturbance itself as a guide. This Jony probed grimly, held to what he could discover. The way took him, not back to the vast pile where the stone woman and the sleeper in the rock waited, but down one of the smaller side streams of stone which was much narrower. Here the piles on either side appeared to lean out above him, as if at any moment they might free themselves into individual blocks and crash down to blot him out.

Jony had to conquer his own growing uneasiness in order to hold to that center of mental disturbance which marked Geogee. He drew closer with every stride, at least he was sure of that much. Then—his head turned, as if jerked, to the right. In there!

As all the other holes, the one beside him had no barrier, nor did any stone figure stand there in welcome or dismissal. Within it was quite dark. For the first time Jony raised his voice:

"Geogee!"

The boy's name echoed hollowly, until Jony was almost sorry he had called. However, in answer, something scuttled from an inner section of the pile, threw itself frantically at Jony, head burrowing against him, thin arms in an imprisoning grip about his middle.

Geogee was shaking so much that his sudden onslaught nearly upset Jony in return. Though the older boy still held tightly to his staff, he dropped his other arm about Geogee's shoulders, holding him in a tight answering grasp. When that shivering seemed to lessen a little, Jony spoke again:

"Geogee," he repeated the name quietly and firmly, hoping to break through that terror which manifestly filled the other, get from him a necessary answer. "Geogee, where is Maba?"

Geogee gave a little cry. Nor would he even look up at Jony. Rather he rubbed his face more strongly against Jony's breast.

Jony held onto his calm as best he could. He must break through, learn what had happened so he could find the girl.

"Where ... is ... Maba?" He spoke very slowly and evenly, spacing his words with all the impact he could summon.

Geogee gave a kind of wail, but he did answer. "The wall took her. It swallowed her up!"

➤ FIVE ◄

Whatever had happened, Jony realized, Geogee believed what he had just said was true. But—a wall which swallowed?

Jony himself gulped down his fear as best he could. He wanted nothing so much as to run with Geogee, get free of this place which, taking on the evil memories of the cages in the dusk, was far more alarming than any trap. Only—there was Maba. He could not leave her here. Instead he must get Geogee quieted enough to make better sense.

He caught the braid of the boy's hair in a firm hand, exerting enough pull on it to bring Geogee away from him so he could view the twin's convulsed face in what small light was here. Rutee had made him promise—never use the control.

But Rutee could not have foreseen this situation. Jony must free Geogee from the clutch of his wild terror long enough to discover what had happened. Or else . . . or else Maba might be lost.

Conquering, at least for this moment, his own

uneasiness, Jony gazed steadily into the boy's eyes. They were fixed, staring, as if Geogee still watched something so utterly horrifying that he was caught within that moment of horror as a prisoner. Jony used his mind-touch, soothing, trying to break through the fear barrier.

The younger blinked; his mouth twitched. Jony concentrated. He was here—Geogee was not alone—they must find Maba! As he had earlier spoken emphatically, he now fed those thoughts.

Geogee's frantic grip on him was relaxing. Jony knew he was getting through. His own impatience warred with the necessary overlay of calm. While they wasted time here—what could be happening to Maba? He firmly shoved aside such thoughts; at present his task was to learn all Geogee knew.

After a time that seemed to stretch endlessly, Jony made a question of her name: "Maba—?"

Geogee loosed his hold, stood away. His face was now calm. Jony remembered the mind-controlled from the cage days, hated what he saw. But otherwise—he did not really have Geogee under full control, he had only managed to reach beyond the boy's fear as he had had to do.

"Back there," Geogee gestured to a darker portion of the den and another opening. "We were back there..."

Jony wet dry lips with the tip of his tongue. To go into that darkness...But it had to be done. He scooped up his staff. At least he could probe shadows with that, not walk straight into disaster unprepared. His sense told him there was no enemy, no living enemy that he could recognize within these stone heaps. Yet from the heaps themselves came a strange awareness, which to him was a warning such as he had never known before.

"Back here." Geogee was already pattering away into the dark. Jony quickly followed.

They went through two of the open spaces which had wall holes giving a small amount of light. Then Geogee halted in the third, facing what gave every appearance of a completely solid erection of stones. Yet the younger boy advanced toward this as if he saw an opening invisible to Jony.

"Maba—" Geogee reached out his hand. "She put her hand right there." With that he forced his palm flat on the stone.

There was a dull grating sound. Under Geogee's push not only the block he touched, but those above and below moved. The boy, off-balanced, stumbled forward through the black hole now open. Jony aimed his staff. The stones were swinging back again to seal Geogee in, but they were stopped by the stout length between.

Jony heard Geogee cry out. Then he levered frantically with his shaft. The stones opened again more fully, but he could see their strength had nearly bitten through the wood.

There was no help for it, he must follow into whatever secret the wall concealed.

He groped through, heard the stones crunch behind him. Panic filled him. This was a cage, worse than those of the Big Ones; it was dark and the wall was solid. And... He took a single step away from the edge of this new cage. His foot did not meet a surface; there was nothing there!

With a cry Jony fell into that nothingness.

His fall was not far. Only after he landed heavily,

he was on a slope down which he continued to slide, though he struck out with his staff trying to find some hold, some way of staying that slip ever downward. So intent was he on such struggles, that it was a moment or two before he realized that he was not moving over a rough stone surface which would have stripped his skin by the friction. Rather under him was soft stuff which gave at the pressure of his exploring fingers and then rose again. It was as if this strange way of traveling had been devised with maximum safeguards against injury.

Down and down, Jony had no way of judging how far this slippery passage reached.

"Geogee!" he shouted, waited for some answer.

Finally that came—thin, faint, and Jony believed far away, a mere thread of sound reaching him. He sent a mind probe instantly.

Geogee was again in a state of fear and confusion, but he was alive, unharmed. If there ever was an end to this worm hole, Jony would catch up with Geogee, and, doubtless, with Maba.

The purpose of such a passage—Jony did not even try to guess at that. Was it a trap set long ago to catch any invading the stone heaps? Did each stone heap have one? If so, what bitter enemies had the people here faced?

The dark was no longer absolute. Ahead, Jony saw a grayish gleam of light. And that cheered him. To be out of suffocating darkness was enough to raise his spirits.

Also, he was not sliding so fast now. The angle of the way under his body was less acute. The light increased, coming from a round opening ahead. Jony began to hope that he had reached the end of this nightmare passage.

He could see better, use the staff as a brake, so

that he did not fall through that hole, but crouched at its mouth, to look out warily.

"Jony!" Geogee, his dirty hands smearing at his cheeks where there were the marks of tears, hunkered on the floor of a vast place filled with the gray light. There was no opening to the outer world. In fact, Jony was sure that they were far beneath the ground in some cave. He could not see nor understand where the light came from. But he accepted thankfully that it was there.

Before him was a very short drop to the floor. Jony jumped, then thought-quested. Something... He swung away from Geogee, facing out into the wide open of that space. Maba—that way!

He stooped over Geogee, drew him up onto his feet. "Come!" He must find Maba and then a way out. To climb up the passage he had just descended might be impossible. Jony shrugged away such speculation. Let him find Maba, perhaps then further exploration would show them an escape.

"Jony, I want out of here!" There was a shrill note in Geogee's voice.

Jony could have applied the calming influence again, but his concentration was needed to guide him to Maba.

"We'll get out," he gave assurance which might be a lie, but which must serve him at present as a tool. "But first we find Maba."

"Where is she?" Geogee demanded, his head turning from one side to the other as if he sought her within eyesight.

"This way." At least Jony was confident of that much. He kept hold of Geogee's shoulder, urging the boy on. At least Geogee seemed willing enough to go.

As they struck out straight across the center of the open space Jony noticed the open space itself was much larger than he had first guessed, stretching farther and farther ahead. He caught sight of other holes in the walls, similar to the one through which they had come. It would seem that this was some central meeting place for many such.

There was an utter silence here, a deadness which did not exist in the shadowed heaps above where small life had made hiding places and dens of their own. Jony shook his head impatiently. He had the odd sensation that the deadness also blanketed thought, that it was becoming harder and harder to retain his guiding tie with Maba. How far had she gone? He was startled when Geogee suddenly shouted: "Maba!"

The name echoed, re-echoed, so that it seemed many Geogees cried that aloud. The boy whimpered and crowded closer to Jony.

"Please," he said, "I don't like this place, Jony. And Maba—where is she?"

Jony was wondering if the girl was on the move, straying farther and farther ahead of them all the time. He knew she was there, but when would they catch up?

The hole openings along the walls were no longer to be seen, while the open space through which they trotted was narrowing. Now they moved between two walls without any breaks in them at all. At the same time the gray light grew stronger, changing hue. It was then Jony saw the barrier ahead.

This was not like the walls on either side, but gleamed a little, while in it was a crack placed vertically. An opening they could force? He hoped so. Maba?—his mind-call went out. To his relief he knew that at last she was close, perhaps only behind that barrier.

When he reached the surface Jony could see that the crack indeed marked an opening. But there was no manner of pulling it open. When he pushed, it closed only more firmly. Again he tried his staff, working the now splintering tip into that crack, exerting all the leverage he could.

Slowly, reluctantly, the crack widened; the door was opening. Jony's hands were slippery with sweat as he worked. Then Geogee joined him, adding a small measure of strength to the effort. Inch by inch they won until they had opened a space wide enough for both to slip through.

Jony stopped short. The contrast between what faced him now and the stark corridor which had led them here was so great it took a moment for his eyes to adjust. Here was color in plenty, so much that it battered against one, dazzling and deluding the sight. Ribbons of brightness were along the walls, and, between the same type of stone tree trunks that Jony had seen in the largest pile, were stacked tightly, from the floor under them to the surface high overhead, blocks of color, no two alike. Some of those blocks were transparent, like the one which held the sleeper, so that he saw many objects piled inside them.

The glitter and brilliance of this place bothered Jony. There was no sign of Maba, yet she was here; his sense told him that. Lost perhaps among the ranges of blocks.

"Maba!" He raised his voice in the loudest shout he could summon.

"Jony . . . ?" Her answer was low-voiced, drawing

him to the left, along that painted wall. Now that he
could focus on one single part of this cluttered place
he could see that those colors made up pictures. Not
too far ahead Maba sat, her feet straight out before
her, her dirty, dusty face turned up, staring intently
at what was just before her.

"Maba!" Geogee broke from Jony's side, ran toward
his twin. "What—"

She raised her hand to point, never looking in her
brother's direction at all, her voice eager and alive.

"Geogee—Jony—look! People—like us . . . see!"

The paintings on the wall had a strange look about
them. They did not exist on a flat surface, but somehow
stood out and away from that, with the semblance of
figures only partly caught in the stone, a portion of
their forms protruding beyond.

The section Maba had chosen to study showed a
number of females who were doing things with their
hands which Jony could not understand. Before them
were a number of boxes of different sizes and shapes,
on which were dots in various colors. The women
appeared to rest their hands upon some of these
dots. Piled about them at foot level were a number
of things, among which all he could recognize with
any certainty was a roll of woven substance, very
much finer than their own kilts or the knottings of
the People. Some objects reminded him unpleasantly
of articles which had been in use in the labs of the
Big Ones, save that these were of a brighter color
and a shape more pleasing to the eye.

He glanced at the next picture. Here were males,
and they each had in hand one of those red rods such
as he had seen in the hands of the sleeper. One man

pointed his rod, and a beam of light was pictured as springing from its tip to strike a rough, unshaped rock. A little farther on was a rock which was its twin, but that had one side smoothed and squared. Jony guessed that those in the picture used their light beams to cut stone, even as the People used sharp stones to hack some length of wood to proper measure.

That such could possibly be done he knew from his memories of the ship's lab. But that was a power of the Big Ones, and therefore evil. Jony frowned at the picture. The men in it looked not unlike those of the mind-controlled the Big Ones caged.

"Look!" Maba picked up something which had lain on the floor beside her, flaunted it at Jony. "See what I found!"

The substance fell in graceful folds between her hands, and he realized that it was cloth—not coarse and heavy as their own clumsily woven kilts, but smooth, soft, beautiful. The color was a clear green, like the leaves of some plants, and, over that, waved a pattern of clusters of small flowers. Jony's hand went to his head. The sprig he had broken off earlier that day had not survived. He had wanted for a moment to compare that with the pictured ones on the cloth, for by his memory they appeared very similar.

"I shall wear this—so—like that one . . ." Maba stood up. She let fall her kilt, struggled to drape the length of green about her in imitation of the covering on the painted woman she had pointed to. Deep in Jony his extra sense stirred in warning. He did not want to see Maba strutting back and forth before that picture, the cloth clutched about her thin brown body. This was—wrong!

"No!" Jony moved on that instinct, snatching at the material before Maba could hold it more tightly. Becoming aware of what he was doing, she cried out, clinging to it stubbornly. There was a ripping sound. The cloth tore so that the larger part was in Jony's hands; she only held the end.

The stuff was so soft, seeming to cling to his skin. He wadded it together in a fierce gesture, threw it from him.

Maba stared incredulously at the ragged scrap she held. Then she let that fall, to rush at Jony with her hands balled into fists, pummeling him with all her strength.

"You—you spoiled it!" she gasped. "You tore it!"

Jony dropped the staff he had caught up again, took her by the shoulders, held her away, kicking and flailing her fists. The girl screamed in sheer anger, and he shook her sharply until she stopped and began to cry.

But she smeared away her tears, as if angry that she shed them, and continued to glare at Jony.

"You spoiled it!" she repeated, her eyes hot with anger.

"Listen!" Jony shook her again. "Now, you listen to me, Maba. Do you remember what happened to Luho? Do you?"

Her eyes were held by his level stare. "She—she ate the yellow thing that smelled good..."

"And after that?"

"She—she hurt bad, real bad. And—and—she died..." Maba's voice trailed away. Then some of the fierceness came back into her face. "But I didn't eat any yellow thing, Jony. I had—had something nice."

"Did Luho think she had something nice?" he

continued, hoping to drive home his meaning by reason alone.

"Yes. But that was growing, Jony. It was a live thing. Mine wasn't a live thing. They made it, I think—" she gestured toward the women on the wall. "It wouldn't hurt me."

"You don't know, Maba. Luho didn't listen when she was told strange things must be handled carefully. This place, it does not belong to the People, nor does it belong to those who are like us either—"

"But they are, Jony! Look at them; you can see! Maybe Rutee was wrong, maybe the sky ship brought her back to this, her own world." Maba spoke faster and faster.

Jony shook his head. "No, Rutee would have known. The People never lived on her world. Think about the hoppers, Maba. Remember how they catch the pincher ones?"

"They—they can make themselves small and they hide a part of their bodies—so they look like a pincher—" she replied. "You mean," her head turned away from him now so she could gaze searchingly once more at the wall, "You mean—these people could be like hoppers—make themselves look like us . . . ? But, Jony, how could they know about *us*? This place is old. It must have been here before Rutee and you came out of that ship, before we were born."

"Not to catch us. But I mean that, though they look more like us than the Big Ones, they could be as different really as the hoppers are from the clawed ones. Do you understand?"

She looked back at him and then once again at the pictured wall.

"Yes. Only what if you're wrong, Jony? What if they are really our kind? Jony"—she pulled away from his loosened hold—"those things over there." She pointed eagerly now to the ranks of colored squares and oblongs. "Those can be opened up and they're full of things. Things like what you tore up. And others—just come and see, Jony!" She caught his hand and pulled him toward the nearest of the squares. Before they reached that, Geogee came running.

"Look what I found!" he shouted. He waved over his head a red rod, swinging it around so that light flashed from its surface.

Jony, again with only instinct to guide him, made a grab. Their hands met on the surface of the rod. From its tip shot a beam so brilliant that Jony was temporarily blinded. He heard screams from the twins, the clatter of something metallic falling, as he reeled back against the wall, his hands pressed protectively over his eyes.

"Geogee—" somehow he managed to get out, "leave that thing—leave it alone!"

"I—I can't see, Jony..." Geogee's voice approached a scream. "Jony—Maba—"

"It's all right." Maba answered him. "This is me, Geogee. Take my hand. That—that thing. It... Jony," her voice trembled. "Where the light went... there just isn't anything! Jony, what happened?"

He blinked, his eyes were tearing, but he could see, as if through a watery haze. His first horrible fear was dulled. The red rod lay on the floor. He made a careful detour around it to reach the children. Maba had her arms about her twin, was hugging him close, but she was looking beyond him and Jony followed her line of sight.

Where the top row of squares had been piled upon a firm base of their fellows there was—as Maba had reported—nothing. The power of that lancing light certainly was a threat which seemed now to him worse than the devices the Big Ones had used.

Had the twins learned their lesson? Nothing here must be touched again. They had no idea what a careless mistake might loose. What if Maba had been in the line of that beam? Jony shuddered, feeling more than a little sick at the answer his imagination offered. He picked up his staff. Now he moved in on the twins.

"We must get out of here," he said tersely.

As he did not see any way of going back up that sliding hole, they would have to explore this storage place further. But there would be no more opening of boxes, no more touching anything which belonged to the people of the stone heaps. No wonder Trush had shown such a marked dislike for the traces these people had left behind!

The twins, now very subdued, joined him readily. They walked together down between those rows of containers, past the clear-sided ones in which strange objects tried to ensnare their curiosity.

The pictures on the wall beside them changed continually. While the first had shown the people of this place in semi-incomprehensible action, these were scenes from outside the city showing reaches of land such as the three knew from their own wandering across it. Then Jony was halted by a vivid scene.

A sky ship! The Big Ones *had* been here before! Yet, as he peered more closely, he was not quite sure... This ship seemed different in outline, though he would

not swear to that. His own glimpse of the outside of
the alien ship had been limited. It was enough that
these people used sky ships. In his mind that linked
them with the Big Ones, and he no longer wondered
at the strange weapon or tool Geogee had found.

"Jony!" Maba had not done more than glance at the
picture which had so excited him. She was ahead again,
pointing at another. "Look—there are the People!"

There they were indeed, seeming alive, ready to
walk away from the wall and join them, Trush, or
Voak, or Yaa. But they... Jony's lips thinned and his
hand tightened on his staff—These People went on
fours, which the People did not, unless the footing
was very bad and they had need for extra bursts of
speed. And around their bodies were straps from
which hung cords. The People here were prisoners;
some—some were pictured in cages!

Jony snarled. Just as he thought, those who had
lived here had the same evil nature as the Big Ones
even though they looked like himself! The People
in their time had escaped, just as Rutee and he had
gained freedom. Evil—he felt now he could sniff the
evil in this as if as rank and air-filling as the stench
of the Red Heads!

"What were they doing?" Maba asked still intent
on the picture. "Why do the People have those things
on them?"

"Because," Jony said between his teeth, "they were
prisoners—prisoners of evil ones. As we were once.
Oh, let us get out of here!"

He pulled her on. There must be some way out;
he had to find it!

> SIX <

They finally reached the end of that huge space. Jony was unable to judge just how large it was because of all that was crowded into it. Here stood another gleaming door, twin to the one he had forced open at the other end. To his surprise, just as he was wondering how effective his mistreated staff might prove for another such assault, Maba moved confidently forward. Standing on tiptoe, she put her two hands as far up as she could reach so that they met in a slight depression.

"Maba!" Jony was reaching to snatch her back when he saw that the door line was enlarging, reluctantly. They could catch a faint grating sound from within the wall, the first sound save those they themselves had made to be heard here at all.

The crack was wide enough open now for Maba and Geogee. But Jony did not trust it in the least. He turned about, grabbed at the stacked colored boxes, catching one which yielded to his tugging. With this he wedged the door panel, holding it open.

They passed into another gray-lit, plain-walled passage. However, this slanted upward, and Jony hoped that that meant they would eventually reach the surface and freedom. He had no idea of what this place was, save that the ones who had built the walls with their rods had apparently gathered therein things which they had made and perhaps treasured.

There was a crackling from behind; Jony whirled, shaft ready. All he saw was that the brace he had put in the doorway was being crushed by the weight of the closing panel, though the debris kept it from closing completely.

Maba—how had Maba learned the secret of the doors? He was more than a little puzzled by that. Now he asked her directly.

"I could see there was a line," she answered promptly. "And I kept feeling along up and down. 'Cause that's the way the wall opened before—when I put my hands on it." She smiled with that particular smile she used at times when she believed that she had been clever. Maba was only too ready to believe in her own powers, and lacked the wariness which Jony had learned in the cages when he was far younger than she was.

"Jony," Geogee had been scuffling along, frowning a little, as if some thought was troubling. "Those People on the wall—you said they were prisoners—like you and Rutee. But the others, the new ones, they looked like us, not as you said the Big Ones do. If they were like us—why would they shut up the People, make them wear those straps around their necks, stay in cages?"

"You heard what I said to Maba," Jony gave the best answer he could summon. "Just because those in the pictures look like us, that doesn't mean they were

like us *inside*. We know the Big Ones are bad, and
they look different, so we learned from the beginning
to be afraid of them. But the mind-controlled—they
were like us. Yet they did just what the Big Ones
told them. So unless we were sure, we could not
trust them, ever."

"Then those in the pictures were mind-controlled?"
Geogee demanded.

"I don't know." Jony could not somehow believe that
the very alien Big Ones were responsible for the building of this place. The sky ship picture had alarmed him
at first glance. But then, Rutee had told him his own
people had such ships. That was how she and Bron had
come to the world where the Big Ones had caught them.
There might be different kinds of sky ships. In the wall
pictures there was no hint of Big Ones.

All he was certain of at that moment was that this
was a place which threatened them. The sooner they
were out of it and back in the open country they
knew, the better.

"I'm tired," Maba said suddenly. "And I can't go
fast any more, Jony. I'm hungry—"

"I'm hungry, too!" Geogee reinforced that promptly.
"I want to get out of here, Jony. We keep going up
and up but we don't see outside."

He was right. The slope they followed kept them
going up and up, but Jony had no way of measuring
how far down the tube descent had taken them in
the first place.

"We'll get out—soon—" he tried to make his assurance sound convincing. The trouble was he had no
idea whether he spoke the truth or not. And he was
hungry and thirsty too. He wanted to run, but both

children were lagging, and he knew that he could do no more than keep them encouraged and moving forward, even though their pace slowed.

"I'm tired," Maba repeated again with more emphasis. "I don't think I can keep on walking up and up, Jony."

"Sure you can," he rallied her. "You're so clever about doors, Maba. We'll need your help if we find another one up ahead."

She continued to look doubtful, and she was climbing very slowly indeed. Geogee bettered her, was farther ahead, so that Jony had to call him back. What worried the older boy was that the strange light filling these under-surface passages was distinctly fading the farther they climbed. Jony had no wish to lose contact with either child in that complete dark which he had met before.

"Listen," Jony spoke sharply. "You, Maba, take hold of this!"

He held out the half-splintered shaft, thinking when they last got out of here he would need to make another. As the girl closed her hands on the butt end, Jony called ahead:

"Geogee, wait right where you are." When they caught up to the impatient boy, Jony pulled him into line with his twin. "Take hold—right here, and don't either of you let go. I want to know where you are in the dark."

He held the crook part in his own hands as he walked in the lead. This last part of the climb was at an even greater angle, and Jony made it slowly, fearing that either twin might lose its link. At last before him was an opening (without any of those sliding panels, Jony was thankful to see), and they came out onto a level space.

Here was a freshness of air, yet walls arose about them. It was dark enough so that Jony moved very slowly.

Finally he caught sight of small, sharp sparks of light ahead. Whether those meant more danger or not he could not tell. But he had to have some guide to center on, and those were the only such he could find. Linked by their hold on Jony's staff, the three came at last to a place the older had been before, in that great heap which was the heart of the forbidden place. There on its dais, glittering with living fire, was the block of stone which held the sleeper.

Those dots of color had been bright in the daylight, but in the dark they were even *more* alive, some sparkling, some burning with a steady glow. Jony wanted no part of this place, but at least he now knew where they were. "What's that?" Geogee asked.

"I don't know," Jony answered shortly. "But I do know where we are *now*. And we can get out of here easily—Come on!"

They skirted the stepped blocks which supported the container of the sleeper, and continued on down the dark way, moving around the stone woman. In this manner they found again the river of stone which would lead them out of this danger zone.

Danger zone it was. Jony's skin prickled with more than just the chill of the night air. He felt as if an emanation rayed out from all these piled blocks, alerting his warning sense, although he received nothing specific, just a general feeling of uneasiness and the need to get as far away as possible.

Maba stumbled and fell. She sat on the ground. "I—I can't get up, Jony. My feet hurt. I'm so tired."

There was only one thing to be done. Jony thrust

his staff at Geogee. "Carry that and stay close," he ordered. He stooped and picked up the girl.

Though she looked so small and thin, Maba was a heavy enough burden, and Jony was tired also. But he knew that he could not manage to keep her going on her own now.

They stayed strictly in the middle of the stone path on their way between the piles of stone. Though the night was dark, it was a straight enough guide to get them out and away. Geogee trailed the shaft, the butt bumping against the pavement. However, he did remain close to Jony. Perhaps he, too, felt that undefinable menace which Jony was sure was a part of this place.

They wavered on, passing one side way after another. Twice Jony had to put Maba down and rest a few moments before gathering her up again. She lay, a limp weight in his hold and never spoke. She might have been asleep, but, if so, this was no natural rest. Jony's uneasiness grew. Maba had handled the cloth, wrapped the length around her. She had been longer than he or Geogee in that storehouse of the alien things. Could it be that because of her curious prying, she now lay under some influence from that place resulting in a weakening of her body? Jony wanted to get out—and yet their way seemed longer and longer.

He was breathing in gasps as they passed between the last of the heaps to reach the outer world. There was no moon tonight, and Jony's night sight was not good enough to do more than show the ridge up which he must go to find the clan camp. He was well aware that he could blunder about in the dark and be lost.

Putting Maba down on the ground, well away from the river of stone, he caught at his staff, drawing

Geogee to him. The boy immediately crouched down beside his twin. Jony stood surveying the dark bulk of the ridge. Though he could not communicate by mind-call with the People, he knew that such an effort—if concentrated enough—did in some manner summon them. Just as his plea had brought Yaa when he had called for help for Rutee.

Now he put his full concentration into such a summons. The People did not travel much by night, though their sight was far better than his. But they had already been out seeking the twins and might still be somewhere about. Trush had known Jony had come in this direction in his own search.

Yes! Jony gave a great sigh of relief. Trush, or at least one of the People, was not too far away. He had touched that alien thought pattern which he could not read. Again he concentrated on trying to relay his need.

But, to his surprise and disappointment, as the time passed, no furred form shuffled down out of the brush to answer him. Was that because he and the twins had been in the place of stone? Did the People hold the site in such a degree of either fear or dislike they would now treat Jony and the twins with the same refusal to admit their existence as Trush had turned on the river of stone at their first sight of it?

Jony thought of that picture on the wall, the People in bondage and in cages. Somehow they had won their freedom from that state. However, Jony and the twins physically resembled their one-time captors, and the three had returned to the place of captivity. Could the People now believe that Jony and the twins were indeed to be identified with their ancient enemies?

The thought of that hurt as much as a sudden blow. Since the first moment when Yaa had come out of the storm to aid Rutee, Jony had accepted the People as wiser, stronger, and better than any other life-form he had known, save Rutee herself. They were not the empty shells of the mind-controlled. In fact, as far as Jony knew, they could *not* be mind-controlled. Neither did they hold him captive with the callous disregard of him as a thinking being the way the Big Ones had.

No, in their way the People were the whole world Jony knew and accepted as right and good. They were not the caged ones he had seen, any more than he was of the same breed who had caged them.

"I am here," he thought with all the force he could summon now, "I am me, Jony, the one you have known...I am *ME*."

He had never known how much of his thought-send the People could pick up, whether it was as difficult for them to "touch" him as it was for any message to be sent in the opposite direction. At the moment he could only continue to hope that he and the twins had not been disowned by the clan, that he could influence the watcher up there.

As the moments continued to pass that hope was blunted. The twins could not remain in the open in the night cold. Jony must find them some kind of shelter. Only *not* in the place they had just fled.

"Jony, I'm hungry," Geogee said plaintively. "And Maba—she's sleeping. But she's breathing funny, Jony. I want to go to Yaa. Please, Jony, let's go!"

Jony knelt to gather Maba once more in his arms. Her skin was chill against his, and her head rolled loosely against his shoulder. She was breathing in

shallow gasps. Jony shivered. Like Rutee—the coughing sickness? But that illness struck in the cold time.
He wanted Yaa as much as Geogee did, but dared he
take the children up into the brush?

They simply could not stay in the open any longer.
Somehow he got to his feet, Maba once more in his
hold. Geogee had the staff.

"Up—there—" Jony got out these words.

Geogee did not move. "It's dark," he objected. "And
it's a hard climb—"

"Get moving!" Jony made it an order. He could not
carry Geogee also. He was not even sure he could top
the ridge under the burden of the girl's dead weight.
That silent watcher from the People was still there,
though. It could be that the clansman simply would
not come this close to the river of stone.

Jony began the climb, Geogee scrambling a little
ahead. Over this rough country the older boy had
to exert his strength to the uttermost, testing each
forward step before he set his full weight upon it.

He looked no higher than that which lay immediately
before him, as much as he could see of that in this
lack of light. The climb seemed to take a very long
time, though he did not stop to rest, feeling that if he
dared that he would not be able to get started again.

Thigh-high brush closed about him, and he had
to push through it blindly, dodging the larger bushes
as best he could. The watcher still waited. Up—one
step—another. Somehow, Jony finished the climb,
lurching up onto the crest of the ridge. Once there
he stood, panting heavily. He raised his head, looked
about him for the presence he knew was there.

Hard as the People were to distinguish in the

daytime, that sighting was even more difficult at night. At last Jony caught those luminous circles of eyes. He did not try to advance. Any action now must be initiated by the other.

Geogee moved closer. "It's Voak!" he cried aloud.

Jony already had recognized the clansman leader moving farther into the open under the night sky. There Voak stood, staring at the three, making no gesture of aid or even of recognition.

Geogee halted. "Voak—?" he asked, a very uncertain note in his voice. Plainly the attitude of the other had first surprised, and now daunted him.

Voak was no longer alone. Jony sensed others moving up and in. The People gathered behind the clanleader, hard to see, except for their steady eyes. There was a reserve, a wariness about them which alarmed Jony. Since he could not reach them with mind-touch, he must wait now, let their future actions explain what had happened to cut him and the twins off from that warm feeling of the clan closeness. For cut off he was now certain they were.

Voak raised his staff to beckon. Jony stumbled forward obediently. One of the other People advanced to take Maba from him. He and Geogee followed on their own feet, though Jony did not miss the point that Voak himself had caught Jony's own staff, drawing it easily away from Geogee.

They staggered along, the People closing in about Jony and Geogee in a way which was not protective, but rather gave the feeling that they were now prisoners. So they traveled in silence back to the campsite near the stream.

Voak waved his staff in another gesture, sending

them to their sleep nests. The one who had carried Maba gave her over to Yaa, who carried her back into the family place. Jony knew a little relief at·that. He still trusted Yaa to give the girl care. He did not know what was wrong with Maba. The thought persisted that she might have contracted some illness connected with the place of stones, and he feared how dire that might be.

Geogee came and curled up beside him under their covering.

"Jony," his voice was the thinnest of whispers in the dark as Jony stretched his aching legs and tried to find comfort from the fact that at least they were back in the camp. "Jony, what is the matter? Why do the People hate us?"

Hate them? Jony was not sure that was the emotion which had built the wall so suddenly between them and the only friendly life they had known. Something vital, and perhaps terrible, had happened to their easy relationship with the People. However, he would have to wait for an explanation rather than guess.

"They may not hate us," he tried to find comfort for Geogee. "We could have broken one of their clan rules by going to that place. If that is so, there will be a judging."

Geogee shivered so that Jony could feel the shaking of his body.

"They will beat us with vines!" He was remembering last warm season when there had been a judging against Tigun after he had acted foolishly and been reckless about leading a smaa lizard across their trail, so that the lizard had come hunting them and Hrus had been badly bitten.

"If they do," Jony told him, "or if they try, then they shall beat me only. I was the one who went to the stone place; you only followed."

"No," Geogee sniffled. "We saw you come out. But we wanted to see inside. We knew it was wrong."

"If I had not done it first," Jony continued, "or gone hunting for the stone river, you would not have followed. If Voak thinks we have done wrong, I shall let him know that that is the truth. Now—try to sleep, Geogee."

In spite of his own fatigue Jony did not sleep at once. He had told Geogee the exact truth. The People were reasonable and very just. They would understand that if any punishment was to be meted out, it must be his rather than the twins'. The children had only followed because they had been curious concerning his actions. His own curiosity was what he must answer for.

After a while he dreamed. Again he stood in that place by the block whereon sparkled those dots of colored fire, which could almost be the stars a-glitter in the sky on a cloudless night. From the box slowly arose the sleeper. He raised one hand to the red mask to free his face, so that Jony could look directly on his features.

Jony shrank from seeing; yet a will stronger than his own held him there to watch. While—the face beneath the mask—! It was the same as he had seen now and then dimly reflected from a pool of water— Jony's own! Then the other had reached forth with the rod and tried to make Jony grasp it.

In his mind he knew that, if he did so, power would fill him. He would be so great that his will would be all that mattered. The People, even Maba and Geogee, would be to him as the mind-controlled were to the Big Ones.

One part of him wanted fiercely, so fiercely that it was a pain through his body, to seize that rod. Within his mind, very far away, as if long buried, arose a voice saying that such power was his by right, that he alone was fit to take and wield it. However, another part of him remembered the lab and Big Ones. Jony shook with the force of the battle within him—for he was like two who warred within one body. Now his hand stretched to take the rod, now he snatched it back!

"Jony! Jony!"

He roused dazedly to the sound of his name. There was the gray of early morning around him. But he was not in that place of stones. Over him was the good, familiar arch of tree branches. Then he saw Geogee. The boy's dirty face was a mask of fright.

"Jony!" He had his hands on Jony's shoulders, was shaking him.

"It's all right—" Jony's own mind was coming back, so slowly, from that struggle. His skin was rank with sweat in spite of the chill. He felt weak, as if he had just performed some task which had strained his body strength to the uttermost.

"You were saying, 'No—no'!" Geogee told him.

"It was a bad dream," Jony answered quickly. "Just a bad dream."

However, he could not dismiss memory so easily for himself. Something of that two-partedness remained in his mind. He had wanted the power of the rod; he had hated and feared it. Now, suddenly, he did want to view that sleeper again, to make sure that the mask still lay over the face, that it was not, as in his dream, he who slept.

The People, early as it was, were moving about

the camp. No one looked at Jony or Geogee, or made finger-talk. Laid out on the ground not too far away was a portion of nut cake. Jony gave Geogee a share and wolfed the rest, suddenly realizing how hungry he was.

He had just wiped the crumbs from his fingers when he looked up to see that the males of the clan were gathering in around him. Geogee moved back a little, apprehension plain to read on his face. Jony put his arm protectively about the younger boy's shoulders for a moment, gave him a reassuring squeeze. Then he used both his hands for finger-talk.

"Young ones not to blame. They followed me."

Impassively those ranged about him made no sign in return. Voak reached out and closed a hand-paw on Geogee's arm, drawing the boy away from Jony, pushing him outside their circle, giving him a shove in the direction of the females.

He signed an answer: "Young follow always. Best older do not give them bad trail."

Jony relaxed a little for Geogee's sake. Anything which happened now would rest on him alone. He hoped that Geogee had had enough of a scare so that this lesson would stick with him. Voak was right, he was the one to blame if some law of the clan had been broken.

"Truth spoken," he signed. Then he waited. What would come now—a judging with some punishment to follow?

"You—come—" Voak replied.

He turned purposefully and Jony fell in behind him. Nor were they two alone. Otik of the younger males and Kapoor of the older joined them. No one returned Jony's staff; he drew an ominous conclusion from that omission. Wherever they might be going it was not near the camp, for each of his companions was equipped with a net of journey food.

All the more apprehensive because he had no idea what was intended, Jony went, a well-guarded prisoner, into the beginning of the morning.

> SEVEN <

They headed toward the higher ridges again—not in the direction of the stone place, but more to the northeast. Voak led purposefully, as if he knew exactly where they were bound. The familiar sights of the open country warred with the shadows in Jony's mind. Now it was easy for him to accept that what had frightened him *was* only a dream, born out of yesterday's strange adventure. Somehow he felt a relief from oppression, even though he did not know what the People planned for him.

He would *not* go back to the stone place, to face the masked one and make a choice between the rod and this freedom. Drawing a deep breath of pure relief, he luxuriated in the feel of dew-wet leaves brushing against his legs and the clean, clear air he drew into his lungs.

Though the People's rather clumsy walk might seem less effective than his own loose stride, Jony was forced to quicken that to keep up with his guards. This pushing pace was quite unlike that generally

kept when the clan was on the move. For then they
were apt to seek edible roots, berries, scraper stones,
over a wide area, each some distance from another
as they traveled.

The day was clear, with a bright, warm sun. In fact,
Jony was almost too warm as they emerged from under
the trees to cross a stretch of open land where grass
grew nearly waist high. Those creatures who lived in
that miniature turf jungle fled from them, their flight
marked only as a quick weaving. Here and there stood
some tall spikes of stem, wreathed with blue flowers
around which insects buzzed.

On the opposite side of that open land, brush
began again. Jony had expected Voak to thrust his way
in through it. Instead, the clanleader turned sharply
left, following the base of the rise. Jony was thirsty,
but he had no intention of allowing any discomfort
to make him appeal to Voak now. His pride stiffened
his resolve to ask nothing of his companions.

They had gone some little distance before Jony noted
ends of stones protruding here and there from the soil
of the ridge. These had been squared, though exposure
to the weather had pitted their surfaces, rounded the
edges. In spite of Trush's reaction to the stone path,
the strangeness of the clan since Jony had confessed
his visit to the place which had been made by the
aliens of the pictures, Voak appeared to be heading
on into a section where similar remains appeared.

Nor did the clansmen pause, when, before them
arose series of those same ledges Jony had climbed to
the place where the sleeper lay in his box. Earth masked
these in part, and several small saplings were rooted
along them. Yet it was very plain that once they had

been used to ascend the slopes behind the first ridge. Voak brought the butt of his staff down on each ledge with a thud as he mounted it, as if that gesture was some necessary announcement of their coming.

Kapoor and Otik echoed Voak's movements, their staffs rising and falling in company with his. The three also began to utter sounds, not unlike those they used when they were moon dancing, the notes rising and falling as they went. Jony sensed that both gestures and sounds were meant to protect against some menace which the clansmen thought lay ahead. Moreover, their present attitude was so unlike the sensible dispatch they used when actually attacked that his wonderment grew.

For any meeting with vor birds, or the smaa, there was no pounding of spear butts or calling of voices. The People fought in silence or uttered only a few hoarse grunts now and then. Jony used his own protective sense, sending it questing ahead. He felt naked without a staff in his own hand, and the attitude of his guards aroused his apprehension.

Still, he could pick up nothing. As the situation had been among the heaps of stone, so was it here. The life forces he touched were all that could be found anywhere else in the open. Then Jony tried to fasten on a very elusive emanation of . . . What? He found a disturbing hint of alien energy (though what he picked up was not born of any spark of life). Whatever waited ahead was not alive as he had always known life. No, it was . . .

A fleeting scrap of memory halted Jony. This outflow of energy was very near to what he had felt when he had dared touch palms with the woman of stone!

The clansmen had been so enrapt in their rhythmic thudding of staffs, their united sounds, that Otik and Kapoor gained a step ahead of Jony before they noted that he had stopped. They turned only a little, each reached out a hand-paw, clamping on his shoulders, drawing him up between them again.

There was no escaping their united wills. He must face whatever lay ahead. Realizing that, Jony tried to explore with his sense for what did wait there. It was not true life, of that he was sure. For he could not even pick up a hint of communication as he could with the People, unable as he was to ever reach them completely. However, there did exist somewhere ahead a force of some kind, a power to which his extra sense responded.

During those moments of the climb, Jony felt the odd and disturbing wash of that power. His body might have been plunged into a substance less tangible than water, but which had as strong a current as any good sized river might produce. Did the People also feel this, or was the thumping of staffs and the ululating sounds they voiced in some manner a shield against it?

Voak topped the long line of steps. He paused there, though he did not turn his head to see how far the others trailed him. Instead he quickened the beat of his staff against the bare rock on which he now stood. His voice was louder; the sounds he made faster as if he needed to build up his defense.

The smooth space on which the clanleader stood was large, as Jony saw when they joined the older male. Like the river of stone, the platform extended, a tongue out-thrust from the last of the ledges. Above, the heights had been broken or dug away to give room to that path, and the sides were walled up with stones to retain the earth.

A short distance ahead loomed a tall opening into the core of the hill. That, also, was rimmed with blocks of stone. This must have been the handiwork of the pictured men, Jony was sure. Yet the People appeared to be able and willing to enter here.

Otik and Kapoor echoed Voak's faster beat of staff, his louder voice. They did not glance in Jony's direction, but rather kept their gaze fastened on the opening ahead. They might be waiting here for someone, or something, to issue forth. But there was no hidden life, Jony would swear to that, just a stronger sense of that power he could not understand.

Once more Voak began his march toward the opening, the others falling in behind in the same pattern they had followed since leaving camp. Jony felt a little dizzy. Perhaps his giddiness was caused by the thumping, the cries—or the *thing* ahead. He could not seem to think clearly anymore.

Over their heads arched the edge of the opening. What light shone in from behind showed only a pavement of stone, the walls about. The way narrowed abruptly just within the doorless opening.

On they went, the duskiness increasing as they left the day behind. This absence of light made no difference to the three clansmen, but it added to Jony's feeling of disorientation. Was there never any end to the sounds, to this way?

Then, as if struck dumb in an instant, paralyzed by a stroke out of nowhere, the clansmen were quiet. There was no more thumping, no cries. Jony's hands went to his ears. He could still hear—something, a pulsing like the beat of a giant staff unable to rest. Now he swayed, his body seeming to bend in time to that beat, and he heard a mighty cry out of Voak's thick throat. The sound scaled up and up, until Jony's ears could no longer distinguish it, only he could still feel the vibration of that ululation through him.

What happened was as startling as the moving wall in the city. Dark and shadows split apart. Light shone from beyond: a ruddy light, not gray like that which Jony had faced in the storage places. This radiance pulsed also, as if it were a part of the power which now enveloped him, made his flesh tingle, his mind spin.

Their way being open, Voak continued, still silent. In the red glow of the light the clansmen's fur took on odd new tints. An aura surrounded them, made up of many colors which spun, faded, mingled in a glow until one could not be clearly defined from another, while the tingling of Jony's exposed skin neared real pain.

They had entered a place not unlike those underground ways which he had followed with the twins. But this was not so large. And in the center was—

Jony shrank back. He could not help that momentary reaction. All he had escaped when he and Rutee won free of the ship came flaring back into his mind. For the center of the rounded inner space or cave in which they stood was occupied by a cage!

They were not going to shut him up! Jony's second reaction was as quick and even more fierce than the first. Never would he be in a cage again! The clan could kill him first!

"No!" he shouted his protest, not caring if the People understood or not. But Otik's and Kapoor's combined strength were greater than his. They held him by the arms again, forced him forward, though Jony fought frenziedly for his freedom. He could see no sign of any open door in that barred enclosure ahead. Voak did no more than move a little to one side, watching the boy's ineffectual struggles.

The clanchief dropped his staff to the floor, his hands engaged in an imperative talk sign.

"Look!"

Jony followed the pointing of that dark hand-paw. Now that he was closer he could see that the cage was already occupied—by bones! And below those empty-eyed skulls rested wide collars.

Only the skulls—the bodies—they were not of the People. They were too slender, too small. Who had been imprisoned to their deaths in this place where the dancing light carried the tinge of blood? Also, that light itself—what was it, flashing from a hole in the floor beyond the cage?

Voak squatted heavily and worked one thick arm between the bars of the sealed cage. His fingers closed on the nearest of the wide collars. Bones tumbled as he drew it toward him. He rose, the collar looped over his arm like a massive, ill-fitting bracelet.

The clanchief began to sign slowly, with exaggerated movements of his hands. As if what he must communicate was of the utmost importance and he wished Jony to clearly understand what he would say.

"People," his thumb indicated his own barrel body, "this—" He twirled the collar around, his gesture one of loathing and hatred as he raised it to his neck as if about to fit the band around his own throat. "We do—collar—says—or die. They—" now his pointing was to the bones within the cage, "make collars, use People.

They—" he hesitated as if at a loss, feeling the need to improvise for Jony's better understanding, "find bad things—bad for them. They die fast—only few left. People not die, People break out. Put collars on those, then *they* do what People say. But they already bad sick—die. People no wear collars again—never!" His final gesture of negation resembled a forceful threat.

"Look!" Now Voak held the collar only inches away from Jony's face, as if to make very sure the boy would understand perfectly. With the band so gripped between the clansman's fingers, there sprang out of its edge a row of stiff points. Eyeing those Jony believed they were set so that, once about a throat, those points would cut into the flesh were the head moved out of a single, stiffly upright position.

Voak flipped the end of a finger against the nearest point. "Fang—" he signed. "Hurt from collar—hurt People if *they* wanted . . . Bad. You—" Now he gave Jony an intent, searching stare which traveled from the other's head to his feet and back again. "You cub—People take, help—give food—give nest. But you are like *them* . . . you go to find collar—make People do what you say . . ."

"No!" Jony protested aloud, trying to move his hands in the strongest of the negative signals, but the two who held him did not release him enough for him to complete that denial.

Voak did not seem to hear him. Instead the clansman turned the collar around in his fingers, examining it carefully. Now he pressed again and the band opened. While Otik and Kapoor held Jony immobile, Voak stepped forward and fitted the collar about the boy's throat, snapped the band shut. The circlet was

loose, lying down on his shoulders as Jony bent his
head to stare at it in horror.

"You wear—you remember," Voak signed. "You go
to *them* again—you shall feel fangs also. The People
do not forget. You shall not forget!"

The others had loosed him. Jony reached up to jerk
the band around his neck. Loose as it was, its very
weight made him sick and somehow ashamed. Voak,
the others, turned away as if Jony was no longer any
concern of theirs. He followed them, suddenly struck
by a second and worse fear: that he would be left
here forever in a place where that cage of bones stood
as a dire warning against enslavement of the People.

He ran his fingertips around and around that ring,
seeking whatever catch Voak had found to open it.
But the secret eluded him. Now Jony realized that
the clansman meant exactly what he had signed: the
boy was to wear this symbol of servitude as a warning. If he tried to return to the place of stones, even
worse would follow.

Having set their shaming bondage on him, all three
of the People appeared to lose interest in Jony. They
did not look back as once more they crossed to the
top of the steps and started down. Jony had a feeling
that to Voak and the others he was no longer of the
clan; he had ceased to exist as an equal.

His numb surprise gave way to a beginning flash of
anger. The judgment of Voak and the rest had been
given without a chance for Jony to defend himself.
What had he done? Entered the stone place, come
out again with the twins—that was all!

If, perhaps, he had brought with him the red rod
Geogee had found... Then—

Jony stopped. His dream! In his dream this had been the way he had felt. With the rod in his hand he could have given orders and had them obeyed—or else. He felt his fingers curl now and glanced down to the hand held out before him. In his mind there for a moment he did not imagine himself holding a staff, but the rod. *Had* that been so, in his hot anger for the burden Voak had laid upon him, he might have raised the alien weapon and used it.

No! Jony shook his head vigorously, as if by strong denial he could drive out that momentary wish.

What would he have done to the Big Ones in the past had he had the power to be stronger and greater than they? In his fear for the return of the bondage of his people was Voak any different?

Yes, but Jony in the ship had faced those very ones who had caged Voak and his people, and had set upon most of them the terrible fate of the mind-controlled. While now Jony had not threatened Voak and the rest...

Their feeling for him must have begun because he physically resembled those others: the ones painted on the walls and the stone woman. Yet how did Voak *know* that? Unless for all their aversion, the People *had* explored the stone place, had seen those pictures, the waiting woman. Still Jony was almost convinced that the clansmen had not. This whole country was new to the clan. Then—how did Voak and the rest know that Jony resembled those ancient enemies? Memory, relayed through folktales and myths, could be passed down through generations. But if Voak and the others remembered their former masters with hatred, then why had Yaa ever come to Rutee's aid?

If there were an ancient hatred of Jony's own species dictated by form alone, Yaa would have ignored
the fugitives, even as Voak, Otik, and Kapoor now
did him, leaving woman and child alone to die on a
strange and hostile world.

Yet, until he and the twins had ventured into the
place of stones, the People had accepted them placidly,
without question—or seemingly so—as living creatures
not unlike themselves. Did Voak believe that going
into the stone place awakened in Jony a desire for
that power which the ancients had commanded?

As Jony thought of one possibility after another,
trying to explain actions he could not understand,
his flare of anger died. Voak was wrong to fear him,
but he, Jony, could not tell what long-dreaded terror
ruled the People. To Voak and the rest he might now
seem to be the enemy, or at least one who must be
watched.

If Jony trailed back with them to the clan camp,
what would follow? He did not believe they would
launch any attack against him. But, with a growing
desolation of spirit, Jony began to guess what might
happen. As they had last night, the clansmen would
treat him as one who was not. He had never known
such a punishment before. Usually their justice was
swift, then forgotten. But to be with the clan and yet
not *of* it ... And what of Maba and Geogee? If they
showed sympathy toward him, might not the same
blighting non-existence be laid on them?

Jony dropped on the top ledge. Already the clansmen had reached the bottom of that descent. Not once
had they turned to look back or showed any interest
in him. He felt more alone even than he had on the

night he crouched beside Rutee, unable to ease her pain. His hand rose to that shameful ring about his neck. He *was* in a cage again. As long as he wore that he was caged within himself, even if he had the whole country free before him.

Voak and the others vanished, treading purposefully back the way they had come. Jony made no move to descend and follow. Putting his elbows on his knees, he rested his head in his hands and closed his eyes. He had to think!

There was no purpose to be gained by his being angry. Voak, the others, they must have acted as they thought best for the clan. Jony could not judge their actions, not when he knew so little of what lay behind all this. He tried now to recall, in what detail he could, that picture on the wall, the one in which the People had been shown tied and led about, or caged.

But he had hurried past it so fast he had now only a jumbled impression. The one fact being that the People, as pictured there, were slightly different in form from the clan. None of them had been depicted as walking erect, rather all had been using both hand-paws and feet against the ground. That was the main difference he could now recall.

Had the People changed after they won their freedom? Or had they been forced by their captors to remain animal-like? Jony shuddered. The Big Ones had done such things with the mind-controlled at times. Rutee had told him that the Big Ones had not considered humans as more than animals; animals to be broken, controlled, used for their own purposes. The horror which this had meant for her had been passed on to him, young as he was. Even if he could not know how life had been before the Big Ones had taken over the colony, he realized he was an intelligent being.

Had the People been mind-controlled also? Or did they remember, with all of Rutee's horror, being "animals" to contemptuous aliens? Were the people of the stone place from off this world?

They must have lived here a long time to build that place. And where did the river of stone run? From this stone place to another such, standing at a more distant site? They had had sky ships—those had appeared in the pictures.

Jony's head ached; he was both hungry and thirsty. But he could not shift off the feeling of burdensome weight on his shoulders. In these moments of confusion and despair, he knew that he was not going back to the campsite, at least not now. Voak had set on him the badge of the owned. Somehow he must be free before he returned; free of the collar in such a manner that Voak and the rest could not place it upon him again.

He sat up straight. The world spread out below him seemed very wide, wide and empty! Since the night Yaa had found them, he had never been aloof from the People. Before that, even though their cages had been separated, there was always Rutee. To think of himself as utterly alone was a realization which brought fear—not of anything he could sense or touch, but, in a strange way, of the land, the sky, the whole world about him.

To sit here was no answer to his problem. And to return to the place of cage—if he could return now—was none either. He must find food, water, a—a staff. His hands seemed so empty and useless without a staff.

Unbidden, unwished, once more the thought of the red rod flashed across his mind. Power greater than any staff...*NO!* Jony's lips moved to shape that word. He must prove to Voak that he was not one with the stone people—he had to prove that!

Food, water, a weapon-tool, they came first and foremost. With those he was himself again. Once given those he could think—plan—find some way to free himself of the metal band so cold and heavy about his throat. In time he might be able to discover the secret of its lock and so get rid of it. But he needed, most of all, to return the collar to the clan with their clear understanding that this was not his to wear.

He descended the steps carefully to the way by the ridge. The campsite lay to his left. Jony turned sharply right.

➤ EIGHT ◄

Perhaps this stream he had chanced on was the same one that farther back fed the falls where Maba and Geogee had splashed and played. Only now matters were different. As he went slowly, Jony hunted under upturned, water-washed stones for enough of the small, shelled things to satisfy his hunger. He drank his fill from his cupped hands. At length, with hunger and thirst in abeyance, he looked about him for his third need: a staff.

Traveling along the sand of the stream's lip, he chewed at a handful of tart leaves from one of the plants he knew well as a part of the clan diet. For the moment he had pushed all questions far to the back of his mind, determined to be occupied only by the here and now, though he was unable to forget the weight about his throat, or what it meant.

Foraging proved so good along the stream that Jony disliked leaving the water's edge. But, though he had found pieces of drift caught among the rocks which might have possibilities for a staff, he vaguely mistrusted their smooth, bleached lengths. No, he would have to head outward toward a real stand of trees to locate what he wanted.

Even as Jony made to turn away from the bank, he caught sight of a bright glint from among the rocks just ahead. Curious, he went to see what had been caught there. Another bit of drift? No, for along the side of this piece a length of caked coating had flaked away, to release that gleam which the sun had betrayed to him. He knew of no wood resembling this.

In fact the shaft could not be wood at all. For, when Jony drew it out of the crevice into which it had fallen or been jammed by flood water, the straight length was heavier than any staff he had ever lifted. That coating around the bright slash appeared to be hardened clay, combined with a red substance which powdered off on his hands. Squatting down, Jony chose a stone and began to scrape at his find, his persistence revealing more and more of what he was now sure was metal. This was longer than the deadly red rods of the stone place, and not the same color at all. A little of his old curiosity kept him to the cleaning, first with stone rubbing, and then with handfuls of sand. At last he held something which was not unlike the staffs of the clansmen, though shorter. It even possessed a curve at one end, though that did not altogether resemble those crooks which were such useful tools. This curve (Jony held a cut finger in the flow of the stream) had a sharpened edge which was far more dangerous than any point a clansman could put on his weapon-tool.

The metal sides were pitted with small holes. However, when Jony lifted the rod high, to bring it crashing

down on the nearest large rock with all his strength,
the length did not snap or bend. Instead, the rock itself
was scarred by that stroke. He rubbed it again, this
time with leaves, cleaning off the sand and the last of
the red powder. What he had was, he was sure, a tool
which had been purposefully made, probably by those
people of the stone place. However, the thing carried
no taint of power as the red rods did. In form it was
plainly such a staff as he could never hope to make
for himself.

Jony sat fingering the pole resting across his knees.
The feel was good, fitting to his hand smoothly in
spite of the pitting. He liked the weight of it. And
that cutting, edged part at the top—there were many
uses to which that could be put. He had not taken
this from the storehouse of the stone place, so it did
not seem forbidden. Long ago it must have been
lost, or discarded as useless. Therefore, Jony made
his decision.

Right or wrong, this was his. He had found and
cleaned it. If he must go a long way through this world
for now, then he would have the best protection he
could lay hand upon. He—

Only that shadow across the sand came as a warning! Jony had been so absorbed in his find that he had
not posted the sentry of his mind which was his most
important defense. He did not even have time to get
to his feet to meet an attack launched from the sky.

There sounded a scream, so high and shrill, as to
hurt his ears. The vor screeched aloud its triumph as
it dropped, talons spread, its head weaving back and
forth. Jony swept the staff upward with a frenzied
hope of beating off that plunge. He could see above

the first attacker, two others of that noisome species
sailing about, perhaps the half-grown young of the first.

His wild sweep of the staff connected with the
plunging predator. Only by chance, and no real thought,
had Jony used the end with the curved blade. The jar
of his blow landing sent him sprawling back, while
fear closed in. For he was now totally defenseless
before the death strike of the vor.

However the bird had been beaten out of line
when his blow fell. It screeched again, not in triumph,
but in rage and agony. One of the great taloned legs
flopped loosely. Blood spurted from a deep wound
opened by the sharp edge.

Up the vor soared with a strong beat of wings.
Jony scrambled to his feet, set his back to the nearest rock. The other two birds were plunging down to
meet their fellow. He had not escaped, he had only
earned a breathing space.

Blood trickled down the length of the staff, was
sticky on his fingers. He momentarily transferred hold
of the staff, wiped his hand on the side of his kilt.
Three vors, and, once they went into combat, they
would not sheer off. He had no chance at all.

The wounded one screamed in on a second dive.
But this time Jony was ready. He thought now he
knew a little of what the staff could do. Only it would
be very good fortune if he were able to land another
telling blow. He forced himself to wait until the last
moment of that strike, then brought the staff around
in a sweep into which he put all his strength, aiming to connect it with the long, twisting neck of the
raging creature.

He missed that mark. But the curved blade hit hard

on the near wing about where it met the vor's body. The force of that blow hurled the flying thing away. Now the attacker could only use one wing, beat that frantically, its screams making a din in the air. Unable to continue airborne, the creature fell among the rocks on the other side of the stream, where it flopped and cried, blood spattering far from its two wounds. Jony, hardly able to believe in his escape, had no eyes for it. He strained upward to watch the two above. At that moment he also unleashed his concentrated sense of command. As with the People, he could not enforce his will on the brain of any creatures of this world. But he might be able to confuse them—a little.

The pair continued to circle over his head. So far he could detect no signs that either was preparing to strike. Perhaps because they were young, they were more puzzled, wary, than an adult vor would be. Jony edged back between two rocks. In the open he felt naked. Though these stones rose to only about his shoulder height, he gained a small sense of security when standing between them. Staff in hand he waited.

Then he tensed. One of the vors had made up its mind. Jony caught the slight change in flight pattern which meant attack. Though smaller than the wounded one yet flopping and shrieking across the water, the creature was still a very dangerous opponent. Jony gripped his staff, knowing that again he must wait. Only his superior weapon had saved him so far, of that he was convinced. But he could not rely on that good fortune to continue. He must be ready to—

The vor dropped, this time silently, without warning. Jony readied himself for a swing. He thought he had little chance of striking the neck, but his success

in catching the wing of the other had given him a
lead as to the best way to meet any attack. He swung
again vigorously.

Once more the blow hit home. The vor squalled.
The creature seemed unable to halt its downward
swoop, and hit the sand beyond the rocks, flopping.
Jony took a chance. He burst from his rock defense
and lashed down with several blows. One hit the
darting head, smashing it.

Breathing hard, Jony backed into his poor refuge,
looked up for the third and last vor. Unlike its fellows,
it was not of a mind to carry on the battle. Instead,
after circling twice and hooting mournfully, it flapped
away. Jony stared at the still twitching vor near him,
that other which tried to deny death on the other
side of the water. Two *vors!* He was dazed at the
fact of his escape. His staff was sticky with blood,
more was splashed on him, on the rocks about. But
he was *safe!* Weakly he leaned back on the stones
which half-supported him.

Clansmen killed attacking vors, yes. But only when
working as a team with a thought-out defense plan.
Jony had never known one of the People alone who
had finished off two of the great predators.

Near his feet the second one had gone limp at last.
While that on the far side of the water was moving
only weakly, loss of blood bringing death. Jony forced
himself a stride or two forward, used the blade end
of his staff to prod the near body. There was no sign
of life.

The fetid stench of the creature, together with the
blood about, made Jony queasy. He moved further
upstream. There he not only scrubbed his new weapon

with sand and water, but washed his own sweated body and stained kilt, so that no possible taint of his kill remained.

There was movement downstream. He saw some of the scavengers that were always quick to find any kill dart out of the rock's shade and scuttle toward the body. By tomorrow there would only be well-cleaned bones left. Jony eyed the vicious talons of the dread creatures. Those had uses. He might stay near enough to claim them as trophies when the feasters were done.

Suddenly he smiled grimly. Though the People did not adorn themselves with anything but their food gathering nets, he had a sudden idea. Those talons he might hang from the collar. If he ever returned to the clan and was able to loosen that yoke they had laid upon him, it would please him greatly to have added this proof of his own ability to survive the burden they had put on him as a punishment and warning.

This staff—never had there been one like this! His hands slipped back and forth along the surface, avoiding the sharp hook at the end, caressingly. Jony took time now to study that edged hook with great care. It was shaped not unlike a fang, a giant fang. He had no such natural fighting equipment of his own, as the People carried in their jaws. But now he could boast of a fang in his hand, use it well...

Prudence dictated a withdrawal upstream. Those dead vors would draw more than these small scavengers already busy. Also Jony wanted to get away from the stench of death and blood. He would find someplace near where he could make a night nest. Only, never again must he relax to the point he was unaware of life about him. His own foolish mistake had nearly provided him as fodder for the flying death. He must learn how to use his sense wisely. However, not with such a power of induced concentration that he would not also be conscious of what lay immediately about him. For here there was no one of the clan to give him the illusion of safety while he freed his mind for questing ahead.

He found a good space among rocks and made several trips into a stretch of grassland to pull up that wiry growth in armloads and bring his harvest back to his nest site. As he moved now, Jony kept instantly alert for any return of the vor, any suggestion that there was other danger abroad in this land. The time was still well before the coming of dusk when he harvested fruit from a couple of high growing bushes, returned with it back to his camp. The land here was rich in provender, but there was no sign that any clan had wandered into it. Perhaps there was a roost of vor too near to make the country safely open for the People's accustomed daylight roaming by twos or threes.

As Jony settled into his retreat, he thought once more of Maba and Geogee. Voak had stated the twins would not be held responsible for their visit to the stone place, so he believed that they would not have to fear an exile like his. And Yaa could control Maba, Voak would probably have Geogee under close watch. Neither would be allowed to return to the stone place.

All those questions which had filled Jony's mind in the morning were still to be answered, if he could ever find answers for any of them. The main one which troubled him now was: would his collar shut him off from the People forever? He did not want to consider what that might mean, yet he could not push the thought aside.

To be always and ever alone! There might be other clans near. There were such, he had contact with them during those meetings which were held from time to time. But he guessed that as long as he wore this collar he would not be accepted among any of the People.

Within his heaped nest Jony moved uneasily. It was one thing to spend the night thus, knowing that within arm's reach were curled companions. But he had never been alone. He lay back now, his eyes closed, though he did not sleep. Instead, Jony journeyed back and back, as far as his memory would take him. To escape the present, he thought of the past.

At first he tried to envision details of the lab in the sky ship. He had always been able to recall as mental pictures small scenes when he had wished. What had been the very first memory of all?

He had been with Rutee in her cage. She had patiently told him over and over who he was, how they had come there. They had once been as free as the People. Then the Big Ones had come, and they were caged. Some of their kind the Big Ones killed slowly, studying them as they died. Rutee had looked sick when she had told Jony that, but she had made him listen. Others they made into the mind-controlled. But a few could not be so trained, Rutee was one, he even more so.

The Big Ones had traveled through the sky away from Rutee's world. There had been other worlds visited, too. Other captives, though none resembling Rutee's own people. At last they had reached here. Though Rutee had never known where "here" was.

She had shown Jony the stars at night, pointed to this one and that. But she said that they were s·

"wrong," that none of them seemed the stars she had known when she had lived outside before. Therefore the sky ship had taken them very far from her colony world. There was no chance of their ever getting back to their own kind again.

Her people had also had sky ships. They had flown out from a world which was their own, settled on other worlds. For a long time they had been doing that. Rutee was not even sure just where their first home world was. It had not been the world on which she and Bron were born, before they joined to help make up another colony. Long and far...

Could it have been this world? Was that why he, Maba, and Geogee looked so like the stone people? But Rutee had not known the People, nor heard of them before. However it might still be a world her people had found once and lived upon.

Jony remembered now, with a fierce desire to hold to every fraction of the pictures in his mind, the seasons they had wandered with the clan. From helpless babies Maba and Geogee had grown to bigger, more thinking creatures. Rutee had talked always with Jony about his own kind. She hoped someday that chance might bring one of their scout ships here. So she taught him the speech of her people, even how to trace marks in the sand or on pieces of bark, signs which carried and held the meaning of those words after one had forgotten them.

Then Rutee had died. He missed her very much. Still there were the twins, the clan. He had not been alone. Jony sat up suddenly, his eyes open, fighting fear and loneliness. His hands clenched on his wonder staff. He was fed, he had fought such a battle as few of the People had faced, all by himself. He had a safe camp. But—he wore the collar.

If he only knew more! Could he, dared he, return to the place of stones to learn?

Perhaps those other people, if they were of his kind, even so far divided, had made signs for their words. The dead cannot speak, but signs could speak for them. Would Voak, the clan, know if he attempted such a mission?

Voak's warning was still clear in his memory. However, if he were exiled, what would it mean to Voak that he went back? Jony would never turn against the clan, he could not.

Maba—Geogee? What if Voak used them to punish Jony for breaking the command he had laid upon the boy? No return then—at least not yet. Jony must do nothing which the clanleader could use as an excuse to make trouble for the twins.

Then—where would he go now? He could trail behind the clan on its wanderings. But he did not want to, not on their terms. Either he would return wholly, one of them as he had been before, or he would keep away.

Jony nodded his head vigorously, though there was no one there to witness this affirmation of his decision. So—in the morning he would follow this stream as a guide. It led on up into the higher hills beyond these beginning ridges, toward those mountains where the earth seemed to challenge the sky and the night stars. Perhaps he would find another stone place, one which Voak's people did not watch. There . . . Jony did not know what he could do there, what he honestly wanted to do. But to move on was better by far than to sit here waiting, or to trail behind the clan as if they had a leash fastened to his shame collar, and so led him along at their will.

How he wished now that he had paid more attention to the pictures on the wall of the storage place. He scowled over that loss of opportunity. Odd—though there had been power there—the sensation had not been as strong as it had when they had gone to the place of the cage.

Was that feeling really the power of hate held within the cage itself: hate of the People, hate of those who had died there? Jony had always been able to sense emotions, even physical pain that had troubled Rutee or the twins. To a much less extent he could also sense pain and trouble with the clan. But could such feelings continue to exist after death?

The stone woman—had the shock from her hand been a remembered emotion passing from that cold, impassive palm into his live one—or something else? He knew so little. Impatience burned high in Jony, just as momentary anger had flared after Voak's sentencing. There was so much he did not understand, and he needed to! The desire for knowledge was now like real pain in him.

How had those captives in the cage died? Quickly, or slowly? Had they been left to perish from hunger and thirst? Or fed and prisoned until their spirits died first, and they had no will left in them to live on?

His collar—Jony put both hands to the band at his throat. Did that loose hoop of metal hold the power of past emotion? He could sense nothing directly from it. Any more than he could from the shaft with the mounted fang of death.

Slowly he turned the collar around, taking care lest some touch of his release those tormenting fangs Voak had demonstrated. Under his fingers the surface was smooth. Unlike the shaft, here was no pitting. The thing could be fresh made, though he believed it was of an age he could not begin to reckon.

No power in it. Then where had the power lain in the cage place? Had it been summoned by the sounds the clansmen had made with their thumping and their cries?

Jony tried an experiment of his own. With the butt end of the shaft he began tapping gently on one of the rocks which guarded his nest, trying to keep to the same speed Voak and the others had used. Vibration did run up the shaft into his arm. But he experienced none of that tingling sensation.

Perhaps the sensation came then from the red light. Could one draw upon such power, feed it into one's own concentrated energy? What was the use of thinking that? Jony had no intention of trying to find the place of the cage again. Contrarily, he preferred to travel as far away from its site as he could.

Within the past few days his mind had become crowded with questions, enough to make his head ache. During all the seasons he had roamed with the People Jony had never speculated so much about matters which were not concerned with the daily round of existence. He felt, oddly enough, as if he had just now wakened from a kind of lulling sleep. After Rutee died, he had not tried to share any of his thoughts with the twins. To him they were responsibilities, not real persons. He was to watch over them, not communicate to them his own doubts and uncertainties.

His limited contact with the People themselves had been confined to the level of what was only necessary for the continued well-being of life.

So Jony had ceased much to question where there could be no answering. His discovery of the river of stone had first shaken him out of the dull shell that lack of real companionship had built about him. Jony had always been different, but he had ruthlessly tried to suppress that difference, to be as like the People as he could. Now he was exiled into difference. So his imagination awoke, pricked at him with new questions upon questions.

Nor could he sleep as this new wakefulness possessed him and made him restless. He would have liked to have strode back and forth out in the moonlight, under those stars Rutee did not know, attempting to dull his thoughts again.

For Jony was no longer complacent. He was uneasy, on edge. Somewhere he must find answers— somewhere...

He had been facing downstream. But also he had been looking skyward. The vor did not attack by night, his sense found no menace there.

Then—

Across the sky a burst of vivid fire.

Wha—?

Jony's hands gripped the staff so tightly his knuckles stood out in hard knobs. He trembled as if reeling under some strong blow.

Perhaps because his awareness had been so aroused that he knew—somehow he *knew!*

Had Rutee ever told him? Now he was not sure. But

he was as certain as if he had witnessed the planeting. That had been a sky ship! And it was going to land!

The Big Ones!

Hate drew Jony's mouth tight, brought him to his feet, his wonder staff up and ready. No!

The flashing sweep was gone. He strained to hear any sound. And thought he caught a hint of a far-off roar. Yes, the ship was down. Now the Big Ones would come hunting. The People—the twins—they had no idea of what hellish things the Big Ones could and would do. He must return to the clan, make them listen! Collar or no collar, he had to make them listen.

Jony was already running lightly along the sand on his back trail. All that lay in his mind now was how much time he might have before the Big Ones came hunting for their prey.

> NINE <

A bad fall brought Jony back to his senses. To go charging along without caution at night through this unknown country was stupid. He sat on the sandy ground nursing a skinned shin, eyeing the dark as the enemy it now was.

There was no way of judging how far away that landing of the sky ship had been. Perhaps it had planeted so distantly from the clan campsite that all his fears were unfounded. But, from Rutee's tales, he knew that the Big Ones possessed other means of travel besides the sky ships themselves. They carried within the larger vessels small craft made to grind steadily ahead over any kind of ground, or take into the air for a distance, if there was need.

How soon would those craft be out searching?

Jony beat one balled fist against the ground in frustration. He must get to the campsite, make Voak and the others listen!

Would the stone place draw the Big Ones? He knew from his life among them that they had explored such sites on other worlds, bringing back objects they had stored with care.

Jony got to his feet and, leaning on the sturdy support of his new staff, limped stubbornly on. He would follow this stream which ran in the general direction southward. If it *was* the same as the one that ran near the camp, he had now a sure guide. And, if he took more care, he could travel even in the darkness.

But even the stream side was none too easy a trail. Twice he came upon piled rock barriers through which he had to find a way, prodding ahead with the butt of his staff to make sure each stone was secure before he put his full weight on it. Once he had to make a detour around a pile of drift embedded in the sand, a menace he dared not cross in the dark.

His leg ached and there was more pain if he put too much weight on that foot. However, slowly as he must go, he would certainly reach camp by morning. He could not have traveled too far north after Voak and the others had left him.

The graying of pre-dawn filled the sky as Jony reached the lip of the falls. There was no sign of the People below. The boy half-fell on an outcrop of stone, the throbbing of his leg matched by a weariness throughout his body. Yet he had still to descend the drop beside that veil of water.

Maba? Geogee? For a long moment he played with the thought of using the mind touch to draw the children to him, to relay the message he had come to deliver, the warning. Then he knew he dared not. Neither of the twins was receptive enough to pick up his clear thoughts, though they might be moved to come hunting him. And, if they did that, their own safety with the clan could be endangered. He dared not work through the twins, but must meet Voak face to face.

However, when he concentrated on the camp, he met only a blank nothingness. Not even the flickering in and out of his usual touch with the People answered his probe.

Jony knew panic then, which, if he had not instantly controlled it might have sent him ahead with a recklessness leading to disaster. Nothing—there was nothing there!

The Big Ones! A raid on the campsite already?

Jony crawled to the drop and began to scramble from rock to rock. He had earlier tied his staff to his back with a twist of fibre so that he would have both hands free. Twice his weapon clattered against stones with a sound loud enough to rise above even the rumble of the falls.

Down, down. Now he was near that very place where Maba had been dragged unwillingly ashore, her hair fast in Uga's grip. Jony limped on, leaving his hands free. To enter the campsite with his shaft on his back would surely be a gesture of peaceful intent. As he breathed heavily his mind-sense ranged ahead, intent on picking up the least hint of where the People might be camped.

There was nothing. Just as he found nothing in sight when he came into the glade within the brush screen where there should have been the night nests, the stir of awakening People.

Nests were there, but they were empty. Jony went to that one to which Yaa had taken Maba the last time he had seen her. Under his fingers the withered grass and leaves were cold. By the appearance no fresh foliage had been added, as was usual, the night before.

Therefore the clan had not slept here. They must have moved on! Taking Maba and Geogee where?

Jony slowly circled the edge of the site. He was not really surprised to find the traces of that withdrawal as he reached the south side. The People must have decided they were too near to the stone place, that they were going to change their direction of slow drift.

But it was also to the south that the sky ship had planeted. Was the clan now walking straight into a danger they could not understand?

He made a careful search of the campsite. His gleanings were a food net with a hole in the side, a castoff, and some of the rubbing stones Otik had been putting to use. There was nothing else.

Nor could he throw off the knowledge that he must now do what he swore only yesterday that he would never do, trail behind the clan until he found them. He could only hope that their pace would continue to be normally leisurely, that they followed their usual occupations of food gathering to slow them as they went.

A day—or at least a part of a day ahead. That should not delay too much his catching up. Heartened by that belief, Jony ate the last of the bruised fruit he carried from last night's meal and returned to that southward direction.

This was a trail easy enough to follow. He could readily pick up the broad paw prints of the People here and there where there was a bare stretch of soil, and twice smaller tracks left by the twins. However, their going was different this time, not spread out in a loose numbering of one, two or three, but rather remaining in a close group, all together.

Jony climbed the next ridge, favoring his leg. From here he could look down once more to where the river of stone cut across the open country. He was too far west to see the place where it ended, ridges to the east masking the walls. But any Big One exploring would be able to detect such a site immediately.

The trail of the clan led straight, still compact, down ridge, on to the river of stone. Had they gone up to the heaps? Jony could hardly believe they would. Yet their tracks ended at the edge of that pavement.

He ventured out again on the smooth surface, only to strike directly across. His guess was right, the People had dared make contact with the evidence of all they hated only because there was no other way to reach the ground beyond. There once more he could sight their tracks, still close together.

This very unusual method of travel was a warning in itself that all was not well. He had never known the People to bunch as they traveled, unless they were skirting some ground in which a smaa had hunting trails of its own. There had been no move either, Jony noted, to harvest the heavy seed heads of a growth of vegetation only a short distance away.

South—and straight across the open where the Big Ones (if any of them prowled afar from their ship) could easily sight them.

Jony made the fastest time he could himself crossing that same stretch. Tall as the grass was, the growth could not hide even Maba. And the clan still marched together in an almost straight line. There was a promising darker rise of trees and brush before him, but that was some distance away.

He ate as he went, snatching handfuls of the seed, chewing them vigorously to get what nourishment each contained before he spat out mouthfuls of husks. Dry eating indeed, and he began to long to see the stream again. However, below the falls, the river had taken a curve to head farther west.

As he went, Jony kept his search sense alert. There was, as yet, no contact with the party he sought. Which meant that they had out-distanced him more than he had first guessed. He tried to quicken pace, eager to be under the safe roofing of the trees ahead, since the sky could now be a roadway for the enemy.

The heat of the sun was shut off abruptly as he stumbled under the taller growth he had sought. Here was still an open trail, no wandering from it. Jony could not guess what moved Voak and the others to set aside all their ordinary ways of travel. Or—was it because of him?

Did they wish so much to lose all contact with Jony that they had moved the clan out immediately upon their return, pushing on so he could not easily catch up?

Slow moving as the People generally were, they had great endurance, much more than his own. For some time he had not sighted those smaller prints marking Maba and Geogee's presence. It could be that the twins were now riding on big shoulders, as they had when they were much smaller and tired quickly during a journey.

When he had started out on this trail, Jony had been sure he would catch up with the clan fast enough. His concern had been all for their acceptance or denial of his warning. But, as the day wore steadily on and his own endurance flagged (not only from the ache in his leg, but from sheer weariness), he began to wonder if he were ever going to find them at all.

This wooded country proved to be only a small tongue thrust out from greater thickets to the west. However, evidence of their passing gave him a thin hope the clan had not turned in that direction (where, indeed, they might well have lost him completely), but held to their southward trek as steadily as if they traveled with a definite purpose in mind.

Jony noted now, however, that at last their foragers were out seeking foodstuffs, although none strayed very far from the line of march. Jony himself snatched fruit from the same places in turn. He came at last to a spring and threw himself down in deeply dented, moist, clay to drink. It was plain the clan had found this water earlier. The sight of those tracks renewed his spirit and determination, for they had not been made too long before.

He settled there knowing that he must rest. His weariness wore on him as if the collar was a mighty burden sinking him, under its pressure, to the earth. It was as he lay thus that he heard the new sound.

A humming, buzzing, a little of both, yet not entirely either. But a noise he had never listened to before. His mind searched...

Jony sat up.

"No!" He even cried the word aloud. Then once more he made contact.

Not Maba, no, not Geogee. Patterns of thought reached his mind, as individual as faces were in his sight. He had, in that moment, contacted neither of the twins. But the mind he had touched so briefly, it *was* one of his own kind.

The scattered bits of thought which were his only answer when he tried to communicate so with the People—he was well versed to recognize those. And he believed he could never forget the way the Big Ones thought, though those were as strange to follow, if much clearer.

This—this was like touching Rutee! Not mind-controlled, a free mind—one with the same pattern as his own.

Meanwhile the sound grew louder, more persistent. Jony hunkered back under the largest bush near enough for him to reach. Then he raised his staff and cautiously pushed aside some branches to bare a piece of sky hardly larger than his two hands laid together. In his shock at what his alerting sense had told him, he dared not use his talent again—not yet.

Through his hole he caught only a glimpse of what hovered overhead: not a sky ship, but a vehicle much, much smaller, possessing the appearance of several trees, denuded of both branches and roots and fastened tightly together to form an object curved at either end. Sunlight glinted as the craft swooped over his sky hole and was gone, the ship's brilliance having some of the same quality as the light from his sand-polished staff.

The Big Ones? No, that had been no enemy mind he had touched in that startling moment of contact. Rather some life-form akin to his own rode in the sky on that flying thing!

People from another stone place? One which had

not died long years ago? Jony thought not, The People would have known of their continued existence, he was sure. Then—could this be a ship of his *own* people—such as Rutee had sworn had carried her in the long ago to the colony world?

Jony's excitement flared. Still, caution, taught by the past, kept him where he was, quiet and attentive. Warily once more he tried mind contact. He was sure he could recognize the mind-controlled. If this was some trick of the Big Ones to entice their prey out of hiding...

Jony found the right level of contact, held it. Again only for an instant. For that other had reacted, had felt Jony's invasion, and had met his quest with a sudden alert.

Surely *not* mind-controlled! One of *them* would never have known, or cared. They were too used to being directed by the Big Ones. Jony tried to sort out the jumbled impressions he had gained in what was less than a second of direct touch.

The being above was on scout and he was not used to direct mind contact. But his pattern was Jony's own. And... Jony thought furiously... maybe, just maybe, he could control this stranger for a space. That would be a way to gain knowledge.

But that would be using mind-control! Just what Rutee had feared he might someday try with Maba and Geogee, and had made him promise that he would never do. Still the flying invader was not kin, and Jony desperately needed to learn all he could. He stirred uneasily. Rutee had said: What the Big Ones did to their kind had been wholly evil. And if he did the same, now, how different was he from a Big One?

The flying thing flashed back into view, steadied
almost directly above. Jony stiffened. Could the being
on board trace Jony through his attempt at contact?
The Big Ones had machines which achieved that
very thing, which also made the mind-controlled what
they were.

Stealthily Jony dropped his staff, allowing the
branches to swing back to their proper places. He
had no idea how much the hunter up there could
see, or guess. But he had no intention of lingering
for a meeting that might end up in capture.

Jony crawled on hands and knees. The buzz of the
flyer remained steady; it neither grew louder nor faded.
Which meant that the craft must have the ability to
hover directly above Jony, something no live-winged
thing he knew was able to do.

He was afraid to try contact again. Now he must
depend upon his hearing more than any other sense.
Belly-flat, he found a way which gave him complete
sky cover and wriggled along very slowly indeed.

Could he depend on his hearing now? Dared he
really believe that the sound was a little fainter, as if
he were drawing away from it? He could not count on
that; he might only do the best he could to escape.

His treetop cover thickened until Jony dared to
get to his feet, though he had to weave in and out
here to make any progress at all. Also he had lost the
trail of the People as he crept away from the spring.
There was only one way left to go unless he wanted
to be under observation from the flyer—straight
ahead—which meant south and toward the direction
in which the sky ship must have planeted.

The sound receded, as if the flyer still hovered

near the spring waiting for Jony to betray himself. About him the wood lay unnaturally quiet. All life there might be cowering to listen even as he did. Jony held his own passage to a minimum of noise.

His problem now was the lack of any trail as a guide; and his sense of direction was confused. He tried to fix on some particular tree ahead, reach that, then select another, always dreading to find himself caught in an endless circling. A broken branch, Jony fairly leaped for that. Work of one of the People! Yes, he could distinguish the stripping of leaves and twigs as the limb had been pulled down into the reach of someone taller than himself. Perhaps even Voak. Though Jony searched the ground here, he could find no prints. But there were other fruit vines and branches torn and mishandled. This had to have happened only a short time ago, since sap still oozed stickily from some.

Once more the growth thinned. Jony crouched behind a screen of leaves and branches. Immediately ahead was another open space. And, not too far away, the grass was beaten flat or torn up by the roots. He stared at that evidence of a struggle and was bitterly afraid. This could only mark a site where the People, or some of them, had been attacked without warning. Jony detected no signs of blood. But he did sight a staff, unbroken, and beyond that a net of fruit, half the contents squashed and now attracting insects.

The flyer!

He dared not venture into the open, even enough to examine more closely what evidence lay out there. Working a way about the fringe of the woodland would double both time and distance, but provided the cover he must have. Grimly, Jony began to move to the right along the line of detour. A moment later he dropped, freezing into instant immobility.

The buzz of the flyer was louder. He peered up as best he could without raising his head. Over the trees the alien craft swept, circling once about the place which marked what Jony was sure had been a struggle.

Then, to his unbelievable surprise, a voice sounded out of the sky:

"Joneeeeeeeee..." His own name, only distorted, sounding like a wail.

How did they not only know where he was, but who? This was more frightening than the red-lit chamber of the cage—all he had seen in the stone place—because it was personal, threatened *him* directly.

"Joneeeeeeee..." again that cry.

Was this some new type of mind-control, reaching one's prey by the use of his closest possession: his own name? If they expected him to be lured so, then they must think him mind-controlled himself. And *who* were those prepared to play the Big Ones' old game?

Three times the flyer called him. Jony's anger changed to a sullen determination to track them down, though he could not follow through the air. The idea had now come to him that they must have captured Maba, Geogee, or both, and so knew of him. Safety was gone from this world; he had nothing to depend upon now but his mind, his two hands, and this weapon he had discovered from the past.

He was not fool enough to believe that the metal staff could threaten the sky craft, good as it had proved against the vor birds. However, now the flyer seemed to be giving up the quest. No longer circling, the craft flew straight. Not to the southwest as Jony had confidently expected, but back north. Still hunting him?

He remained in hiding until the faintest of the buzzing stilled. If these others did have Maba or Geogee, if something dire had happened to the clan, he must know. So he believed his way now led south, toward where he had seen the ship planet. He no longer had any hope of finding the clan. And, undoubtedly, any warning he might have given was already far too late; useless.

Jony was driven to rest at last, simply because he was staggering and had fallen twice, in spite of the support of his staff. He made no nest, merely pushed back under a bush and pulled branches down as well as he could to hide his body. Once more he was thirsty, the fruit had only partly allayed his need. However, there had been times in the cold season among the folk when one learned to go hungry and even thirsty. Jony's plight was not a new one, save it came at the wrong season.

Weariness hit him so that he slept. Though even in that sleep he kept his hand on the shaft of his staff. Once more he slid into a dream...

He again visited the place of stones, climbing the ledges to face the woman. There was that which he alone could do, must do. Still he dreaded what would follow, not knowing what the result could be.

Reaching the figure he put out his hand as he had before, laid it palm to palm against her larger one. His body quivered. From that touch there flooded a fire, not to burn his flesh but rather to fill him with a power which he understood dimly he was to hold, contained, until the moment came for its full release.

Filled with that power, still obeying an order he did not understand, Jony went then on into the long space of stone trees, seeking the sleeper. As he looked down, that covered form moved; a hand arose to twitch aside the concealing mask. This time it was not his own features that were revealed. This was Maba. Not as he knew her now, but as she would be seasons ahead when she was as old as Rutee. Nor did she offer him the rod. Instead she signaled for him to come and aid her out of the box, bring her to her feet. This also he had to do.

She threw aside her clinging covering to step outside—and she smiled. But never as he had seen Maba smile. There was in her expression a hint of that look she assumed when she planned a bit of mischief or was stubbornly set on forbidden action—yes, that remained. But over all lay a cold knowledge of power and the will to use it.

That compulsion which had led Jony here and had made him free the one wearing Maba's face, broke. He struck out, not to grasp her rod for himself, but rather to capture the alien weapon, fling that dangerous thing as far from them both as his strength of arm could hurl it. Maba must not do what lay in her mind! That he understood.

Easily she avoided his grasp. Her smile deepened, she laughed. With the end of the rod she pointed to him and her words held a jeering note:

"Animal! Who are you who dares to rise?"

There was a tight strangling constriction in an instant about Jony's throat. He cried out, caught at the collar to tear himself free. Where that had once hung loose on him, now it was tight. From the band dangled a cord. Also, his back—he was being pressed down on all fours in spite of his frantic struggles.

The woman who was Maba caught the point of her rod through the looped cord, drew it to her. She laughed a second time, stepped away from the box which had held her for so long.

"You see," she said lightly, "you cannot be both— man and animal. Animals are ruled, men rule." Her twitch on the cord appeared light but drew Jony after her. She began to descend the ledges, never looking at him now as he followed on all fours at her heels, the animal so easily tamed.

> TEN <

The growth about Jony was sodden with a rain which fell with a steady persistence. That same rain erased any tracks of the People which might otherwise have been traced from that place of disaster in the open. Had all the clan been captured?

Jony roused from a night of unquiet rest, still ridden by that singularly forceful dream. It was seldom possible, beyond a few moments when one first awakes, to remember such details. But he continued to be haunted by vivid memory, just as he had by that earlier vision, when the sleeper, awaking in his box of stone, had worn Jony's own face, not Maba's. The feel of the constricting collar remained with him also. So that, now and then, his hand went half-consciously to his throat to see if the hoop still hung loose.

He caught no sound of any flyer. Perhaps the bad weather had driven it from a stormy sky. However, the same rain and wind did not keep Jony from his steady course south. And, after a climb up another line of ridge land, he came upon what he had sought

ever since that flash of evil-to-come had swept across
the night sky.

Below was a valley cut by a sizable stream, angling
south and west. Not too far from that placidly flowing
water stood a sky ship erect on its fins. About those
supports the ground was charred, blackened, fused
by the force of the beams down which it had ridden
to this landing.

Jony concentrated on the ship. He was quite sure
this one was not as large as that of the Big Ones,
though it was of the same general shape. Perhaps
most sky ships, no matter who piloted them, followed
a like pattern. He had expected a ramp out from an
open hatch, but the body remained sleekly closed, no
manner of opening to be seen at all.

Nearby, however, there rested on the ground the
flyer which had sent him into cover the day before.
Now that Jony could view it from above instead of
below he could pick out the features which made it
readily recognizable as an intricate machine. There was
an over-curved hood covering the top, under which, he
supposed, the pilot and any passengers could shelter
while the thing was aloft.

On the side of the standing ship there was a marking also, though it was dim, as if old.

Jony stirred unhappily. Here his shelter from the
storm was poor, and there seemed to be no way of
finding out what was going on below within the sealed
ship. He wondered if he dared to try a thought-
send—but hesitated. Somehow he was sure it was
by that means he had attracted the attention of the
flyer before. But—

He stiffened, instantly alert. At last something was

happening. A roll-back opening appeared in the side of the ship; a ramp for landing curved out as might a questing tongue. That struck the ground, anchored firmly. Now, down that incline walked a man.

Not a Big One. Jony knew relief, then immediately regained his wary distrust. What kind of men rode the sky? They might be mind-controlled. If the kinfolk of Rutee had at last made their way here ... But then why had they attacked the People?

Maba—Geogee—and how many of the clan were now down there, imprisoned?

The spaceman's whole body was covered with clothing fastened about his arms, his legs, up to his throat. The material was a green-brown in color, making his face seem very dark. His hair had been trimmed into a short stiff brush. Now the invader descended to the end of the ramp, to just stand there, holding something before his eyes, turning the upper part of his body very slowly. As if, through that object Jony could not distinguish very clearly, the stranger was making a careful survey of the very slope upon which the boy crouched.

Did they somehow know he was here? Were they now seeking him again? Jony had dabbed his body with sticky mud and leaves before he had settled here, making the best attempt he could to copy the ability of the People to be one with their background when they chose. Now, with a fast-beating heart, he waited any moment for the stranger below to center directly on him.

What would happen then? Could the invaders loose some vapor into the air as did the Big Ones, leaving him unable to defend himself as they came to collect another prisoner?

However, the other swung past, no longer centering on Jony's perch. Instead he was continuing his examination of the terrain. At last the spaceman dropped his hands, though he still held the object through which he had studied the countryside.

Just then the rain hit with a heavier gust. Apparently the stranger did not care for that. He turned and ran back up the ramp into the open hatch. A moment or so later, the ramp itself was lifted and drawn in. Jony, however, did not relax. The ship was now a cage, the most secure cage he had ever faced.

Should he have tried to fasten on the mind of that watcher, perhaps control him? Had he lost his best opportunity of rescuing those inside? If he only knew a little more! He had been able to work on the Big Ones because he had watched them, studied them with all the concentration Rutee had taught him to use. But Jony knew very well that an approach which might work with one life-form would not serve as well for another. Also, his own advice to Maba held true. This stranger might seem to be kin physically, but that did not mean that he really was.

Jony edged backward from his spy post. Mistrust still held—suppose that watcher *had* detected him, but had been cleverly concealing the fact by his actions? Better be gone from here and find another place from which he could still spy on the ship.

Crawling backward he again came to a complete halt. One of the People—and not too distant! Jony sat up, sure that he was far enough into the brush not to reveal himself to any ship lookout, and stared straight in the direction from which that shadowy touch of mind had come. A space of time as long as several breaths passed before Jony's eyes detected the lurker apart from his brush cover. Otik!

Jony's first impulse was to join the clansman—try to discover what had happened to the rest of the People and the twins. Then he remembered only too well how they had parted. His hand went to the collar. The first gesture must come from Otik; he was very sure of that.

The clansman knew Jony was there; had probably had him under observation all the time Jony himself was spying on the ship. Now Otik's head was turned so his eyes watched the boy. Well as he knew the People, Jony had never learned to read any emotion by the expression of their faces. He could not tell now whether Otik would allow contact at all.

Patience was one of the first lessons to be learned when dealing with the People. They lived by delibera-tion for the most part, and Jony had seldom seen them hurried. He waited, trying to match Otik's impassive stare with an answering one of his own.

Then the clansman hunkered forward, not rising to his feet, but using his hands against the ground as had his ancestors in those pictures. He came forward deliberately and slowly. There was a food net slung about one of his thick shoulders, but he had no staff.

Reaching a position several arms distance away from Jony, he sat back on his heels, his paw-hands dangling loosely between his knees. Otik was young; he had been Yaa's first cub some seasons before she had come to aid Rutee. As yet he had neither the bulk nor the strength of Voak or Kapoor, though he could best Trush in friendly wrestling. Had the clan done as always this year and met with other families, Otik might well have gone hunting a mate.

The clansman continued to sit and stare. Inwardly Jony fought his own impatience. He longed to sign a question, a demand, for all the information Otik could supply. Had others escaped? What had happened back at that trampled space of grass in the open? Only now he must wait until Otik accepted or rejected him.

The paw-hands moved. Otik gestured, grunted also, as if to emphasize the importance of what he would say.

"You go flying thing?" He gave that the quality of a question, not a statement.

Jony had planted his staff close to hand to have his fingers free to answer. Now he tried to keep his gestures as unhurried as he could.

"No go—yet."

"Your clan—they be so." Otik continued.

Jony found it disturbing that the other's face remained without expression, that he could learn so little from Otik's attitude as to what thoughts moved behind those large eyes. He had not really realized until this moment how frustrating it could be when their powers of communication remained so meager. Probably because, his mind now suggested, the daily life of the clan had been so based on the essentials of food, familiar action, and the routine of ways Jony had known for years, that he had not had to improvise any means of conveying messages outside the bounds of those basic elements.

"Not *my* clan," he chose the best answer and the simplest he could think of. "Where Maba—Geogee?" He spoke their names aloud, aware that Otik would recognize those sounds, just as he could recognize and attempt to imitate the sounds which identified each of the clan by name.

"With your clan." Otik signed uncompromisingly. "Those came from sky." He stopped word signs and was acting out with his two paws what must have happened. One set of fingers pattered along the ground, plainly the clan traveling. The other hand flattened, swooped down upon that small band from the air and held in position over it for an instant or two. Then the fingers against the ground went limp, sprawling out flat. The hand representing the flyer scooped them up—made to carry them away.

Both hands returned to signs. "So Otik see."

Jony moistened his lips with the tip of his tongue. He must ask the next question but he feared what the reply might be.

"Dead?" he signed.

Otik made the sign for "not sure," and then, hesitatingly, the one for "sleep."

Perhaps the space people had a stunning device such as the Big Ones used. Jony hoped with all his heart that was so.

"Who?" he signed now. If Otik had escaped—had others also?

"Voak, Yaa," Otik barked the sounds Jony knew, added two more names.

Four of them in all then, as well as the twins. And the rest . . . ?

He did not need to ask, Otik was already signing that those were in hiding, watching. Though what hope they had of getting their people out of the sealed ship, Jony thought, was very small indeed.

"You go—your clan—" Otik repeated his earlier

accusation, or was it simply a statement of fact as the clansman saw it?

"Not mine!" Jony made the gesture for firm repudiation.

Otik's hands were still. Did the clansman believe that? Jony knew of no proof he could offer to back up what he had said. Though he was certain at that moment he did speak the truth.

For a very long instant Otik simply sat and looked at him. Then the clansman made one of those lightning swift moves which could startle even one who knew them well but had become lulled by their usual placid, slow-moving attitude. Before Jony was aware, Otik had Jony's new staff in his hands.

Jony's reaction to grab for it, was, he knew at once, useless. That Otik had taken it at all was ominous. For a staff was its maker's and should not be handled by anyone else.

"You get—where?" Otik signed with one hand, keeping the staff closely gripped with his other.

"Found—by running water. Long time hidden in sand," Jony returned.

Otik inspected the find carefully, running fingertips along the pitted metal of the shaft, even bringing it to his nose for an investigative sniffing down the whole length.

"Thing—of old ones—" he declared.

"I found it—in sand, by running water," Jony returned with all the force of gesture he could muster. He must not let Otik get the idea that he had returned to loot the place of stones.

The place of stones! An idea which was wild, which he was sure no clansman would agree to, flashed into his mind. Against the weapons those of the ship must be able to muster what chance had the clan with their wooden staffs or their strength of body? But, suppose they possessed rods such as the sleeper held, with which Geogee had experimented so disastrously? A beam from one could bring down that flyer; might even eat a doorway into the ship for attackers.

One idea joined another in his mind. Jony breathed faster, unconsciously his fingers flexed in and out as if he were ready to grasp one of those terrifying weapons right now.

There was a honk from Otik which startled Jony out of his own thoughts, back into the present and the realization that there was little hope of doing what he had dreamed in those moments of anticipated triumph.

The clansman had laid down the metal shaft. Once more he regarded Jony with that searching look. Then his paw-hands moved.

"You know a thing to help." Again no question, but a statement. Jony's amazement was complete. How had Otik guessed that? Could it be that, although he was unable to tap minds with the People, the same difficulty did not exist on their side? Such a thought was more than a little frightening.

"You know," Otik repeated. "I smell you know! What this thing?" Smell? Jony was bewildered. How could one *smell* thoughts? The idea was dizzying, but he had no time now to explore it.

"Things—in place of stones—" he took the plunge. Otik could only say yes or no to that. "They better than staff—like things from ship."

Otik made no answer at all. Instead, once more on hands and feet, he backed into the brush, leaving Jony alone. That was probably the end of any contact with the remnants of the clan, Jony decided bleakly. His first move was to secure the metal staff. His second was to think again of his wild idea of turning the finds in the storage place to use.

But the stone dens lay to the north. And suppose Maba or Geogee had already told their captors about the things found there? If so, the spacemen could easily fly that distance, take what they needed, and be away before the People—or Jony—could cover half that journey back on foot.

Maba had been so excited about the finds. Jony could well imagine her telling these strangers about them. Or was Maba a prisoner?

Jony tensed. Movement about him. Not Otik alone, there were others of the People ringing him nearly around, advancing toward him. There was only one opening in their circle, downslope. To take that way of escape would bring him into view from the ship. He could only wait...

His suggestion to Otik might have touched off a reaction which—Jony's hand went to the loose collar. He remembered only too well those concealed fangs within it which Voak had displayed as a warning. On the other hand, he knew he had no chance of escaping from the clan's steady advance, nor could he use the staff—not against them!

Otik, then Trush, Huuf, two of the younger females— Itak, Wugi—none of the older members of the clan. Jony could do little against even Itak and Wugi; he could not choose to fight.

The newcomers squatted down as Otik had done, their staffs beside them where a paw-hand could drop easily to a familiar hold. Otik had something else in his grasp—a coil of the cord they used to weave their nets.

"Talk—" Otik signed.

About his wild plan for looting the storage place among the stone walls? Jony could only guess. He signed slowly, trying to make sure he chose each time the most effective gesture to clarify his meaning. Though, with the limits imposed upon him, he despaired of making them understand or believe what he had to tell.

He told of his own journey underground to a great cave—of the many strange things there. Finally of the rod Geogee had found, and what happened when, in the struggle to get it away from the boy, the alien power had been inadvertently fired. That they would believe in the instant disappearance of what it had been pointed at, Jony was doubtful. They listened, but did they understand?

No one signed a message for him to read as he finished. Instead they spoke among themselves, leaving Jony baffled as always by the succession of sounds which had no meaning for the ears of his species. Each made some comment in turn. Then, though Jony was not sure of what had been said, he sensed that the verdict was against him.

He reached for his staff, though he was sure he could never turn its terrible might against any of the People. But Otik had again gotten paw on that, and it was gone! At length Otik rose to his feet and loomed over Jony.

When Jony tried rising to face the young clansman, the weight of Trush's paw-hands on his shoulders held

him where he was. Otik uncoiled his cord, hooked an
end through the collar, and made one of the deftly
tied knots the People used.

He gave a jerk, bringing the edge of the collar tight
against Jony's throat as if he meant that as a warning.
Then he turned away, and Jony, now released, had to
follow. It was plain that he had worsened his cause
with these clansmen, instead of bettering it. He was
angry now with his own stupidity at voicing a suggestion which must have aroused their deep-set rage
against their one-time captors, turning it toward himself.

The clan had no campsite, but they had taken up
station within a thick covering of brush which would
give them cover overhead if the flyer came cruising.
There were four more awaiting the return of Otik's
squad with their prisoner—three were females, the
fourth old Gorni, who had once been chief, but who
had yielded to Voak as his strength had lessened.

It was to him that Otik went, reaching down to put
the end of Jony's leash in the paw-hand of the old
one. One of Gorni's eyes was covered with a white
film so that he had to always turn his head slightly
to view anything directly before him, as he did now.

But he did not use sign language; instead he gave
the leash a tug which again brought the collar painfully against Jony's flesh. At that rude demand that
he sit, Jony dropped down. Otik also laid the metal
staff before the elder, as if to clinch some argument.
But Gorni only glanced at that briefly.

With his free hand, the other never losing that
tight hold on the leash, the clansman began to sign
very slowly:

"You are now walker on fours. You do what People

say. You are People's *thing.*" He touched the fruit
net looped about him. "This People's thing. You like
this—not People—just *thing!*"

Jony wanted to loop both hands in the leash, tear
it loose from the oldster's hold. He knew better than
to make any such move. He was now a "thing," perhaps having some use for the clan, but without any
freedom to be Jony.

The anger which he had known, young as he was,
when in the cages of the Big Ones, burned in him
once more. Only he could see the side of the People,
too. They did not trust him. What of those the flyer
had taken—the spacemen who looked like Jony, who
resembled the pictures in the storage place and the
stone woman? Perhaps the People had always feared
that Jony himself might revert, to become one with
their enemies. Only when he was small had they tol-
erated him, as they did the twins, as a weak, helpless
thing not to be feared. Then he had directly sought
out the place of stones, aroused in them the fear that
the old days might so return. After that, to add to
their fear, had come the arrival of the sky ship and
the capture of the clansmen. The People were only
doing what they could for their own protection.

What was the worst was that he must have, by
his suggestion of raiding the storage place, aroused
in them a belief that he was intending to take over
once again. They had undoubtedly dismissed his talk
of their finding and using the weapons as being delib-
erate falsification on his part, or as an indication that
he held them in contempt.

Looking at Gorni's impassive face, then glancing
from one to another of those ringing him around,

Jony could see no way of impressing them with the fact of his own innocence of any desire to harm them. Yet he had to do just that.

The ship might lift now, taking with it, into the unknown of the far skies, their own people and the twins! Above all else the People must somehow find a way to prevent that—though Jony could not see now any hope of rescue.

> ELEVEN <

Jony's leash was released by Gorni, only to be fastened by another of those tough knots to a sapling strong enough to resist any attempt of his to break loose. For the moment the boy had to accept the knowledge that he could do nothing. But neither could he believe that this was the end, that the clan would continue to consider him a "thing," and that he might not be able to find some way to rescue those on the ship.

If he could reach Maba or Geogee . . . Just as Rutee had once instructed and trained for the day when he could get to freedom, perhaps he could work through concentration to make the twins aid him now in the same fashion.

Wugi came near enough to place on the ground two fruits and a leaf twisted around about a handful of grass seeds. Even a "thing" was to be fed. And Jony ate the portion hungrily.

His metal staff remained lying on the ground near Gorni. Nor did the elder make the slightest move to examine it as Otik had. Jony eyed the sharp edge of the hook longingly. By the use of that the leash could be easily severed; he freed. But to go where, do what?

Impatience ate at him until he wanted to pound the wet ground with both hands and howl aloud his misery. If he could only make them understand! Concentrate on the ship? Or would such mental touch guide the spacemen here? He wanted...

Otik returned. The young clansman had been away in the brush, perhaps once more spying on the invaders. Going directly to Gorni he conveyed some report. Jony watched, longing to be able to understand. If he could only share such open communication perhaps he might make the People understand the folly of not listening to him. They had, he was sure, little idea of the weapons and instruments which the ship people might use. Jony's own knowledge was only the bits and pieces relayed to him by Rutee, who had, in turn, a very limited grasp of the subject. That, and what he had learned in the lab of the Big Ones. But those scraps of information were certainly infinitely more than the People possessed.

Both Gorni and Otik eyed Jony now. He could guess that what they said had to do with him. At last Otik came to the sapling, loosed that knot and gave a jerk, to signal Jony to follow. A call from behind made Otik turn his head.

Wugi, leaves wrapped about her fingers so she did not touch the bare metal of the staff, had taken up Jony's find. She carried the weapon with the attitude of one disposing of a loathsome thing and held it out to Otik. Plainly this was not to be left behind.

If Wugi did not care to touch the weapon-tool, Otik had no such scruples. He lacked a staff. Perhaps, in

spite of clan opinion, he had a lurking desire to keep
this one. At any length he readily took it into his hand.
Then, with another jerk, but no signed command (as if
Jony now lacked the intelligence to understand such a
thing), the clansman pushed out of their small brush
camp, heading back upslope of the ridge.

The rain was slacking, though periodic gusts struck
them in the open, driven by a new wind. At least the
sky was lighter. Jony could see the position of the
ship and the flyer nearby in clearer detail than he
had earlier. Also the ramp was run out once more,
and there was a cluster of figures gathered on the
lower edge of it. The spacemen now wore coverings
over their heads which made them look unnatural,
as if they were in truth a race as alien as the Big
Ones. But the smaller figure with them—even at this
distance Jony recognized Maba!

As far as he could determine she was under no
restraint, but mingled freely with the off-worlders. As
he caught plain sight of her, she flung out one arm in
a typical exaggerated Maba gesture, the fingers of that
hand pointing north. Telling them of the stone place?

But why was Maba free? Mind-controlled? Memory
supplied that as a very probable answer. Jony's anger
against circumstances, and now against these intruders, flared higher. Maba, to be so controlled! What
Rutee had always feared for any of her children had
happened.

Because of that anger Jony sent a sudden probe,
striving to find out just how much they had taken
over the girl. Was her normal mind totally blank so
that she was only animated by the wishes of the space
people, after the fashion of those blank-eyed captives

of the Big Ones who walked blindly through what life their owners allowed them to retain?

His probe met no barrier, no hint of mind-control! Jony's shaft of Esper power had sharpened to meet the resistance he expected, but instead went straight into Maba's own thought-stream.

"Maba!" Aware that the worst had not happened, Jony was excited. Could he plant a thought of escape—of aid—now?

He watched that small figure eagerly. Her arm had dropped limply to her side, she swayed, and perhaps would have fallen to the ground, had not one of the spacemen caught and steadied her. Jony had put too much force in that contact. He retreated at once, aware of the danger of his move as caution returned too late.

The invader who supported Maba gathered the girl up in one swift movement, turned and ran back up the ramp into the ship. However, his two companions did not follow. Instead they headed for the flyer, throwing themselves through an opening which appeared in its bubble top, as if they sought safety from attack.

Jony guessed that they were aware of his attempt to contact Maba, that now they would again be on search for him. He turned to Otik. Let the clansman understand that Jony's presence was what would draw trouble straight to the People. He signed with all the authority he could bring to the matter:

"Those know I am here—they will hunt—they can track—"

Otik gave that small turn of the head which signified indifference.

"No one can find when People are warned," he returned.

"*They* can," Jony had kept part attention on the flyer. The bubble was closed, the machine rising steadily into the air. "They have a way—"

Was he getting Otik to really listen? If the clansman would not, the People were probably doomed to the same fate as had already swallowed Voak, Yaa and the rest.

"Show—You go—that way—"

To Jony's momentary relief, Otik dropped the leash before he pointed with the metal staff along the ridge, away from that section where the clan had gone to cover.

Jony began to run, scrambling down under the roofing of the brush, indeed leading any chase away from the others. He had not the slightest hope that the People could match the weapons of the strangers. But he had once mind-befuddled a Big One, and he might just have a chance to do the same with these new invaders. If he could escape detection, and was sure he had, he would head back to the stone place, arm himself with the most potent weapon he could find there. Unless, with Maba's help, the strangers got there first.

Why was Maba helping these invaders if she was not mind-controlled? The question haunted him, but Jony could give no real time to such a problem now. He must use all his wits to try and escape that flyer whose buzzing grew ever louder.

The leash dangling behind him caught once on a bush with a backward jerk which nearly swept him off his feet and brought the collar constrictingly tight against his throat. Jony tore the cord loose and then made a tight roll of the end about his waist, unable to take the time to pick the knot on the collar. Here ground was rough and the rain had slicked clay into greasy slides, so that twice he lost his footing and tumbled down.

He kept to cover with all the skill he had learned when in vor bird country. Only that buzz overhead was continuous; they were apparently able to follow him with the same ease as if they saw with their own eyes every movement he made, every dodge and evasion he tried. Then—

Jony stumbled forward on feet which suddenly refused to support him. A sense of weakness, of floating, made him feel as if he were no longer trying to run, but rather rested on air which was moving... He made one last desperate attempt to hold on to his consciousness—and lost.

His head hurt. That was the next thing of which he was truly aware: a headache so strong, so vast, that it filled not only his skull but his whole body. At the same time a sour nausea moved him into retching. When that shaking passed, he endeavored to lie very quiet. For a little then the pain seemed to lessen.

He opened his eyes. Then shut them quickly as light (a glaring light which had nothing of the sun's glow in it) stabbed deeply, adding to the pain in his skull. Sounds—

Jony tried to concentrate on the sounds. Those of wind in the grass and across brush? No. Here was a murmur of a voice, but he could not make the effort to try to understand what words came so faintly.

Scent—smells...

Jony's body went rigid with the old fear. Once, long ago, he had been used to such smells. In the lab of

the Big Ones. He was back—back there! The horror
of it left him trembling.

See—he must see! He forced his eyes open; endured
the pain that glaring light caused. There was a smooth
expanse over him—not the sky. He must be in the
flyer—or even the ship!

His old hatred of the cage came back full force.
As he forced his head to turn slowly, his eyes to
remain open, he discovered he was lying full length
on some support he could not see. Facing him were
the furnishings of a lab—NO!

Maybe he uttered some sound aloud, for a body
moved into his limited range of vision. Someone stood
within touching distance. And that face bending above
so that the stranger could observe him was not that of
a Big One. Or even of a mind-controlled. There was
too much intelligence in those eyes, the expression
on the dark face too alert and knowing. That this was
one of the spacemen Jony now had no doubt.

"How do you feel?"

Jony blinked. He understood the words, save that
they were accented differently from the speech Rutee
had taught him, which he used with the twins. Rutee's
people?

Making what seemed to him to be an exhausting
effort, Jony asked slowly in return:

"Who . . . are . . . you . . . ?"

The stranger nodded as if the fact that Jony could
speak at all was encouraging.

"I am Jarat, the medic."

"I am in the ship—" Jony did not quite make that
a question, he was already sure of the answer.

"In sick bay, yes."

"Maba...Geogee..." he hesitated then and licked his lips unsure whether he dared ask his final question. Would it awaken the suspicion of this—this—medic (whatever that could mean)? "The People...?"

"Maba and Geogee are safe with us," Jarat replied.

But he said nothing about Voak, Yaa, the others. Were they—*dead?*

"How is he?" Another had moved up beside Jarat, to stare down at Jony. "Can he answer any questions yet?"

"Let him get orientated first, Pator. You know what a stunner can do—"

The one Jarat had addressed was plainly impatient, Jony thought. Ask him questions, about what—the People? The place of stones? In that moment he made up his mind, he intended to answer nothing until he knew what had become of the People, if he were now a prisoner in this place which reminded him so much of the old captivity.

He closed his mouth tightly, his return stare nearly a glare of defiance. Whether the spacemen understood his attitude or not, Jony could not guess, but the second did step back out of the range of Jony's sight, leaving Jarat there alone.

The medic held something in his hand which he touched to Jony's upper arm. There was no pain from that contact; instead there followed a soothing of the ache in his head, then throughout his body. Unconsciously he relaxed against the pad on which he lay.

"That better?" Jarat did not wait for any answer. "Take this now—"

He put a tube to Jony's mouth, and, without wanting to in the least, Jony allowed it between his lips.

"Give a good hard suck," Jarat ordered.

Jony obeyed. Warm liquid was the result, and he swallowed. That, too, seemed to have not only a good taste but a pleasant reaction on his body.

"Take a nap," Jarat was smiling. "When you join us again you'll find yourself a lot better."

He was as authoritative as if Jony were mind-controlled after all. The boy's eyes did close, and he was almost instantly asleep. This time sleep without dreams.

When Jony roused, there was no change in the light about him. But the pain in his head was gone, he felt rested, relaxed as he had not in a long time. Levering himself up on his elbows, he looked carefully around.

The place in which he lay had some of the same equipment he remembered from the lab, but all made to a much smaller scale. And there were no cages. As he made sure of that, Jony gave a gusty sigh of relief. He had half-expected to see the People shut up so, awaiting what torments their captors would devise, as his kind had suffered with the Big Ones.

His head felt light and he was a little dizzy, as he might have been had he not eaten for too long a time. But he was able to sit up, swing his scratched and bruised legs over the edge of the narrow shelf-like place on which he had been lying.

They had taken his kilt away and—his hands suddenly went to his throat. The collar! That was gone also. Naked, he stood beside the shelf, steadying himself with one hand as he looked around. There were many boxes, shelves with things on them—all objects he could not name. But as far as he could see there was no one about.

Jony tried a few steps, still holding on to the shelf. He was stronger, able to manage. Letting go his anchorage, he began a tour of the cabin, eager to find the door. He had no idea if he could get out of the ship unnoticed. But no one could be sure of anything until an attempt was made.

Just as he reached the one wall which was bare of shelving, though it had no opening in it that he could mark, there came a small sound. That sought-for door appeared, directly before him, with a suddenness which held him immobile through sheer amazement.

The spaceman who had named himself Jarat stood there. For a second or two his astonishment seemed equal to Jony's. Then he smiled and stepped in quickly, the open slit closing firmly behind him, though he did nothing to make it do so.

"So—you are not only awake, but ready to begin living again, Jony?"

"How did you know my name?" Somehow Jony resented slightly this greeting. The assurance of it made him feel young, small, on an equality with the twins in an odd way he could not define.

"Maba—Geogee. Did you forget they joined us?"

Jony edged back until he felt the shelf against the small of his spine.

"They did not join you," he said. "You captured them. As the Big Ones used to take their prisoners. What will you do with us?"

"Take you home," Jarat said.

"This is home." For Jony, for the twins it was. He had been so long on the Big Ones' ship he could not remember any other Outside except this one.

"You *are* human, you know," Jarat still had that

note of one reassuring a cub as he spoke. "From what the children have told us you escaped from a Zhalan slave ship, you and your mother. They were born here, but it is not your world."

He slid a bundle of cloth off his arm, dropped in on the shelf near Jony.

"Brought you a ship suit. Ought to be close to your size—try it on. Captain Trefrew wants to speak to you as soon as he can."

Jony drew the bundle to him. If he put that on, he would be one with these ship people. And what of Yaa and Voak? Perhaps if he seemed willing to obey orders, he could not only discover what had happened to the clansmen, but also be able to help them.

Jarat had to show him how to seal the front of the one-piece garment which so entirely covered the body that it also included soft-soled pieces for the feet. Jony felt queerly stifled, too well enfolded, when he had it fastened up properly.

The medic looked him over critically. "Not too bad. That mop of hair would never fit inside a helmet. But, for the rest, you'll do."

Do for what, Jony wondered? He asked no questions now, hoping that he could discover what he needed to know about the ship without anyone guessing his purpose. Though this spaceman had claimed him as one of his own kind, Jony felt no kinship with him.

There were men and there were animals. Rutee had told him that her people had once used, almost uncaringly, animals as tools. Then *they* had become in turn the "animals," tools of the Big Ones. The People must have been animals as long as those of the place of stone had ruled, and afterwards...

His hand went to his throat again, still feeling that he should encounter the collar there. The clan had made him an "animal" for their purposes as a warning and a punishment.

"Strange to you, eh?" Jarat said. "Ask any questions you want—I know you have a lot to catch up on."

Jony shook his head. What the medic said was true, but not in the way Jarat meant it. He had not tried any mind-contact since he had awakened here, being cautious about that. Could he, if he wished, control Jarat? Make the other lead him to the People, free them all, as he had done with the Big One to arrange Rutee's escape? He did not know and, as yet, he was too wary to try.

But Jony used his eyes as they went; tried memorizing their path through this wilderness of the ship as he would have searched for landmarks Outside. There was no sign of either Maba or Geogee, nor did Jony ask for them yet. Better simply obey orders and wait until he could learn more by himself.

He was aware, however, that his companion glanced at him intently now and again as if expecting more from him. Not that Jony paid too much notice; the ship itself held most of his full attention.

They went down a short way and came to a center well up which climbed a series of steps. The medic swung onto this; Jony followed. His feet, covered for the first time in his life, felt clumsy, and he went carefully.

Twice they passed other sections of the ship above, coming to a third. This time the medic swung off once more into a second short passage. Before him the wall opened to let Jarat through. Jony followed, hiding, as he hoped, his growing sense of being trapped.

This must be the captain. The man was seated at his ease. When he gestured, the medic went to the wall and snapped down two other seats, one of which he took, motioning Jony to the other.

Jony occupied only the very edge of that. In the first place to be seated so far above the ground felt unnatural to him, secondly he was too tense inside to relax much.

"So you escaped a Zhalan ship," the captain began abruptly. "And that years back. You have no idea of your home world?" His words came impatiently, as if Jony presented a problem he could have done without.

"Rutee said," Jony broke silence for the first time, "that it was a new colony. She and Bron had chosen to go. Then the Big Ones came...Bron could not be mind-controlled and he fought in the lab. They killed him." It was a story which had never meant too much to him though Rutee had hurt when she spoke of it. He always sensed that hurt when she told it.

"And you?"

"I was very small. They left me with Rutee in the cage. I don't remember back beyond the cages."

"This Rutee—your mother—she was mind-controlled?"

"No!" Jony scowled at the captain. "Some of us they could not use so. Most they dumped. Rutee thought they wanted her to find out why. They used their machines on her many times..."

He shivered, hating this man for making him remember how Rutee had been dragged from the cage, how they would bring her back later. Sometimes seeming as if she were dead, at others moaning and holding her head, crying out if even he came close to her for a while.

"And you—?"

"They could not control me either. But they did not try much. Rutee thought they were keeping me until they got to their own world—wherever that was. She did not know why."

"And the twins?"

Jony's inner anger grew. Just as he had known and felt all Rutee's pain, so he had known her shame and despair. But this was the truth so he would tell it. Let these spacemen know what the Big Ones could do to the helpless.

"They put me in another cage, then they gave her to a mind-controlled male," he said starkly.

There was silence in the cabin. Jony did not look at either of the spacemen.

He heard the captain say a word he did not understand, sharply and bitterly. But the memory of Rutee had fired Jony into what might be recklessness. He arose abruptly from his seat to face the spaceman. Keeping his voice as even as he could, fighting down impatience and fear, he demanded:

"Where is Yaa?"

> TWELVE <

"Yaa?" repeated the captain. He spoke as if he could not identify the name. "You mean Maba. She is with—"

But Jony interrupted, determined here and now to learn the truth. "Yaa, the female of the People. You took her and Voak, and two others back there in the open."

"The female—" Jarat stirred. "She is—" Then he stopped abruptly, perhaps reading Jony's expression better than Jony could that of the captain. Jony rounded on the medic sharply.

"She is where? Have you killed her?"

Jarat shook his head. "Of course not! Specimens are—" Again he paused, almost in mid-word.

Jony fought to retain his self-control, in order not to show either of these strangers his instant hostile reaction.

"Yaa," he said with a deliberation which he hoped would make an impression on the two, "saved Rutee's life. She took the twins when Rutee died. Now—what have you done with her?"

Jarat's eyes dropped from Jony's compelling stare. So the boy turned again to the captain.

"I ask you—what have you done with the People?"

It would seem that he was not going to get a quick answer from the commander of the spacemen either. So Jony unleashed his search-sense, sending it straight into the captain's thought pattern.

A confused picture, but clear enough to bring to Jony a snarl, similar to the guttural utterances of an angry clansman, as his own answer to what he learned.

Yaa imprisoned among machines not too different from those of the Big Ones. Yaa, perhaps, mind-controlled! Jony's horror and anger fed the power of his concentrated talent.

The captain was shaking his head, his hands moved jerkily toward his belt, toward what Jony knew must be his weapon. The boy hurled at the officer all the force he could muster. Finally the man slumped in his seat and slid limply to the floor.

Jony was already turning toward the medic who had risen abruptly to his feet, openly alarmed. Once more the boy concentrated, thrusting ruthlessly into a mind which was wide open to his probe.

"Yaa," he ordered, "take me to Yaa!"

Jarat fought, attempting to raise barriers which Jony, in his fear and ire, overrode easily. Though for how long he might be able to do so he did not know. Stiffly the medic turned to the door, walking as if he fought with every muscle to regain command of the body Jony was forcing to answer to his own purpose. No promise to Rutee could hold now, not after what Jony had read in the captain's mind when he asked for Yaa.

They left the captain lying on the floor of the cabin. Jony did not know how long the spaceman would remain unconscious, and he was afraid he could not control two at the same time. He must reach Yaa and the others as soon as he could.

"Jony!" Maba's voice from below. But Jony did not allow himself now to think of anything which would break his hold over Jarat.

The medic began a slow descent of the central ladder, Jony impatient to force him ahead. He could feel the struggle of the other against his dominion, and he bore down with all the pressure he could exert.

"Jony!"

They had descended two levels. Maba stood there, beside the ladder, her eyes alight. Jony did not even glance at her. For the moment Maba did not count. She was free among these; Yaa, the others, were not.

"Jony, what is the matter?" She caught at his sleeve as he went past her. He freed himself with a quick jerk, intent upon controlling Jarat, keeping the medic moving.

"Jony . . . !" Now she sounded frightened. That did not matter in the least, though he was aware she had started down after them.

They were past the level from which Jony had first come, down by the next one. So far they had been lucky not to encounter any other of the crew. Jarat stepped away from the ladder on this level, stood swaying.

His face was wet with sweat as he made a maximum effort to break Jony's control. Jony himself felt the drain of that power which he must use to keep the other both his prisoner and his guide. For Yaa—Voak—the People—he could do it!

"Jony—why—?" Maba's voice.

He shook his head against the irritation of her attempt to gain his attention. Jarat, staggering as he went, still battling control, headed down the passage, a very short one.

The medic raised his hand very slowly, his inner reluctance to do this thing strong even in that curtailed movement. Now Jarat's palm rested against the wall for an instant. Then, as had those in the place of stones, the wall itself parted, and they came through into the very place Jony had feared might exist.

The stench of fear here was as strong as the strange smells of the ship. There was Yaa, braced against the wall, metal bands holding her upright, her head encased in a helmet from which sprouted wires of uneven lengths. The purr of a machine was loud; louder still came a plaint which nearly unnerved Jony.

He looked away from Yaa to the other side of the place of torment. There Voak was fastened the same way. His head had fallen forward; his great eyes were closed. He might be asleep, save that that sound issued from his slack mouth.

Another of the spacemen bent over the purring machine, his eyes intent upon a lighted square at its top.

He gave Jarat a quick glance and went back again to his watching.

"Amazing, simply amazing," he commented. "The reading is unique."

"Yaa!" It was not Jony who cried that. Maba had caught up with them. Now she ran across to reach the furred figure against the wall. But the spaceman at the machine was too quick for her. He threw out one long arm and fended her off, fighting.

Jony had been shaken by the confirmation of his worst fears. His control wavered. Jarat broke free, whirling, his hands flying to his belt and weapon which hung there.

No staff, but—From a table nearby Jony snatched up a length of wire, making it into a lash. The People used braided vines so, and he had learned. That loop flipped out, catching about Jarat's wrist.

"What's going on?" Maba's struggles still kept the other spaceman fully occupied. "What do you think you're doing?" He gave Maba a shake which did not in the least subdue her.

Jony moved in against the medic. The People wrestled and Jony knew their tricks. Whether they could save him now he had no idea. His body slammed hard against Jarat's, driving the man back against a table, jarring loose things which crashed to the floor. But the spaceman struck back swiftly, body-shaking blows Jony did not know how to counter.

He had only one weapon—and used it. Into the other's mind he sent a blighting concentration of all the force he could summon and aim.

Jarat, his hand raised for another attack, stumbled forward, and went to his knees among the breakage from the table. Jony used his wire thong, bringing the other's wrists together behind his back, lashing them together.

"Jony!" Maba's cry was one of warning.

He hunched around. The other spaceman held her with one hand. In the other was a belt weapon pointed directly at him. Jony must make a last effort, though he was not sure how much of the force he could still summon. But he once more used his talent for assault.

The face of the spaceman twisted. He cried out

with a queer rising scream. Maba, loose, sprang for his weapon hand, using her wiry strength to wrest the arm out of his grip. Before Jony could move, she turned it on its owner, pressed a button on the butt.

Her victim flopped forward, falling face down beside the still writhing Jarat.

"Him—too!" Maba leveled the stunner again.

"Don't kill—" Jony began, but she laughed recklessly.

"These don't kill, they just make people sleep." She pressed the button and Jarat also subsided.

Maba looked down at the spacemen, then she gazed up at Jony.

"I didn't know, Jony, truly I didn't!" she begged him to understand. "I didn't know what they did to Yaa..."

"Now you do," he answered shortly. "And I don't know if we can get out of here."

He was already at Yaa's side, working on those bonds which kept her thick-set body immobile. There was some trick to the fastening, as there had been a trick to the collar, and he could not discover it. They must hurry. The captain might already have recovered and alarmed the whole ship.

"Please, Jony," Maba hovered at his side. "I didn't know..."

He was fighting those stubborn bonds, pressing here and there, tearing with his fingers. What kept them fastened?

How had the Big Ones operated these things? Jony racked his memory without gaining any coherent answer. He backed away a step or so, and struck against the machine over which the spaceman had been so busy at their entrance. Could the machine control the locks? That was not impossible. But which of the many buttons in rows across it were the right ones? He feared to experiment lest he harm Yaa the more.

"Jony," Maba pushed close to him. "Look here." She held the weapon and was shoving it in his direction. "Could you use this to break..."

He did not want to touch the thing. Like the red rod, it represented a force he neither understood nor wanted to use.

"Drop that!" he ordered.

"No! With it we can get out of here, Jony. We can just put to sleep anyone who tries to stop us."

He adjusted his thinking. She was right. With that to defend the door of this place, they might have more time to work on the bonds which held Yaa and Voak.

"Jonnnneeee—"

Startled he looked around. Voak's head was up, his huge eyes open wide. He had twisted his powers of speech mightily to utter that croak which approximated Jony's name. That he had something of the utmost importance to communicate, the boy knew. But his paw-hands were helpless, he could not sign any message. And Jony's sense could not connect enough to receive any real illumination.

The boy realized that Voak was making as great an effort of will as he himself had done earlier when he had held Jarat in control and forced the medic to lead him here.

Opening his mind as far as he could, Jony stared deep into the clansman's eyes. The—the place of buttons! He laid his hand on the edge of it. Voak's muzzle rose and fell eagerly. If the clansman knew...

"Maba," Jony gave the order crisply. "Go to the door. Be ready to use the weapon."

She nodded, detoured around their unconscious captives, stationed herself directly before the portal. The stunner, steadily grasped in both her hands, was raised breast high, held ready.

Jony began to hold his index finger over the buttons in their rows. He knew Voak was watching. But there came no signal.

Did the clansman understand? He was sure Voak did; that he was feverishly waiting for Jony to reach the right one.

None of the first row, or the second. But, as Jony's fingertip hovered over the first one of the third row, Voak gave quick, vigorous assent. Jony applied pressure.

There was a click, and the bands holding Yaa snapped loose, as did Voak's also. The clansman lumbered across the cabin, reached his mate's side, to support her body against his while Jony raced to free her head from the network of wires. Voak's tongue caressed the fur of her cheek, and, uttering a weak small sound, she opened her eyes.

"Jony, I hear them coming!" Maba called.

There was a thudding from without, as if many feet pounded down that ladder at a speed which suggested attack was imminent. Jony got to Maba, grabbing the weapon from her.

"You hold it so," she told him, "and press that!"

"Where are the others—Geogee, the People?"

"Geogee went with the ones who wanted to see the stone place," she told him. "I don't know where they put Corr or Uga."

"And maybe we can't wait to find out," Jony returned grimly. He wondered if any one of them would win free of the ship. He might be able to control Jarat or any of the other spacemen one at a time. However, he was sure he could not extend that domination over the entire crew at once. He glanced at the prisoners on the floor. Could they be used as a bargaining point?

A grunt from Voak drew his attention. The clansman was leading Yaa away from the wall. Her eyes were only half-open. It was apparent she moved only because her mate urged her along. With one hand Jony made the sign for "danger," indicating the door.

Voak grunted again and dipped his nose in assent. With his paw-hands he continued to pet and smooth Yaa gently, giving voice to a series of small rumbles.

Then, out of the air about them, a voice spoke:

"Attention—red alert . . . You in the lab. Jony . . . Maba . . . !"

For a single moment Jony thought that had been spoken by one of their prisoners. Only, when he glanced down, he saw that both men were still under the influence of Maba's weapon. Then who—and how . . . ?

He stared around wildly, searching for the speaker. Maba caught his arm, stood on tiptoe, her lips forming words silently, so he stooped closer and caught her whisper:

"They talk so from cabin to cabin. That is the captain."

Perhaps she could recognize the voice, but to Jony the order had an inhuman tone, cold and distant.

"Are you listening?" the unseen asked. "You cannot get out. Neither can you, Jony, use Esper against us again. Try . . ."

Such was the compulsion of that command, Jony did. His thought-probe struck against an unbreakable barrier. The force of the meeting hurled his own power back at him like a blow, so he wavered on his feet.

"Jony!" Maba's anguished cry forced him out of that backlash. So, he thought bleakly, the only weapon he truly knew how to use was lost to him.

"Do you understand?" continued the voice. "We can dampen you as much as we want, knock you completely out, as we did before."

Perhaps they could. He had no measure of what forces they could control in turn.

"Use your intelligence," the words came out of the air to plague him. "You are completely in our hands. There is no escape..."

Jony threw back his head. That last had held an arrogant assurance which something in him refused to accept. Now he spoke aloud: "Use *your* intelligence," he countered. "We have two of your people here."

"Just so. But if you attempt to bargain with them as hostages, we shall not play. You can remain where you are until you are hungry enough to agree to come out peacefully."

Before Jony could frame any answer to that, if the captain were still listening, Maba raised her voice with a tone he knew of old:

"You told me Yaa was all right!" she shouted. "You said you would let her and Voak, and Uga, and Corr go. But you hurt her! You *are* like the Big Ones after all!"

Her face grew flushed as her voice rose higher. Maba had always had a quick temper, now she was fast approaching the peak of one of her tantrums. She spun around, seizing the nearest object from the shelf on her right. Then, with a deliberation which spelled her full intent to do the most harm she could, she advanced on the box which had controlled the bands

that had held the People prisoner. Raising a heavy
bar in her hands, well over her head, she brought it
down with all her might on the machine.

The glass panel on its top splintered. There was a
flashing of sparks from the interior below.

"Try it now!" she shouted. "Just try to use this to
hurt Yaa again—or anyone else!"

Gripped by a frenzy close to hysteria, the girl battered at the machine. Jony made no move to stop her.
In fact he was a little envious that he had not seen
that obvious form of retaliation himself. Destroy the
lab equipment, and the spacemen could not use it to
torment any other prisoners they might take.

"Stop her! Stop her, you fool!" The man who had
operated that installation at last raised his head from
the floor waveringly, watching, with a shadow of horror on his face, Maba's destructive attack.

"Why?" Jony asked. "So you can use it on the People? She's right, you're no better than the Big Ones."

"You don't understand." The man tried to crawl
toward the scene of action. Jony stepped swiftly
between him and Maba, though the obvious distress of
the spaceman had given him the beginnings of an idea.

"She'll burn out the circuits!" The man's voice was
half a howl now. "We'll all be fried in a backlash."

"Better that than end in your cages," Jony held his
outer calm. The fear of this stranger was convincing—
perhaps they were in danger. If they were, so much
the better for his own poor hope of their survival.

"Maba—" Jony stepped behind the girl, catching her
arms as she raised them above her head to deliver yet
another attack on the very battered machine. There was
a strange, unpleasant odor leaking from the box now.

"Let me go!" She thrust against him.

"Not yet," Jony returned. "Perhaps we can exchange something..."

Maba wriggled her head about so she could look up into his face.

"How about that?" Jony spoke directly to the spaceman who was struggling to move closer. Beyond him the medic lay; his eyes, too, were now open. "Now listen very carefully, both of you. I think Maba has the right idea, I think this whole lab should be smashed. I don't like cages, I don't like people who look like me but act like Big Ones. I don't like my friends being hurt. Do you understand that?"

"We weren't hurting them—we were testing..." the spaceman returned.

"I have been tested—so," Jony said. "I have seen what happens to lab 'animals.' You believe these People are animals, don't you?" He bore in fiercely. "You need not make up an answer to please me, I can read what you really think—"

Jarat spoke first. "What do you intend to do now? Captain Trefrew cannot be pushed..."

"I can let Maba continue with her work here," returned Jony, "even join her. You see, having been a lab captive once, I have no intention of ever being so again. It is much better to be dead—"

"But," protested the other spaceman, "we have no intention of touching you or the children. Ask her—" he indicated Maba with a lift of his chin, "whether she has not been very well treated."

"I don't doubt it in the least," Jony returned. "You accepted her as one of your own kind. But you see, we do not accept you as one of us! That is the problem for you to consider. We are of the People—" he motioned towards Yaa and Voak.

Whether the clanspeople had understood any of this exchange, Jony did not know. He was glad to see that Yaa was looking brighter, that she no longer leaned weakly against her mate. Perhaps if, by some uncommon stroke of fortune, they could get out of the ship she would be herself again.

"You are human stock," Jarat said.

"We are of the People," replied Jony with the same firmness.

"What will satisfy you?"

"Free passage out of this ship, with your prisoners." He waited, his hold dropping away from Maba.

"If you have any way of talking to your captain," he added a moment later, "you had better do it. If not—when Maba gets tired—I shall take over, with a great deal of pleasure."

> THIRTEEN <

"You heard him captain," Jarat raised his voice a little. "I can assure you he means what he says."

There was silence except for a very faint buzzing out of the box Maba had assaulted. The spaceman who had tended that watched it now with the same apprehension one would feel on a cliff where vors were known to roost. It was plain that he now feared his own machine; was no longer master of it.

"Captain!" It was his turn to call out. "I-20 is building to critical!"

"Order your men away from our path, the other two of the People set free—" Jony restated his demands. "We have nothing to lose but our lives, and in your hands that is an escape of another kind. I know."

When there was no answer, he turned resolutely to Maba. "Give me that!" He reached for the bar she had used to such purpose.

"No!" the word was like a scream from the spaceman. "You'll—the backlash—You don't understand what you're doing!"

Jony shook his head. "The answer is that I do, very well indeed."

"The girl. You can't let her die."

"I would," Jony said slowly and distinctly, "kill her with my own two hands rather than let her remain here with you."

Maba laughed. "He would do so," she nodded vigorously. "When Jony promises, he does as he says he will. And if he does not smash your machine, then I shall. You lied to me about Yaa and Voak. Uga is my cub-kin. Do you understand!" She leaned forward, her face only inches away from that of the struggling man. "We are of the same season, Uga and I—and so kinbound. Jony, do it!" She straightened and shifted her fierce glance from the spaceman to the machine. "He is afraid; they are all afraid! Do it, Jony!"

He raised the bar.

"Captain!" The last appeal from the spaceman was frantic.

Jarat did not add to that protest, he was eyeing Jony narrowly as if trying to assess just how much of this was the truth. What he read in Jony's face must have convinced him.

"Captain," his voice was more controlled than that of his fellow. "He does indeed mean it. After all, we cannot judge these castaways by our own knowledge... not yet."

"Your passage out—" the words came gratingly as if the captain was forced against his will to utter each. "But we are not finished—"

"Our passage out," Jony returned.

"They lied before, they can do it again!" Maba flashed, but Jony had already thought of that.

"You will raise the barrier, the mind barrier," he said. "I shall not try control, but I will know it if your men plan against us."

Again no answer for a long moment. Then: "Very well." He could sense the fury behind that agreement.

Now he used the mind-sense. Yes, the barrier was gone. He motioned Maba to the door, Yaa and Voak were already there. The portal slid open. Outside there was no one. Jony held to his probe, spacemen were above, below...

"Down—" he gestured to the ladder. If Yaa could not negotiate that descent, he did not know what they could do.

But her strength seemed to be returning. Maba scrambled down first, then Voak followed, Yaa moving more slowly behind him. Jony came last, concentrating on locating every indication of life ahead and behind as his sense sought them out.

Luckily they were only one level above that from which the ramp stretched open to freedom. And below, awaiting them, huddled the two younger People. Maba threw her arms about Uga's furry shoulders, hugged her.

"Out!" Jony made that order urgent. But the People did not need his command, they were already padding down the ramp, into freedom. He followed. So far, his mind-search told him, no one within the ship had stirred. But once they were outside they would be highly vulnerable. Then would the captain keep his side of the bargain? Jony distrusted that as much as he would any bargain with an enemy.

They were crossing the open now, heading to the ridge. Uga and Corr appeared unaffected by their imprisonment, but it was plain that neither Voak nor Yaa had their old strength or were able to move at the best speed the People could keep.

Jony played rear guard. He still had the stunner taken from the spaceman, as well as the second which he had twitched out of Jarat's belt before he had left, and which he now entrusted to Maba.

She raced ahead, to stand halfway up the ridge, facing back toward the ship. Jony had no idea how far the range of those weapons was. He only hoped that Maba might cover their retreat from her position as well as he could from his rear guard station.

Luckily the flyer was gone. With that overhead they would not have any chance at all. Could those within the ship now perhaps strike out at them with some longer range attack? He knew so little...

The People had passed Maba's stand. Uga and Corr had already crested the ridge. He knew they would get under cover with all possible speed. Yaa and Voak followed.

At the foot of the rise Jony faced around as Maba had done. His mind-probe was blotted out again. Back in the ship they had once more raised that barrier. Which could mean attack to come!

"Jony." Maba's voice—"Come—"

He went, with a burst of speed. Yaa and Voak were out of sight. Maba had moved to the crest where she stood, still on guard. He was breathing hard as he came level with her.

More than anything now he wanted to set that rise of solid earth and stone between them and the ship. He still could not quite believe that they had gained their freedom.

Jony watched the ship closely, more than half-expecting to witness an exit of force to trail them. Or would the spacemen wait for the return of the flyer to start pursuit? Geogee! In the stress of their breakout he had forgotten about the boy. What had they said—Geogee had gone to guide the spacemen to the place of stones. Jony had no doubts that meant the storage place. The power rods...!

Glancing around he saw no sign of the People. The fugitives had melted away into the brush cover with their usual skill at concealing themselves. Maba pulled at the sleeve of the garment the ship's people had forced on him.

"They—they'll come after us, Jony?" she asked that as a question.

"Maybe they're waiting for the flyer."

"Geogee—he's with them, Jony."

"I know. We'll have to get him away, too." But at the moment he was more worried about what the boy could have shown the spacemen. The captain, those on board the ship, had displayed no dislike for the children, not until Maba had turned against them. Could he believe Geogee was safe—for now?

"You must tell me," he rounded on Maba, "all you can about them. What are they doing here?"

Maba's expression was one of trouble. "They want to come here—to have a colony, Jony. There was a big fight—somewhere 'way out there—" with the hand not holding the stunner she motioned to the sky. "The Big Ones, they were driven away from this part of space. Now these people hunt new worlds for more colonies."

"This world *has* its People," Jony looked down over

her head to the bush into which Yaa, Voak and the others must have gone. "These spacemen cannot just come and take it."

"Jony," she moved closer to him. "Maybe they can. They showed us things. They have a big box and you sit there watching it. Inside the box are pictures and the people in them move and do things. They showed us how they live on other worlds. Jony, there're lots and lots of them. There must be more than all the trees you ever saw," she was plainly reaching for some kind of comparison to make the biggest impression on him. "And they have a lot of sky ships, bigger ones than this one. They say that they need more room for their people, and they were so glad to find this world. Because they can breathe here, and it is like others where they already live."

"But it is not theirs," he repeated. "It belongs to the People!"

"Did it always, Jony? Remember what we saw in the pictures..."

He seized the girl fiercely by the shoulders, stared straight down into her astonished face.

"That was wrong, Maba. The People are not animals, *things* to be used—"

He remembered at that moment what Voak had said to him when they had set the collar about his neck. Things to be used—like a staff, or a fruit net—a *thing* not a person. The People had won free from that once, such bondage must never be set on them again.

"But, Jony, what can we do to stop them?" Maba came directly to the point. "The spacemen can make people go to sleep with these things," she waved the stunner. "They can fly right over us and do that. That's the way they caught us. The People won't even be able to get near enough to them to fight back."

This was the unwelcome truth and he had to face it. Added to that was the possibility that Geogee might this very moment be showing the spacemen the weapons of the stone people. Jony had no idea *what* he and the clan could do, but he was also certain that they must not allow these others to take this world without a struggle. It remained to be seen what the People would think or do for their own protection.

"Come!" He started down after the vanished clanspeople. If he could only communicate fully with Voak! At such a time as this sign language fell woefully short.

He half-expected to be met by Otik, at least when they got into the bush cover. But there was no sign of any of the People there. Now Jony used his special sense, searching for the faint impressions they had for him. Nothing—near. The People were on the move, which was only what he could expect. They would travel as far from the ship now as they could.

And he could send no message to halt them. That they were angling northward again was the only promising bit of evidence for him.

The brush, through which he had learned long ago to slip with a minimum of obstruction, caught at his ship garment over and over and over again. His body felt hot and sweaty, his skin was chafed where the material rubbed against neck, armpit, along his thighs. At least Maba was not so encumbered.

She did not have the kilt she had worn, but her new covering was only from neck to knee. Jony guessed it had been improvised, there being no ready garment on the ship small enough for her to wear. She was able to slip and duck, weave in and out far faster than he could.

They had trail enough to follow and the People had certainly learned quickly that one must keep under cover. Jony kept listening for the buzz of the flyer. Did those in the ship have any far ranging means of communication to recall that?

As he went he fired questions at Maba, and she answered as readily and promptly as she could. Her account was of very good treatment, that Jarat and the captain had both questioned her and Geogee as to their past. The twins, not seeing any danger, had poured out in return all they knew. The spacemen had been particularly excited about the stone place.

"They might well be," Jony returned grimly to that, "seeing what could be hidden there—"

"You mean the rod Geogee found—that one that made things go away," Maba agreed. "He told them about that. They wanted to see one."

Jony could well guess that they did. What had he and the twins done to the People who had given them life? Brought the space ship? No, that might have landed if Jony and the twins had not explored the place of stones. But to give the spacemen guidance to the secrets hidden there!

In spite of the steady progress of the clan Jony and Maba caught up with them by nightfall. They were not challenged by Otik who was plainly on sentry, but neither were they welcomed. He only stared at them as they went by into the campsite, where the nests were very small and thin, meaning a short rest only.

Voak squatted by his mate who lay full length on

the biggest and best of that bedding. He was flanked on either side by Uga and Corr, and Jony thought it plain that they were sharing with the rest the details of their imprisonment and treatment on board the ship.

The boy held Maba by his side when she would have sped to Yaa. Not until he had some form of acceptance from Voak and the rest would he know whether they could stay, were once more clankin in the way which would matter most.

Voak was silent as he surveyed Jony and the girl. It was Yaa who voiced some rumbles in their talk. Her mate glanced down at her, then back at Jony. Getting ponderously to his feet, he crossed to face the boy squarely. His bulk and height made Jony seem small, unimportant, or so he felt. But at least the clanchief was not ignoring him as he half-expected he would. The collar was gone, but it had not been loosened by the People. In Jony's mind it still lay about his throat until he won full fellowship with them again.

"Ship thing"—Voak's hand arose to sign—"bad."

Swiftly Jony made answer. "Bad!"

"People—sky thing—like—you."

Jony could not deny that outward appearance. He cast around frantically for some comparison he could use to suggest that outward and inward should not be confused.

"Hoppers, Jony," Maba produced the possible key, "remember hoppers and pinchers!"

The comparison he had once made for her! If Voak would only accept that belief. Jony gestured. His hands moved in the sign for hopper, then for hide and hunt—and then for the pincher—and again hide. The People all knew of that strange method of concealment which the hopper could use and how often it deceived the chosen prey.

Having so outlined something which they already knew Jony launched into his parallel thought.

"Sky ones—hoppers. Jony, Maba, Geogee—pinchers. Look alike—different."

Voak appeared to consider the idea.

Jony plunged on. "Jony captured—find Yaa, find Voak, Corr, Uga—make them come out of bad place."

Now that Voak could not deny.

The boy continued, "Jony not clankin to ship bad ones, Jony clankin to Voak, Yaa."

He waited tensely. This was his bid for acceptance. If Voak refused to believe, then he and Maba would be no-kin—alone—in spite of what they had done to free the People.

From where she lay Yaa again spoke. Voak moved uneasily, his head turned a little toward her and then back again.

"Geogee—take bad ones—place of stones," Voak signed.

"Geogee not know what happened to Yaa, Voak. Geogee, Maba, not told. Think all well."

Would Voak believe that either?

"Bad ones find power to make People *things*. Place of stones have power to do so."

Jony signed assent and then daringly added, "People must keep bad ones from taking power."

Voak's jaws opened, displaying his most formidable fangs. He scowled as he did when facing a smaa or a vor.

"Voak—People—have no this"—he turned and

caught the staff out of Trush's paw-hand, shook it in Jony's face—"like bad ones. Those have sleep sticks. Voak go to sleep before getting near to bad ones."

Jony pulled the stunner from the front of his ship suit.

"Sleep stick for Voak." He held it out.

But the clansman retreated a step. "Bad thing. Not for People."

"Better for People than to be in ship again."

From those massed around behind Yaa old Gorni pushed. He held the metal staff Jony had found. Now he pointed the curved tip of this straight at the boy's breast.

"Give paw!" he signed.

Jony transferred the stunner to his left hand, extended the right. Before he could resist, Gorni had caught his wrist, held on in an unbreakable hold. In spite of the clansman's advanced age his physical strength could not be matched by any off-worlder.

He dropped the sharp point of the staff, piercing the skin on the back of Jony's hand. Then he dipped his muzzle and sniffed long at the bubble of blood forming there. The meaning of his action was lost on Jony. But he believed from the small stirs of the watching People, that to them this act held some vast importance.

Gorni gave a last sniff, raised his head. "Smell right," he signed. "Clankin."

Jony gave a great sigh of relief. What the smell of his blood had to do with acceptance, he could not tell. Only it was very apparent from the attitudes of those Gorni had so reassured, that he was again one of them. And, being one of them, he must now try to make them understand the danger from the sky ship. Not only for the present, but in days to come.

If Maba was right—that this one ship was the forerunner of a colony—then they were in desperate straits and must move. In what direction and how, Jony did not know. It might be they were already defeated in that instant when the ship had made a safe landing. But he refused to accept that; he dared not believe such a thing could happen.

With more confidence than he had felt for a long time, Jony signed to Voak: "People must not let bad ones take any power things from place of stones."

Voak hunched his massive shoulders a little. Almost Jony could believe that the clansman felt the same breath of defeat which had touched his own thoughts.

"How stop?"

How indeed? Jony could give him no answer yet. Perhaps if they returned there he could tell. But would Voak agree to break the rule of the People and enter a place the clan held in such disgust and dread?

"We must find a way. What they take—" In his mind Jony could picture very vividly the use of a red rod with intent, not chance the way Geogee had done. "What they take could be very bad."

Voak made the down and back muzzle assent of his species. "People go far—bad ones not find."

"Bad ones can move through the air faster than People can travel." Jony hoped that Voak would agree that was true. He, himself, was under no illusions as to how successful the flyer and the sky ship were.

Perhaps Voak wanted to deny that, but he could not. Instead he made a dismissing sign which Jony must obey. Taking Maba's hand, the boy crossed to the other side of the campsite, allowing the People to discuss the matter in their own way. Only he was sure of his own plans.

"Jony, what if they won't go to the place of stones?" Maba asked.

"I shall have to go anyway," he told her. Best get that settled now.

"And me," she said promptly.

"No! You will stay with Yaa and the People." He was going to be firm about that.

Some of her old rebellion countered that order instantly. "I won't! I know more about the place of pictures than you do. I found the way in. If you try to go without me, I'll follow."

She would, too, he had no doubts about that. Nor did Jony believe that the People would make any move to prevent her.

"Geogee's there," she was continuing. "And, Jony, Geogee, he likes Volney, he follows him around all the time. Volney has promised him he can learn to fly a sky ship someday. I don't think Geogee would listen if *you* told him they're bad. But he might listen to me."

"Who is Volney?" Jony demanded.

"He's the one of them who knows how to make things go up and travel in the air," Maba explained. "Geogee is all excited about the machines. He told them lots about what he saw in the place of stones. And I heard them talking, they think some of those old people left very important things there. Geogee will want to stay with them, not us, unless we can make him understand."

She was very serious about this, and Jony knew that she was telling the full truth. The tie between the twins was a deep one, it could well be true that Maba could accomplish more in making Geogee understand the danger threatened by these strangers than he ever could. But he hated to take her with him into what might be not only hopeless but a dangerous struggle.

"I will go!" She returned to her own statement of fact.

Before he could find any answer, Voak broke from the cluster of the People, came toward them. Jony could read nothing, of course, in that furred face, but Voak's paw-hands were moving.

"We go—to see..."

At least he had won that much, thought Jony, soberly, but not in triumph. He could be entirely wrong, leading them all into danger. There was only that instinct within him saying stubbornly that this was all which was left for them to do.

> FOURTEEN <

Their party did not approach the place of stones (which Maba said the spacemen referred to as a "city") by the way Jony had done so before, openly down that solid river which flowed directly into its heart. Once Voak had assented to this journey, he had taken command of their small party, leaving behind the females and the young under orders to move off to the west, into a region of deeper and more impenetrable woods which they hoped would be a barrier against any more attacks from the flyer.

Their own return journey north had followed, at the best pace of the People. Even Jony, impatient as he was, realized the wisdom of not becoming too tired before they reached their goal. Such progress demanded the better part of two days of travel, with only a short interval of rest during the dark hours.

Once more they crossed the open fields about the river of stone before working back into those ridges which Jony believed were near the place of the cage. This passage took them almost the whole of another

day before they reached a ridge point from which the
city could be viewed, not from the front, but directly
from the rear.

Jony sighted no sign of the flyer. However, the
machine could have set down on the far side of the
cluster of rising walls. As he lay near Voak, concealed
by the grass and brush on the crest, the boy used his
own method of locating who might be below.

Even if those on the flyer had been warned in some
way (Maba stated positively the off-worlders were able
to communicate even at a distance by using machines)
to set up that same mind barrier the ship people had
used to repel his control, the very fact they did this
would be assurance they were still here.

He sought Geogee, fixing a picture of the boy in
his mind, sending out a probe to pick up the familiar
pattern of the twin's thought processes. Jony encountered no barrier—and—yes! So faint was it that he was
not sure he could track the touch with any certainty
to where Geogee was. But he *had* caught it.

Voak raised himself head and shoulders from the
ground. His wide nostrils expanded, to flatten again
visibly. Then the clansman ducked his head in the
gesture of agreement before Jony had a chance to
report his own findings.

Crabwise, Voak retreated from the top of the ridge.
Jony slipped after him. When that bulk of earth and
stone wall stood between them and the city, the
remainder of Voak's people drew in to meet the scouts.

"Scent—strong—they—there." Voak signed.

He looked gravely at Jony who was trying to think
of what to do next. Whether the ship had warned the
men in the city was unknown. If the off-worlders had

been so alerted, then the chance of his own party's success was lessened.

Remembering the stone-walled dens, Jony knew that there were places in plenty where one could play hide-and-seek. Thus the People, with their natural tendency to take cover efficiently at need, might still well work their way in secretly. Only, the strangers had the superior weapons, that could operate at a distance and far more effectively. Also—would the People even consent to enter the city?

His companions were talking in their own speech. Jony sat quietly, his hands clasped on the metal shaft which had been returned to him, frowning a little as he thought of one ghost of a plan and then another, rejecting each in turn. Then he remembered, with sudden and complete clarity, the cage in the mountains. Why it came to him at that moment he did not know.

There lay the evidence that the People, in the past, had been able to deal with those having superior weapons, and very effectively! He hunched forward and his change in position must have registered on Voak. For the clanchief swung his head a little to again eye Jony with that steady regard.

The next move depended on how much Voak could or would tell Jony, and then on whether the People would trust him fully. He longed bitterly for the power to read their thoughts, more so than he ever had in his life before. But he...

Voak signed: "What do?"

Had the clansman guessed that Jony did have, at last, a nebulous idea? One, however, that depended so much on others, having so many flaws even he could see, that it might also fail?

"The People were there," Jony tried to sort out in signs what he must learn, if they would let him. He pointed to the ridge behind which lay the city. "They wore collars, they were things..."

Voak made no assenting gesture to that. Jony refused to be daunted.

"How People be freed?" He made his question boldly.

For a long instant he was afraid Voak would refuse to answer. There came a series of sounds from others about, until Voak signed silence with a paw-hand. His muzzle sank forward until it nearly rested against the pied-fur on his chest. Jony waited.

Maba, who had squatted beside the boy, moved. Jony put out his own hand in a signal to be still. This time he could guess that Voak was weighing the idea of telling, by doing so perhaps breaking some old rule of his own kind.

At last the other raised his black-skinned hands, beginning to sign slowly, as if he wanted to make very sure Jony understood.

"Those—were sick. Many died. People did not die. People strong. People break collars—out of cages... They make trap. Catch those—take them out—away from place where those had strong things to hurt—to kill. Put in place they could not get strong things— Those die. People free. Not again collars for People."

An illness had weakened the makers of the city and left them open to a rebellion of the People. This trap...

"In the place of stones," Jony asked, "there was a trap?"

Voak dipped his head.

"It is still there?"

"Long time—who knows?" came the clansman's answer.

"Could you find it?" Jony persisted.

Again that moment of silence before the People spoke together. Finally Voak replied: "No know."

"Would you seek for it?" This was one of the first of the most important points he must make. Jony had persuaded the People to approach the city, but would they actually enter it?

"Why?" Voak's counter question was a single gesture.

"If the trap there, perhaps catch these also," Jony answered.

"They no sick, they have bad things. Make People go sleep—wake in sky ship again."

"I go—alone . . . place of stones. I find those, make them think I am clankin. They listen, I tell of things to be found. Take them to trap."

There, he had outlined his poor plan, and, even as he had proposed it, Jony knew that there were so many ways it could go wrong. If those on the ship had contacted the party in the city, then they would know Jony for the enemy. And . . .

"I go," Maba said, first aloud, and then in sign for the People to read. "Don't you see, Jony," she added in speech, "I can say you made me believe things were wrong. But I have changed now, and I need to be with Geogee, that I want to be friends with them. They know me, they would believe me sooner than they would you."

"No!" Jony's refusal was sharp. There was logic in what she urged. Only, if any message had come from the ship, those down in the city would be aware of the important part the girl had played in their escape.

"They would believe *me*," she repeated with much of her usual stubbornness, "before they would you."

Voak could not have understood their exchange. However, he arose ponderously to his feet, the rest moving with him.

"We go—place of stones." He made a statement of that, as forceful as an order.

They did not descend the ridge in plain sight of any who might have been watching, as Jony half-feared they might, but turned more to the east. Voak took the lead; Trush and old Gorni fell in behind him. Then came Jony and Maba, the others furnishing a rear guard. Their path led along a narrow valley below the ridge, heading on toward those taller heights behind the city.

And, as the clansmen had earlier done on their visit to the cave of the cage, the People strode along in a matched step, bringing their staffs (those who had them) butt down against the ground with a regular thumping. As yet they had not raised their voices, but Jony was worried. Such a noisy advance could possibly betray them to some machine of the flyer. Only he knew better than to try to urge caution on the People at this point. They knew the danger. Undoubtedly they were moving to counteract it in their own way.

The valley became a very narrow slit. Then, for the first time, Jony saw stones cropping out of the thin soil. The city builders had been here also.

It was against certain of those stones (he could not tell why, for their choices seemed to follow no pattern that Jony could determine) that the clansmen now thudded their staffs. The resulting sound was hollow and echoing. Jony tried to listen beyond that muffled pounding, fearing to hear the buzz of the investigating flyer.

At last the valley came to an abrupt end in a wall which a fall of earth had revealed completely. The stones which formed this obstruction were not all alike. Even with the weathering and discoloring to confuse the eye, Jony could make out the outline of a former opening into which rougher and less finished rocks had been forced as a plug.

Two of the clansmen drew apart, stood thumping the butts of their staffs, not against those stones sealing the old opening, but aiming at the solid wall on either side. Voak, Trush, and Otik padded forward, extending their claws to pry between the plug rocks, digging to free them from their long setting. Jony pushed up to join them. Motioning the clansmen back, he inserted the point of his metal staff into those crevices, digging free soil, levering them apart.

They cleared the way at last, to be faced by a dark opening from which issued cold, dank air. Jony uneasily surveyed the way ahead. He had no liking for venturing into an unknown dark.

Then Voak signed to him. "Give staff!"

Amazed, Jony gaped at the other's outstretched paw-hand. For a moment he thought that the clansman again mistrusted him, wanted him unarmed as they advanced. So his grasp on the weapon tightened. He was determined not to yield.

Voak must have read his fears, for once more the clansman's fingers moved.

"Must have staff—need for going."

Well, Jony and Maba still had the two stunners they

had brought from the ship. And Voak certainly knew
more about this hidden way than he did. Reluctantly
the boy passed over his find to the clansman.

Voak raised the metal length, seemed to weigh it in
hand for the best grip, before he sent the butt thudding against the wall, his round, furred head unmov-
ing as if he listened for some necessary answering
sound. The thump was certainly sharper and clearer
than that which came from meeting of the wooden
ones with the wall. Voak gave one last mighty swing,
to clang against rock, and then advanced, passing
into the dark passage, thumping the staff as he went.
The others fell into the same line of march they had
earlier held. As they went, Maba's hand caught Jony's
and her fingers tightened.

"Where are we going?" she asked in a voice hardly
above a whisper.

"Into the city—somehow," he answered her, trying
to make his tone casual and reassuring. Though, as
the light behind them grew dimmer and dimmer, the
way before darker, he found it hard to hold to any
high pitch of confidence.

The beat of the staff butts continued regularly. Jony
wished he knew the reason for this. Was the gesture
one only of ceremony, to be used when approaching
a place forbidden now to their kind? Or did that
pounding have a more definite and practical purpose?
At least this passage remained level; there was no
sudden drop to slide down into the unknown as had
been part of his earlier adventure.

The air was flat and held strong earthy odors. Jony's
head began to ache a little, a condition increased by
every thump of staff butt.

The boy tried to guess what lay about them in the dark. It seemed to him this was no longer a narrow passage but a wider space, for he fancied there was a different ring to the faint echoing of their pounding. If he turned his head for a second or two, he could catch the faint gleam of his companions' eyes.

Maba said nothing, but her grip on his hand continued very tight, and he could gauge her tenseness by that. Jony longed to give her some assurance that there would soon be an end. But that he could not know.

Again, as had happened earlier, there grew slowly a show of gray light ahead. Shortly, the light showed that they were indeed in a much vaster open area. Voak kept to a straight course between two rows of the stone pillars. Was this another part of the storehouse? If so they must be doubly on their guard, or they might be betrayed by the noise the People continued to make. But there were no signs of any of those boxed containers, no paintings on the walls. This was only a bare, grim-looking burrow revealed in a limited amount of dusky light. They neared another wall. At last Jony could make out against that a series of ledges which the people of the city had used to gain heights above.

Voak had not thumped for the last two strides, nor had any of the others. His head now stretched to the highest angle he could hold it, so his muzzle pointed up the rise of the ledges. There was light enough for Jony to see that the clansmen were sniffing.

To Jony's less sensitive nose there was nothing to be scented but the musty smell which had hung about them ever since they had entered this way. But he knew that the People were far better endowed than he.

Whatever Voak searched for, he seemed satisfied. Without any signed explanation, he began to climb. Now there was no pounding with their staffs, they moved in that absolute silence their big hind paws could keep when there was need.

Before long they emerged into the full light of sunset. That rich glow lay in a broad path directly to the head of the ascent, as if to welcome them, issuing through a wall slit placed well above Jony's head. He looked around, and, not too far ahead, saw the place of the sleeper. The hidden underground ways had led them straight to the heart of the city.

As the clansmen hesitated for the first time, Jony pressed past them. Sounds kept him from advancing very far. Voices, surely; only so muffled that he could not make out separate words. The spacemen—down in the passage to the storage room!

Geogee? Once more Jony concentrated on reaching the boy. No barrier here as he had feared. The force of his thought swept swiftly into the boy's mind. Too swiftly, too forcefully perhaps. Jony withdrew. Had Geogee betrayed them to the others with his shock as Jony made contact?

He wriggled the stunner out of the front of his ship garment where he had stowed it for safekeeping. If their party could now only take the spacemen by surprise while the invaders explored below...

Voices coming nearer... Jony did not really have to make any warning sign. The People had already melted away into the shadows, Maba with them. Jony slipped from one pillar to the next, using those huge rounds of stone for cover just as he would the trees of a wood.

He was nearly opposite the other entrance, and he already had proof that the spacemen were doing more than just exploring below. After all, they had had some time to select from the stores of the city people. So there was a tall stack of the colored boxes built up in a wall-like pile, their brilliant hues all mixed together. In how many were power rods? Jony could not possibly guess, and he had no time to investigate. For two of the suited invaders advanced into the open, another box carried between them.

They were pulled to one side by the weight of what they carried. Jony took a long chance to aim in a way which he hoped would catch them both. He pressed the firing button.

One slumped, the other gave a startled cry, dropped his end of the box, staggered a step or two, until Jony caught him full on with a second beam. The noise of the box hitting the floor—that cry! Had the sounds given the alarm to the party still below?

Voak and his clansmen needed no orders. They flitted silently between the pillars, caught up the two unconscious men, bundling them fast in large nets they had brought with them. How many more of the enemy were here? Maba had thought that four had gone with the flyer from the ship with Geogee; but she was not sure.

Now Jony struck in another fashion. He could not aim at either of Geogee's two other companions with mental compulsion, because he neither had them in view, nor knew them well enough to form a mind-picture. However, through the boy, he ought to be able to deal easily with the opposition, as he had once before.

Rutee—his far off promise! Only Rutee could not have foreseen such a situation as this. She would certainly not hold him to any word, if keeping such meant ill to the People who had saved her and her children.

Geogee! Jony aimed an order with the same precision as he had just used the stunner.

Come!

He had the boy! Geogee was obeying.

Come!

Geogee must have been well up the ascent from the storage room, because their contact was so clear, so immediate. Jony held communication to top pitch, until the smaller form of the boy did appear in the open, his eyes as wide and set as any mind-controlled. Jony winced at the sight. But this must be done.

Now Maba ran lightly forward, caught her twin by a dangling hand, hurried him with her, back into the dusk behind where that single high window laid its path of light.

"What's with the boy!" Spoken words Jony could pick up and understand.

"Maybe he can't take this hole any longer. I'm beat out myself. Let's call this the last—for now."

"The last? It will take us months to clear out that place. What a find! I don't think anything like it—so complete—has ever been uncovered before. Who were these city builders? They look like pure Terran stock in those pictures."

"Could be. There were a lot of colony ships which took off and just went into nowhere as far as the records are concerned. Or colonies of colonies of colonies. What I'd like to know is what happened to..."

The speakers had reached the top of the ramp. Again they carried between them a box. However, directly in their path lay the first which the now-prisoners had dropped. Sighting that, the newcomers stopped short.

"Down!" One of them loosed his end of their own burden, fell to the floor behind it. His fellow was only a fraction late in following him. What had alerted them Jony could not tell. But he heard them slithering along behind the barrier of that loot they had already brought out. He shot the stunner twice. Apparently its power could not penetrate that barrier. And, when he tried mind control, he met with the dampening effect of some safe coverage.

They were heading for the open by the sounds, to get out to their flyer. He could guess that much. And, also, if they reached that and were able to rise he and the People would have lost.

Jony began to run along the other side of the boxes. Would one of the invaders now produce a power rod and use it? He could taste his fear, but that did not slow his desperate chase.

> FIFTEEN <

The off-worlders broke from behind the end of the line of boxes. Raising his stunner, and aiming as best as he could, Jony was about to press the firing button when he himself was struck. Not by any blow, but with that same weakening of the muscles, that inability to keep on his feet which had made him easy prey for the spacemen before. Only this time he did not lose consciousness; even though he wilted forward, to lie face down, unable to raise or turn his head.

Geogee! Jony received in his still-alert mind the impact of the twin's anger and fear. He could hear the thud of running feet. The escaping spacemen must be well on their way out of the building. But Geogee did not accompany them.

Once again Jony tried mind-touch, control, if he could force it. Now he met the same barrier which the ship people could raise. He fought with all his will against the inert disobedience of his body, but was unable to break whatever bonds held him.

Jony heard the whisper of footsteps from behind.

Geogee? Another spaceman? A clutch on his shoulder rolled him over, to lie limply, staring up at Geogee.

The boy scowled down at him. He wore not only a smaller version of the ship garment, but, now, over his head, a bubble-like covering which was far too large, shifting back and forth on his shoulders, so that he had to raise a hand constantly to steady it in place. However, in his other hand, at the ready, was a stunner.

"Geogee..." Though he was not able to move, Jony discovered he could shape that name with his lips, utter it as a low whisper.

If the other heard him, he made no sign. Instead he walked around Jony, picked up the stunner he had dropped when he fell under attack. Geogee thrust that extra weapon into the front of his clothing, as if it were very necessary to make sure of such possession at once.

Then, for the first time, he spoke: "What did they do with them?"

Jony had no idea what he meant. He struggled to give voice in that whisper. "Who—do with what?"

"With Volney, Isin. I saw the People take them, back there." Geogee settled his helmet straight, then waved his hand toward the rear of the long hall.

So the People had gone, taking with them their prisoners. Jony accepted that with difficulty, startled at first by the fact that they had deserted him. Geogee leaned closer.

"I said—where are they going to take them?" His eyes blinked nervously, he fidgeted. Though Jony could not now use the mind-touch, he was well aware that Geogee was in a state of great excitement, perhaps even fear.

When Jony did not answer at once, Geogee brought the stunner around, pointing the rod straight at his victim's head.

"I can give you another shot," he shrilled. "You won't ever know anything after that!"

"And if I don't know anything," Jony returned, "how can you find out what you want? Geogee, this is me, Jony! Why are you doing this—?"

Geogee's eyes flicked from side to side as if he expected at any moment to be attacked from another direction.

"You let *them* take Volney," he burst out. "Those animals—they'll kill him! You—you—" His accusation ended in a sputtering, as if he could not find any name evil enough for Jony.

In turn he was struck silent as another voice called from behind the line of boxes: "Geogee?"

"Maba! What are you doing here? Let me alone!" For a moment Geogee's concentration on Jony was broken. Had the other been able to move he might have used that instant well. But, in spite of his will, his body remained inert.

"What are *you* doing, Geogee?" the girl countered. She advanced into the line of Jony's sight. Both her hands were empty, the stunner she had carried was gone.

"I want to know where they took Volney!" her twin repeated loudly. "I saw them drag him off; he and Isin! They'll maybe kill him..."

The twin was lashing himself into a stronger display of anger and fear than Jony had ever seen him exhibit before. Now he actually swung the stunner around to point at his sister.

Ignoring the menace of that weapon, she walked forward boldly, facing Geogee across Jony's body. Her face was as calm as if they had both awakened in a clan nest that morning and there had been no fatal interruption to the peace of their lives.

"The People won't kill them," she stated firmly.

"How do you know? Animals! They always kill when they're threatened." Geogee spat back. "And how did you get here, away from the ship?"

"I came because he brought me," she indicated Jony. "Don't we always have to do as he wants, if he controls us?"

Geogee laughed, a reckless note high in sound. "Not anymore! I've got this." He thumped the helmet, which slipped so that he had to hurriedly right it once more. "Jony didn't know about it—so I could grab it when he let me go—when I got to you, too. They know about what Jony can do. But he can't control me anymore. Not now. He can't do anything at all but just lie there. Eh, Jony?"

He stared down at his captive; the grin on his face was not a pleasant one.

"Rutee made you promise," he hissed, "that you would never try to control us. But you did! You learned a lot from the Big Ones. But I've learned more—from Volney. I can control *you*, Jony. See, I'll show you how—"

Turning up the butt of the alien weapon he made some adjustment there, and then, with a flip of the wrist, aimed once more at Jony, sending whatever power that weapon emitted to travel the full length of his victim.

There was a tingling in Jony's flesh. Circulation

might be returning to some limb which had gone numb. But, though Jony attempted at once to move, he was still in thrall to that terrible inertia.

"Get up!" commanded Geogee.

To Jony's sudden horror then, his body, if slowly and disjointedly, did move. Fear filled his mind—he was *controlled!* Yet this was not the same way as the Big Ones practiced such captivity. He was sure that the effect was different.

Once on his feet he swayed back and forth, his own mind fighting desperately to take over command of his body. He felt enmeshed in an unseen net of alien strength. Geogee backed away, stunner still aimed at Jony's middle. And Jony was drawn to follow, staggering, wavering, but on his feet and moving in obedience to that pull.

"You see?" Geogee laughed again. "Now Jony can't control us, but we can him! We'll march him right to the flyer. Varcar and Hansa, they're there. We'll take him back to the ship. The captain will know what to do with him."

To Jony's surprise and dismay Maba echoed that laughter. "Clever Geogee," she praised her twin. "How did you know how to do that? When you took my stunner you didn't tell me how you could..."

"Volney showed me when I told him about Jony. Volney knows more than Jony could ever hope to. Volney likes me. He says when we go back with them he'll see I'm taught how to be a pilot, learn to run their machines. Volney says I learn things easier than any boy he's seen, that I have a very good brain. Volney..." Geogee's face twisted again into that ugly scowl. "Volney! Those animals have Volney! We must get him free. Jony knows where they are; he's going to take us there—right now!"

"Jony doesn't know everything," Maba answered. "He tried to make the People come here, fight the spacemen. They came, but they wouldn't fight. They don't want to fight, but just run away. And now they've run off and left Jony. They won't take Volney and the other far; they're afraid of the space people. If we went after them, left Jony... He doesn't go fast when you make him move—we could stop them. You have that," she indicated the stunner. "You can take Volney away from the People easily. But we have to hurry now to catch up."

Geogee came to a halt, his attention once more passing from Jony to the girl. Jony was sick inside. What had happened to Maba? On board the ship she had aided in their escape; he could not have carried that through without her quick wit. And he had allowed her to come here because he knew that she did have influence over Geogee. Only now she was using that influence to set Geogee, armed with his alien weapon, on the trail of Voak and the others. Since she had come out of the shadows, she had not once looked straight at Jony nor given any indication that she was in opposition to her brother.

"Leave Jony?" Geogee said thoughtfully. "But they want Jony, they want to learn how he can control us. Volney said maybe he is a mutant."

"What's a mutant?" Apparently that was new to Maba.

"Someone who is changed from the rest, I guess. But they want to know about Jony."

"Easy enough," Maba made a slight face. "Leave

him here. You can stun him again, or just leave him
controlled like this. He won't be able to get away.
If we wait, the People may be able to hide Volney
before we can catch up."

"They aren't *People!*" Geogee still did not relinquish
his wary attitude toward his captive. "Volney said they
don't have that high a reading on the scale. They're
not like us at all. Jony is stupid, always telling us how
great they are. About leaving him here...I don't know."

"Oh, come on," Maba was growing impatient. "You
know he can't get away, not if you leave him controlled.
Anyway, those who went to the ship—they'll be back."
She gestured to the heaped boxes. "They're never
going to leave all this, or you, or Volney and Isin."

Slowly Geogee nodded. Though he watched Jony
measuringly, he lowered the weapon slightly.

Now Jony made the move he had decided upon
during that short exchange when both the twins apparently ignored him. He allowed his body to slump once
more to the pavement, as if he could no longer obey
the controls. Until he fell he was not sure that he
could do that much of his own will. So at this small
assertion of his desires, he regained a little of the
confidence Geogee's actions had drained out of him.

"Look at him!" A foot kicked lightly against his
shoulder, its movement was all he could see of the
twins in his now limited field of vision. "You think
he's going to escape?"

"All right," Geogee conceded. "He won't be able to
get away. And I'd better not give him another raying.
Volney says they want him to be all right when they
examine him."

"Geogee!" thought Jony. Who or what was this

Volney that the off-worlder had been able, in a period of days, to wipe out all Geogee's ties with those he had known since birth? He himself had hated the spacemen hotly when he had seen Yaa as a focus for their experiments. Now that hatred grew into a cold purpose within him. If they could so persuade Geogee, then they were even more like Big Ones. Geogee might not have the outward appearance of the mind-controlled, but he was thinking along a pattern these others had dictated. And for that also Jony wanted a reckoning. And Maba...

He had begun to sense she might be playing some game of her own. But that he dared trust her...no, of that he was not sure. If she did guide Geogee after the People, then even a small chance of victory would be lost.

Jony listened to the footfalls pacing away from him. He was not sure whether he could do anything to break the invisible bonds Geogee had netted around him. While the boy was in sight and could bring his weapon to bear again, he dared not even try.

Only deep silence now. Still Jony made no attempt to struggle. He was gathering all his power. Also what Maba had said: that the two spacemen who had fled might return, haunted him, kept him listening, until he decided he dared not wait any longer.

He concentrated on his right hand where it lay touching his cheek, willing fingers to move. There was a barrier there, yes, but not so great a one that he could not achieve a stirring. So heartened, he poured in all the strength he could summon. His fingers clawed, crawled ahead, as might the legs of a lethargic insect.

Though he had still very little real strength, he could move! How long would it take for the full influence of the weapon to wear off, if that ever would? He might have so very little time left. Palm lay flat now in the thick dust—stiffen wrist, raise arm, other hand the same. Now—heave!

Weakly, Jony brought himself up, though he felt that at any moment his arms might collapse and let him fall forward once again. He must do better! Somehow he fought to his knees. His head ached, waves of dizziness, in which all about him swung back and forth, assailed him.

That he could rise to his feet was clearly impossible. But he could still crawl. Crawl he did, half-choked by the dust his hands stirred up so close to his hanging head.

He was headed, he thought, toward the open front of the building where stood the stone woman. And he hoped that, in the open air, he might regain more of his strength. If he were allowed that long.

To his right were the piled boxes. Then shortly, just before him, the steps which raised the coffer holding the sleeper. How far was that point from the outer door? He could not remember now.

Jony crawled through the silence of the stone place. He believed that he felt a little stronger as he went. The exercise might be breaking some of the hold over him. But he could not yet rise to his feet, and he must reserve all he could of his energy, lest he be called upon to exert himself fully by yet some other trial.

To the next pillar . . . and the next . . . and then a third. His throat was parched by the dust; he sneezed and coughed. But he would not pause, nor dared he

even try to see how far away was his goal, for that
might dishearten him.

The sound of his own panting, wheezing progress
was suddenly overtopped by another noise. He knew
that, had feared for a long time to hear it again:
the buzz of an airborne flyer. Would the spacemen
swoop overhead, use one of their weapons to stun
anyone within the pile whether they could see their
prey or not?

Sweat streaked through the dusty mask over Jony's
face. He shivered as he crawled, waiting for such a
blow to fall. However, the buzzing grew fainter. Were
they in retreat toward the ship? Or else winging out
to quarter over the ways of the city, hunting signs of
any other party?

One pillar, another . . . His hands grew sore and raw
as, his palms planted hard on the stones, he writhed
and dragged himself forward to win the length of
another open space.

Around him it was lighter! He must be nearing
the outer door. Now he must think past that simple
arrival in the open which had been his first goal. What
would he do next? Crawl down into the city, wearily
along the stone river? The open country beyond was
too far, and he would be instantly sighted from the
air were the flyer to return.

No, best seek out one of the other dens, hide until
he knew whether time could make him whole again.
If the only way one could recover from a stunner
attack was through some agency of the spacemen,
then he did not know what would become of him.
That lurking fear he now resolutely battled into the
far depths of his mind.

Jony came at last to the foot of the stone woman. His hands were so painful he could not force them into action again. Helplessly, almost hopelessly, he leaned his head and shoulders against the figure, and thereby was able to look back down the way he had crawled.

His heart labored so that his breath came in short gasps; and there was a mist which came and went before his eyes to cloud the back trail. Jony squinted, trying to center on one shadow among the many. Had there been movement back there?

Geogee, Maba, returning? Had the twins so quickly lost the trail of the People? Jony felt he should care, should try for action. Only he was too tired, too strengthless, to do more than crouch where he was and wait for whatever fate moved there to come upon him.

That shadow which was no shadow advanced so slowly. Jony longed to shout to the lurker, urge a confrontation. He was so worn with effort that he wanted a swift ending, not this eternal wait . . .

It was . . . Otik!

Of all whom he might have expected, the clansman was the last. Nor could Jony tell whether Otik was a fugitive from some lost battle, a scout of the People, or had returned for Jony's own sake. He did not even have strength at this moment to raise his raw, scraped hands to sign out any question.

Straight toward him padded the clansman. Otik was nearly as tall as the stone woman behind which Jony sheltered, and he moved with some of that same ponderous solidity which was Voak's. As he loomed over Jony, the boy saw that he carried two staffs: his own laboriously made one of wood, and the metal-fanged one from the river bed.

Somehow Jony raised his shaking hands, signed a single name in question: "Voak?"

Otik gathered both shafts into the crook of his arm, leaving his hands free for reply. "To the place of the cage."

So the People were taking their new captives to that same safekeeping which their ancestors had used to hold their ancient enemies. That is, unless the twins caught up with them, and Geogee fought for the off-worlder who had come to mean so much to him.

"Geogee—Maba?" Jony uttered the names aloud knowing that Otik would recognize those sounds.

"No see," the clansman replied.

With the dignity of his race he lowered himself, to balance on stooped legs. Even so foreshortened Jony had to look up a little to meet his eyes.

"You hurt." Otik might have been gravely concerned or merely curious. Jony, well shaken out of his old belief that he was an integral part of the clan, could never accept again that unquestioning feeling that he was one with the People, so was now not able to guess what lay behind the other's question.

"Strange weapon"—the sign language lacked so much that he needed when he would talk with his old companions—"make me weak, must crawl not walk."

Otik gave an assent gesture. He must have seen the tracks of Jony's painful progress through the wide hall.

"Geogee do," he made answer. "Geogee go with ship ones."

How much the People had witnessed Jony could not tell. But the certainty with which Otik signed that made him sure the clansman had seen the attack on Jony.

"Geogee"—Jony forced his weary hands through the motions—"hunt People. Want shipmen free."

"Geogee"—Otik remained unruffled—"no go right way. He—Maba go other side. Tracks in dust say so."

Jony drew a long breath of relief. Then he had been right in his second guessing about the girl. She was not leading her brother to cut off the clansmen, but rather in the wrong direction to gain them time. How long she might be able to continue that deception Jony did not know. Neither was he in the least happy about her wandering in this city. And what would happen when Geogee realized he had been tricked? The younger boy might not turn on Maba; their tie was close. But he would hurry back here to make sure of Jony, try to force from Jony where Volney had been taken. Jony had no doubt of that at all.

"Must get away," he signed.

Otik made no answer. Rising to his big feet again with more agility than his bulk of body would suggest, he reached down, hooked one paw in Jony's armpit and drew the other up with no more difficulty than if Jony had been no larger nor heavier than Maba.

With Otik's support Jony could stand. When the other moved, he was able to stumble along upright. The clansman did not turn back toward the shadowed interior from which he had come, rather edged on for the open.

However, as they rounded the stone woman, Jony dragged back for an instant or two. Otik turned his head, stared. What came suddenly into Jony's mind was so wild a thought that it could well have been born out of some disorder in his thinking processes. It was now, when he half-faced the stone woman, when memory moved sharply in him, that he wanted to try an act which might be the height of folly, or else the wisest action he had ever chosen.

He signed to Otik to wait, pulled a little away from the clansman, steadying himself with a hold on the stone figure. Slowly he brought up his bleeding, dust-engrained hand. It was hard to lift, as if it were also a heavy chunk of unfeeling stone.

Jony forced his wrist higher, flattened palm, straightened his fingers. Then, with a purpose he could not have logically explained, he half-stepped, half-fell forward, so that his flesh rested as it had once before against the age-pitted surface of stone.

Only what it met did not feel like stone. This was warm, strange. Jony could find no word to describe the sensation. Not the flash of instant response which had frightened him before. No, this was different. It was as if from the larger, immobile hand there flowed into his, rising, ebbing, rising again, an unknown form of energy. Perhaps a man long athirst and chancing upon a spring and drinking his fill might have so experienced this wondrous expansion of well-being, of restoration.

Through his palm, down his arm, into his body—more and more and more! Though Jony did not realize it, tears spilled from his eyes, tracking through the dust on his face. He wanted to sing, to shout—to let the whole world know this wonder happening to him!

➤ SIXTEEN ◀

Jony was not himself again—he was much more. He stood as tall as a Big One, as strong as Voak! With his hand he could flatten the walls about him, snatch a flyer out of the air, overturn the sky ship, so that it could never fly up and out to betray them! He could...

Somewhere deep within Jony's mind fear flared. No—no! He dared not be like this. Yet he could not draw back from that wonderful contact through which flowed the power; his palm of flesh seemed united to the stone by an unbreakable bond.

NO!

As he had exerted his talent in the past for control, now he called upon it to sever this dangerous contact. His determination resulted in a sudden sharp cutoff. The stone hand sent him spinning away, rejected him as harshly as before it welcomed him gladly.

Jony would have fallen down the series of ledges, save that he struck against Otik. The clansman stood rock-still, an anchorage for Jony to cling to momentarily.

Otik neither put out an arm to steady, nor a

paw-hand to repulse the other. He merely stood
and let Jony hold to him, until the reaction to that
break in energy flow subsided. The boy drew several
deep breaths. What secret of the city builders he
had tapped he had no way of knowing, but he was
not reckless nor unthinking enough to try it again.

However, it *had* given him back a body obedient
to the orders of his mind. For that he was thankful.
Now he signed to his silent companion:

"Find Geogee—Maba—"

Otik surveyed him from head to foot. Then he
made answer by holding out the metal staff without
further sign. Jony took the weapon eagerly, running
his hand along its length. That hand, though still
dust-grimed, bore now none of the raw marks left
by his long crawl. Nor either did its palm when he
turned that to the light. His whole strength of body
was renewed, as if he had slept well, eaten heartily,
and had borne no burdens of mind for a long time.

Otik moved back into the shadows of the long hall
behind the stone woman. Here, as Jony hastened to
catch up, he saw those waiting boxes. If there were
only some way to prevent their ever being taken from
this place! To think of their contents in the hands of
the spacemen!

Only there was no time now to deal with these.
Even if the two who escaped on the flyer returned
with an attack force, they surely would be more intent
on discovering the whereabouts of their men than
transferring loot. At least for the present.

The clansman never turned his head to look as he
padded by; that pile of boxes did not appear to exist
for him. They skirted the rise of blocks which held

the sleeper's box, kept on. It was when they passed
the opening through which they had earlier emerged
from the lower ways that Jony grew uneasy.

If Maba had not guided Geogee by that passage,
where in this pile had she taken him? How far did this
hall extend? Were there more passages, other ways?
He saw that the path of sun which had struck across
the floor from the wall opening had since vanished.
The time must be closer now to nightfall. And if the
twins were lost here in the dark . . .

Jony believed there was more to fear in this ancient
place than even a vor or Red Head. Recalling the
impulse which had made him unite touch with the
stone woman, he was surprised at his recklessness.
That that had healed and strengthened him was only
good fortune. The same flow of energy directed at
one of the twins might even kill!

Otik slowed down. His heavy head swung from
side to side, as he turned his gaze directly to the
floor, examining its surface. In this more shadowed
portion Jony could make out a few traces in the dust;
undoubtedly Otik could read them more clearly. As
it grew darker he would have to depend more and
more on the clansman.

Unless . . . he sent out a questing thought. And
touched—very faintly—Maba! Jony's confidence
rebounded. As it had happened once before in this
pile, he had his own guide to follow.

They had not reached the end of the hall when
Otik turned right, Jony only a stride behind him. In
the wall on that side there was another opening. Jony
tried contact again . . . faint still—and not steady! Her
pattern seemed to weave in and out, as did the only

touch he could ever have with the People, a sense of presence rather than real contact. It had never been so before with the twins. Perhaps Geogee was using some other covering trick Volney had taught him.

The thought of Volney gave Jony certain grim satisfaction. He could picture the spaceman in the cage of the People. At least there the off-worlder could do no more harm. What was the man's power over Geogee? It appeared to Jony that the stranger had, in a new fashion, used mind-control on the boy, erasing all Geogee's former life and associations, or reducing them to something best forgotten, and implanting new desires to make the twin one of the enemy.

As he thought of Geogee, Jony's confidence in Maba was again a little undermined. She had been with the ship's company long enough to be influenced. It was only the vivid memory of her smashing their cherished machine (an act he was sure had not been arranged for his benefit), which persuaded Jony that the girl had not also been mind-warped by the off-worlders.

The door led, not into another tunnel or place of descent, but into a series of small sections above ground. From the third of those they emerged into the open. They now faced the portion of the city which lay behind the huge central pile, completely unknown to Jony. There was no straight river of stone here to serve as a guide out to the country.

Instead, confronting them was a space of ground on which no stone had been laid or built. This was covered by a thick tangle of vegetation, presenting as thick a barrier as the stone walls behind. Even Otik gave a surprised grunt when he surveyed it.

Between that impenetrable tangle and the place

from which they had just emerged there existed a thin ribbon of clear ground. The trail left on that was plain to read. Those they followed had turned to the left, keeping to that narrow pathway.

Dusk was closing in. Jony's sense picked up several forms of small life living within the safe mat of vegetation. Also he listened for something else: that ominous buzz from the air announcing a return of the flyer with more men; men armed with weapons against which the People had no chance. He longed for the stunner Geogee had taken from him, weighed the metal staff in his hand, and knew how little use that would be in a struggle against the off-worlders.

In the half-light he saw Otik's hand move in the sign for water. The clansman's sense of smell could pick that up where Jony's could not. A moment later Otik's staff whirled up at ready. Jony sensed no danger signal of his own, but it was apparent that the clansman was highly suspicious of something. Jony tried mind-seeking. He caught Maba, to his gratification, closer and clearer. Geogee must still be wearing the too large helmet which cut off such contact. But there was nothing else. Except from the section before them there came a complete absence of the small life signals he caught elsewhere.

Otik halted abruptly. His nostrils were fully extended. Even Jony could now catch a faint, sickening stench, as if ahead some rot lay open under the sky.

Scenting that, the boy needed no other warning from his companion. Here, in the heart of the stone place, was a colony of Red Heads! But the twins had gone this way! Had the children blundered into this worst of dangers without any warning?

Otik still held his head as high as he could, sniffing audibly. That they should venture through any part of country those plant-beasts patrolled was pure folly. Over the Red Heads none of Jony's talent could prevail, any more than he could force the People themselves to his bidding. With growing apprehension, he surveyed their surroundings. That wall to the left had no openings big or little. To their right the thick vegetation was far too entangled to crash a path through. Any attempt to do so would shred his skin, even slash Otik, in spite of the other's thick fur covering.

Where *were* the twins? That Jony could still mind-reach Maba meant she was alive—one small hope granted him.

To his utter surprise Jony saw Otik move again. Not in retreat, as the boy had entirely expected, but on along the same path. Jony trailed behind, for this way was too narrow for them to go abreast. The plant-beasts were the one enemy even the People did not face, yet Otik was proceeding as if he believed they had a chance!

The stench grew stronger, while coming dark added to Jony's wonder at Otik's recklessness. Once night had fallen the Red Heads would be mobile, at their most dangerous. He brought his own staff into a good position for a slashing blow, such as he had used with the vor, but it would offer no defense to the stupefying vapor the things broadcast when in action.

An arch of stone arose before them, and, when they moved just under that, the whole scene ahead changed. The matted growth drew sway. Though it still formed a wall of its own, there was a far greater open space here.

In the middle of that open area was a large pool

which possessed an edging of vigorous plant life. Yet over its murky waters coasted none of the winged things one would naturally find at such a spot. This scene was silent, devoid of any life save that which was ground-rooted.

Spaced around the turgid and unpleasant looking stretch of water were the Red Heads. In terms of general growth, this collection was stunted, rising hardly higher than Jony's shoulder at their tallest. Their red, bulbous tips were faded-looking, more of a sickly, yellowish shade. And many of them had lower leaves which were only rotting stubs.

Also, the blossomheads were canted at crooked angles, as if the creatures were too weakened to hold them straight. Yet a stir ran through their company as Otik and Jony drew nearer, such movement as a wind might raise when furrowing the grass on the open plain. This growth might be sickly, even dying, but the things still knew when prey approached.

Jony sprang forward. Aroused by his very loathing of the creatures, he swung his staff so the sharp fang could bite into the nearest stem. There was a dull thunk of sound as the metal sheared in. A liquid of such putrid smell as to make him gasp sprayed forth as the head of the thing fell to one side, attached now to the plant only by a thin strip of outer bark.

The plant-beasts moved so sluggishly that Jony was encouraged, leaping to attack the next in line. Had Geogee used the stunner on them? Or had some illness of their own species half-crippled the plants so that they could be so easily dealt with? He did not know; he was only thankful that these were not the virile species he had seen elsewhere.

Perhaps Otik had been fired by his example and the
results Jony was getting. For the clansman stumped
out in turn. His wooden staff could not sever stems
as Jony's more efficient tool was doing, but he beat
down upon red blossoms, which burst under his attack,
stripped away leaves with the vigor of his swings.

The two crossed the plot where the plant-beasts
festered, to reach the opposite side beyond the pool.
Here was another stretch of stone-paved open, cutting through it a runnel of dark water which either
fed or drained the pool. The smell rising from that
was noxious in the extreme. Then Jony, fired by his
easy victory over the enemy the People feared so, was
nearly caught in a trap set by his over-confidence.

The last Red Head had been crouching in the stream,
its rooted feet sucking up the moisture. If the fate of
its fellows had alerted it, it had not chosen to move,
either in defense or flight—then. Now, directly in Jony's
path, the plant-beast straightened with a snap to full
height. And this one was truly a giant among the poor
wizened dwarfs of the company. Taller than Jony, its
ball head displayed a deeper, glowing red, visible even
through the growing dark. The boy could see that
expanding bag beneath the blossom, ready to empty
its cloud of blinding, stupefying pollen in his direction. Its two long upper leaves, lined with fang thorns,
were already reaching confidently in his direction.

With a cry Jony leaped back as one of the leaves
lashed viciously, nearly sweeping him from his feet.
He crouched low, metal staff in both hands, sharp
cutting edge up. If the creature released that pollen,
he might have only an instant, perhaps two, before he
collapsed. Then Otik would have little defense in turn.

Those leaves were reaching again; while the under, more slender growths gathered around the mouth of the pollen bag, ready to fan the discharge toward Jony. The boy would have no time, no chance to get close enough to slash at the ball head as he had when meeting the weaker growths.

His hand slid along the shaft of the staff; he raised it shoulder high, hurled it, the point of its fang aimed at the red blossom. A leaf whirred out to slap that weapon down, moving with such speed Jony's eye could hardly follow. So it deflected the staff.

But, as the weapon fell, the point ripped across the bag of pollen, cutting those areas of tension which worked to expel tire deadly burden. The lower leaves waved wildly. Some of them clutched, pulled at the opening of the bag. But that had shrunk back and was closed so that the beating of the growth about it brought no responsive scattering of lethal pollen.

Jony retreated step by step, still facing the thing. One of the spiked leaves had closed loosely about the staff. The plant-beast might be trying to raise the metal length, thrust it back upon its owner with a deadly purpose. Only the fibers and leaf surface could not contract tightly enough, so that the staff slipped out of its hold, clanged on the stone, and then rolled.

It still lay too close to those raking leaves for him to hope to retrieve it, Jony decided. He dared not risk such a try. So he began to move left. The plant-beast turned to match him as it struggled out of the water runnel. If its roots got a good purchase on the ground, Jony would have no chance at all. However, those fibers slid over the smoothness of the stone as if unable to find any stable grip. The whole creature rocked unsteadily from side to side like a storm-struck tree, as it strove to rush him. Awkward or not, the Red Head lost none of its threat that Jony knew. He was forced to slip and dodge, in evasion, never relaxing his watch upon its deceptively clumsy movements. The smaller lower leaves worked vigorously at the limp pollen bag, squeezing around that appendage. Manifestly the thing was still trying to release its deadly cloud by such pressure. The fanged upper leaves darted and lashed, until it required all of Jony's strength and speed to keep beyond its reach.

He retreated while the plant-beast followed, unable to spare a single instant of inattention to locate Otik who might now have a chance to reach the metal staff lying on the pavement. Jony had only one hope, that the clansman could take up that weapon and use it in place of his less efficient one.

Back! That time an edge of leaf raked Jony's arm, slashing the material of the ship suit as clean as if cut by a blade, leaving a smarting, shallow, blood-drawn line on his skin. Two of the roots writhed, began to uncoil from their normal tangle. Both crept out toward him; he could be tripped... Once down, he would be a helpless victim. Even if Otik moved in then, Jony would be already dead, caught between the fanged leaves, his body impaled on their armor to feed the hunger of this night-walking horror.

He dodged, skidded, caught his balance again just in time. As Jony gasped for breath, his whole body chill with fear, he saw a flash, brilliant in what light remained. Otik had the metal staff at last; the clansman swung it with all the force of his huge, strongly muscled arms.

Its sharp edge bit home just under the ball head, slashed on—not as easily as it had severed the stalk of the smaller creature, but with force enough to cut clean across. The blossom ball tumbled free, to be caught by a wildly flailing toothed leaf, which closed instantly, crushing it completely. Still the creature continued to totter on ahead; but Jony, keeping out of its path, no longer drew it after him. Rather it smashed straight on until its writhing roots tangled with each other and it fell forward.

There prone, it rolled back and forth on the ground. A paw-hand closed on Jony's arm tearing the ripped sleeve yet farther, jerking him back with a mighty heave as a puff of thick, dusty-looking vapor rose from the struggling creature. At last the pollen was loosed. Only there was no concentrated effort to wave it toward the prey, so the dust settled back quickly over the still heaving body.

They made a wide detour around the thing, allowing all the room they could to the lashing upper leaves, the snapping curl and uncurl of the roots. Otik shambled along at fastest pace one of the People could achieve. Jony wanted to sprint ahead, but he could not desert the other.

Once across the paved space they came to another opening which gave onto a smaller, stone-laid walk place lined with structures on either side. Otik paused there, once more sniffing. He was again fully intent on their search with the single-minded stolidity of his kind.

Once away from the dying plant-beast, he had handed the metal staff back to Jony, who took opportunity, offered during their pause, to tear loose the rest of the sleeve of his garment, with that wiping all he could of the evil smelling stains from the fang edge. Hurling the rag as far as he could from him, he was ready to go on. He felt almost weak with sheer relief.

It was then that the quiet of the early evening was broken by a cry which brought him out of his concern with the battle.

"Maba!" Though Jony had not tried mind-search since they had encountered the Red Heads he recognized that voice with his inner sense as well as his ear.

"Maba!" He called once, then knew the folly of that. He must not alert any danger which faced the girl, give knowledge that help was on the way. But he did know she was along this way, within one of the side dens. Jony began to run, not waiting to see if Otik would follow.

Before he reached the right opening Maba cried out again. There was such terror in that scream Jony picked up a stab of her fear. Something—someone—threatened her. But where was Geogee with the stunner? Surely...

Here was the hole which led to Maba. Jony slowed his pace sharply, trying to creep in without noise. The alien coverings on his feet prevented such a soundless advance. He wished he had had time to shed this hated garment.

The space within was very dark, with only lighter spots to show the wall openings. Jony must use his eyes as well as he could, but he could employ the talent too.

As he had shared Rutee's pain in the long ago, now he knew the full force of Maba's terror. And he could not get any idea of what menaced her from the disjointed thoughts marred by her strong emotion.

He listened. Though there was no sound in the outer part of this den, from beyond came a broken whimpering. Maba! Only—he could pick up no other life trace, not even that blocked-out deadness which marked Geogee while wearing the helmet. Maba—alone...?

Jony did not take the straight path from the outer opening to the other large one he could see ahead. Instead he chose to slip along the wall. He dared not give full concentration to touch with Maba, only keep an outer alert to prevent sudden attack.

Now! His hand was on the side of that other opening. The dark inside seemed to whirl about oddly, as if the air therein was full of black particles in constant motion. Jony lifted the staff, thrusting it tentatively through the opening. He waited a long moment, his imagination painting for him an only half-visible lurker, something which could close upon any who entered even as the fanged leaves of the plant-beast had tried to do.

But in his slow sweep the cutting part of the staff moved freely enough. Jony slipped through quickly, got his back to a solid wall, held his weapon at ready. A scream sent him into a half-crouch, so sure of some attacker that he could almost see one existing as part of the dark itself.

"No!" Maba cried out from the other corner of the room.

"Please, Geogee, don't leave me. Geogee...?" There was a broken pleading in her voice which tore at Jony.

"Maba..." he called softly. Her mind was such a whirlpool of frantic panic he could not get through to her. "Maba!" He dared only try to reach her by voice alone.

She did not call again, but he could hear a harsh breathing which was more like half-strangled sobs.

Jony moved away from the wall. He was sure now that only fear itself filled this darkness. Slowly he approached the corner in which he could very faintly see a huddled body.

She cried out again. "No—go away!"

"Maba," he tried to make a soothing call of her own name. "This is Jony."

Her ragged breathing continued. Then—

"Jony?"

That he had gotten that much of an intelligent response from her was promising. He went to his knees, felt out in the dark, his hand finding and moving along her shuddering body. There was something abnormal about the way she lay. Had she been injured, maybe by one of the plant-beasts? But where was Geogee?

Moving slowly, gently, mainly by touch, Jony gathered her up into his arms. Her skin felt chill and her shivering did not ease. He must get her out of here into some kind of light so he could see her hurts, whatever those might be.

She did not move of her own accord, but her breathing seemed less labored.

"I hoped, Jony. I did hope so you would come," she said brokenly. "I knew that maybe you couldn't. Because Geogee did that to you. But I just kept on hoping that somehow you would."

He cradled her close against him and strode for the door.

"Where is Geogee?" he asked.

Her shivering was worse. And her voice was very low when she answered: "He—he just went away."

› SEVENTEEN ‹

Out in the open, even though they were still sur-rounded by the stone dens, Jony drew a deep breath of relief. Maba's head rested heavily against his shoul-der, as if she had no control over her muscles. In his arms her weight was flaccid. Geogee must have used the stunner on her!

But, as he went, Jony could feel the fear draining from her. That was the poison which had tormented her as she lay in the strange darkness. As he reached the open Otik was waiting, his large eyes surveying the girl. The clansman signed: "She was struck by the evil..."

Jony nodded assent.

Nostrils widened as Otik turned toward the den in which Jony had found her. "There is none else here."

Again Jony agreed. Even in this dim light he could see Maba's eyes were open. She watched him. Now tears gathered to brim over, run down her cheeks.

"Jony," her voice was hardly above a whisper, she might have exhausted all its power during her own ordeal by terror, her screams through the night, "Geogee—he used the stunner, on *me*. Then he went off..."

"Why?" Jony made his question blunt, hoping thus to get a sensible answer out of her quickly.

"He said I was helping the People. He—Jony, he's all changed in his head somehow." Her words were choked now with the same sobs which made her body quiver in his hold. "He—he hates the People because he thinks they have done something to Volney. Volney means more to him than I do...and you...and Yaa, and Voak, and all of us! Why, Jony?"

For that he had no answer. "Do you know where he went?" he asked what might be now a matter of importance. Geogee lurking in the city, hostile. Suppose the boy was hiding out somewhere among these dens, ready to use a stunner without warning? Jony could not guess what so altered Geogee's thinking. But if he would do this to Maba, then indeed perhaps he was mind-controlled by some subtle method the spacemen practiced.

Jony let his mind search free. He could not contact Geogee directly while the other wore that protective helmet, but perhaps he could pick up the boy near by that very blank he touched. Only he met nothing he could so define.

"He is hunting for Volney," Maba continued. "Jony, I feel so queer...what if I never am able to move again? Jony!" Once more her hysteria was rising.

Jony drew her closer. "It will pass," he assured her. "With me it did."

Or had that full recovery been because he had taken into his body the strength the stone woman had to give? And—Jony caught at this new idea—could it possibly be that such a strength could be passed in turn from person to person as well as from the stone to him?

He lowered the girl to lie on the pavement in the beginning light of a slowly rising moon.

"Maba, listen to me. I am going to try to break you free. I do not know whether I am able to do this, but I can try."

"Oh, yes, Jony!" Her voice was so eager that he was disturbed. Perhaps he was doing wrong to give her even a fraction of hope that this would work. Bending closer, he took one of her hands in each of his, held them fast. Then he began to concentrate on sending, not the mind-thrust he had always used, but rather a sensation of returning energy into her body. When there followed a slight tingling of his flesh, he had to stifle quickly his own sense of wonder and triumph, keep his mind occupied only by the need to pass to Maba a portion of that strength he had won from the stone woman.

"Jony—Jony, I can feel!" she cried out. "Oh, Jony, it is true you can make me feel!"

He, in turn, was aware of a feeble flexing of her fingers within his hold. Then her limp arms arose a fraction, her head moved from side to side on the stones as if she must learn for herself that this was again possible.

She was sitting up, though still weak enough to need his support, when Otik joined them. Jony had not even noticed the clansman missing. Now as he stood there, he held not only his staff, but Jony's. He must have gone into the blackness of the den to get that.

"I thought maybe you would never find me," Maba said, the remains of her sobs still making her voice shaky. "I thought I would just lie there . . . maybe forever!"

"But you did not." Jony put what he hoped would be a bracing briskness into his voice. "Now, do you have any idea of where Geogee was heading?"

"It was the helmet, you see," she answered, and then went on to make her explanation clearer. "He believed me at first. I thought I could lead him far enough away from the People so that he could not hurt them. But I didn't know about the helmet, except that you could not mind-control him if he wore it. I didn't know *they* could!"

"How?" Jony's instant distrust of any of the equipment used by those from space gave him a core of belief already.

"There is a way they can talk through the helmets—I didn't know about that, really, Jony. I thought they had to use those boxes they have in the flyer and the ship. But there are talk places in the helmets, too—inside somehow. And Geogee heard Volney calling through his. He knew somehow that the call came from another direction. But he did not tell me at first. We came to the place where the Red Heads were," she shuddered. "Geogee, he used the stunner. They all went stiff and did not move so we could pass them. But, when we got here, he was all of a sudden very mad. He yelled at me about taking him the wrong way. And he said he'd show me what it meant to tell lies! He—he wasn't like Geogee at all! Those space people made him like them. I got afraid, Jony; he was so strange. So I ran, and then I tried to hide. But he found me and used the stunner.

He laughed, Jony, he just stood there and laughed. Then he said he'd find Volney all right; Volney would tell him just how to go. Only first he was going back and get one of those rods. And when he had that—he'd know what to do with it, too..."

Jony tensed. Geogee running wild with one of the destructive rods! Supposing he did, by some chance, find the People and their prisoners? He believed now that Geogee was as much under the control of this Volney as those poor creatures of his own species had been when in tire lab of the Big Ones.

"We have to stop him," Jony said more to himself than to the girl. Nor dared he keep the seriousness of this action from Otik. Still kneeling beside Maba he signed to the clansman what had happened as best he could.

Otik said nothing in return. Rather he turned around, facing the way down which they had come. Once more he was sniffing. Then he made a negative gesture. Whichever way Geogee had gone, he had not doubled back. Now Otik did something that Jony had very seldom witnessed among the People: he went down on all fours, bringing his massive nose close to the pavement about them. Several shambling steps away from the door of the den he stopped short, made a prolonged inspection by smell, and then raised a hand-paw to beckon.

Clearly Otik had found the trail. But, though Jony knew that they must follow, he did not want to take Maba. She had recovered in part, but that she could keep up, he greatly doubted. Yet he could not leave her here alone in the dark either.

As he hesitated, Otik moved back. His head went

down to sniff at Maba. Then, without wasting time on explanations, he stooped ponderously and picked up the girl, setting her on his shoulders, one thin brown leg on either side of his short neck. In this manner the People carried small cubs on a long trail, and Otik moved as if Maba's weight were nothing.

The problem of her transportation was only part of it. If Geogee was waiting in some ambush . . . But perhaps Otik could give warning of such danger also, and they really had no choice. Once more Jony took up his fang staff; Otik already held his. Letting the clansman take the lead, they moved on between the dens.

Jony went uneasily, glancing from one side to the other, trying to see farther into shadowed holes. He feared Geogee, yes. But also, by night, this place of stone had an uncanny kind of life which was beyond his powers to explain. It was as if, just beyond the fringe of his natural range of vision, things moved, so that he was aware of a vague fluttering he could not really see. In addition there was a dampening of spirit; not fear, as Jony had known it so often in this place of many surprises, but rather as if the inner core of his spirit was weighted down with a vast burden he could not understand.

He wanted nothing more than to flee from the sight of all these dens, get out into the open land which meant freedom. Yet he must follow Otik who now turned left into an even narrower slit running between high walls. They were heading back in the direction of the central building again, for Otik had made a second turn, moving with the certainty of one following a well-marked, open trail.

Before them reared a wall taller than the others, and in it an opening, through which the clansman padded confidently. Here the moonlight was brighter. Jony saw in detail the bulk of the structure ahead. Yes, he was certain now that they had come around, back to the place of storage. At least they were approaching the place from a different direction than that treacherous path of vegetation where the Red Heads rooted.

Otik did not lead them to one of the large ground-based openings, but to a smaller one up in the wall. He halted there, his muzzle just topping the lower edge of it, and sniffed. Jony needed no gesture to understand that this had been Geogee's entrance.

It was easy for Jony to clamber through it and gather Maba as Otik handed her in. But the clansman found entrance more difficult. His thick body was never intended for climbing, and the hole itself was a tight wedge. However, Otik made it.

The darkness within, away from that hole, was almost as thick as that in the den where Jony had found Maba. Now the three linked hands, Maba's in Jony's; his fingers grasped in Otik's strong hold. It was plain that the clansman's night sight would still be their guide.

All Jony could make out were shadows, with here and there one of the tall pillars looming up near them. Maba had uttered no sound since their journey had started. He was glad that she seemed able to make her way on foot here without weakening.

They came to the door they sought by a different angle so that Jony at first did not quite recognize the opening. Then he knew this was the one through which his own party of clansmen had invaded the city.

Otik paused there, sniffing deeply. He even took a step or two toward the front of the large space as if to verify his discoveries. Then he resolutely returned to the entrance.

The way was too dark to see any tracks. Otik himself was only a black bulk in this deep dusk. Now the clansman caught Jony's hand again, drawing him toward the opening. If Otik were certain that Geogee did have some way of following Volney...

They were almost within the long-walled run when Jony heard a dread sound even through the stones of the great den. The buzz of the flyer! Faint—but growing stronger. Volney had been able to guide Geogee. Was he also in communication with those coming to his rescue? And with the air speed of the flyer...

Otik had been listening too. Now he grunted, jerked at Jony's hand. Apparently the need for speed had also impressed him.

They went on at this swift pace, the best the clansman could produce in times of great necessity. Jony feared that Maba could not keep up; but she continued to trot along beside him with the ease she had shown when they had traveled across country, before the evil of the stone place and the sky ship had broken into their safe lives.

Down the passage they went, coming out into the open land among the ridges. Jony believed that he knew their destination now: the place of the cage above in the heights. At least Otik kept on to the northeast. That Geogee must still be ahead, he was not certain. And what of the rest of the clansmen who had retreated with their prisoners?

Jony's throat was dry; he was vaguely aware once

more of both hunger and thirst. And what of Maba? She still made no complaint; but she did stumble frequently, and finally fell. Jony dropped back beside her. Then Otik, grunting something in his own tongue, once more scooped her up.

From time to time Jony sent out a questing probe. He had not yet picked up that deadness which he thought might identify Geogee. Instead he touched on an awareness which heralded one of the clansmen. That brief contact heartened him for a second spurt of effort.

The path they followed was so confused, winding from one ridge valley to the next, that Jony worried from time to time if Otik himself knew where they were bound. Yet the clansman never hesitated, turning right or left with the authority of one following a well-marked trail.

Now—yes! In the moonlight Jony saw the ledges rising. This he knew—the way to the cage place. And, at the top of that climb, hunched in the moonlight like a craggy rock, was Voak. Otik set Maba on her feet at the foot of the ascent. He took not only his staff, but Jony's, and began to drum with their butts. Jony threw his arm around Maba's shoulders, aiding her as they climbed.

At the crest Voak stood in the bright moonlight. He made no gesture of welcome; neither did he bar their way, but only turned and walked ahead, his own staff raised to thump in unison with Otik's two. They had slowed their pace to walk with a ponderous dignity. Then Voak raised his deep voice, echoed by the younger clansman.

"Jony—" Maba began.

He tightened his hold on her. "Hush!" he gave a single whispered warning.

Once more he felt that tingling. Only this time it was heightened, striking him as a series of small shocks. He refused to allow himself to think of what that power might do, this must be followed to the end.

The red-lighted cave opened before them. There was the cage. Only this time it held not bones, but living bodies. Here were the two spacemen and Geogee, who crouched near one. The boy's helmet was gone and he looked as if he had been rolled in mud and dust. But as far as Jony could see he was unharmed.

If the clansmen had imprisoned their captives, they had not yet collared them. But their off-world weapons and helmets were laid out in a row on the floor just beyond the bars of their prison. Stunners—and one of the red rods! Jony's fingers curled. He wanted nothing more than to seize upon that, hurl the thing so far away no one could chance on it again.

"You—Jony!" It was the spaceman who had been Geogee's companion. He advanced to the front of the cage, caught the bars with his hands.

Jony dropped Maba's hand. He paid no attention to the hail from the off-worlder. Instead he concentrated on Geogee. He read his thoughts, his memory; he reached as far as he could into the other's head.

Each new discovery he sorted out, filed to incorporate in his own store of knowledge. But what had happened to Geogee? He was—alien! Not mind-controlled as Jony had known that state before, with the boy's personality erased either temporarily or entirely, so that he knew only such thoughts as his captors wished. No, Geogee's mind was as alive as it had ever been; it was simply that he had somehow accepted an entirely different way of thought.

Geogee now held hot resentment against the clansmen. They had trapped him in a net, spoiled his chance to rescue the man beside him, to prove himself worthy of Volney's interest.

Worthy! Jony knew bitterness at that. He could read all Geogee's thoughts concerning himself. And now began to examine his own feelings in relation to the boy. Because Geogee and Maba were Rutee's, he had given them all the protection and care he could. But he never had felt toward them as he had toward Rutee, that he was a part of them, and that they were, in a way, a part of him. No, perhaps he felt revulsion because they had been born to Rutee by will of the Big Ones, the children of a mind-controlled who had taken Rutee by force. Deep down Jony hated the act which had brought them into the world. Only the promises to Rutee and his own control of his emotions had given him a friendly surface relationship with the twins.

Had the children always sensed this reserve in him, even if they could not read his thoughts? Perhaps. Now Geogee had discovered in this spaceman someone to whom he felt truly akin. The boy's mind had opened to this man, had taken in greedily and joyfully all the other had to offer. Geogee was mind-controlled by his own choice. He longed only to be another Volney.

So, having found Volney, he was now prepared to turn fully against Jony, accepting Volney's values without question. Geogee—Geogee was lost.

Was Maba also? But there was no time now to think of Maba. Jony must deal with Geogee, Volney, and the other one. That the three could be kept he c as the People had imprisoned the others was impossible; not with their flyer already cruising, hunting...

But neither must they be allowed to use their wills on the People, this world!

Jony could see in Geogee's mind the distorted picture of the People as the spacemen judged them: great shambling animals to be dealt with as one deals with a slight obstruction which can be easily swept away. The People would not last against the might the invaders could summon.

Once more Jony searched Geogee's memory, soaking up all he could of Volney's teaching, seeking a way out for his people. He burrowed for all the details concerning the ship-communication. What he found there—but he must have time to think!

Geogee was on his feet in the cage, his face a tight grimace. He had not protection against Jony's invasion, still he was fighting dully. Jony withdrew, and Geogee lunged against the bars, his voice suddenly raised in a scream of defiance.

"You let us go, Jony! You make them let us go!" He was once again a small boy swept by temper tinged with fear.

"He's right, you know." Volney watched Jony narrowly. There was a lazy curl to his lips as if he saw in the other nothing to fear, that he himself, in spite of being a caged prisoner, had full command of the situation. "I don't know how these animals have managed to influence you, but—"

Jony gave him a long, measured look, then tried swiftly to probe. His mind-thrust was met by a locked defense, even though Volney wore no blanketing helmet. The spaceman threw back his head to laugh derisively.

"That you can't do, my friend. We have sensitives among us, too—but trained ones."

At the same time he spoke, he counter-probed. Jony could feel his attack. However, though Jony had not consciously raised any barrier, the other could not penetrate. Volney was putting full force in his desire to reach Jony, perhaps to implant his own ideas as he had with Geogee. But those pulses of power did not reach as he intended.

The easy curve faded from the other's lips. His mouth became a grim line. Those eyes stared straight into Jony's, as if by the power of an unblinking stare alone he could force a way for his power to enter.

"You cannot," Jony said, knowing that he spoke the truth.

The other relaxed. "So it's a standoff," he said. Jony did not recognize the word, but understood its meaning. "We'll get you, Jony, you know that. Sooner or later."

Jony thought of the returning flyer, of those it might have brought with it. He knew Volney was right, yet he had no intention of surrender. Now he spoke aloud. "You have no right here. This world belongs to the People."

"Did they build that city?" countered Volney. "You, yourself, know of the status they had there. Animals— pets—things to be owned. We tested your People. They are not of a mind pattern to be considered equal with human beings within the range of galactic law. That city is a storehouse. A find such as men make once, perhaps, in a thousand years. This world—our breed need this world."

"You need, so you take," Jony replied. "The Big

Ones needed; they took. We were then the animals
within their labs. I have been caged. I have seen what
they did—for sport—to increase their 'knowledge.'
Yes, they considered it gaining of knowledge from our
torment, blood, death. You would do the same here,
as you tried with Yaa, with Voak. Animals? You and
the Big Ones are less than animals. Not even the Red
Heads torment before they kill, and they kill only to
live. You would take this world and make it yours,
but you shall not!"

What Jony had gained from his probe of Geogee,
what had lain as vague ideas in the back of his mind,
now came together in a grim pattern. He was not
quite sure of his counterplan as yet, only in general
outlines. But whatever he could do, he must.

A hand slipped into his; Maba had moved forward
to stand beside him, just as Geogee stood beside
Volney radiating defiance.

"You—" she spoke to Geogee, "what have they done
to you, Geogee? Yaa—they hurt Yaa! When you were
sick, she carried you, and hunted a long time for the
leaves to make you well. Yaa is real; Voak is real. They
are not just things to be used. They are our *people.*"

"People?" Geogee cried out in a choked voice, his
face flushed. "The ship's people are ours, and you know
it. They've come to take us home, to live as we should,
not wandering around with a pack of animals, with
him"—he flung out a hand to point to Jony—"telling
us what to do, getting into our minds and making
us obey him! He's got you mind-controlled and you
don't even know it. But I guess the mind-controlled
don't—not when they're caught forever and ever..."

Jony had not heard more than a jumble of words.

Gently he released Maba's hold. Then he took two steps to where the weapons of the strangers lay on the rock. Geogee's helmet was there, too. That was an added aid in what he must attempt.

He picked that up first, tried to settle it on his head, but the thick club of his hair prevented it. Impatiently he reached for the metal staff Otik held. Using its sharpened edge, he sawed through the hair, dropping that to the ground. Now the helmet would go on. He reached for the nearest stunner and the red rod.

Voak moved to bar his way.

"What you do?" the clanchief signed.

Jony had only one answer. "What I must to make sure the People remain free."

Apparently Voak believed him, for the clansman stepped aside. Jony took up the stunner with one hand, the rod with the other.

"You can't do anything, you fool," Volney's voice reached even inside the helmet. He sounded very confident.

"Do not be sure," Jony answered as he turned toward the entrance of the place of the cage. There were many ways his poor plan could go wrong. He could only hope to try as hard as he could to make it succeed.

➤ EIGHTEEN ◄

One chance in how many? Jony shook his head. If Geogee had been right in what he had learned from Volney, such counting seemed almost like an action of a bad dream, like comparing one blade of grass to all the rest which grew in one of the wide-bottom lands. Could that be true? That the chance against the spacemen finding this world had been as small as that? Volney's own reckoning—might that be depended upon?

And if that ship never lifted from this planet, never returned to base with its burden of information concerning this world, then the chances of any such coming again were far reduced. One man—to defeat a ship? That, too, might rank with the impossible. He could only try.

"Calling Spearpoint. Come in Spearpoint! Can you read me!"

Jony's head jerked, one hand flew up to the helmet on his head. Whose voice rang in his ears? The sound had a metallic rasp he could not associate with normal speech. Then he understood. The communicator in the helmet was working. Those who had come in the flyer must be trying to locate the rest of their party.

The voice had changed now to an annoying buzz which made him want to free his head. Until he discovered that grew louder or lessened as he turned this way or that among the ridges, heading back toward the city through the night.

A possible guide! He could follow the volume of the sound to bring him to the flyer party. But he must not contact them yet. There was a greater need...

Jony could picture in his mind that row of looted boxes the spacemen had been bringing from the storage room. Those were bait, and they were also the danger. He swung the rod in his hand. The alien weapon weighed much less than the metal shaft which he had left with Voak, but, as he knew, this was far more deadly. How many of these lay encased there? Only one or two might be needed to win this battle with the off-worlders.

Jony filed that plan in the back of his mind and concentrated on the buzzing guide which he had not expected to bring him so easily to his goal. He traversed the ridge valleys at a steady trot. Hungry, yes, he was hungry, thirsty too. But since he had taken on that flow of energy from the stone woman, neither of those states of body seemed able to slow him. There was no time to answer his own physical needs.

Twist, turn, right and then left, with the sound growing, fading ever in his ears. At last he could see the lump of the city, silver and black in the moonlight. The buzz urged him left toward the far side. However, that was not yet his goal.

"Spearpoint come in!" Again the words, imperative and demanding.

Jony could not have replied, even if he had wanted to. These spacemen spoke to each other in patterns which they had set up before they ventured out of their ship. Even Geogee had not been able to supply him with the key to such.

The buzz dwindled. Entering the city from this angle, Jony was deliberately heading away from the ship. However, he had only to lift his head to see the rise of the pile which was his present goal. Though again he had to work from one of the paved ways to another until he came out on the main river of stone. Shadows afforded him protection. Jony dodged from one pool of them to the next, keeping to the best speed he could.

He had become adjusted to the directorial sound in his helmet. Still, as once again the voice suddenly cut through the steady buzz, he was startled into a quick halt.

"Last broadcast came from that center structure. We can only start a search from there..."

Those from the flyer were headed in the same direction! Hearing that, Jony threw away caution and began to run. He must get there before they did. What off-world weapons besides the stunners they might carry he did not know; Geogee's information had only concerned those. But if the spacemen could lay hands on the rods, knew their use...!

Gasping a little, Jony reached the ledges, looked up into the dim opening where stood the stone woman. As he scrambled up that ascent, he kept his eyes on her. Was that power which had flowed into him from her touch also something he must make very sure *they* did not use? He could not tell.

As Jony stood once more before her, gazing into that calm face, into the eyes which stared over his head at the city, he raised the rod. To do this was fighting a part of himself. What was her purpose? Had she been set here to guard in some way what lay in the den behind? Or the sleeper? This was no time for speculation. But he could *not* blast her into nothingness, not yet.

He thudded past her, running down the lines of stone trees toward the block of the sleeper, and beyond him those rows of boxes. The light in the great inner den was scant, yet something in the clear face portion of the helmet gave him power of seeing as well as if he had come here by a mid-day height of sun.

Jony reached the end of that pile of boxes. What did lie within them? Wonders of the vanished people, more than he could guess? For a second or two his curiosity and desire to learn battled with his purpose. Surely not all could contain things deadly to life. Or could they? The People must have known of this wealth, of what would be to them treasures, all these years since they had escaped the city. Yet they had turned their backs on everything to do with their former masters. At this moment it was better to accept the judgment of the clan than his own desire to explore for forbidden knowledge.

Resolutely Jony raised the rod, found that button near the base, set his thumb firmly over it. He aimed at the pile and pressed. This time the flame of the flash did not blind him—perhaps the helmet eyeplate helped. Instantly those containers at which he aimed simply were not, leaving not even dust to mark where they had once stood. Again, he raised the weapon and pressed. A second pile was gone. However, at his third attempt there was no answering flash, though he thumbed the button furiously with all his strength.

What was wrong! Did the devastating energy within the rods only last for two or three times use? Jony looked about wildly. Where could he find another? In the boxes left before him?

He leaped for the nearest, grabbed at its top and pulled. There was no response. Fastenings like those on the cages in the Big Ones' ship? Holding down his impatience, he examined the upper edges, searching for some indications of locks. With his fingers he alternately pressed and pulled. All at once the lid yielded, and Jony tore it up and back furiously.

The glitter of what lay within was visible even in the dusk. He ran his hand through the contents. Smooth bits of bright metal, sparkling stones...but no rod.

"That's the place, right ahead, captain!"

Jony whirled about. Those words resounding within his helmet were a startling warning that he had no more time for searching. Rod? The only one which remained that he knew of was that in the sleeper's hands. He caught up the one he had tossed aside, moving swiftly up to stand beside that stone in which the sleeper was encased. For the first time he dared to run his bare hand across the transparent surface of the block. It felt far smoother than stone to his touch. Could he break through it? Holding the dead rod in both hands, as Maba had fiercely beat upon the machine in the ship, so did Jony bring down the useless weapon upon the smooth lid on the block.

Once, twice. There was no sign of any cracking or breaking. Jony tried to strike in the same place each time, hoping that the concentrated pounding

could bring about such results. The surface remained
unmarked.

When again he used his fingers over the area
where he had been striking there was no promising
roughness to his touch. Was this sealed in some way
as were the boxes?

Falling to his hands and knees, Jony began a closer
inspection of the rim where that clear surface joined
the sides. He pressed and pulled, striving to wedge
the end of the rod into some invisible joint as a lever.
But there was no spot he could find to apply such
a pressure.

Getting to his feet again, wild with frustration,
Jony looked down in despair at the red mask of that
shrouded form, and the rod. He had no time to search
those other boxes—no time!

Once more he ran his hand down the length of
the box. If he could only locate some join, some sign
that there *was* an opening! Then—

Jony stiffened, jerked his hand away. He stared at
the box in wild astonishment. Just as his first touch
against the palm of the stone woman had informed
him that he had tapped an unknown source of energy,
so had he now gained a similar shock.

Tentatively he leaned closer, using just the tips of
his fingers to trace a space immediately above the
mask which covered the unknown's face. There was
something there, no fissure. No, his fingers told him
that what he could not see was an area shaped like
the hand of the woman.

He marked its outward edging by the tingling
response of his own flesh. To his eyes there was no
evidence of any such marking. Jony reached forth

his hand, poised it above that unseen space which seemed attuned to energy. Was this the lock of the box; so different from the cage locks he had been able to handle long ago?

"Spread out!" Once more the order rang in the helmet. "Under as much cover as you can."

No more time! Jony brought his hand down on the place over the mask.

A charge of energy flashed back from that contact, into his body. Was this a protective device to make sure that the sleeper was not disturbed? It was too late for fear now; he could not withdraw his hand, even when he put his full will and strength to do that. Rather, there came a sensation of his flesh and bone being firmly entrapped, being drawn down into the clear substance of that cover. Yet his eyes assured him that was not so. Instinctively Jony countered with that very personal weapon of his own talent. He concentrated his full will on the opening of the box, the freeing of his hand.

Now! Suddenly a network of fine cracks ran out and away from where his fingers rested. Those merged, as more and more appeared, becoming thicker, shattering so that splinters dropped away from their cleavage to lie on the sleeper. Then Jony was free as the whole portion he had touched gave away.

Only that did not end the crackling of the protective cover. The breaks still ran on and on, until they reached the stone rim. All that clear substance fell away in small broken bits, some as fine as dust. There was a puff of air, cold, smelling of acrid liquids, which Jony vaguely identified with the lab.

He had no time for any exploration or examination.

Nor did he want in the least to disturb the mask on the sleeper's face. Instead his freed hand grabbed for the rod, drawing it out of that light grip. If only the rod still worked!

Without another glance at the sleeper, Jony descended in two leaps to the floor of the wide-walled den. He leveled the button, pressed, not quite daring to hope until he saw the results.

Flame answered. The boxes were gone!

He kept on raising and lowering the weapon of the unknown, working with wild haste to clear the floor of all those boxes the spacemen had brought out of the storage place. What still lay below there must be completely destroyed also, though he might not have time to do it now.

"Captain—there ahead! Who's that?"

Jony instinctively dodged behind the nearest tree of stone. He had accomplished this much. Now he had to face the invaders and carry out the rest of his impossible plan. He swung up the rod. The energy which had disposed of the boxes might now blot out men!

Only he found he could not press that button. He raged inside at this unexpected inability to blast into nothingness his own kind. Instead he groped for the stunner.

There were four—no, five of them—slipping from the shadow of one pillar to the next. They all carried arms held at ready. But two (he could not tell them apart with their heads all encased in the bubble helmets) had weapons which were different, probably more potent than stunners.

Jony aimed at the first of those. The figure buckled slowly, fell face down, his weapon skidding out of his loosened grip along the floor. Jony saw the others whirl at the sound of that fall.

One of them darted toward the weapon. Jony used the stunner again.

"Stay back!" That order was sharp. "Whoever he is, he's over there. Use the laser, Mofat!"

A beam of eye-dazzling light sped, to wreathe the pillar behind which Jony had sheltered for his second shot. As if the stone were a tree struck by lightning, it blazed up. Heat scorched Jony's hand as he crouched in what he knew now was not a safe hiding place.

"Must have fried him, captain!" the second voice was exultant.

But what the captain might have added to his first command was lost. There was a sound throughout the whole den—not one that the ear could pick up, rather a vibration which filled the body. And Jony's mind! He put his hands to his head, tore off the helmet. His brain! He ... what was happening to him?

Dimly now he saw those others reel into the open. They, too, were tearing at their head coverings, throwing them down, as if to wear those protections was a torment they could not bear.

And the den was no longer dark. There was light from the glowing pillar. Also there beamed radiance from another site: the box in which the sleeper had lain. All those bits of colored glitter about its sides were on fire, brilliant enough to affect one's eyes. And the shrouded form which had lain within was rising, but not as a sleeper leaves his bed; only the masked head lifted slowly on stiff and unbending shoulders.

The sleeper stood erect now. However, nothing about the shrouded form suggested he was alive.

There was no rippling movement in any of the limbs, no turning of the masked head; nor did he attempt to leave the box.

From the air about them thundered sounds, words that Jony at first could not understand. But then—the pain in his head was gone. At that moment he was filled with an exultation, a sense of power which lifted him beyond all weariness of body, all confusion of mind.

He stood up. *This was the Awakening, as had been foretold*—by whom, asked a part of him who was still Jony—*but he had no time for questions now. He must make sure that all was safe.* Without fear, Jony stepped into the open, toward those others who still twisted and moved feebly. He raised the rod.

Danger must be swept from the place of the Great One ...

No! That was not right. Jony shook his head trying to clear it. He felt as if he were now two people— being swept first this way and that. *Use the force. Blot out those who came in anger and greed.* No ... protested the other Jony.

He could not think straight. *Kill*—no! *Destroy*—no! The two orders contradicted each other with a rising need for action. On the next "no" he fired—with the stunner.

The intruders crumpled. *See—they were safely quiet now. The Great One was safe. He must approach, make ready the return of ...*

Jony moved with swift strides up toward the standing figure wearing the blank metal mask. The roused sleeper was as stiff as the stone woman. Stone Woman? *Gulfa of the Cloud Power.* A name floated out of somewhere into his mind. *Gulfa, who would never die because of the forces sealed within her. But this was not the hour of Gulfa. This was the Hour of the Return . . . the Awakening which was designed to be—*

Jony climbed the steps, moving to face the masked one. As he went he mouthed words he did not know nor understand. *Gulfa had rightly entrusted him with the power to rouse the sleeper. Now he must use it.*

He put out his hand. *The mask! Draw aside the mask so the Great One could breathe, could live again. For this one act alone had he been born, been schooled*—the half-memory, the purpose which had flowed to him from Gulfa's touch was strong.

However, in him now struggled that same queer doubt which had kept him from first using the rod to destroy those who had come unbidden into the place of the Great One. There was another fear. He must *not* take the mask from that head. *That was untrue, this was his great mission: to return the Great One to the world. No . . . yes . . .*

No!

Jony came aware, fully conscious, as one might wake from sleep. This was his once dreamt nightmare of terror. He was himself, Jony. He was not tied to this *thing* of dread rising out of a broken box!

He swung up the rod, pressed the button.

There was a far-off sound, like a thin scream of uttermost despair.

Nothing stood in the box. Jony lurched closer to look within. Nothing lay there now. Somehow he had been saved from a danger he did not understand, but which he sensed was greater than any this world or the spacemen had ever threatened.

Shuddering, he turned around. The bodies of the

invaders lay on the floor. He did not know how this thing had come to pass; but he had won this part of the battle against double odds.

Jony descended to inspect his prisoners. They were all unconscious. From them he took their weapons, gathered these into a pile, and used the rod.

Now—for the ship.

He found the flyer easily enough. They had left a guard; but Jony's helmet, his ship's garb, gained him the entrance. Once more he disarmed and destroyed a weapon, letting the guard see plainly what he did. Under the threat of a similar raying, the spaceman flew him back to the towering ship.

Jony stood below the star-pointing bulk of the ship, gazing up its side into the heavens where dawn had already broken. A ship which never returned—it would not be the first one lost on such exploration. This party had come here purely by chance. The only records of what they had discovered were on board. Those would never be delivered now to the distant authority who meant to make this world theirs.

Perhaps, in time, there would come another ship— by chance. But then the People would be warned, ready. Jony would see that this story would be kept alive so that they would know what must be done if that did happen.

Men of his own kind had built this ship, had had the courage to take it into the far reaches of space. He could understand their pride of achievement when he looked upon it. Only, in truth they had not achieved very much. Things they could make: machines to obey them—to set them among the stars—to live in new worlds. But they had other machines which they took pride in using. Jony grimaced at what he had seen in the lab—Yaa in the grip of equipment set to tear the secrets of her life out of her.

Perhaps the men his act would leave here for the rest of their lives would never understand. Perhaps some of them could learn—in time. Jony did not care, or know. He was only aware of what he must do.

Men were not "things." Nor were "animals" things— to be used, discarded, experimented upon. All had life-force in common and that life-force was a precious gift. Man could not create it. If he destroyed a machine, as Maba had destroyed the one in the lab, that could be rebuilt. But if the invaders had destroyed Yaa during their ruthless quest for knowledge, who could make her live again?

Men, the Big Ones—all the arrogant kind who believed that their will should rule...

Slowly Jony began to walk around the ship. Geogee's information had been sketchy, but the older boy had learned enough to guess what he must do. He had destroyed the motor power of the flyer and stunned the pilot before he had left it. Now this larger craft must die in turn.

With the rod of the Great One, Jony took careful aim at the casing above the fins on which the ship balanced. How many levels above lay its motor power he was not quite sure. But he was going to hold the rod on his target until he had done all the visible damage he could.

Under the glare of the ray a hole appeared raggedly in the smooth casing of the ship. Through that Jony continued to pour the energy he did not understand. He could feel the pulsation of the power as it left the rod. There could be no repairing the destruction he now wrought. Then he turned in a half-circle to cut away the fins, so that the ship crashed to the ground, broken, dead, and harmless. There was still life inside, he could sense that. Men bewildered by his attack. He had no quarrel with them now. They would be weaponless, helpless—forced to come to terms with this world—not dominate it.

For a long moment Jony surveyed the crumpled bulk. He dropped his stunner to the ground, and destroyed that in turn. The rod he must keep—for a while. Until he was sure all danger from the invaders was over.

What would happen to them after this was up to them. If they learned to accept the People, they might eventually become one with this world. If they could not, then they must exist as best they might.

Jony took the helmet from his head, hurling it away. He tore at the fastening of the ship garment, dropped that onto the ground. The wind about his body felt fresh, clean. He touched his throat once, remembering the collar. But he, Jony, was not a "thing"; he was a man. As Voak, Otik, all the rest were men—and would remain so.

Turning his back on the fallen ship, Jony began to walk north into a new future.

➤ EPILOGUE ◄

"Hey—Lookit this! A box all torn up and, gee, Johnny, there's a dead kitten in it!"

"Let's see. Boy, think of someone throwing out a kitten just like it was old rubbish or something."

The cat raised her head at the sound of voices. She was not yet wary or abused enough to fear such sounds. They had always meant food, warmth, comfort. She mewed.

"Well, I'll be! Now, lookit here—in this old fridge! There's a cat, and one—two—three kittens. I'll bet they were all in that old box! What are you doing, Johnny?"

"Doing? I'm going to take her back home. Here, you empty out this bigger box. Get those rags over there. No, you dummy, don't take those wet ones on top, get the dry ones. There ought to be some still dry underneath."

"Your Mom is going to have fits if you turn up with a cat and three kittens. 'Member how she took on 'bout that old dog?"

"Sure. But he got a good home with the Wilsons, once we fed him up and cleaned him, and everything. This is a good cat. See, she likes me. See her rub against my hand? Anyway, I wouldn't leave anything here just to die—nothing at all. Sometimes I just don't dig people. They don't care about animals. You'd think they were broken toasters or something. Throw 'em out and forget them!"

"Well, you can't be a one-man army to save all the animals—"

"Maybe not—but I tell you, if *somebody* doesn't start doing something—then someday..."

"Someday what? Animals get back at us? Shut us up in cages? Leave us on dumps? That what you mean?"

"I dunno. I just have a feeling we've got to learn how to live so everything has a fair chance. There was something I read once, had to learn it for my book report. 'Animals are not brethren nor underlings, but others, caught with ourselves in a net of life and time, fellow prisoners of the splendor and travail of earth.'"

"Huh? What's all that mean in plain talk now—"

"That we're all part of this world together—and—well, we've got to learn to live together in another kind of way. Or else we've all lost."

"You and your books! Come on anyway. I'll give you a hand with the box..."

A thousand years later and half the galaxy away, Jony rubbed his throat again. He could scent the camp of the People. He wore no collar, nor did they. No iron cages waited for either of them—alien to each other though they might be. He threw his arms wide, and the feeling of freedom made him almost giddy.

BREED
TO COME

With appreciation for their invaluable aid in research,
my thanks to my resident people-in-fur
(in order of seniority)

Timmie
Punch
Samwise
Frodo
Su Li

and to the valiant memory of

Thai Shan
Sabina
Samantha

who were with us for far too short a time.

Man is old enough to see himself as he really is—a mammal among mammals. . . . He is old enough to know that in the years to come he may be crowded out like the prehistoric monsters of the past, while life breaks out in some ascendant form that is better suited to survive. . . .

—Homer W. Smith, *Kamongo*

What monstrous folly, think you, ever led nature to create her one great enemy—man!

—John Charles Van Dyke

> 1 <

There was a light breeze, just enough to whisper through the leaves. Furtig lay belly down on the broad limb of the tree, hunter-fashion, but his claws were still in his belt loop, not strapped on. No sniff of that breeze brought any useful scent to his expanded nostrils. He had climbed the tree not for a base from which to make a good capture-leap, but to see what lay beyond. However, now he knew that he must climb higher still. The leaves were too thick a screen here.

He moved with sinuous grace. Though his ancestors had hunted on four legs, Furtig now went on two, save when time pressed and he had to take to a fast run. And he was very much at home in the treetops. For those ancestors had also been climbers, just as their active curiosity had led them into exploration. Now he drew up from his perch into smaller branches, on which he balanced with inborn skill.

At last he gained a crotch, and there he faced through an opening what he had come to see. He had chosen a tree on a small hill, and the expanse before him was clear.

The first nips of frost had struck the country, though by day a gentle warmth returned. Tall grass rippled between him and those distant, monstrous shadows. The grass was brown, and it would not be long before the cold season. But first came the Trials of Skill.

Furtig's black lips pulled tight, and he opened his mouth on a soundless battle snarl. The white curve of tearing fangs showed their pointed tips. His ears flattened in folds against his rounded skull, the furred ridge along his back lifted, and the hair on his tail puffed.

To those who had known his ancestors, he would be a grotesque sight; for a body once well fitted to the needs of its owner had altered in ways strange to nature. Rounded forepaws had split into stubby fingers, awkward enough but able to accomplish much more in the way of handling. His body was still largely furred, but there were places where the fur had thinned to a light down. There was more dome to his skull, just as the brain beneath was different, dealing with thoughts and conceptions earlier unknown. In fact it was that brain which had altered most of all. Feline, Furtig's ancestors had been. But Furtig was something which those who had known those felines could not have accurately named.

His people did not measure time more than by certain rites of their own, such as the bi-yearly Trials of Skill when a warrior gave the best evidence of his prowess so that the females could pick a mate. One noted the coming of winter cold, and the return of spring, summer's heat when one drowsed through the days and hunted by night. But the People did not try to count one year apart from the rest.

Though it was said that Gammage did things none other of the People thought of doing. Gammage—

Furtig studied the bulk of buildings on the other side of the fields, lairs of the Demons. Yet Gammage feared no Demon. If all the stories were true, Gammage lived yonder in the heart of the lost Demon world. It was the custom for first-rite warriors to speak of "going to Gammage." And once in a long while one would. Not that any returned—which argued that the Demons still had their traps at work, even though no Demon had been seen for generations.

Furtig had seen pictures of them. It was part of the regular scout training to be taught to recognize the enemy. And, while a youngling could be shown one of the Barkers, a Tusked One, or even a vile Ratton in the flesh, he had to depend solely upon such representations of Demons for identification.

Long ago the Demons had gone from their lairs, though they had left foul traces of their existence behind them. The stinking sickness, the coughing death, the eaten-skin ills—these had fallen on the People too in the past, for once they had been imprisoned in the Demons' lairs. Only a small handful of them had escaped.

The memory of such deaths had kept them away from the lairs for many lifetimes. Gammage had been the first to dare to return to live in the Demons' forsaken shells. And that was because his thirst for knowledge had taken him there. Gammage came of a strange line differing yet again from many of the People.

Absently Furtig brought his hand to his mouth, licked the fur on it clean of an itch-causing leaf smear. He was of Gammage's own clan line, and they were noted for their boldness of curiosity and their differences in body. In fact they were not too well regarded. Once more his lips wrinkled, his tail twitched a little. Warriors of his family did not find it easy to take a mate, not even when they won in the Trials. Their restlessness of spirit, their habit of questioning old ways, of exploring, was not favored by any prudent cave mother who wished security for future younglings.

Such would look in the opposite direction when Gammage's kin padded by. And Gammage himself, awesome as he was, had little repute nowadays. Though the clans were willing enough to accept the infrequent, but always surprising, gifts which he had sent from the lairs in times past.

The hunting claws, which clicked softly as Furtig shifted his weight, were one of Gammage's first gifts to his people. They were made of a shining metal which did not dull, break, or flake with the passing of years as did the shards of metal found elsewhere. Set in a band which slipped over the hand, they snapped snugly just above the wrist, projecting well beyond the stubby fingers with tearing, curved hooks, like the claws one grew, but far more formidable and dangerous. And they were used just as one used one's natural defenses. A single well-placed blow could kill one of the deer or wild cows Furtig's people hunted for their staple food.

In war with one's kind they were forbidden. But they could be worn to face the Barkers, as those knew only too well. And with the Rattons—one used all and any weapons against those evil things. While with the Tusked Ones there were no quarrels, because of a truce.

Yes, the claws were from Gammage. And from time to time other things came from him, all designed to lighten the task of living in the Five Caves. So that the clans were respected and feared. There were rumors that another tribe of the People had settled lately to the north of the lairs, but so far none of Furtig's people had seen them.

The lairs—Furtig studied those blots on the landscape. They formed a long range of mountains. Was Gammage still there? It had been—he began to count seasons, tapping them off with a finger—it had been as many as fingers on his one hand since any word or gift had come from Gammage. Perhaps the Ancestor was dead.

Only that was hard to believe. Gammage had already lived far past the proper span of any ordinary warrior. Why, it had been Furtig's great-great-grandfather who had been Gammage's youngling in the last of the families born before the death of his mate and his departure for the lairs. It was also true that Gammage's blood lived longer than most. Fuffor, Furtig's father, had died in a battle with the Barkers, and he was then the only one of his years left at the Five Caves.

Nor had he seemed old; his mate had had another pair of younglings that very season, and she was the fourth mate he had won during the passing of seasons!

If it was not that so much of Gammage's blood now ran in the tribe there might be trouble. Once more Furtig snarled silently. Tales grew, and dark tales always grow the faster and stronger. Gammage was in league with Demons, he used evil learning to prolong his life. Yet for all such mewling of stories in the dark, his people were eager enough to welcome one of Gammage's messengers—take what he had to offer.

Only, now that those messengers came no more, and one heard nothing from those who had gone to seek Gammage, the stories grew in force. At the last Trials Furtig's older brother of another birth time had won. Yet he had not been chosen by any mate. And so he had joined the far scouts and taken a western trail-of-seeking from which he had never returned. Would it be any better for Furtig? Perhaps less—for he was not the warrior-in-strength that Fughan had been, being smaller and less powerful, even though his rivals granted him speed and agility.

He supposed he should be in practice now, using all those skills for the Trials, not wasting time staring at the lairs. Yet he found it hard to turn away. And his mind built strange pictures of what must lie within those walls. Great had been the knowledge of the Demons, though they had used it ill and in a manner which later brought them to defeat and death.

Furtig remembered hearing his father discuss the dim history of those days. He had been talking with one of Gammage's messengers about some discovery the Ancestor had made. That had been when Gammage had sent his picture of a Demon; they were to beware any creature who resembled it.

Before they had died, the Demons had gone mad, even as sometimes the Barkers did. They had fallen upon one another in rage, and were not able to mate or produce younglings. So without younglings and with their terrible hatred for one another, they had come to an end, and the world was the better for their going.

Gammage had learned this in the lairs, but he also feared that someday the Demons might return. From death? Furtig wondered. Great learning they had had, but could any living creature die and then live again? Perhaps the Demons were not rightly living creatures such as the People, even the Rattons. Someday— someday he would go to Gammage to learn more.

But not today, not until he had proven himself, shown all the Five Caves that the blood of Gammage was not to be ill-considered. And he would waste no more time in spying on the dead lairs of Demons either!

Furtig swung out of the tree, dropping lightly. This was the outpost of a small grove which angled back to become an arm of the forest country, the hunting territory of the Five Caves. Furtig was as at home in its shade as he was in the caves.

He stopped to tuck his hunting claws more tightly into his belt so that no small jangle would betray his passing, and then flitted on, his feet making no sound on the ground. Since he wanted to make speed he went to all fours, moving in graceful bounds. The People stood proudly upright when it was a time of ceremony, thus proving that the Demons who always walked so were no greater, but in times of need they fell back upon ancestral ways.

He planned to approach the caves from the north, but at first his course was west. That would take him by a small lake, a favorite feeding place of plump ducks. To return with an addition to the cave food supplies was always the duty of a warrior.

Suddenly a whiff of rank scent brought Furtig to a halt, crouching in the bushes. His hand whipped to his belt, reached for the claws, and he worked his hands into them with practiced speed.

Barkers! And more than one by the smell. They were not lone hunters like his own people, but moved in packs, centering in upon the kill. And one of the People would be a kill they would enjoy.

Courage was one thing, stupidity another. And Furtig's people were never stupid. He could remain where he was and do battle, for he did not doubt that the Barkers would speedily scent him (in fact he wondered fleetingly why they had not already done so). Or he could seek safety in the only flight left—aloft.

The hunting claws gave him a firm grip as they bit into tree bark, and he pulled himself up with haste. He found a branch from which he could view the ground below. Deep in his throat rumbled a growl he would not give full voice to, and with flattened ears and fur lifted on his spine, he watched, eyes aslit in a fighting face.

There were five of them, and they trotted four-footed. They had no one such as Gammage to supply them with any additions to the natural weapons of fangs. But those were danger enough. The Barkers were a third again as large as Furtig in size, their strong muscles moving smoothly under hides which were some as gray as his own, others blotched with black or lightened on belly and chest with cream.

They wore belts not unlike his, and from three of these dangled the limp bodies of rabbits. A hunting party. But so far they had found only small prey. If they kept on along that way though (Furtig's soundless growl held a suggestion of anticipation), they were going to cross the regular ranging ground of the Tusked Ones. And if they were foolish enough to hunt them—Furtig's green eyes glistened. He would back the Tusked Ones against any foe—perhaps even against Demons. Their warriors were not only fierce fighters but very wily brained.

He hoped that the Barkers would run into Broken Nose. In his mind Furtig gave that name to the great boar leader. The People could not echo the speech of the Tusked Ones, any more than they could the sharp yelps of the Barkers—though no reasonable creature could deem those speech. At the rare times of truce communication, one depended on signs, and the learning of them was the first lesson of any youngling's education.

Furtig watched the Barkers out of sight and then worked his way around the tree, found a place where he could leap onto the next, and made that crossing skillfully.

He was still growling. To see Barkers invading the hunting territory of the Five Caves was a shock. He would waste no time duck-stalking. On the other hand he must make sure that those he had seen were not outscouts for a larger pack. There were times when packs changed hunting territories, driven out by larger packs or by lack of game.

If such a pack were coming into the woods, then Furtig's warning would carry a double impact. He must back trail on those he had seen for a space.

For a time he kept to the trees, where he left no trail to be sniffed out even though, unlike the Barkers and the Tusked Ones, his people had no strong body odor. They hunted by sight and hearing and not by scent as did their enemies.

As a final precaution Furtig opened a small skin pouch made fast to his belt. Within was a wad of greasy stuff; its musky smell made his nose wrinkle in disgust. But he resolutely rubbed it on his feet and hands. Let a Barker sniff that and he would get a noseful as would send him off again, for it was the fat of the deadly snake.

Down again on the ground, Furtig sped along. As he went he listened, tested the air, watched for any sign that the home woods had been invaded in force. But he could not find anything save traces of the small party he had seen.

Then—His head jerked around, his nose pointed to a tree at his left. Warily he moved toward it. Barker sign left there as a guide, but under it—

In spite of his disgust at the rankness of the canine scent, Furtig made himself hold his head close, sniff deeper. Yes, beneath that road sign of the enemy was another, a boundary scent—of the People, but not of his own clan.

He straightened to his full height, held his arms overhead as far as he could reach. Scratches, patterned scratches, and higher than those he could make with his own claws. So the stranger who had so arrogantly left his hunting mark there had been larger, taller!

Furtig snarled aloud this time. Leaping, he slashed with his claws, managing to reach and dig into the other's sign, scouring out that marking, leaving the deeper grooves he had made. Let the stranger see that! Those deep marks crossing the first ought to be a warn-off to be heeded.

But the forest was getting far too crowded. First a hunting party of the Barkers, now a territory marking left by a stranger, as if Fives Caves and its clans did not exist at all! Furtig abandoned his back trailing. The sooner the People learned of these two happenings, the better.

However, he did not throw away caution but muddled his trail as he went. If any scout tried to sniff out the reptile scent, he would be disheartened by these further precautions. But this took time, and Furtig had to make a wider circle to approach the caves from a different direction.

It was dusk and then night. Furtig was hungry. He rasped his rough-surfaced tongue in and out of his mouth when he thought of food. But he did not allow himself to hurry.

A sudden hiss out of the night did not startle him. He gave a low recognition note in return. Had he not sounded that he might well have had his throat clawed open by the guard. The People did not survive through lack of caution.

Twice he swung off the open trail to avoid the hidden traps. Not that the People were as dependent on traps as the Rattons, who were commonly known to have raised that defense to a high art in the lairs. For, unlike the People, who distrusted and mainly kept away from the Demon places, the Rattons had chosen always to lurk there.

The Five Caves were ably defended by nature as well as by their inhabitants. None of them opened at ground level. High up, they cut back from two ledges with a straight drop below. There were tree-trunk ladders rigged to give access to the ledges.

But these could be hauled up, to lie along ledge edge, another barrier to attack. Twice the caves had been besieged by packs of Barkers. Both times their defenses had been unbreakable, and the attackers had lost more pack members then they had slain in return. It was during the last such attack that Furtig's father had fallen.

Within, the caves cut deeply, and one of them had a way down to where water flowed in the ever-dark. Thus the besieged did not suffer from thirst, and they kept always a store of dried meat handy.

Furtig's people were not naturally gregarious. Younglings and their mothers made close family units, of course. But the males, except in the Months of Mating, were not very welcome in the innermost caves. Unmated males roved widely and made up the scouts and the outer defenses. They had, through the years, increased in numbers. But seldom, save at the Trials of Skill, were they ever assembled together.

They had a truce with another tribe-clan to the west, and met for trials with them that they might exchange bloodlines by intermating. But normally they had no contact with any but their own five families, one based in each of the caves.

Furtig's cave was at the top and north, and he swung up to it quickly, his nose already sorting and classifying odors. Fresh meat—ribs of wild cow. Also duck. His hunger increased with every sniff.

But as he entered the cave, he did not hurry to where the females were portioning out the food but slipped along the wall to that niche where the senior member of the clan sat sharpening his hunting claws with the satisfaction of one who had recently put them to good use. So apparent was that satisfaction, Furtig knew Fal-Kan had been responsible for the cow ribs.

Though his people's sight adjusted well to partial darkness, there was light in the cave, a dull glow from a small box which was another of Gammage's gifts. It did not need any tending. When the first daylight struck into the mouth of the cave it vanished, coming alive again in the dusk of evening.

Gammage's bounty, too, were the squares of woven stuff that padded the sleeping ledges along the walls. In summer these were stowed away, and the females brought in sweet-scented grasses in their places. But in the cold, when one curled up on them, a gentle heat was generated to keep one warm through the worst of winter storms.

"Fal-Kan has hunted well." Furtig squatted several paces away from his mother's eldest brother, now sitting on his own sleep ledge. Thus Furtig was the prescribed respectful distance below him.

"A fat cow," Fal-Kan replied as one who brings home such riches each morning before the full heat of the sun. "But you come in haste, wearing trail destroyer—" He sniffed heavily. "So what danger have your eyes fastened on?"

Furtig spoke—first of the Barkers and then of the strange boundary sign. With a gesture Fal-Kan dismissed the Barkers. They were what one could expect from time to time, and scouts would be sent to make sure the Barkers were not pack forerunners. But at the story of the slash marks Fal-Kan set aside his claws and listened intently. When Furtig told of his counter-marking, the Elder nodded.

"That was well done. And you say that these slashes

were not deep. Perhaps no more deeply set than these could do?" He held out his hand, extending his natural claws.

"So it looked." Furtig had long ago learned that caution was the best tone to take with Elders. They were apt to consider the opinions of the young as misled and misleading.

"Then this one did not know Gammage."

Furtig's open astonishment brought him to the discourtesy of actually interrupting an Elder.

"Know Gammage! But he is a stranger—not of the Five Caves—or of the western People. Gammage would not know him."

Fal-Kan growled softly, and Furtig, in confusion, recognized his error. But his surprise remained.

"It is time," Fal-Kan said in the throat-rumbling voice used for pronouncements against offenders of cave custom, "that one speak clearly about the Ancestor. Have you not wondered why we have not been favored by his attention lately, during this time of your growing—though it would seem by your actions that you have not in truth progressed far beyond a youngling?"

Fal-Kan waited for no answer but continued without a pause.

"The fact is that our Ancestor"—and he did not say Honored Ancestor or use any title of respect—"is so engrossed by this fear of returning Demons which has settled in his head that he raises voice to unite all People—as if they were of one family or clan! All People brought together!" Fal-Kan's whiskers bristled.

"All warriors know that the Demons are gone. That they slew each other, and that they could not make their kind anymore, so they became fewer and fewer and finally there were none. Whence then would any come? Do old bones put on flesh and fur and come alive again? But the Ancestor has this fear, and it leads him in ways no prudent one would travel. It was learned the last time his messenger came that he was giving other People the same things he had sent here to the caves.

"And—with greater folly—he even spoke of trying to make truce with the Barkers for a plan of common defense, lest when the Demons returned we be too scattered and weak to stand against them. When this was known, the Elders refused the gifts of Gammage and told his messenger not to come again, for we no longer held them clan brothers."

Furtig swallowed. That Gammage would do this! There must be some other part of the story not known. For none of the People would be so sunk in folly as to share with enemies the weapons they had. Yet neither would Fal-Kan say this if he did not believe it the truth.

"And Gammage must have heard our words and understood." Fal-Kan's tail twitched. "We have not seen his messengers since. But we have heard from our truce mates in the west that there were truce flags set before the lairs in the north and strangers gathered there. Though we do not know who those were," Fal-Kan was fair enough to add. "But it may well be that, having turned his face from his own kin when they would not support his madness, Gammage now gives to others the fruits of his hunting. And this is a shameful thing, so we do not speak of it, even among ourselves, unless there is great need.

"But of the hunting sign on the tree, that we must speak of—all warriors together. For we are not so rich in game that we can allow others to take our country for their own. And we shall also tell this to the western kin. They come soon for the Trials. Go and eat, warrior. I shall take your words to the other cave Elders."

➤ 2 ◄

The visitors had been in sight of the cave scouts since midafternoon, but their party did not file into their usual campsite until after nightfall. This was the alternate season when the western clans came to the caves. Next season Furtig's people would cross country for the Trials.

All the young unmated warriors who were to take part in the coming contests scattered along the in-road (unless their Elders managed to restrain them with other duties). Though it was ill mannered to stare openly at their guests, there was naught to prevent their watching the travelers from cover, making comparisons between their champions and those marching in the protect circle about the females and younglings, or, better still, catching glimpses of their Choosers.

But to Furtig none of those were as attractive as Fas-Tan of the cave of Formor. And his interest was more for probable rivals than for the prizes of battle the other tribe could display. Not, he reflected ruefully, that he had much chance of aspiring to Fas-Tan.

Through some trick of heredity which ran in her family, she had odd fur coloring which was esteemed, along with the length of that fur, as beauty. The soft fur about her head and shoulders was nearly three times the length of that sprouting from Furtig's own tougher hide, and it was of two colors—not spotted or patched as was often the case but a dark brown shading evenly to cream. Her tail, always groomed to a silken flow, was also dark. Many were the fish-bone combs patiently wrought and laid at the message rock to the fore of Formor's cave, intended by the hopeful to catch the eye of Fas-Tan. And to know that she used the work of one's clumsy hands was enough to make a warrior strut for a day.

Fas-Tan would certainly have first choice, and with her pride, her selection of mate would be he who proved himself best. Furtig had not the least chance of catching her golden eyes. But a warrior could dream, and he had dreamed.

Now another thought plagued him. Fal-Kan's revelations concerning the folly, almost the treachery of Gammage, hung in his mind. He found himself looking not at the females of the westerners, but at the fringe of warriors. Most had hunting claws swinging at their belts. However, Furtig's eyes marked at least three who did not wear those emblems of manhood, yet marched with the defenders. A warrior could gain his claws in two ways, since they no longer came from Gammage. He could put on those which had been his father's if his sire had gone into the Last Dark, or he could challenge a claw wearer and strive for a victory that would make them his.

Furtig's claws had been his father's. He had had to

work patiently and long to hammer their fastenings to fit his own hands. If he were challenged tomorrow by one of the clawless and lost—He dropped his hand protectingly over the weapons at his belt. To lose those—

However, when he thought of Fas-Tan there was a heat in him, a need to yowl a challenge straight into the whiskered face of the nearest warrior. And he knew that no male could resist the Trials when the Choosers walked provocatively, tails switching, seeming to see no one, yet well aware of all who watched.

And he was the only contender from the cave of Gammage this year. Also, since his brother Fughan had brought home no mate, he was doubly held to challenge. He wriggled back into the brush and headed for the caves.

As he pulled up into his own place, he gave a small sigh. Trials were never to the death; the People were too few to risk the loss of even one warrior. But a contender could be badly mauled, even maimed, if the Ancestors turned their power from him.

Only Gammage, Furtig's most notable Ancestor, was not here, even in spirit. And it seemed, after he had listened to Fal-Kan, that Gammage had fallen from favor with his own kind. Furtig squatted by the lamp box and lapped a mouthful or two of water from his bowl as he thought about Gammage.

Why did the Ancestor fear the return of the Demons? It had been so long since the last one had been seen. Unless—Furtig's spine hair raised at the thought—deep in the lairs they still existed. And Gammage, creeping secret ways there, had learned more of their devilish evil than he had shared. But if that were true—no, he was certain Gammage would have sent a plain message, one which might even have won some of the People to join in his wild plans.

Elders sometimes took to living in the past. They spoke to those who had gone into the Last Dark as if such still stood at their sides. It came to them, this other sight, when they were very old. Though few lived so long, for when a warrior grew less swift of thought, less supple of body, he often died suddenly and bloodily by the horns and hoofs of hunted prey, from the coughing sickness which came with the cold, of a hundred other perils which always ringed the caves.

Only such perils might not haunt the lairs. And Gammage, very old, saw Demons stalking him in the shadows of their own stronghold. Yes, that could be the answer. But you could not argue with one who saw those gone before. And Gammage, moved by such shadows and master of the lair wonders—why, he could even be a menace to his own People if he continued in his folly of spreading his discoveries among strangers! And even—as Fal-Kan had said—among his enemies! Someone ought to go to Gammage in truth, not just in the sayings of young warriors, and discover what he was doing now. For the good of the People that should be done.

Going to Gammage—it had been four trials ago that the last one who said that had gone, never to return. Foskatt of Fava's cave. He had been bested in the contests. Furtig tried to recall Foskatt and then wished he had not. For the image in his mind was too like the one he had seen of himself the last time he had looked down at the other-Furtig in the smooth water of the Pool of Trees.

Foskatt, too, had been thin, narrow of shoulder and loin. And his fur was the same deep gray, almost blue in the sun. He also had been fond of roving on his own and had once shown Furtig something he had found in a small lair, one of those apart from the great ones in which Gammage lived. It was a strange thing, like a square box of metal, and in its top was a square of other material, very smooth. When Foskatt pressed a place on the side of the box, there appeared a picture on the top square. It was Demon-made, and when the cave Elders saw it they took it from Foskatt and smashed it with rocks.

Foskatt had been very quiet after that. And when he was beaten at the Trials, he had gone to Gammage. What had he found in the lairs?

Furtig fingered his fighting claws and thought about what might happen tomorrow; he must forget Gammage and consider rather his own future. The closer it came to the hour when he would have to front an opponent chosen by lot, the less good that seemed. Though he knew that once a challenge was uttered, he would be caught up in a frenzy of battle he would neither want to avoid nor be able to control. The very life force of their kind would spur him on.

Since it was not the custom that one tribe should stare at another in their home place, those of the caves went to their own shelters as the van of the visitors settled in the campgrounds, so Furtig was not alone for long. In the cave the life of his family bubbled about him.

"There is no proper way of influencing the drawing of lots." Fal-Kan and two of the lesser Elders drew Furtig aside to give him council, though he would far rather have them leave him alone. Or would he? Which was worse, foreseeing in his own mind what might happen to him, or listening to advice delivered with an undercurrent of dubious belief in their champion? Fal-Kan sounded now as if he did wish there was some way to control the selection of warrior against warrior.

"True." Fujor licked absentmindedly at his hand, his tongue rasping ever against the place where one finger was missing, as if by his gesture he could regrow that lacking member. Fujor was hairier of body than most of the cave and ran four-footed more often.

"There are three without claws," Fal-Kan continued. "Your weapons, warrior, will be an added inducement for any struggle with those. Some will fight sooner for good weapons than a mate."

Furtig wished he could pull those jingling treasures from his belt and hide them. But custom forbade it. There was no escape from laying them on the challenge rock when he was summoned. However, he dared speak up out of a kind of desperation. After all, Fal-Kan and Fujor had been successful in their own Trials. Perhaps, just perhaps, they could give him some manner of advice.

"Do you think, Elders, that I am already defeated, that you see the claws of my father on the hands of a stranger? For if this is so, can you not then tell me how the worst is to be avoided?"

Fal-Kan eyed him critically. "It is the will of the Ancestors who will win. But you are quick, Furtig. You know all we can teach you. We have done our best. See that you do also."

Furtig was silenced. There was no more to be gotten

out of these two. They were both Elders (though Fujor only by right of years, not by any wisdom). Fe-San, the other Elder, was noted for never raising his voice in Fal-Kan's presence.

The other males were younglings, too young to do more than tread the teaching trails by day. Lately they had had more females than males within the cave of Gammage. And after every Trial the females went to the victors' caves. The family was dwindling. Perhaps it would be with them as it had been with the cave of Rantla on the lower level, a clan finally reduced only to Elders and to Choosers too old to give birth. Yet Gammage had founded a proud line!

Now Furtig ate sparingly of the meat in his bowl, scrambled onto his own ledge, and curled up to sleep. He wished that the morning was already passed and the outcome of his uncertain championship decided. Through the dark he could hear the purring whispers of two of his sisters. Tomorrow would be a day of pride for them, with no doubts to cloud their excitement. They would be among the Choosers, not among the fighters.

Furtig tried to picture Fas-Tan, but his thoughts kept sliding in more dismal directions—he pictured a belt with no claws and an inglorious return to his cave. It was then he made up his mind. If he was a loser he was not going to take the solitary trail his brother had followed, or remain here to be an object of scorn for the Elders. No, he was going to Gammage!

The morning cry woke Furtig from dreams he could not remember. Thus they had not been sent by any Ancestor to warn him. And Furtig, as he dropped from his sleep place, felt no greater strength. The thought of the coming day weighed heavily on him, so much so that he had to struggle to preserve the proper impassive manner of a warrior on this day of days.

When they gathered on the pounded-earth flooring of the Trial place, Furtig had to join the line of Challengers as confidently as if he were San-Lo himself, there at the other end. San-Lo was easily counted the best the caves could produce. His yellow fur with its darker brown striping was sleek and well ordered, seeming to catch the morning sun in a blaze, foretelling the glory which would soon rest on him in the sight of both caves and westerners.

Furtig had no illusions; of that company he was certainly the least likely to succeed. There were ten of them this year, with a range of different fur coloring making a bright pattern. Two brothers of the gray-with-black-striping, which was the commonest; a night black, a contrast to his two black-and-white brothers, a formidable trio who liked to hunt together and shared more companionship than others of their age group. Then came a stocky white with only ears and tail of gray; two more yellows, younger and lighter editions of San-Lo; a brown-striped with a white belly; and last Furtig in solid gray.

Their opponents were more uniform, having originally come from only two families, according to tradition. They were either all black, or black-and-white in various markings.

The Choosers were lying at languid ease on top of the sun-warmed rocks to the east of the combat field, while the Elders and the mated gathered north and south. Now and then one of the Choosers would wantonly utter a small yowling call, promising delights for him she would accept. But Fas-Tan did not have to attract attention so. Her superb beauty already had registered with them all.

Ha-Ja, who was the Eldest of the Westerners, and Kuygen, who held the same status at the caves, advanced to the center of the field. At a gesture each brought forward the first warrior in each line, holding a bowl well above the eye level of the contestants. Those raised their hands and drew, keeping their choices as concealed as they could. So it went, two by two, until Furtig had his chance. He groped in the bowl, felt the two remaining slips of wood, and pulled out one.

Once they had all drawn, each contestant smoothed a small patch of earth and dropped his choose-stick on it. Ha-Ja called first:

"One notch end."

San-Lo showed his fangs and gave a low snarl of assent.

Kuygen gestured to the westerners. The duplicate lay at the feet of a powerfully built all-black, whose tail was already twitching. At least, by the look of him, San-Lo would be fairly matched.

Both advanced to the center rock, tossed their hunting claws with a jangle of metal on the stone. At least in this battle there would be no forfeiture of weapons.

Together Ha-Ja and Kuygen made signal. The warriors went to full ground-crouch, their tails alash, ears flattened, eyes slitted. And from their throats came the howls of battle. They circled in one of the customary challenge moves, and then the black sprang.

Their entanglement was a flurry of such fast tearing, rolling, and kicking with the powerful hind feet that the spectators, accustomed as they were to such encounters, were hardly able to follow the action before the warriors parted. Tufts of fur blew from the battle site, but they were yowling again, neither seeming the least affected by the fury of their first meeting.

Again that attack, vicious, sudden, complete. They rolled over and over on the ground and fur flew. The emotion spread to the spectators. Waiting warriors yowled, voicing their own battle cries, hardly able to restrain themselves from leaping at each other. Even the Elders added to the general din. Only the Choosers held to their studied languor, though their eyes were very wide, and here and there a pink tongue tip showed.

San-Lo won. When they separated the second time, the black had lowered tail and backed from the field, raw and bleeding tears on his belly. The champion of the caves strutted to the rock to pick up his claws, dangling them in an arrogant jingle before he returned to his place in line.

The fights continued. Two of the cave warriors surrendered to the visitors. Then there were three straight wins for Furtig's clan. But his apprehension was growing. The matching of pieces was leaving another warrior on the western side as formidable in size as the one who had stood up to San-Lo. If the favor of the Ancestors was against Furtig—

And it was. His neighbor on the cave line bested—but just—his opponent. Furtig must face the powerful warrior. Also—no claws swung from the other's belt, so he had to face the thought of not only one defeat but two.

Dreading what was to come, yet knowing it must be

faced, he went dutifully to the rock, tossed his claws there with a reluctance he hoped was not betrayed.

At least he could make the black know that he had been in a fight! And he yowled his challenge with what strength he could muster. When they tangled, he fought with all the skill he had. Only that was not enough. Sheer determination not to give in sent him twice more to tangle with those punishing clawed legs, fangs which had left wounds. It was a nightmare to which there was no end. He could only keep fighting—until—

Until there was blackness and he was lost in it, though there were unpleasant dreams. And when he awoke in the cave, lying on his own pallet, he first thought it was all a dream. Then he raised his swimming head and looked upon the matted paste of healing leaves plastered on him.

Almost hoping, he fought pain to bring his hand to his belt. But there were no claws there. He had plainly lost, and those weapons which had been Gammage's good gift to Furtig's father were gone with all his hopes of ever being more in the caves than Fu-Tor of the missing hand.

They had patched him up with the best of their tending. But there was no one in the cave. He craved water with a thirst which was now another pain, and finally forced his aching and bruised body to obey him, crawling through the light of the night lamp to the stone trough. There was little left, and when he tried to dip out a bowlful his hand shook so that he got hardly any. But even as he had fought on when there was no hope of victory, he persisted.

Furtig did not return to his ledge. Now that he was not so single-minded in his quest for water, he could plainly hear the sounds of the feasting below. The Choosing must be over, the winners with the mates who had selected them. Fas-Tan—he put her out of his mind. After all she had been only a dream he could never hope to possess.

His clawless belt was the greater loss, and he could have wailed over that like a youngling who had strayed too far from his mother and feared what might crouch in the dark. That he could stay on in the caves now was impossible.

But to go to Gammage armed and confident was one matter. To slink off as a reject from the Trials, with his weapon lost as spoils of victory—In some things his pride was deep. Yet—to Gammage he must go. It was his right, as it had been his brother's, to choose to leave. And one could always claim a second Trial—though at present that was the last thing he wanted.

However, Furtig had no intention of leaving before he proclaimed his choice. Pride held him to that. Some losers might be poor spirited enough to slink away in the dark of night, giving no formal word to their caves—but not Furtig! He crawled back to the ledge, knowing that he must also wait until he was fit for the trail again.

So he lay, aching and smarting, listening to the feasting, wondering if his sisters had chosen to mate with victorious westerners or within the caves. And so he fell asleep.

It was mid-day when he awoke, for the sun was shining in a bright bar well into the cave mouth. The ledges of the Elders were empty, but he heard noises in the parts within. As he turned his head one of the younger females almost touched noses with him, she had been sitting so close, her eyes regarding him unwinkingly.

"Furtig." She spoke his name softly, putting out a hand to touch a patch of the now dried leaf plaster on his shoulder. "Does it hurt you much?"

He was aware of aches, but none so intense as earlier. "Not too much, clan sister."

"Mighty fighter, in the cave of Gammage—"

He wrinkled a lip in a wry grimace. "Not so, young-ling. Did I not lose to the warrior of the westerners? San-Lo is a mighty fighter, not Furtig."

She shook her head. Like him she was furred with rich gray, but hers was longer, silkier. He had thought Fas-Tan was rare because of her coloring, but this youngling, Eu-La, would also be a beauty when her choose-time came.

"San-Lo was chosen by Fas-Tan." She told him what he could easily have guessed. "Sister Naya has taken Mur of Folock's cave. But Sister Yngar—she took the black warrior of the westerners—" Eu-La's ears flattened and she hissed.

Furtig guessed. "The one I battled? He is a strong one."

"He hurt you." Eu-La shook her head. "It was wrong for Sister Yngar to choose one who hurt her brother. She is no longer of the cave." Once more she hissed.

"But of course she is not, sister. When one chooses, one is of the clan of one's mate. That is the way of life."

"It is a bad way—this fighting way." She chewed one claw tip reflectively between words. "You are better than San-Lo."

Furtig grunted. "I would not like to try to prove that, sister. In fact it is a not-truth."

She hissed. "He is strong of claw, yes. But in his head—does he think well? No, Fas-Tan is a fool. She should pick a mate who thinks rather than one who fights strongly."

Furtig stared at her. Why, she was only a youngling, more than a season away from her own time of choice. But what she said now was not a youngling kind of thing.

"Why do you think so?" he asked, curious.

"We"—her head went up proudly—"are of the cave of Gammage. And the Ancestor learned many, many things to help us. He did not so learn by fighting. He went hunting for knowledge instead of battles. Brother, females also think. And when I grow trailwise I shall not choose—I shall go to Gammage also! There I shall learn and learn—" She stretched forth her thin furred arms as if she were about to gather to her some heaping of knowledge, if knowledge could be so heaped and gathered.

"Gammage has grown foolish with time—" He spoke tentatively.

Once more she hissed, and now her anger was directed at him.

"You speak as the Elders. Because some do not understand new things they say that such are stupid or ill thought. Think instead on what Gammage has sent us, and that these may only be a small part of the great things he has found! There must be much good in the lairs."

"And if Gammage's fears are the truth, there may also be Demons there."

Eu-La wrinkled a lip. "Believe in Demons when

you see them, brother. Before then take what you can which will aid you."

He sat up. "How did you know I was minded to go to Gammage?"

She gave a soft purr of laughter. "Because you are who you are, you can do no other, brother. Look you." She brought out from behind her a small bag pulled tight by a drawstring. Furtig had seen only one such before, that being much prized by the females. It had been made, according to tradition, by Gammage's last mate, who had had more supple fingers than most. But it had not been duplicated since.

"Where got you that?"

"I made it." Her pride was rightfully great. "For you—" She pushed it into his hand. "And these also."

What she produced now were as startling as the bag, for she had a pair of hunting claws. They were not the shining, well-cared-for ones which had been his. There were two points missing on one set, one on the other, and the rest were dull and blunted.

"I found them," Eu-La told him, "in a place between two rocks down in the cave of waters. They are broken, brother, but at least you do not go with bare hands. And—this I ask of you—when you stand before the Ancestor, show him this—" She touched the bag. "Say to him then, shall not a female of the cave of Gammage not also have a part in the learning of new things?"

Furtig grasped both bag and claws, astounded at her gifts, so much more than he could have hoped for.

"Be sure, sister," he said, "that I shall say it to him just as you have said it to me."

> 3 <

Furtig crept forward. It was not yet dawn, but to his eyes the night was not dark. He had chosen to cross the wide expanse of open space about the western fringe of the Demons' lair by night—though a whole day of watching had shown no signs of life there. Nor had he, during this patient stalk across the grass-covered open, discovered any game trail or sign that aught came or went from the buildings.

But the closer he approached the lairs, the more awe-inspiring they were. From a distance he had been able to judge that their height was far greater even than that of the cliff which held the Five Caves. However, he had had no idea how high they were until he neared their bases. Now he had almost to roll on his back to see their tips against the sky.

It was frightening. Furtig felt that to venture in among those banks of towering structures would be to set foot in a trap. As Gammage had? Was it death and not the reception afforded his unwelcome ideas which had kept the Ancestor silent these past seasons?

Though his sense of smell was no way near as keen as a Barker's, Furtig lifted his head higher and tried to distinguish some guiding odor. Did Gammage's people mark the boundaries of their territory here as they would forest trees, though with scent not scratches? He could detect the scent of the dying grass, got some small whiffs of the inhabitants of that flat land—mice, a rabbit. But nothing seemed to issue from the lairs, though the wind blew from there, rippling the grass in his direction.

On all fours, Furtig advanced with the stealth of a hunter creeping up on unwary prey, alert to sounds. There was a swishing which was the wind in the grass, some rustlings born of his own movements, which could not be helped unless one could somehow tread air above the blowing fronds. A frantic scurrying to his left—rabbit.

The grass came to an end. Before him was a stretch of smooth stone—almost as if the lairs had opened a mouth, extended a tongue to lap him in. There was no hiding place beyond. He would have to walk across the open. Reluctantly, Furtig rose on hind feet.

It was well enough to creep and crawl when one had the excuse of keeping to cover. But he did not intend to enter the lairs so. There was something in him which demanded boldness now.

He paused only to slip the claws over his hands. They were inferior, and did not fit his hands smoothly, but he had worked them into the best condition he could. And, while he never ceased to regret the loss of his own fine weapons, he was deeply grateful to Eu-La for her gift. Armed, he was now ready.

A quick dart took him across into the shadow by

the first wall. There were regular breaks in that, but set so high he could not reach any. Surely there must be some guide to Gammage, some trail markings to lead in a newcomer. For it was well known that Gammage welcomed those who came to him.

Furtig continued to sniff for such a marker. There was a smell of bird. He could see streaks of droppings on the walls. But nothing more than that.

With no guide he could only work his way into the heart of the lairs, hoping to pick up some clue to those he sought. However, he went warily, making use of all shadows he could.

And, as he went, awe of those who had built all this grew in him. How had they piled up their cliffs? For these erections were not natural rock. What knowledge the Demons had had!

Sunrise found him still wandering, at a loss for a guide. He had come across two open spaces enclosed by the buildings. They were filled with tangles of vegetation now seared by fall. One surrounded a small lake in which water birds suddenly cried out and rose with a great flapping of wings.

Furtig crouched, startled. Then he realized that he could not have been the reason for that flight. Then—what had?

At that moment he caught the hot scent, rank, overpowering. And he snarled. Ratton! There was no mistaking its foulness. Rattons—here? They clung to the lairs of Demons, that was true, yet it was thought they had not spread far through those.

Furtig edged back into the hollow of a doorway. At his back the door itself was a great unbroken solid slab, and it was closed. As it was about six times his own height and gave the appearance of strength, he had no hope of opening it. And if he were sighted, or scented, in this place he would be cornered.

The Rattons did not fight as the People did but more like the Barkers, sending many against one. Though Furtig was much larger than any of their kind, he could not hope to stand up to a whole company of them. His tail twitched sharply as he watched the bushes about the lake and used his nose and ears to aid his eyes in locating the foe.

Though most of the water birds had flown, at least three of their flock were in difficulty. For there was a beating of wings, harsh cries at the far end of the lake. Furtig could not see through the screen of bushes, and he was not about to advance into what might be enemy territory. Suddenly the squawking was cut off, and he thought the hunters must have finished their prey.

His own plans had changed. To go into Ratton-held lairs—no! And he imagined now what might have been Gammage's fate—well-picked bones!

But could he withdraw without being hunted? Furtig was not sure whether the Rattons hunted by scent or by ear and eye. His only recourse was to befuddle his trail as well as he could. And in the open he could not do that.

Furtig tried feverishly to remember all he had heard concerning the Rattons. Could they leap, climb, follow the People so? Or were they earthbound like the Barkers? It seemed he was soon to prove one or the other.

On either side of the door behind him was a panel in the wall. These were set higher than his head, even when he stretched to his full height. The one to his right was intact. But the other had a break in its covering, leaving only shards of stuff in the frame.

Furtig crouched and leaped. His fighting claws caught on the edge of those shards and they splintered. He kept his hold and kicked his way in. He found himself on a ledge above a dusky floor. It was narrow, but he could balance there long enough to survey what lay beyond.

There were objects standing here and there, a heavy dust covering the floor. He surveyed that with disappointment. Not a track on it. When he dropped he would leave a trail the most stupid tracker could follow. Furtig teetered on the ledge, undecided. The dead air made his nose wrinkle, and he fought the need to sneeze. His half-plan now seemed rank folly. Better to stay in the open—He turned his head to look out. There was a flash of movement in the bushes near the door.

Too late! They were already closing in. He needed speed now to reach a place where he could wedge his back as he turned to face his attackers.

He made a second leap from the ledge to the top of one of the objects standing on the floor. His feet plowed into the soft dust and he skidded nearly to its far end, pushing the dust before him, before his claws held fast.

The room had two doors, both open arches, neither barred. What he wanted now was to get to the very top of this lair, and out into the open, where he would perhaps have a bare chance of leaping to the next lair, just as he would leap from tree to tree to escape ground-traveling enemies.

There was little choice between the doors, and in

the end he took the nearest. This gave onto a long passage from which opened other doorless rooms—rather like the caves. Save that these promised no security.

Furtig wasted no time exploring, but ran at top speed past those doorless openings to the end of the hall. Here was a door and it was closed. He tried to insert claw tips in the crack he could see and was answered by a slight give. Enough to set him tearing frenziedly at the promise.

When it did open far enough for him to slip his body through, he gave a convulsive start backward. For, opening at his feet, was a deep shaft. There was nothing beyond the door but a hole that might entrap a full-sized bull. In his fear Furtig spat, clawed at the edges of the door.

It was too late. The momentum of his assault on that stubborn barrier pitched him out into empty space. He had closed his eyes in reflex as he went, fear filling him, forcing out sense and reason—

Until he realized that he was not falling like a stone pitched from one of the cave ledges, but drifting downward!

Furtig opened his eyes, hardly aware even now that he was not on his way to a quick death. It was dark in the shaft, but he could see that he was descending, slowly, as if he rested on some solid surface that was sinking into the foundations of the lair.

Of course it was well known that the Demons commanded many powers. But that they could make thin air support a body! Furtig drew a deep breath and felt his pounding heart lessen its heavy beat a fraction. It was plain he was not going to die, at least not yet, not so long as this mysterious cushion of air held. Thinking about that, he grew fearful again. How long would it hold?

He wondered if he could aid himself in some way. This was almost like being in water. One swam in water. Would the same motions carry one here? Tentatively Furtig made a couple of arm sweeps and found himself closer to the wall of the shaft. He reached it just in time to see the outline of another door, and tried to catch at the thin edge around it with his claws. But those scraped free and he was passed before he could make any determined effort. Now he waited, alert to another such chance as he drifted down. Only to be disappointed.

A sound from above! The faint squeal echoed in the shaft. Rattons up there! Probably at the door he had forced open. Would they take to the air after him? Furtig flexed his fingers within the fastening of the claws. He had no liking for the prospect of fighting in mid-air. But if he had no choice he had better be prepared.

However, it seemed that those above were not ready to make such a drastic pursuit. Perhaps if they could not sight him they would believe that he had plunged to death. Unless they, living in the lairs, knew the odd properties of the shaft. If so, would they ambush him on landing?

Alarmed at the thought, Furtig kicked out and thrust closer to the wall, searching as he drifted down for any signs of an anchorage he could use. But he must have waited too long. The walls here were uniformly smooth. And, though he drew the claws despairingly along, hoping to hook in some hole, he heard only the rasping scrape of those weapons, found nothing in which they could root.

He could not judge distance, and time seemed strange too. How long, how far, had he fallen? He had entered the lair at ground level, but this descent must be carrying him far under the surface of the earth. Though he knew security in caves which reached underground, yet this was something else, and the fear of the unknown was in him.

He was falling faster now! Had that cushion of air begun to fail? Furtig had only time to ready himself for what might be a hard landing before he did land, on a padded surface.

The dark was thick; even his night sight could not serve him. But he could look up the shaft and see the lighter grayish haze of what lay beyond the door he had forced.

Furtig tested the air for Ratton stench but was only a fraction relieved at its absence. There were other smells here, but none he could identify.

After a moment he straightened from the instinctive crouch into which he had gone and began to feel his way around the area. Three sides, the scrape of his claws told him, were walls.

His whiskers, abristle on his upper lip, fanned out above his eyes, gave him an additional report on space as they were intended to. The fourth wall was an opening like the mouth of a tunnel. But Furtig, remembering his error at the door above, made no quick effort to try it.

When he did advance, it was on all fours, testing each step with a wide swing of hand ahead, listening for the sound of the metal claw tips to reassure him about the footing.

So he crept on. The tunnel, or hall, appeared to

run straight ahead, and was the width of the shaft. So far he had located no breaks in its walls, at least at the level of his going. Now he began, every five paces, to rise and probe to the extent of his full reach for any openings that might be above.

However, he could find none, and his blind progress continued. He began to wonder if he were as well trapped by his own recklessness as the Rattons could have trapped him by malicious purpose. Could he somehow climb up the shaft if he found this a dead-end way?

Then his outthrust hand bumped painfully against a solid surface. At the same time there was a lightening of the complete dark to his right, and a sharply angled turn in the hall led him toward it.

Furtig's head came up, he drew a deep breath, testing that faint scent. Ratton—yes—but with it a more familiar, better smell, which could only come from one of his own people! But the People and the Rattons—he could not believe any such combination could be a peaceful one. Could Gammage have carried his madness so far as to deal with Rattons?

The Ratton smell brought an almost noiseless growl deep in his throat. But the smell of his own kind grew stronger, and he was drawn to it almost in spite of himself.

Furtig discovered the source of the light now, a slit set high in the wall, but not so high that he could not leap and hook claws there, managing to draw himself up, despite the strain on his forearms, to look through.

All that short glimpse afforded him was the sight of another wall. He must somehow find the means of remaining longer at the slit. Whatever was there must lie below eye level, and the odor of the People was strong.

Furtig had his belt. Slowly he pulled the bone pin which held it about him, unhooked the pouches of supplies, and laid the belt full length on the floor. He shed the claws and clumsily, using his teeth as well as his stubby fingers, made each end of the belt fast to the claws, testing that fastening with sharp jerks.

Then he looped the belt around him, slipped the claws on lightly, and leaped once more for the slit. The claws caught. He jerked his hands free, and the belt supported him, his powerful hind legs pressed against the wall to steady him.

He could look down into the chamber. His people— yes—two of them. But the same glimpse which identified them showed Furtig they were prisoners. One was stretched in tight bonds, hands and feet tied. The other had only his hands so fastened; one leg showed an ugly wound, blood matted black in the fur.

Furtig strained to hold his position, eager to see. The bound one—he was unlike any of the People Furtig knew. His color was a tawny sand shade on his body; the rest of him, head, legs, tail, was a deep brown. His face thinned to a sharply pointed chin and his eyes were bright blue.

His fellow prisoner, in contrast to the striking color combination of the blue-eyed one, was plain gray, bearing the black stripes of the most common hue among the People. But—Furtig suppressed a small cry.

Foskatt! He was as certain as he was of his own name and person that the wounded one was Foskatt, who had gone seeking Gammage and never returned.

And if they were prisoners in a place where there

was so strong a stench of Ratton, he could well guess
who their captors were. If he had seen only the
stranger he would not have cared. One had a duty to
the caves and then to the tribe, but a stranger must
take his own chances. Though Furtig hesitated over
that reasoning—he did not like to think of any of the
People, stranger or no, in the hands of the Rattons.

But Foskatt had to be considered. Furtig knew
only too well the eventual fate of any Ratton captive.
He would provide food for as many of his captors as
could snatch a mouthful.

Furtig could hold his position no longer. But he
took the chance of uttering the low alerting hiss of
the caves. Twice he voiced that, clinging to the claw-
belt support.

When he hissed the second time, Foskatt's head
turned slowly, as if that effort was almost too much.
Then his yellow eyes opened to their widest extent,
centered on the slit where Furtig fought to keep his
grip. For the first time Furtig realized that the other
probably could not see him through the opening. So
he called softly: "Foskatt—this is Furtig."

He could no longer hold on but slid back into the
tunnel, his body aching with the effort which had kept
him at that peephole. He took deep breaths, fighting
to slow the beating of his heart, while he rubbed his
arms, his legs.

His tail twitched with relief as a very faint hiss
came in answer. That heartened him to another effort
to reach the slit. He knew he could not remain there
long, and perhaps not reach it at all a third time. If
Foskatt were only strong enough to—to what? Furtig
saw no way of getting his tribesman through that hole.

But perhaps the other could supply knowledge which would lead Furtig to a better exit.

"Foskatt!" It was hard not to gasp with effort. "How may I free you?"

"The caller of Gammage—" Foskatt's voice was weak. He lay without raising his head. "The guard-has-taken-it. They-wait-for-their-Elders—"

Furtig slipped down, knew he could not reach the slit again. He leaned against the wall to consider what he had heard. The caller of Gammage—and the Ratton guard had it—whatever a caller might be. The guard could only be outside the door of that cell.

He picked up his belt, unfastening the claws. Now—if he could find a way out of this tunnel to that door. It remained so slim a chance that he dared not pin any hopes on it.

He stalked farther along the dark way. Again a thin lacing of light led him to a grill. But this one was set at an easier height, so he need not climb to it. He looked through into a much larger chamber, which was lighted by several glowing rods set in the ceiling.

To his right was a door, and before it Rattons! The first live ones he had ever seen so close.

They were little more than half his size if one did not reckon in the length of their repulsive tails. One of them had, indeed, a tail which was only a scarred stump. He also had a great scar across his face which had permanently closed one eye. He leaned against the door gnawing at something he held in one paw-hand.

His fellow was more intent on an object he held, a band of shining metal on which was a cube of glittering stuff. He shook the band, held the cube to one ear. Even across the space between them Furtig caught the faint buzzing sound which issued from that cube. And he guessed that this must be Gammage's caller—though how it might help to free Foskatt he had no idea. Except he knew that the Ancestor had mastered so much of Demon knowledge in the past that this device might just be as forceful in some strange way as the claws were in ripping out a Ratton throat.

Furtig crowded against the grill, striving to see how it was held in place, running his fingers across it with care so as not to ring his weapon tips against it. He could not work it too openly with Rattons on guard to hear—or scent—him.

The grill was covered with a coarse mesh. He twisted at it now with the claw tips, and it bent when he applied pressure. So far this was promising. Now Furtig made the small chirruping sound with which a hunter summons a mouse, waiting tensely and with hope.

Three times he chirruped. There was a shadow rising at the screen. Furtig struck. Claws broke through the mesh, caught deep in flesh and bone. There was a muffled squeak. With his other hand Furtig tore furiously at the remaining mesh, cleared an opening, and wriggled through, hurling the dead Ratton from him.

On the floor lay the caller. The scarred guard had fled. Furtig could hear his wild squealing, doubtless sounding the alarm. It had been a tight fit, that push through the torn mesh, and his skin had smarting scratches. But he had made it, and now he caught up the caller.

He almost dropped it again, for the band felt warm, not cold as metal should. And the buzzing was louder. How long did he have before that fleeing guard returned with reinforcements?

Furtig, the caller against his chest, kicked aside the bars sealing the door and rushed in. He reached Foskatt, hooked a claw in the other's bonds to cut them. But seeing the extent of his tribesman's wounds, he feared the future. It was plain that with that injury Foskatt could not walk far.

"The caller—give it to me—" Foskatt stared at the thing Furtig held. But when he tried to lift a hand it moved like a half-dead thing, not answering his will, and he gave an impatient cry.

"Touch it," he ordered. "There is a small hole on the side, put your finger into that!"

"We must get away—there is no time," Furtig protested.

"Touch it!" Foskatt said louder. "It will get us out of here."

"The warrior is mad," growled the other prisoner. "He talks of a thing coming through the walls to save him. You waste your time with him!"

"Touch it!"

Foskatt made no sense, yet Furtig found himself turning the caller over to find the hole. It was there, but when he tried to insert a finger, he discovered that his digit was far too thick to enter. He was about to try the tip of a claw when Foskatt batted clumsily at his arm, those deep ridges in his flesh, cut by the bonds, bleeding now.

"No—don't use metal! Hold it closer—hold it for me!"

Furtig went to his knees as Foskatt struggled up. Foskatt bent forward, opened his mouth, and put forth his tongue, aiming its tip for the hole in the cube.

➤ 4 ◄

Foskatt's head jerked as if that touch was painful, but he persisted, holding his tongue with an effort which was manifest throughout his body. At last, it seemed, he could continue no longer. His head fell back, and he rested his limp weight against Furtig's shoulder, his eyes closed.

"You have wasted time," snarled the other prisoner. "Do you leave us now to be meat, or do you give me a fighting chance?" There was no note of pleading in his voice. Furtig had not expected any; it was not in their breed to beg from a stranger. But he settled Foskatt back, the caller beside him, and went to cut the other's bonds.

When those were broken, he returned to Foskatt. The stranger had been right. There was no chance of escape through these burrows, which the Rattons knew much better than he. He had wasted time. Yet Foskatt's urgency had acted on him strongly.

The stranger whipped to the door. Even as he reached it, Furtig could hear the squealing clamor of gathering

Rattons. He had failed. The only result of his attempt at rescue was that he had joined the other two in captivity. But he had his claws at least, and the Ratton forces would pay dearly for their food when they came at him.

"Fool," hissed the stranger, showing his fangs. "There is no way out now!"

Foskatt stirred. "The rumbler will come—"

His mutter, low as it was, reached the stranger, and his snarl became a growl, aimed at them both.

"Rumbler! He has blatted of none else! But his wits are wrong. There is no—"

What he would have added was forgotten as he suddenly whirled and crouched before the door, his bare hands raised. However, for some reason, the Rattons did not rush the prisoners at once, as Furtig had expected. Perhaps they were trying to work out some method whereby they could subdue their captives without undue loss on their part. If they knew the People at all, they must also realize that the Rattons on the first wave in would die.

Furtig listened, trying to gauge from sounds what they were doing. He did not know what weapons the Rattons had besides those nature had given them. But since they frequented the lairs, they might have been as lucky as Gammage in discovering Demon secrets. Foskatt pushed at the floor, tried to raise himself. Furtig went to his aid.

"Be ready," his tribesman said. "The rumbler—when it comes—we must be ready—"

His certainty that something was coming almost convinced Furtig that the other knew what he was talking about. But how that action of tongue to cube could bring anything—

The stranger was busy at the door. He had pulled some litter together, was striving to force into place rusty metal rods as a bar lock. Even if that worked, it could not save them for long, but any action helped. Furtig went to aid him.

"This should slow them—a little—" the stranger said as they finished as well as they could. He turned then and padded across the room to stand beneath the wall grill high overhead. "Where does that lead? You were behind it when you signaled—"

"There is a tunnel there. But the opening is too narrow."

The stranger had kept one of the pieces of metal, too short to be a part of their barrier. Now he struck that against the wall in a rasping blow. It did not leave more than a streak of rust to mark its passage. There was no beating their way through that wall.

He strode back and forth across the cell, his tail lashing, uttering small growls, which now and then approached the fury of battle yowls. Furtig knew the same fear of being trapped. He flexed his fingers, tested the strength of his claw fastenings. In his throat rumbled an answering growl. Then the stranger came to a halt before him, those blue eyes upon Furtig's weapons.

"Be ready to cut the net with those." His words had the force of an order.

"The net?"

"They toss nets to entangle one from a distance. That was how they brought me down. They must have taken your comrade in the same fashion. He was already here when they dragged me in. It is only because they were awaiting their Elders that they did not kill us at once. They spoke among themselves much, but who can understand their vile chittering? One or two made signs—there was something they wished to learn. And their suggestion"—the hair on his tail was bushed now—"was that they would have a painful way of asking. Die in battle when they come, warrior, or face what is worse."

The Rattons were trying to force the door now. How long would the barrier hold?

Furtig tensed, ready to face the inpour when the weight of those outside would break through. Foskatt pulled himself up, one hand closing upon the caller, raising it to his ear. His eyes glowed.

"It comes! Gammage is right! The rumblers will serve us! Stand ready—"

Then Furtig caught it also, a vibration creeping through the stone flooring, echoing dully from the walls about them. It was unlike anything he had experienced before, though it carried some tones of storm thunder. It grew louder, outside the door, and once more the enemy squealed in ragged chorus.

"Stand back—away—" Foskatt's husky whisper barely reached Furtig. The stranger could not have heard it, but, so warned, Furtig sprang, grasped the other's arm, and pulled him to one side. The stranger rounded on him with a cry of rage, until he saw Foskatt's warning gesture.

As if some supreme effort supplied strength, Foskatt was sitting up, the caller now at his mouth, his tongue ready, extended as if he awaited some signal.

Then—there was a squealing from the Rattons which became a hysterical screeching. These were not battle cries but rather a response to fear, to a terrible, overpowering fear.

Something struck against the wall with a force that certainly the Rattons could not exert. Thudding blows followed, so close on one another that the noise became continuous. The door broke, pushed in, but that was not all. Around its frame ran cracks in the wall itself; small chunks flaked off.

Together Furtig and the stranger backed away. No Ratton had sprung through the opening. The prisoners could see only a solid, dark surface there, as if another wall had been erected beyond. Still those ponderous blows fell, more of the wall broke away.

Yet Foskatt, showing no signs of fear, watched this as if it were what he expected. Then he spoke, raising his voice so they could hear over the sounds of that pounding.

"This is one of the Demons' servants from the old days. It obeys my will through this." He indicated the caller. "When it breaks through to us we must be ready to mount on top. And it will carry us out of this evil den. But we must be swift, for these servants have a limit on their period of service. When this"—again he brought the caller their notice—"ceases to buzz, these servants die, and we cannot again awaken them. Nor do we ever know how long that life will last."

There was a sharp crash. Through the wall broke what looked to be a long black arm. It swept around, clearing the hole. Instantly, at its appearance, Foskatt thrust his tongue into the opening in the cube. The arm stopped its sweeping, was still, as if pointing directly to them. Behind it they could see the dark bulk of the nimbler, solid as a wall.

"We must get on it—quick!" Foskatt tried to rise but his weakened body failed him.

Furtig, at his side, turned to face the stranger.

"Help me!" He made that an order. The other hesitated. He had been heading for the break in the wall. But now he turned back, though it was plain he came reluctantly.

Together they raised Foskatt, though their handling must have been a torment, for he let out a small mewling cry at their touch. Then he was silent as they somehow got him through the broken door, raised him to the back of the boxlike thing.

It had more than one of those jutting arms, all of them quiet now. And it was among their roots that they settled their burden. How the thing had arrived they could not determine, for they could see no legs.

But that it had come with ruthless determination was plain by the crushed bodies of the Rattons lying here and there.

Once on top, Furtig looked to Foskatt. How did they now bring to life this Demon nimbler? Would it indeed carry them on?

"Brother!" Furtig bent over his tribesman. "What do we now?"

But Foskatt lay with closed eyes, and did not answer. The stranger growled.

"He cannot tell you. Perhaps he is near death. At least we are free of that hole. So—I shall make the most of such freedom."

Before Furtig could hinder him, he jumped from the top of the servant and ran in long leaping bounds into the dimness beyond. But, greatly as he was tempted to follow, the old belief that one ought not to desert a tribesman held Furtig where he was.

He could hear distant squealing. More Rattons must

be gathering ahead. Now he no longer believed that
the stranger had made the best choice. He could well
be heading into new captivity.

As would happen to them unless—Furtig pried at
Foskatt's hold on the caller. Tongue tip had gone in
there, and the servant had come. Again tongue tip,
and the rumbler had stopped beating down the wall.
Therefore the caller ordered it. If that were so, why
could Furtig not command it now?

He brought it close to his mouth. How had Foskatt
done it? By some pressure like the sign language?
Furtig knew no code. All he was sure of was that
he wanted to get the rumbler away from here, back
to Gammage, if that was where it had come from.

Well, he could only try. Gingerly, not knowing
whether the caller might punish a stranger without
learning for attempting to use it, Furtig inserted his
tongue and tried to press. A sharp tingling sensation
followed, but he held steady.

There was an answering vibration in the box on
which he crouched. The arms pulled back from the
wall, and the thing began to move.

Furtig caught at Foskatt lest he be shaken loose as
the rumbler trundled back from the wall and slewed
around, so that the arms now pointed toward the
broken door of the room.

They did not move fast, no faster than a walk, but the
rumbler never paused. And Furtig knew a new feeling
of power. He had commanded this thing! It might not
take them to Gammage as he wished it to do, but at
least it was bearing them away from the Ratton prison,
and he believed that those slinkers would not dare to
attack again as long as Foskatt and he rode this servant.

Foskatt's warning of the uncertain life span of the Demons' servants remained. But Furtig would not worry about that now. He was willing to take what good fortune was offered in the present.

They slid away from the light of the Ratton-held chambers. But now the rumbler provided light of its own. For two of those arms extended before it bore on their ends small circles of radiance.

This was not a natural passage like the cave ways; the Demons had built these walls. Furtig and the wounded Foskatt rumbled past other doorways, twice taking angled turns into new ways. It would seem that for all the sky-reaching heights of the lairs aboveground, there was a matching spread of passages beneath the surface.

Furtig's ears pricked. They had not outrun, probably could not outrun, pursuit. Behind he heard the high-voiced battle cries of the Rattons. At least he was well above their heads on the box and so had that small advantage.

Hurriedly he used Foskatt's own belt to anchor him to the arms of the rumbler, leaving himself free for any defense tactics needed. With the claws on his hands, he hunched to wait.

Strange smells here. Not only those natural to underground places, but others he could not set name to. Then the nimbler halted in front of what seemed a blank wall, and Furtig speedily lost what small confidence had carried him this far. They were going to be trapped; all this servant of Gammage had bought them was a little time.

But, though the rumbler had halted, its outthrust arms moved. They were doing nothing Furtig could understand, merely jerking up and down, shining round spots of light on the wall here and there.

There was a dull grating sound. The wall itself split in a wide crack, not such as those arms had beaten in the prison wall, but clean, as if this was a portal meant to behave in this fashion. As soon as the opening was wide enough, the rumbler moved on into a section which was again lighted. Furtig looked back; the wall started to shut even as they passed through. He gave a small sigh of relief as he saw the opening close. At least no Ratton was coming through there!

But the rumbler no longer moved steadfastly; rather it went slower and slower, finally stopping with its arms curled back upon its body. Now it looked—Furtig's woods-wise mind made the quick comparison—like a great black spider dying. When the rumbler ceased to move he lifted the caller to his mouth, readied his tongue. This time there was no tingling response to his probing. It must be as Foskatt had warned—the servant had died, if one might term it so.

There was light here, and they were in another corridor with numerous doors. Furtig hesitated for a long moment and then dropped to the floor. Leaving Foskatt where he was, he went to the nearest opening to look within.

The room was not empty. Most of the floor was covered with metal boxes, firmly based. And there was an acrid smell which made him sneeze and shake his head to banish it from his nostrils. Nothing moved, and his ears, fully alert, could not pick up the slightest sound.

He returned to the rumbler. If that could not carry them farther, and Foskatt could not be transported, what was he to do? When he was the merest youngling, he had learned the importance of memory patterns, of learning the ways of the People's tribal hunting grounds until those became a matter of subconscious recall rather than conscious thinking. But here he had no such pattern as a guide, he had only—

Furtig scrambled up to sit beside Foskatt. There was one thing—If they had in truth been heading toward Gammage's headquarters when this journey began, he could try—He closed his eyes, set about methodically to blank out the thought of what lay immediately around him.

He must use his thoughts as if they were ears, eyes, nose, to point to what he sought. This could be done, had been done many times over, by some individuals among the People. But Furtig had never been forced to try it before.

He had never seen Gammage, but so well was the Ancestor fixed in the mind of all who dwelt in the caves, that he had heard him described many times over. Now he tried to build in his mind a picture of Gammage. And, because the Ancestor was who he was and had been to his tribe a figure of awe and wonder across several generations, doubtless that mind picture was different from the person it represented, being greater than reality.

As he had never tried before, Furtig strove now to think of Gammage, to discover where in the lairs he could find this leader. So far—nothing. Perhaps he was one of those for whom such searching did not work. Each of the People had his own abilities, his own weaknesses. When the People worked together, one could supply what another lacked, but here Furtig had only himself. Gammage—where was Gammage?

It was like picking out the slightest ripple in the grass, hearing a sound so thin and far away that it was not true sound at all but merely the alerting suggestion of it. But a warm flush of triumph heated Furtig. It was true—he had done it! That sense would lead him now. Lead him. He opened his eyes to look at Foskatt.

What of Foskatt? It was plain that the other could not walk, nor could Furtig carry him. He could leave, return later—But perhaps that wall which had opened and closed was not the only entrance. One dared not underrate the tenacity of the Rattons. Long before Furtig could return with help, Foskatt could be captive or dead.

Suppose that somewhere in one of these chambers along this way he could find another of these servants, one which could be activated? It would do no harm to go and look, and it might be their only chance.

Furtig began the search. But he found himself moving slowly, needing to stop now and then to lean against the wall. All of a sudden, now that the excitement of their escape had died, he needed rest. He fed on some of the dried meat from Eu-La's bag. But it was hard to choke down even a few mouthfuls of that without water. And where was he going to find water?

Determinedly Furtig prowled among those metal boxes set in the first chamber, finding nothing useful. Stubbornly he went on to explore the next room.

This was different in that it had tables, long ones, and those tables were crowded with masses of things he did not understand at all. He backed away from one where the brush of his tail had knocked off a large basin. The basin shattered on the floor, and the sound of the crash was magnified a hundred times by echoes.

Furtig's startled jump almost brought him to disaster. For he struck against what seemed a smaller table, and that moved! He whirled around, expecting an attack, snarling. The table went on until it bumped against one of the larger tables.

Warily Furtig hooked his claws lightly about one of its slender legs. Very cautiously he pulled the small table back. It answered so readily, he was again startled. Then he mastered surprise, and experimented.

The surface was high, he could barely touch the top with his chin when he stood at his tallest. There was a mass of brittle stuff lying across it, and when he tried to investigate, it broke and powdered, so that he swept it off, leaving a bare surface.

But he could move the table!

Pushing and pulling, he brought it out of the room, back to the side of the rumbler. Luckily there was only a short space between the two levels, the table being a little lower. He was sure he could get Foskatt from one to the other.

Blood was seeping again from the matted fur about Foskatt's wound by the time Furtig had finished. He settled the unconscious tribesman in the center of the table, hoping he would not roll, as there was no anchorage here.

He fastened his belt to the two front legs of the table and then slung the end over one shoulder. It was a tight fit, the table bumping continually against his back and legs, and if it had not rolled so easily he could not have moved it. Resolutely he set out down the corridor.

There were times following, which could have been
night and day, or day and night, since Furtig could
no longer measure time so here—times when he
believed that he could not go on. He would hunch
down, the table looming over him, breathing so hard
it hurt his lower ribs. His whole body was so devoted
to pulling the table that he was not really aware of
anything save that he had not yet reached the place
to which he must go.

On and on, and there was no end, from corridor
to room, across room, to another hall. The lights grew
brighter, the strange smells stronger. He was never
sure when the vibration in the walls began. It might
have started long before his dulled senses recorded
it. There was a feeling of life here...

Furtig leaned against the wall. At least there was
no smell of Ratton. And they were still heading in
the right direction.

Then he really looked about him. The corridor
down which they had just come ended at a wall. And
if this was like the wall the servant had opened, well,
he did not have the ability to get through it. Leaving
the table, he shambled forward to examine it better.

What was happening to him? This was the bottom
of a shaft, much the same as the one he had fallen
down earlier. But now—he was going up! Gently, as
if the air itself was pushing him.

Frantically Furtig fought, managed to catch hold of
the shaft entrance and pull out of that upward current.
As he dropped to the ground, he was shaken out of
that half-stupor which had possessed him.

It was plain, as plain as such a marvel could be,
that here the shaft reversed the process of the other

one. And it was also plain that Gammage—or what his search sense had fastened on as Gammage—was above.

Would this mysterious upward current take the table also? He could only try. Pulling, he got it into the shaft. Foskatt's body stirred, drifting up from the surface. So—it worked on him, but not on the table. Wearily Furtig accepted that, kept his hold on his tribesman as they began to rise together.

It took a long time, but Furtig, in his weariness, did not protest that. He watched dully as they slid past one opening and then another. Each must mark a different level of these vast underground ways, even as the caves opened from two ledges. Up and up—

Four levels up and Furtig's search sense gave the signal—this one! Towing the limp Foskatt, he made swimming motions to take them to the opening. And he had just enough strength to falter through, out of the pull of the current, to the floor beyond.

He lay there beside Foskatt, panting, his sides and back aching from his effort. What now? But he was too worn out to face anything more—not now. And that thought dimmed in his mind as his head fell forward to rest on his crooked arm.

➤ 5 ◄

Furtig came out of sleep, aware even before he opened his eyes that he was not alone. What he sniffed was not the musky scent of Ratton, but rather the reassuring odor of his own kin. With that, another smell, which brought him fully awake—food! And not the dried rations of his traveling either.

He was lying on a pallet not unlike those of the caves. And, waiting beside him, holding a bowl which sent out that enticing fragrance, was a female he had never seen before. She was remarkable enough to let him know he was among strangers. And he gaped at her in a way which should have brought her fur rising, set her to a warning hiss.

Fur—that was it! Though she had a goodly show of silky, silvery fur on her head and along her shoulders, yet on the rest of her body it was reduced to the thinnest down, through which it was easy to see her skin.

And those hands holding the bowl—the fingers were not stubby like his own but longer, thinner. Furtig did not know whether he liked what he saw of her, he was only aware that she was different enough to keep him staring like a stupid youngling.

"Eat—" She held the bowl closer. Her voice had a tone of command. Also it was as different as her body was from those he knew.

Furtig took the bowl and found its contents had been cut into easily handled strips. As he gnawed, and the warm, restorative juices flowed down his throat, he came fully to attention. The female had not left and that disconcerted him again. Among the People this was not the custom—the males had their portion of the caves, the females another.

"You are Furtig of the Ancestor's cave—"

"How did you—"

"Know that? Did you not bring back Foskatt, who knows you?"

"Foskatt!" For the first time since his waking, Furtig remembered his tribesman. "He is hurt   the Rattons   "

"Hurt, yes. But he is now in the healing place of the Demons. We"—there was pride in her tone—"have learned many of the Demons' secrets. They could heal as well as kill. And every day we learn more and more. If we are given the chance we shall know all that they knew..."

"But not to use that knowledge to the same purposes, Liliha."

Startled, Furtig looked beyond the female. The soft tread of any of his race should not be entirely noiseless, but he had been so intent he had not been aware of a newcomer. And looking up—

"Famed Ancestor!" He set down the bowl with a bump which nearly shook out what was left of its contents, hastened to make the gesture of respect due

the greatest Elder of them all. But to his pride (and
a little discomfort, were the full truth to be known),
Gammage hunkered down by him and touched noses
in the full acceptance of the People.

"You are Furtig, son of Fuffor, son of Foru, son
of another Furtig who was son of my son," Gammage recited as a true Elder, one trained to keep
in memory clan and tribe generations through the
years. "Welcome to the lairs, warrior. It would seem
that your introduction here has been a harsh one."

Gammage was old; the very descent lines he had
stated made him older than any Elder Furtig had ever
known. Yet there was something about him which
suggested vigor, though now perhaps more vigor of
mind than of body.

Like the female's fur, though she was clearly young
and not old, Gammage's body fur was sparse. And
that body was thin, showing more bony underlining
than padded muscle.

He wore not just the belt common to all the People
but a long piece of fabric fastened at his throat, flowing back over his shoulders. This somehow gave him
added stature and dignity. He also had about his neck
a chain of shining metal links and from that hung a
cube not unlike the one Foskatt had carried. While
his hands—

Furtig's gaze lingered. Whoever had he seen among
the People with such hands! They were narrower, the
fingers longer and thinner even than those of the
female. Yes, in all ways Gammage was even stranger
than the old tales made him.

"Eat now." Gammage gestured to the bowl. "Within
the lairs we need all the strength food can give us.

Rattons"—his voice deepened to a growl—"Rattons establishing their own place here! Rattons attempting to gain Demon knowledge! And so little time perhaps before we shall be called upon to face the Demons themselves." Now his voice became a growl without words, the sound of one about to offer battle.

"But of that we can speak later. Furtig, what say they of me now in the caves? Are they still of like mind—that I speak as with the mindless babble of the very young? The truth, warrior, the truth is of importance!"

And such was the compelling force of the Ancestor's tone that Furtig answered with the truth.

"The Elders—Fal-Kan—they say that you plan to give Demon secrets to strangers, even to the Barkers. They call you—"

"Traitor to my kind?" Gammage's tail twitched. "Perhaps in their narrow viewing I might be termed so—now. But the day comes when the People, plus the Barkers, plus the Tusked Ones, will have to stand together or perish. Of the Rattons I do not speak thus, for there is that in them akin to what I have learned of the Demons. And when the Demons return, the Rattons may run with them to overturn all our lives."

"The Demons return?" Listening to the note of certainty in the Ancestor's voice made Furtig believe that Gammage was sure of what he said. And if he truly believed that, yes, would it not be better to make truce even with Barkers against a common and greater enemy?

"Time!" Gammage brought those odd hands of his together in a clap to echo through the room. "Time is our great need and we may not have it. We have so many lesser needs, such as the one which took Foskatt into that section of the lairs we had not fully explored, seeking hidden records. But, though he did not find what he sought, he has alerted us to this new danger, a Ratton base on the very edge of our own territory. Let the Rattons learn but this much"—Gammage measured off between two fingers no more than the width of one of them—"of what we have found here, and they will make themselves masters, not only of the lairs, but of the world beyond. Say that to your Elders, Furtig, and perhaps you will find they will listen, even though they willfully close their ears to a worse threat."

"Foskatt was seeking something?"

Gammage had fallen silent, his eyes on the wall beyond Furtig, as if he saw there something which was as plain to be read as a hunting trail, and yet to be dreaded.

"Foskatt?" Gammage repeated as if the name were strange. Then once more his intent gaze focused on Furtig. "Foskatt—he was hardly handled, near to ending, when you brought him back to us, warrior. But now he heals. So great were the Demons—life and death in their two hands. But they played games with those powers as a youngling plays with sticks or bright stones, games which have no meaning. Save that when games are played as the Demons play them, they have grim consequences.

"They could do wonderful things. We learn more and more each day. They could actually make rain fall as they pleased, keep the sun shining as they would. There was no great cold where they ruled and—But they were not satisfied with such, they must do more, seeking the knowledge of death as well as of life. And at last their own learning turned against them."

"But if they are all dead, why then do you speak of their return?" Furtig dared to ask. His initial awe at seeing Gammage had eased. It was like climbing a mountain to find the way not so difficult as it had looked from the lowlands. That Gammage could impress, he did not doubt. There was that about him which was greater than the Elders. But he did not use it consciously as they did to overawe younger tribesmen.

"Not all died," Gammage said slowly. "But they are not here. We have tracked them through this, their last lair. When I first began that search we found their bodies, or what was left of them. But once we discovered the knowledge banks we also uncovered evidence that some had withdrawn, that they would come again. It was more concerning that second coming that Foskatt sought. But you will learn, Furtig—There is so much to learn—" Again Gammage gazed at the wall, rubbing one hand on the other. "So much to learn," he repeated. "More and more we uncover Demon secrets. Give us time, just a little more time!"

"Which the Rattons threaten now." Liliha broke into the Ancestor's thoughts, amazing Furtig even more. The fact that she had not withdrawn at Gammage's arrival had surprised him. But that she would speak so to the Ancestor, almost as if to an unlessoned youngling, bringing him back to face some matter which could not be avoided, was more startling yet.

However Gammage appeared to accept her interruption as proper. For he nodded.

"True, Liliha, it is not well to forget today in

considering tomorrow. I shall see you again and soon, cave son. Liliha will show you this part of the lairs which we have made our own."

He pulled the fabric tighter about him and was gone with the speed of a warrior years younger. Furtig put down the bowl and eyed the female uncertainly. It was plain that the customs of the caves did not hold here in the lairs. Yet it made him uncomfortable to be left alone with a Chooser.

"You are not of the caves," he ventured, not knowing just how one began speech with a strange female.

"True. I am of the lairs. I was born within these walls."

That again amazed Furtig. For all his life he had heard of warriors "going to Gammage," but not females. But that they carried on a normal manner of life here was a minor shock. Until he realized the limit of his preconceptions concerning Gammage's people. Why should they not have a normal life? But whence had come their females?

"Gammage draws more than just those of his own tribe," she went on, as if reading his thoughts. "There are others of the People, on the far side of the lairs, distant from your caves. And over the seasons Gammage has sent messengers to them also. Some listen to him more closely than his blood kin seem to." Furtig thought he detected in that remark the natural air of superiority which a Chooser would use on occasion with a warrior.

"There is now a new tribe here, formed from those of many different clans," she continued in the same faintly superior tone. "It has been so since my mother's mother's time. We who are born here, who learn early the knowledge of the Demons, are different in ways from those outside the lairs, even from those who choose to join us here. In such ways as this do the In-born differ." She put forth her hand, holding it in line with Furtig's. Not with their flesh, making contact, but side by side for comparison.

Her longer, more slender fingers were in even greater contrast when held against his. Now she wriggled them as if taking pride in their appearance.

"These"—she waved her hand slightly—"are better able to use Demon machines."

"And being born among those machines makes you so?"

"Partly, Gammage thinks. But there are also places the Demons use for healing, such as that in which Foskatt now lies. When a mother is about to bear her younglings she is taken there to wait. Also, when she first knows she has young within her, she goes to that place and sits for a space. Then her young come forth with changes. With hands such as these I can do much that I could not do—"

She paused, and he finished for her, "With such as mine." He remembered how he had used his tongue, as had Foskatt, in the cube hole. Perhaps, had he had fingers such as Liliha's, he need not have done that.

"Such as yours," she agreed evenly. "Now, Gammage would have you see the lairs, so come. We have," she told him, "a thing to ride on. It does not go outside this one lair, though we have tried to make it do so. We cannot understand such limitations. But here it is of service."

She brought forward something which moved more swiftly than the nimbler on which they had ridden out of the Ratton prison. But this was smaller and it had two seats—so large Furtig was certain they had been made to accommodate Demons, not People.

Liliha half-crouched well to the front of one seat. Leaning well forward, she clasped a bar in both hands. He guessed that she was uncomfortable in such a strained position, but she made no complaint, only waited until he climbed into the other seat.

Then she drew the bar back toward her. With that the carrier came to life, moved forward smoothly and swiftly.

That there was need for such a conveyance became clear as they swept ahead. And things which astounded Furtig at first became commonplace as he saw other and more awesome ones succeed them. Some, Liliha told him, they did not understand and had found no way to use—though teams of workers, specially trained by Gammage, and at intervals under his personal supervision, still tried to solve such problems.

But the learning machines, those Gammage had early activated. And the food for them was contained in narrow disks wound with tape. When Liliha fitted one of these into a box and pressed certain buttons, a series of pictures appeared on the wall before them. While out of the air came a voice speaking in a strange tongue. Furtig could not even reproduce most of the sounds.

However, there was another thing, too large to wear comfortably, which Furtig put on his head. This had small buttons to be fitted into the ears. When that was done, the words became plain, though some had no meaning. One watched the pictures and listened to the words and one learned. After a while, Furtig was told, he would not need the translator but would be able to understand without it.

Furtig was excited as he had not been since he had forced himself to face up to the Trials, knowing well he might lose. Only this time it was an excitement of triumph and not of determination to meet defeat. Given time (now he could understand Gammage's preoccupation with time in a way no cave dweller could) one could learn all the Demons' secrets!

He would have liked to have lingered there. But the chamber was occupied by Gammage's people, one of whom Liliha had persuaded to allow Furtig to sample the machine, and they were plainly impatient to get along with their work. Perhaps they had allowed such an interruption at all only because Furtig had been sent by Gammage.

For Furtig was not finding the warriors here friendly. They did not show the wary suspicion of strange tribesmen. No, this was more the impatience of an Elder with a youngling—a none-too-bright youngling. Furtig found that attitude hard for his pride to swallow.

Most of these workers displayed the same bodily differences—the slender hands, the lessening of body fur—as Liliha. But there were a few among them not different, save in coloring, from himself, and they were as impatient as their fellows.

Furtig tried to ignore the attitude of the workers, think only of what they were doing. But after a space, that, too, was sobering and disappointing. He, who was a trained warrior, a hunter of some note, an accepted defender of the caves (a status which had given him pride), was here a nothing. And the result of his tour with Liliha was a depression and the half-thought that he had much better return to his own kind.

Until they reached Foskatt. They stood in an outer

room and looked through a wall (for it was the truth that here you could see through certain walls). Within was a pallet and on it lay the tribesman.

The lighting in the room differed from that where Furtig stood with Liliha. Also it rippled just as wind rippled field grass. Furtig could find no explanation of what he saw there. There was light, and it moved in waves washing back and forth across Foskatt.

The wounded warrior's eyes were closed. His chest rose and fell as if he slept, rested comfortably without pain or dreams. His wounded leg was no longer bloody, the fur matted with clots. A scar had begun to form over the slash.

Furtig, knowing how it might have gone had Foskatt lain so in the caves, how many died from lesser wounds in spite of the best tending their clanspeople could give them, drew a long breath. It was but one more of the wonders he had been shown, yet to him, because he could best appreciate the results, it was one of the most awesome.

"This can be done for the coughing sickness?" he asked. He had set his two hands flat on the surface of that see-through wall, pushed so close even his nose touched it.

"This can be done for any illness," Liliha told him, "as well as most hurts. There is only one it cannot cure so."

"That being?" A certain shading of her voice had made him turn his head to look at her. For the first time he could see uneasiness in her expression, the superiority gone.

"Gammage found a thing of the Demons. It spouts a mist—and when that meets flesh—" She shuddered.

"It is the worst handwork of the Demons we have seen. There is no halting what happens to one unfortunate enough to be caught in the mist." She shivered again. "It is not even to be thought upon! Gammage had it destroyed!"

"Ah, and what do you think now of the lairs, Furtig?"

Gammage stood behind them. His sudden appearances—how did the Ancestor manage thus to arrive without warning?

"They are full of marvels."

"Marvels upon marvels," the Ancestor agreed. "And we have hardly touched the edge of what is stored here! Given time, just given time—" Once more he stared at the wall, as if his thoughts set a barrier between him and those he addressed.

"What I do not understand"—Furtig dared now to break in upon that withdrawal—"is why, when the Demons knew so much, they came to such an end."

Gammage looked at him, his gray frost-furred face alight.

"It was because they were greedy. They took and took, from the air, the earth, the water. And when they realized that they had taken too much and tried to return it, they were too late. Some went—we cannot yet read their records well enough to know how or where. They seem to have flown into the sky—"

"Like birds? But they were not winged, were they? Those I have seen represented..."

"Just so," Gammage agreed briskly. "But we have good evidence that they had some means of flight. So, a number of them flew away. Of those who were left—well, it seems that they worked very hard and fast to find some way of restoring the land. One of their attempted remedies became instead their doom. We have found two records of that.

"What developed was an illness like our coughing sickness. Some it killed at once. Others—it altered their minds so they became like those Barkers who foam at the mouth and tear madly at their own kin. But with all it had one sure effect: They bore no more younglings.

"Also—" Gammage hesitated as if what he would say now was an important thing, a wise utterance of an Elder. "This sickness had another effect. For it made us, the People, the Barkers, the Tusked Ones, even the Rattons, what we are.

"This is the thing we have learned, Furtig. We were once like the rabbits, the deer, the wild cattle we hunt for food. But we had some contact with the Demons. There is good evidence that some of us lived with them here in the lairs, and that"—his voice grew deeper, closer to a warrior's growl—"that they used us to try out their discoveries, so we were their servants to be used, killed, hurt, or maimed at their will.

"But it was because of this that we grew in our minds—as the Demons dwindled and died. For they forced on us their fatal sickness, trying to discover some cure. But us it did not slay nor render sterile. Instead, though our females had fewer younglings, those younglings were different, abler in ways.

"And the Demons, learning too late that they had set those they considered lowly servants on a trail which would lead those servants to walk as their equals, tried then to hunt them down and slay them, since they wished not that we should live when they died. But many escaped from the lairs, and those were our forefathers, and those of the Barkers, and the Tusked Ones.

"The Rattons went underground, and because they were much smaller, even than they are today, they could hide where the Demons could not find them. And they lived in the dark, waiting, breeding their warriors.

"The hunting of our people by the Demons was a time of great pain and terror and darkness. And it set in us a fear of the lairs, so great a fear that it kept our people away, even when the last Demon met death. That was a disservice to us, for it cost us time. And even now, when I send to the tribes and tell them of the wonders waiting them here, few conquer their fears and come."

"But if we learn the Demon's knowledge," asked Furtig slowly, "will not all their evil learning perhaps be mixed with the good, so that in the end we will go the same way?"

"Can we ever forget what happened to them? Look about you, Furtig. Is there forgetting here? No, we can accept the good, remembering always that we must not say 'I am mightier than the world which holds me, it is mine to be used as I please!'"

What Gammage said was exciting. But, Furtig wondered, would it awake the same excitement in, say, such an Elder as Fal-Kan? The People of the caves, of the western tribe, were well content with life as it was. They had their customs, and a warrior did this or that, spoke thus, even as his father before him. A female became a Chooser and set up her own household, even as her mother. Ask them to break such patterns and be as these of Gammage's clan, who paid more attention to learning the ways of Demons than to custom? He could foresee a greater difficulty than Gammage could imagine in that. Look at what the Elders now said of the Ancestor, in spite of his years of free giving, because he had tried to breach custom in a few of their ways.

➤ 6 ◄

While he was with Gammage, listening to the Ancestor, inwardly marveling at the fact that it was because of the will and curiosity of this single member of his own cave that the lairs had been invaded, that its secrets were being pried open, Furtig could believe that this Elder was right. Nothing mattered save that they learn, and learn in a race against time with some invisible enemy who might at any moment arrive to do battle. And that the only weapons which would adequately protect them were those they still sought in that time race.

However, Furtig's own part was not only insignificant but humiliating. For he, a seasoned warrior, must return to the status of youngling, studying with those half his age, even less. For learning here did not go by seasons reckoned from one's birth, but rather by the speed with which one absorbed lessons in the instruction rooms.

He wore that ill-fitting headgear until his head ached. So equipped, he watched pictures flit across the wall, listened to that gabble of voice wherein about every third word had no meaning for a hunter-warrior. And those in the room sharing these periods of instruction were all so young!

The air of superiority worn by the lair people chilled him, seemed to erect an unscalable barrier. The adults Furtig dealt with were curt, always hurried. If they had any leisure, they spent it in some section to which he had not been invited. None were interested in Furtig as an individual, but merely as another mind to be pushed and pulled through learning.

His resentment grew, coloring what he learned. Though at times there were things so interesting he forgot his frustrations and became genuinely enthralled. He was especially fascinated with the series dealing with the latter days of the Demons—though why they had wished to leave such a sorry record, save as a warning, he could not understand.

He learned to hate as he had never hated the Barkers, though his detestation of the Rattons approached it, when he saw those sections dealing with the hunting down of his own people after they had not only proven to be able to withstand the disease wiping out the Demons, but had benefited in some ways from it. The ferocity of the Demons was a red madness, and Furtig, watching them, broke into growls, lashed his tail, and twice struck out at the pictured Demons with his war claws. He came to himself to see the younglings cowering away from him, staring as if the horrible madness of the Demons had spread to him. But he was not ashamed of his response. It was so that any warrior would face the enemy.

During this time he saw nothing of Liliha. And

only once or twice did Gammage make one of his sudden appearances, ask a little vaguely if all were well, and go again.

Furtig longed to ask questions, but there was no one who showed enough awareness of his presence to allow him to do so. What did they all do? Had anything at all been discovered to hold off any Demons who might return? What and what and what—and sometimes who and who and who? Only there was no one he could approach.

Not until one day when he returned to his own chamber, that in which he had first awakened and which apparently had been given to him (the lairs were so large there was no end to the rooms to be used), and found Foskatt sitting on his bed.

It was like meeting a cave brother—so Furtig thought of the other now.

"You are healed?" He really did not need to ask that. There was only the faintest trace of a scar seam, hardly to be seen now, where mangled flesh had once oozed blood.

"Well healed." Foskatt's upper lip wrinkled in a wide grin. "Tell me, brother, how did you get me here? They say that we were found at the door of a rise shaft. But I know from my own hunting in the ways below that we were far from that when we had our last speech together. And what became of that Ku-La, who was with us in the stinking Ratton pen?"

Furtig explained the break-through of the rumbler. Foskatt nodded impatiently. "That I know. But how did you control it? I must have gone into darkness then."

"I did as you did, used my tongue in the cube," Furtig replied. "We put you on the top of the rumbler

and it carried us—but the stranger you name Ku-La
would not come. He went on his own. And since the
Rattons were everywhere"—Furtig gave a tail flick—"I
do not believe he made it."

"A pity. He would have been a useful contact with
a new tribe. But if you used the caller—how did you?
Touch starts the servants, yes, but you would not know
the proper touch for a command."

"I put in my tongue and it started," Furtig repeated.
"I gave no command—"

"But what did you think when you did that?" Foskatt persisted.

"Of Gammage and the need for reaching him."

"Just so!" Foskatt got to his feet and began to stride
up and down. "It is as I suspected—one touches, but
it is not the touch alone as they have said, the pressure
once, twice, and all the rest they would have us learn. It
is the thought which directs those! For you have proved
that. You knew no touch pattern, you merely thought of
where you would like to be—and it traveled for you!"

"Until it died," commented Furtig, "which it did."

"But if it died, how then did you have any guide
through the ways?" Foskatt halted, stared at Furtig.

"I—" Furtig tried to find the proper words. "I tried
hunting search—"

"The person tie!" Foskatt's eyes grew even wider.
"But you did not know Gammage, had no tie with him."

"None except that I am of his blood kin in direct
descent," Furtig agreed. "I do not know how I was
able to do this thing, but I did. Had I not, neither
one of us would be standing here now." He added to
his tale the finding of the moving table, their arrival
at the shaft, rising to the right level via that.

"Has Gammage heard this?" demanded Foskatt when he had done.

"No one has asked how we got here. They probably think you played guide." For the first time Furtig realized this. He had been overwhelmed by the wonders of the lairs, yet no one had asked him questions in return.

"But he must be told! Only a few of us can so depend upon hunting search." Foskatt's moving tail betrayed his excitement. "And never have I heard of a case wherein it could be used if the two involved were not close. This may mean that there are other changes in us, ones which are important." He started for the door as if to hunt immediately for Gammage. Furtig moved to intercept him.

"Not yet. Not until we are sure."

"Why not? Gammage must hear, must test—"

"No!" That was almost a warning growl. "In this place I am a youngling, fit only for lessoning with those still warm from their mothers' nests. If I claim some talent I do not have, then I shall be rated even less. And that I will not have!"

"So once did I believe also," Foskatt answered. "But all that matters is learning something to add to the knowledge of all."

Now it was Furtig's turn to stare, for it seemed Foskatt meant that. Of course a warrior stood ready to defend his home cave. But, except when pressed by battle, a warrior was concerned not with others but with himself, his pride. And to keep that pride, those who lost at the Trials wandered. If he had not done so himself, he would have been less than an untried youngling in the eyes of his own clan. Yet now Foskatt calmly said that he must risk the jeers of strangers for no good reason—for to Furtig the reason he offered was far from good.

"Do you think I was welcomed here, by any but Gammage?" Foskatt asked then. "To stand as a warrior in the lairs one must have something to give which others recognize as worthy of notice. And since the In-born have always had the advantage, that is difficult. It is a Trial in another fashion from our own."

"How did you then impress them with your worth?"

"By doing what I was doing when the Rattons took me. It would seem that the gain of one kind of knowledge is sometimes balanced by the loss of another. How learned you the hunting lands of the caves, brother?"

"By running them, putting them in my mind so I could find them day or night."

"Yes, we have a place here"—Foskatt tapped his forehead with one stub finger—"to store that knowledge. Having once traveled a path we do not mistake it again. But the In-born, they do not possess so exact a sense of direction. If they go exploring they must mark that trail so that they will know it again. And with the Rattons invading, that is the last thing we want, trails to direct the enemy into our territory. Therefore we who have not lost that inner sense of homing, we do the scouting. Look you, Furtig, do you not see that you have something more of benefit even than that which is common to all of us? If we can find out how you are able to fix upon one you have never seen, use him as a guide, then we shall be even more free to explore."

"Free to face Rattons? You can trace them by the stink alone."

"Rattons, no. Any one of us could spy upon Rattons. Nor does that duty need us going on two feet or four, or will soon. For the In-born have recently found another device of the Demons which moves through the air—though it has no wings. As it moves so it gathers pictures of what lies beneath it and sends those back to be viewed at a distance—"

"If Gammage has such a thing, why did he not use it to see you taken by the Rattons and come to your aid?" Furtig interrupted. He had seen many marvels here, but the idea of a flying picture taker—Only, Foskatt was not making up a tale for younglings; it was plain he meant every word.

"For two reasons. First it has not been tested to the full. Second, it is again as with the other servants; these spy boxes fly only for a short space. Then they ground and there is nothing to be done to get them aloft again. Either the Demons had some way of infusing life into them at intervals, or they have grown too old to be trusted.

"But what I went to find was knowledge. You have seen the disks of tape which are fed into the learning machines. It is from these that Gammage and others have learned all they know about the machines and secrets of the Demons. However these disks are not stored in one place. We have found them here, there, in many places. Though why the Demons scattered them about so is a mystery. Gammage has a theory that all of one kind of learning was kept together, then the kinds separate. A little time ago he found what may be a guide to locate several different stores, but that was guessing. Much we learn here must be connected by guessing. Even when we hear the

Demons' words, we know only perhaps half of them. Others, even though many times repeated, we are not sure of. When we can add a new word, be sure of its meaning, it is a time of joy.

"It has long been Gammage's hope that if we uncover all the tapes, use them together, we can learn enough to run all the servants of the Demons without the failures that now make them unreliable. And with such servants, is there any limit to what we may do?"

"Some, perhaps," Furtig said. "Did the Demons not think that once also? And they were limited in the end. Or so it seems."

"Yes, there is that danger. Still—what if the Demons return, and we are again their playthings—as we were before? Do you wish that, brother?"

"Playthings?"

"So they have not shown you that tape yet?" Foskatt's tail twitched. "Yes, brother, that we were—playthings of the Demons. Before the time when they began to use us in other ways—to learn from our torments of body what some of their discoveries would do to living creatures. Do you wish those days to return?"

"But this feeling Gammage has, that they will return—why is he so sure?"

"At the centermost point in the lairs there is a device we cannot begin to understand. But it is sending forth a call. This goes to the skies. We have tried to destroy it, but it is safeguarded too well to let us near. And it has been going so since the last Demon died.

"We have discovered the records of those Demons who took to flight when the last days came. If they escaped the disease which finished their tribe here, then that device may call them back."

So serious was Foskatt's tone that Furtig's ears flattened a little to his skull, his spine fur ridged. As Gammage had the power to enthrall when one listened to him, so did Foskatt now impress his companion with his conviction of this truth.

"But Gammage believes that if he has the Demons' own knowledge he can withstand them?"

"It will be a better chance for us. Which would you choose to be in battle, a warrior with claws or without? For weapons support one at such times. Thus we seek all these stores of disks to learn and learn. It may be even the next one we find which will teach us how to keep the servants running. But, as I said, Gammage thought he had heard such a store place described, and I went to seek it. The Rattons took me. They work with traps, brother, most cunningly. Since it was not known they were in that part of the lairs, I was taken. Nor can I hold my head high, for I was thinking more of what I hunted than the territory I moved through. So I suffered from my own carelessness, and would have paid full price if you had not come."

"But you would go again?"

"I will go again when I am needed. Now do you see, Furtig, what we have to offer here? We can be the seekers, using all the craft of the caves. And if it happens that you have something to better that seeking—"

Furtig remained unconvinced. "Not until I have proven it for myself," he repeated stubbornly.

"Prove it then!" Foskatt retorted.

"How can I? If I trail through Gammage again," Furtig pointed out, "then I am doing no more than our people have always been able to do."

"Not all our people. You know that well. It is a talent which varies."

"But it is not uncommon. I could fasten on you, on Gammage—and it would not be extraordinary. You found my sensing strange because I used the Ancestor when I had never seen him."

Foskatt limped a little as he strode back and forth, as if his wound plagued him somewhat. Now he sat down on the bed place.

"Let me tell Gammage, or better still, tell him yourself. Then perhaps he can see a way to test this—"

"I will think about it." Furtig held stubbornly to his own will. He was interested by all Foskatt had told him, impressed by the other's belief in the Ancestor and what he was doing here. But he wanted a chance to prove to himself that he need not fear the scorn of the In-born before making a bold claim.

"Did you know really what you sought when you fell into the Ratton trap?"

"A secret place holding learning tapes—but this, Gammage thought, was larger than most by the reference to it which he had discovered. He wanted to find more dealing with the skyward call. We had avoided that section, for twice we lost warriors to the protective devices of the Demons. Only at this new hint of the store place Gammage asked for volunteers, and I said I would go. For we of the caves have keener senses to detect what may lie in wait in places of danger. I was passing through what we thought a safe section when I was entrapped."

Foskatt seemed convinced that the cave-born had certain advantages over the In-born. Or did he cling to that thought because he, too, smarted from the superior airs of the In-born? Was he convinced, or had he convinced himself? It did not matter; Furtig was not going to put himself on trial until he could prove that he had something to offer. Though it seemed that Foskatt's story contained a clue as to how he might do so.

"How close were you to this place you hunted when the Rattons took you?"

"Some distance. I was taking a circle trail because I was not sure of Demon traps. Part of the first ways fell in with a loud noise when I tried to reach the signal."

"Closing off that section of the passage?"

"No, only the main trail. Look—"

From his belt pouch Foskatt brought out a slender stick. Its point, drawn along the floor, left a black line easy to see. With quick marks and explanations, he began to show Furtig the sweep of the underground ways. Though Furtig had never seen such a way of displaying a trail before, he grasped the advantages of this and commented on them.

"But this writing stick is nothing! Wait until you see—no, better—come and see!"

He put the stick away, scrambled up, and made for the door. Furtig, drawn along by his enthusiasm, followed Foskatt to his quarters.

Those were indeed different from the bare room in which Furtig had made his home since coming to the lairs. Here were two tables, their tops well burdened by masses of things Furtig was unable to sort out in the single glance or two he had time for before Foskatt drew him to the bed place, pushed him down to sit, and caught up a small box.

This was about as large as his two fists set together, and he pointed it at the wall. As with the learning devices there appeared a picture there, but this was a series of lines only. However, after a long moment of study Furtig began to recognize a resemblance between them and the ones Foskatt had drawn.

Foskatt wedged the box steady beside Furtig on the bed and then went to stand by the picture, thrusting his hand into it as he explained.

"We are here now!" An emphatic scrape of claw on the wall distorted the picture. Beginning so, he launched into a description of this corridor and that, up and down.

"If you have such as this," Furtig asked when he was done, "why do you need to search out these new trails in person?"

"Because these"—Foskatt came back and gave the box a tap and the picture disappeared—"are limited in what they show—each one portrays only a small section of the lairs. And if you cannot find the right box you have no guide."

"All this—" Furtig pointed to the mass of things on the tables. "What have you here?"

"Many things of worth for a scout. See, with this, one can carry food which is hot, and later open it and find the food still hot."

He turned a thick rod around in his hands. It split in two neatly.

"Food hot? But why should food be hot?"

"Wait and see!"

Foskatt put down the two pieces of rod and went to another box, much larger than that which had given the wall pictures. He took up a bowl in which

Furtig could see a strip of meat, scooped the meat out, placed it within a mouth opening on the box, and snapped the opening shut.

Within seconds Furtig sniffed such an odor as he had never smelled before. It was enticing and his mouth watered. Before he knew it he had given one of the small mews a youngling utters when he sees a filled food bowl. And, startled, he was ashamed.

Foskatt might not have heard. He opened once more the mouth of the box. The meat he took out was now brown and the odor from it was such that Furtig had to force himself to sit quietly until his tribesman offered it to him. It tasted as it looked, different from any meat he had ever mouthed, but very good.

"It is cooked," Foskatt said. "The Demons did so to all their food. When it is so treated and put into carrying things such as these"—he picked up the rod again—"then it does not turn bad for a long time. One can carry it and find it as hot as when it came from the cooker. Then there is this—" He picked up a band which went around his middle like a belt. It had been rather clumsily altered to fit Foskatt, and at the front was a round thing which, at his touch, blazed with light.

"This can be worn in a dark place to make light."

There seemed to be no end to Foskatt's store of Demon-made treasures. There were slender, pointed rods one could use for a multitude of purposes. Something he called a knife—like a single straight claw mounted on a stick—which cut cleanly.

In fact Furtig was shown so many different devices so hurriedly that he lost count, and it all became just a whirling mass of strange but highly intriguing objects.

"Where got you all these?"

"When I go seeking new trails I bring back things small enough to carry. Sometimes I can see their use at once. Other times I turn them over to others for study. Now here—"

Another box. This time at his touch no picture appeared on the wall, but a portion of its lid rolled back and within—!

Furtig did not muffle his hiss of astonishment.

It was as if he were very tall, taller than the lairs, and stood looking down into a part of the country near the caves. Animals moved there, he recognized deer. But they were not moving as the wall pictures moved, rather as if they lived as very tiny creatures within the box. Furtig put out a finger—there was an invisible cover, he could not touch.

"They are—alive?" He could not believe that this was so. Yet the illusion of reality was so great he still had doubts that such a thing could be if it were not real.

"No, they do not live. And sometimes the picture changes and becomes—Watch!" Foskatt's explanation ended in a sudden exclamation.

The world within the box was hidden in a gathering fog. Then that cleared and—Furtig began to shout:

"The caves! There is Fal-Kan and San-Lo. It is the caves!"

➤ 7 ◄

When Furtig glanced around Foskatt was not watching him, but staring at the cave scene as if he, too, found it astounding. Then Foskatt's hand shot out, his fingers tightened about Furtig's arm.

"Think," was his order. "Think of some particular place—or person—and look at this while you do so!"

Just what he meant Furtig could not understand. But when he heard the urgent tone in the other's voice he did not mistake its importance. Obediently he looked at the box—though what he should "think" about momentarily baffled him.

The scene of the tiny world was again obscured with the fog, the caves hidden. Then—just why he did not know—a mind picture of Eu-La as she had watched him leave on this venture came to him from memory.

Mist cleared, revealing a small rise north of the caves. But that was not quite the scene he remembered. Somehow small differences were vivid: more leaves had drifted from the trees, a patch of silver frost was on the grasses.

Then a figure climbed to stand, facing him. Eu-La, but not as he had seen her last. Again certain subtle differences marked the passage of time. Furtig had a jog of guilty memory when he thought of how she had asked him to speak for her to the Ancestor and of how, until now, he had forgotten. He must do that for her as soon as possible.

She shaded her eyes with her hands as if she stood in the full glare of the sun. No, this was no memory picture which Furtig was in some manner projecting into the box. It was independent of any memory of his.

"Who is she?" Foskatt demanded.

"Eu-La, who is of the Ancestor's cave kin. She is daughter to the sister of my mother, but much younger than I. At the next Trial of Skill she may go forth to another cave. Alone among the People she wished me well when I came to Gammage."

Mist once again, hiding Eu-La. When it faded, there was nothing inside, only empty dark. Furtig turned almost savagely upon his companion. He felt now as if he had been made the butt of some game in which he did not know the rules and so appeared stupid.

"What is this thing? Why does it make me see Eu-La and the caves when we are far off?"

Again Foskatt paced up and down, his tail swinging, his whole attitude that of a warrior disturbed in his mind.

"You have again proved, brother, that you have something new to our knowledge, though these lairs are full of things always new to us. That box has shown many pictures from time to time. At other times it is dark and empty as you now see it. I have looked upon the caves through it, seen distant kin of mine as I remember them. Only now you were able to summon, yes, summon, one person and see her perhaps as she lives and moves at this very hour! This is perhaps allied to that talent which guided you to the Ancestor. Do you understand? If we can use these"—he gestured to the box—"and see by only thinking of a person or thing we would look upon—"

He paused, his eyes agleam, and Furtig thought that now he was caught by a new idea.

"Listen, brother—look now at this and think of learning disks!"

Furtig thought of such disks as he had seen fed into the learning machines.

Straightaway a small picture, though dim, blurred, and fuzzed, came into view. There was the learning room in which Furtig had spent such weary hours. Two of the younglings were wearing the head bands, and Liliha tended the machine into which the disks were fed.

They saw the room for only a moment or two. Then it blurred and was gone. Nor could Furtig bring it back.

He said as much. But Foskatt did not appear too disappointed.

"It does not matter. Perhaps you are not so familiar with the disks. But what does matter is that you could do this. Do you not see? If we can learn your secret, such boxes as these will keep us in contact with one another though we are apart. What would scouts not do to have such devices!"

What it would mean as an aid in hunting was immediately plain. If the caves could be so equipped, one would never have to fear a surprise attack from a Barker. Scouts in the field could send in early alarms. Or perhaps the boxes could even be hidden and watched from the caves without the need to use scouts! Furtig's thoughts leaped from one possibility to the next, and his excitement grew.

"It may be that only you have such a talent, brother," Foskatt said, interrupting Furtig's line of thought. "Unless this is a thing which can be learned. But the Ancestor must know of it—come!"

Seizing the box, Foskatt herded his companion out of the chamber. They tramped along corridors Furtig remembered from his first tour, coming to one of those shafts where air could so remarkably carry one up or down. Liliha had earlier admitted that the People had never been able to discover what particular device of the Demons governed this. But their workings had been discovered by Gammage on his first penetration of the lairs when he had fallen into one. And they were now accepted by his clan as matter-of-factly as the cave people would accept a trail.

So borne aloft, they went past three more levels, emerging in a place which startled Furtig, though with all he had seen in the past few days his ability to be surprised should by now have been dulled. They appeared now to be standing on a ledge with one side open to the sky. There was such a sensation of height as to make Furtig crowd back against the stone wall, avoiding that open space.

"There is a wall there, though it cannot be seen."

Foskatt must have sensed his unease. "See here, brother." He walked calmly to the far edge, raised one hand, and rapped against an unseen surface.

As Furtig observed more closely, he sighted here

and there smears on that transparent covering. More than a little abashed at his display of timidity, he made himself join Foskatt and look out, fighting the strong feeling that he was standing on the edge of a drop.

They were far above the ground level here. A strong morning sun, which awoke points of glitter from the sides of many of the upward-shooting towers, beamed warmly at them. Furtig stared in wonder. From the ground level he had marveled at the height of the lairs. But from this vantage point he could see even more. He had had little idea of the extent of the buildings before. They seemed to go on and on forever. Even in the far distance there was a hint of more. Had the Demons covered most of this part of the world with their buildings?

"Come—later you can climb higher if you wish, see more. But now is the time to tell Gammage this new thing."

Foskatt set off at a bold stride. In spite of his knowledge of the invisible wall, Furtig kept a path closer to the building. They rounded a curve. From this angle he could see a green shading which could only be trees at a distance. It was as if in that direction the lairs narrowed and one could sight open country beyond.

The corridor ended in a bridge connecting two of the towers. Foskatt trotted out on this as one who has made the journey many times. Furtig, in spite of his discomfort, paced close behind, keeping his attention focused strictly on the path ahead, glancing neither right nor left.

He had always thought that heights did not bother him—nor had they in the cave world. But this was not that natural world, and now, his body tense, he hurried until he was almost treading on his companion's heels in his eagerness to get to the solid security of the building ahead.

This time their way was not invisibly walled; instead they were in the lair chambers. Here the walls were lighted with a brilliance that ran in swirls and loops, patterns which Furtig found he did not care to examine too closely.

Also, here the floor was soft under his feet, being covered with a material which yielded to pressure when he stepped. Without being asked, Foskatt offered explanations as they went.

"This is the manner of all those rooms where the Demons once lived. They have many unusual things— springs of hot and cold water which flow at the touch. Sounds—listen, now!"

But he need not have given that order. Furtig was already listening to a sound, or a series of sounds, such as he had never heard before. They certainly came from no living creature, but apparently from the air about them. Low sounds, lulling in a way. At the moment he could not have said whether he liked what he heard or not; he only listened and wondered.

"What makes it?" he asked at last.

"We do not know. It does not come regularly. Sometimes we walk into a room and sounds begin, stopping when we leave. Sometimes they start with the coming of dark, just as certain lights come on then. There is so much we do not know! It would— will—take the lifetimes of five times five of such long-living Ancestors as Gammage to learn only a few of the mysteries."

"But Gammage does not believe we will have such time undisturbed?"

"He is increasingly fearful of the Demons' return. Though just why he fears this so strongly he has not told us. If there were more of us—You see, brother, Gammage believes one thing. When our people fled from the lairs and the torments of the Demons, they were not all alike. Oh, I do not mean different in color and length of fur, shape of head—the usual ways one differs even from a litter brother. No, we differed inside. Some were closer to the old Ancestors who were born for generations here in the lairs, whom the Demons controlled and used as they pleased.

"But others had the change working more strongly in them. And so their children, and children's children differed also. Though all the People grew in knowledge and were different from their older kin, still they were so in varying degrees.

"Gammage himself differed greatly, so greatly he was almost cast out as a youngling from the caves—until he proved his worth. But he believed early that there was a way to learn more and that that lay hidden in the very place of horrors his people shunned. So he came back. And to him from time to time came those who also had seeking minds, who were restless, unhappy for one reason or another in the life of the outer tribes. It was this very restlessness that he put to service here. And those who settled, took mates, who absorbed more and more of what the lairs had to offer, and produced the In-born, still more changed. It is Gammage's belief that no warrior is drawn to the lairs unless he has that within him which reaches for what is hidden here.

"It is his hope, his need, to bring all the People here, to make open to all the ways of learning, of healing"—Foskatt's hand went to the wound seal on his leg—"so that we can be as much masters here and elsewhere in this land as the Demons were. But mainly so that we can stand firm and safe when the Demons return, and not be hunted for their pleasure. For that was how they served our Ancestors."

As he talked they went from the chamber with the twisting lights on the walls through a series of further rooms. These were furnished with more than just beds and tables. There were hangings on the walls with pictures on them, many seats, and even large pads, as if someone had heaped up five or six thicknesses of bed pallets to make soft puffs. And crowded in among these were a great medley of things—boxes, containers, other objects Furtig did not know.

It reminded him of the crowded state of Foskatt's quarters. Here, too, there had been an ingathering of things found throughout the lairs.

Among these moved several of the In-born, though none of them paid any attention to the two newcomers threading a path here. These workers were females. Some sat on the chairs or puffs intent on bits and pieces laid out on low tables before them. Others stood over devices which purred or clinked or made outlandish noises.

"All small strange devices are brought here," Foskatt needlessly informed him. "First Gammage and his Elders, those who have worked the longest and know best the dangers which might exist, inspect them. In the early days there were accidents. Dolar has no hand on one wrist because of an incautious examination of a new find. So each is tested. When they are sure that it is not dangerous, it is given to those who try to unravel its secrets. For these gathered here have the best hands for that."

Furtig saw what his companion meant. The fingers of those at work here were indeed as unlike his own stubby ones as Liliha's—longer, less clumsy in movement.

It was Liliha herself who stood in the doorway of the third room. She folded, with quick, graceful turns of hands and wrists, a long strip of material which seemed bulky until she dealt with it firmly. Then it made a neat and surprisingly small pack.

To Furtig's surprise she gave them the customary greeting of the cave people:

"Fair morning and smooth trail, warriors."

"And a fair morning to you, One-Who-Chooses," he replied.

"One-Who-Chooses," she repeated. "Yes, of that custom I have heard, warrior. Though we do not altogether follow it here. If you seek the Ancestor, he is within. A new find, Foskatt?" She looked to the box.

"No. Just perhaps a new use for an old one. You see, Liliha, even we who are not seekers-in-depth may make discoveries also."

Did Foskatt then sound defensive, as if he had a need to outdo the In-born in some way? If he did, Furtig could well understand that emotion.

"All knowledge is three times welcome," was Liliha's answer. Once more she was industriously flipping the fabric into those smooth, much-deflated folds.

Gammage was not alone in that last chamber. He was seated on one of the wide seats of the Demons', all of which were raised just the wrong distance from the floor to be comfortable for one of the People, unless the feet were drawn up.

Beside him on the same seat was a powerfully built warrior with a notched ear and a long scar on his jaw. His one hand rested on his knee, and he gestured with his other arm as he talked. There was no fur-backed hand on that arm; instead, it ended in a ball of metal equipped with claws, and a cuff which was lashed to his own flesh and bone. This must be Dolar, Furtig reasoned.

The other there, a Chooser, was plainly of the Inborn, just as Dolar was of the out-country. Her fur was silky black, and around her neck was a chain of bright stones. She wore bands of a like nature about her wrists.

Both she and the battered warrior showed no welcome to those who entered. But Gammage gave a purring call:

"What have you, Foskatt? It seems that you come in haste with something new."

"It is one of the see boxes," the female broke in. "Of these we have plenty—amusements for younglings."

To Furtig's secret satisfaction, Foskatt caught her up quickly. "Not used as this brother can use it!"

"How?" Gammage squirmed off his seat and came to them. "How do you use it?"

Between them Furtig and Foskatt explained. Then Furtig demonstrated. He produced two pictures, the first of the caves, the second of Eu-La.

In that small, vivid scene she was busied with a number of strips cut from hide. These she twisted and turned in a fashion which seemed to Furtig useless. And it was apparent she was frustrated at not achieving what she attempted. But Gammage uttered an exclamation.

"Lohanna, see what this young female does!"

At his call the In-born looked. After a long moment of close attention she turned on Furtig almost accusingly.

"Who is this youngling?" she demanded, as if Furtig were attempting to conceal a matter of importance. He remembered his promise to Eu-La—this was the time to carry it out. And he freed the bag from his belt.

"She is Eu-La of Gammage's cave. This she made and asked me to show to Gammage."

The Ancestor took the bag, turned it about as if it were indeed some treasure newly discovered, then passed it to Lohanna. She studied it with the same attention and then said to Gammage:

"She is one we should have with us, Elder. Though she is not of the In-born, yet see what she has wrought. And what does she there?" She gestured to the picture. "She rediscovers by herself one of the secrets of the Demons—doing it clumsily, but from her own mind! The old strain is not finished in the Out-World!"

"So it seems. And we shall try to bring her, Lohanna. Now—" Gammage looked to Furtig. "So you can make the picture become what you wish—How?"

"I do not know how. I think—and there is the picture of the one I think of. Not as I remember them last, but perhaps as they are at present. But how can I be sure? I do not know it for the truth!" He was not going to claim any talent which could later be proven false. In spite of Foskatt's enthusiasm, Furtig was stubbornly determined to walk cautiously before the In-born.

"Tell him how you were led through the lairs—"

Reluctantly Furtig added that piece of information.

"Not so strange." For the first time the metal-handed Elder commented. "We have long known that certain of us can be so guided—"

"But the point Foskatt would make," Gammage said, "is not that Furtig was guided, but that he used it with one he did not know, had had no contact with before. So it would seem his use of that talent is also different. If such a change breeds true, we can hope for much in the future. Yes, Furtig, our brother here has been right to urge you to tell us this. Now, what else can you see—perhaps here in the lair?"

Furtig took the box. The picture of Eu-La had vanished in the fog. Should he try to see an unpeopled place—or one with people? He tried to fasten on the prison room in which he had found Foskatt, but the box remained dark.

"It will not show me a place without people," he reported.

Gammage did not seem in the least disappointed. "Then your ability must tie with a living thing. Well, can you think of a person in the lairs—"

Furtig chewed his lower lip and thought. Then an idea flashed into his mind. It would be the highest test of his ability. He summoned to mind the picture of the second Ratton guard he had seen before the prisoners' cell.

To his surprise and delight the fog gathered. The picture which emerged was blurred, but not so much that he could not distinguish part of it. And small sounds from two of those with him indicated that they saw also.

There was the Ratton. But he lay on the floor of the guard room. A piece of rubble, probably dislodged by the battering of the servant, pinned his leg to the floor. However, he still lived, for reddish eyes glinted and Furtig saw his mouth open as if he called for some help that would never come. Perhaps his fellows had left him to die because he was now useless.

"The Ratton guard!" Foskatt cried out. "Him I have seen! And that place—"

The blurring was complete, the scene vanished.

"That was one of the guards who held me!"

"So it would seem you can pick up other than our own people!" Gammage was excited. "Yes, these boxes, if others can learn to use them so, will become far more than just something to amuse younglings. Lohanna, would it not be well to check immediately on all those who have used them idly to see whether they were thinking of anything when they did so, or if they had any control over their viewing? If they can control it—or only a small number can control it—"

"Scouts," the warrior broke in. "Send scouts and turn this on them—you could have instant warning of what they viewed. We could prepare for attacks in good time." He raised his false hand and used its harsh talon tips to scratch his chin.

Lohanna was already at the door. "You shall have the answer as soon as possible, Elder," she assured Gammage.

"Lohanna knows very much about the learning machines," the Ancestor told Furtig. "I only wish we had more of the ancient records—"

Foskatt stirred. But Gammage was continuing: "Do not take those words of mine as a complaint of

your failure to find such records. We had no idea
the Rattons had invaded that section of the lairs in
force. It is a great danger that they have. We dare
not underestimate them in any way. They breed in
greater numbers than we do. Though the same illness which changed us in the beginning also cut the
numbers of our litters, the Ratton females have many
offspring in a single season.

"And among the Rattons are those whose cunning
has greatly advanced, so that they have their own
seekers of Demon knowledge. Being small, they can
slink along ways we cannot follow. It would be very
difficult to seal off any part of the lairs so that they
could not find their way in. Also, they have their traps.

"We have certain Demon weapons. But, like the
servants, those are uncertain as to performance and
to depend upon them in time of need and then have
them fail—" He shook his head. "But still, the records
we have found reference to—they must lie in the very
territory the Rattons have invaded. Should they find
them first—and I am firm in the conviction that they
have among them those who are able to put Demon
learning to use—then we may be in a very dangerous
position. Time—we have so little time!"

➤ 8 ➤

There is only one thing to do," Foskatt said slowly. "I shall try again. Though this time, being warned, I do not think I shall be entrapped." There was dour determination in his voice.

Gammage shook his head. "Remember, younger brother, you are but fresh out of the place of healing. Your wound may seem closed, but if you were put to some severe test this might not hold. Do you not remember what happened under similar circumstances to Tor-To?"

For a moment Furtig thought Foskatt would protest. Then his tribesman gave a sigh. "But who then can go? And if the Rattons have taken over that part of the lairs, will we ever be able to reach the records if we wait longer?"

"He is right," the deeper half-growl of Dolar rumbled. "Were I but able—" His speech became a full growl, and he brought his metal hand down upon the edge of a table with such force that the claws left deep indentations in its surface.

"Dolar, my close-brother, were you able, yes. But this needs youth and quickness of body such as we have both long since lost."

To his inner astonishment, some other seemed to take over Furtig's voice then, for he heard himself saying:

"I am warrior trained and skilled, Elder. Also I have the homing sense which before led me through unknown ways. Let me know just what to search for and—"

"No!" Gammage was emphatic. "We must have you here, to work with the box, to learn how you are able to do this. Can you not see that is of the greatest importance?"

"More," Dolar asked, "than saving records from the Rattons? We have but six now of the warrior Out-World breed, and the other four are abroad on missions to contact tribes. If Foskatt cannot go, dare we send an In-born? They cannot learn the ways without many journeys under guidance. Those we cannot give them. But now this matter of boxes—let Foskatt and this young warrior try between them such sendings. If they find they can use it as a scout might, then there may be a way out of this difficulty."

His sensible suggestion carried, and so for the rest of that day and part of the night, taking only short rests and eating the trail rations they carried with them, the two played a hunt and search game through the echoing corridors of the aboveground lairs. When Furtig set off to wander, Foskatt sought him with the box. At first they were defeated over and over again, Foskatt seemingly unable to pick up any clear picture. Though once or twice the mist formed, enough to encourage him to keep on trying.

Just as they were ready to surrender to disappointment, Furtig, returning to the point where he had left his partner, discovered Foskatt wildly elated.

"You stood in a room where there were shining strips on the walls!" he cried out hoarsely. "And then you went and put your hands against one of the strips. On its surface was a second you who also put forth his hand to meet you palm to palm!"

"That is right." Furtig slumped against the wall. "That is what I did just before I started back. Then it works for you, too!"

When they returned with the news of this small success, they were greeted with a disturbing report from another scout. He had tried to reach one of the tribes of the People reputed to have hunting grounds to the north, only to be cut off by a pack of Barkers who, it appeared, were settling in.

Gammage paced up and down as if his thoughts would not let him sit still. His tail switched and his ears were a little flattened. Had not Furtig known that in the lairs Trials were forbidden, he would have believed the Ancestor was preparing to offer challenge.

"In the records there is proof that the Barkers were, even more than we, the slaves of the Demons, licking the ground before their feet—which the People, owned though they were, never did! I had hoped—But that is another matter. If the Barkers now ingather about the lairs, can we believe that is a sign pointing to Demon return? Perhaps the Demons have in some secret manner signaled the Barkers to them. Though if the Barkers remembered the Demon end here as well as we do, they would not be so quick to answer such a call."

"The Barkers," offered Dolar, "are rovers, not liking settled lairs. Other times they have come near, but they never stayed for any length of time."

"Hunting parties, yes," Gammage agreed. "But this time they bring their females and young. Ask of Fy-Yan, who has been three suns watching them. We must have knowledge—"

"Which perhaps we can gain for you, Ancestor," Foskatt said. "We can use the box. I have seen Furtig afar in it."

Gammage turned with the quick grace of one seasons younger. His yellow eyes glowed.

"Sooo—" In his mouth the word became a hiss, almost akin to the warning one uttered when entering a hunting country. "Let us lay hands upon those records and perhaps we can hold the lairs. Even if the Barkers continue to be our enemies."

"Continue?" Dolar clicked his claws. "Think you it can be otherwise? Do you also fear that they might swear truce with Rattons?"

"Not impossible. In times of war it is best never to say in advance this can be, that not. Be prepared for any danger. And I say to all of you, though perhaps I have said it so many times before that the words will have no effect, with Rattons one cannot be sure of anything! Remember that well, Furtig, if and when you go into ways where they can be found."

Furtig thought he needed no warning. His hatred for the creatures, together with his earlier brush with them, had been enough to arouse all his caution. No warrior ever trusted anyone or anything, save his own clan brothers and the lair which gave him shelter.

He listened, impatiently but curbing the outward

show of that, to all the information and instructions which those who had explored the ways could provide. Foskatt gave him directions—vague enough—as to what he sought. He was to watch for certain marks on walls—which might or might not be there—and would have the use of a secondary guide.

This was a cube similar to that with which Foskatt had summoned the rambler. But its buzzing had another use. They had discovered a season back that this sound was emitted when the cube was brought near Demons' record disks.

With this instrument, and trail supplies, Furtig at last descended to the lower runways of the lairs. As yet they had no knowledge as to how far the Rattons had penetrated, though they had stationed scout-guards at important checkpoints to warn of any spillover into their home territory. Metal servants of the Demons could also be used for this service and Furtig passed some of these on the way.

At last he slid into the dark of those tunnels, which could be runways for either the People or their enemies. There were doors here, but he wasted no time in exploring. This was not the area of the reputed cache. He moved noiselessly along, depending upon both ear and nose for warnings. The smell of Ratton he would never forget, and that warning the enemy could not conceal.

As a hunter he knew that many of the wild creatures had senses of smell far superior to his own. The Barkers did. But his hearing and his sight, which was hardly limited by the dim grayness of these ways, were his own weapons.

There was not complete darkness here. At long

intervals small vertical bars were set in the walls to emit a dull light. Whether those had once been brighter and had dimmed through the years was not known. It was enough that the light aided the sight of the People.

Furtig had eaten, drunk, and slept before he had set out on this quest. At his belt a packet of food was balanced by a container of water. They did not expect him to be away too long, but he was prepared for possible delays.

Under his feet dust formed a soft carpet, but he trod so lightly that little of it was disturbed. His one hand was never far from the butt of a new weapon Dolar had given him out of their small store. The difficulty was that it was too big to handle with ease, having been fashioned to fit a hand much larger than his own. In order to use it at all (one leveled the barrel and pressed a firing button on the butt), Furtig had to discard his familiar and useful claws.

But having seen it demonstrated, Furtig was certain that the results might well outweigh those disadvantages. For when the button was pressed a vivid crackle of white (as if the Demons had indeed tamed lightning and compressed it into this weapon) shot forth like a knife of light. What that touched ceased to exist at all! It was indeed a fearsome thing. But, like all the Demon treasures, it was erratic. Explorers had found many of these, yet only a small number worked. It was as if they had been drained of life during the long time they had lain unused.

Furtig turned from the main passage into a narrower one and began to count the dim lights in the wall. At the fourth he stopped to look down. There was a grating such as had given him entrance to free the prisoners—that was Foskatt's first guidepost.

Kneeling, Furtig slipped on his claws. With their added strength he was able to hook into the grating, work it out of place. Foskatt had warned him how sound carried and he was sure it had been his own handling of that grating which had alerted the Rattons, so Furtig moved very slowly.

As he worked he thought about Foskatt, hoping that their practice had proven the truth: that the other was now picking up the picture of where he was. Having held that concentration on his part as long as he could, Furtig found the grating loose, laid it on the floor, and ran his hand into the lightless space beyond.

It was large enough for him to crawl into, but Furtig hesitated. If the Rattons were suspicious, they might well have rigged another trap. Yet this was the only known way in since the fall of roof and walls had closed off the corridor passages ahead.

Carefully Furtig lifted the grating, fitted it back into place. He had made his decision. To follow exactly in Foskatt's path was folly. During his time of instruction in the lairs he had been shown various types of Ratton traps. Some of them were practically undetectable. Therefore he must find another way in. Or Foskatt must be able to suggest a possible other trail, knowing the ways of the lairs.

Furtig squatted on his heels and once more concentrated on a mental picture, this time not of what he was doing, for Foskatt's pickup, but of Foskatt himself.

The picture was vivid in his mind. Furtig closed his eyes—now, he might be looking directly into the other's face. He shaped his need for further information. This was something entirely new he was trying. Could he communicate this way—even with Foskatt's see box as an aid?

Ways—

Furtig could not be sure of that. Was he receiving a message from the other, or was it only that he wanted an answer so badly that his mind deceived him?

"On—right—down—"

Furtig opened his eyes. He was certain that was not his own thought. On—right—down—On along the passage, right—down—Well, it was either believe that to be a message or try a passage which could be a trap. And of the two alternatives, he would rather believe that he had received a message.

So he left the grating that had been Foskatt's entrance and padded on. The passage ran straight, with no breaks except a few doors. Then Furtig could see a wall at the end—a dead end with no turn right or left, only a last door to his right.

Furtig turned in there. The room was bare of any furnishing. The only break in its walls was the door through which he had entered. There were two floor gratings; a distinct current of air flowed from one of those. Furtig went to his knees to better sniff at it.

No Ratton stench, nothing but the acrid odor common to all these levels. There was a good chance that he had bypassed the dangerous territory. At least he must now chance this or fail without even trying.

The grating resisted his efforts to free it. Furtig had to use force with his claws to lever it out. When he lowered it to the floor and swept his hands within, he discovered that this was even more spacious than the area beneath the first grating.

He crouched for a long moment before he entered, once more making a picture that Foskatt might or might not be able to pick up. Then he took from his belt one of the tools Gammage had provided. It was no longer than the palm of his hand when he pulled it from the loop, but when he pressed it here and there it unfolded longer and longer, until he held a slender pole twice his own height in length. This detect was his only protection against traps, and he must use it with all the skill he could.

Resolutely he crawled into the duct. The interior was large enough for him to go on hands and knees, but it was too dark for his sight to aid. Instead he must depend on that thin rod as he edged slowly forward, sweeping it back and forth, up and down, to test for any obstruction. Explorers had used these successfully to set off traps in confined spaces. But they had failed, too. And at that moment such failures were to be remembered vividly.

Suddenly the point of the device struck against solid surface ahead. A crosswise sweep, a second vertical one met opposition all the way—There was a wall ahead, yet air continued to flow—

Side walls? Furtig tapped right and left: only solid surface. Which left only up or down—and down had been Foskatt's message. Furtig slid the detect along the flooring of the duct. There was an opening. By careful tapping he measured it to be a wide one. He edged closer, hanging his head over the rim, trying to discover the length of the drop, what might be below.

He folded the detect, put on his claws, and swung over. There were places in the walls to set claw tips so that he did not slide down too fast. But it was a chancy trip, and he had no idea how long that descent lasted. It seemed to his aching arms, his tense body, far too long. Then he came, not to the end, but to another cross passage leading in the right direction.

Thankfully, Furtig pulled into that and lay panting, his whole body sweating and weak. It was not until some small measure of strength returned that he pulled out the detect rod, stretched it again to explore by touch.

The new passage was smaller than the one from which he had come. It was necessary to wriggle forward on his belly. But it pointed in the right direction, there was no smell of Ratton, and he had no excuse not to try it.

It was prod, slide, prod, a very slow advance. But his detect found no more barriers. Now there was even a faint glimmer of light to be sighted ahead. It was so welcome, Furtig hurried more than he had dared since he had entered the ducts.

Soon he peered through what could only be a grating. But, like that of the Ratton prison, this was set not at floor level but near the ceiling, so that he had to squeeze close to it in order to get even a limited view of the floor.

He was just in time to witness action. Rattons! Even before he saw them, their foul smell arose. Furtig froze, afraid of making some sound. But with that stench came the smell of blood and that of his own People. His stiff whiskers bristled.

He could hear sounds almost directly below his perch, but the angle was such that he could not view what was happening. There was a low moan of pain, a vicious chittering in the Ratton tongue. Then a body rolled out far enough for him to see it.

Though the fur of the prisoner was matted with blood, he was able to recognize Ku-La. So the stranger had not made his escape after all! He was not only back in Ratton claws but had suffered their cruel usage. That he still lived was no mercy. And his end would mean only one thing, food for the Rattons.

Plastered against the grating, Furtig listened, as if he could do that not only with his ears but with his whole body. He could hear small scuffling noises, a few chitterings. Then those grew fainter, stopped. He was certain after a long wait that the Rattons had gone, leaving no guard here.

Ku-La's own actions proved that. He was striving to raise his battered head from the floor, making efforts, which brought cries of pain out of him, to somehow reach his bonds with his teeth. But the Rattons were no fools; he had been well and skillfully tied. His struggles did not last long. With a last moan he went limp as if even that small effort had finished him.

Ku-La was not of Furtig's clan, and one did not champion strangers. But—common blood—he was of the People. And his fate might be Foskatt's, or Furtig's.

Furtig started to move away from the grating, but he discovered that something would not let him go in comparative safety, leaving Ku-La to Ratton-delivered death. He edged back and began to feel about the edge of the grating. At first he thought that too tightly set, that fate had decided for him, giving him no choice.

Then there was a click which startled Furtig into instant immobility. After listening, and hearing nothing to suggest the enemy had returned, he began once more that patient prying and pulling.

To work the grating loose in those confined quarters

was difficult, but Furtig managed it. Once more he had recourse to his belt and the various tools and aids he carried. Wound there was a length of cord, seemingly too thin and fine to support even a youngling. But this was another of the Demons' wonders, for it could take greater weights than Furtig.

He used the grating to anchor one end. Then, as he had used vines in the trees, he swung out and down. Furtig hit the floor in a half-crouch, ready to take on any Ratton. But the door was closed; there were none there.

Sighing with relief, he moved to the captive in a single leap. Ku-La stared up at him in wide-eyed amazement but made no sound. Nor did he attempt to move as Furtig slashed through his bonds. The extent of the other's injuries made Furtig sick, and he was not sure he could save him. If Ku-La was unable to follow him into the duct, perhaps it would be his choice to ask for a throat slash and go out as a warrior should, rather than linger in the enemies' hold.

Furtig extended his hand that the other might see his claws and understand the choice it was his to make. Ku-La's blue eyes regarded those claws. Then he moved, slowly, painfully, levering himself up, looking not to the promise of a clean and speedy death, but to the cord dangling beyond. He had made his choice, and Furtig was forced to accept it.

For a moment he was bitterly resentful. Why did he have to turn aside from a vital mission to aid this warrior who was not of his clan, to whom he owed no duty at all? He did not understand the impulse that had brought him to Ku-La's aid, he only mistrusted it and the difficulties into which it had plunged him.

Ku-La could not get to his feet, but he crawled for the end of the cord with such determined purpose that Furtig hurried to help. How he could get the almost helpless warrior aloft he had no idea. And he was driven by the fear that at any moment the Rattons might return. In the end he managed by looping the cord about Ku-La, then returning aloft to pull with all the strength he could summon.

Had the distance been greater, Furtig could not have done it. But somehow he had the energy left to bring that dangling body within reaching distance of the opening. Then Ku-La himself, with what effort Furtig could imagine, raised one arm to the edge and drew himself within.

Wasting no time in trying to tend the other's hurts, Furtig hurried to reset the grating. Only when he had done that did he squirm beside Ku-La, unhook his water container, and let the other drink—which he did in a way that suggested that his thirst had been almost as great a torment as his wounds.

"Where now?" Ku-La's whisper was very weak.

Well might he ask that! Furtig's impatience flared again. In this tight duct he could only tug the other on. He was sure Ku-La could not climb up the vent down which he had come. It could well be that he should leave the other here, momentarily out of harm, and go on his own mission. As he was considering that, the same idea must have come to Ku-La, for he said: "They will seek—"

Naturally they would. And they would not be long in finding the grating. It would take them some effort to reach the opening, but Furtig could not gain much satisfaction from that. He set to work to see if he could wedge the grating more securely. He broke off a length of his detect and rammed it well into place. They would have some trouble breaking that.

"We can only go on," he said at last. But how far—and to where? The pace Ku-La could keep—His concern over the other had indeed put him in awkward straits; it might even lead to disaster.

Perhaps Ku-La could help. Let them get away from the grating, and he could ask the other what he knew of this section of the lairs.

"Can you crawl?"

"While there is breath in me," replied the other. There was that in his tone akin to some blood-oath promise. Furtig believed he meant it.

He put out his hand, caught the other's right arm, and hooked Ku-La's fingers into his own belt.

"Hang on then and let us go!"

➤ 9 ◄

They lay together in the small space the meeting of three ducts provided. Furtig could hear Ku-La's harsh gasping and knew, without need for confirmation, that Ku-La had come to the end of his strength. Yet he himself found that he could not just crawl on and leave the other to die in this hole. That drag upon him produced a dull anger in him.

It was Ku-La who spoke first, his voice a thread of sound which Furtig had to listen to well to hear at all.

"No—farther—"

So he was accepting defeat. Furtig should now feel relief. It was as if Ku-La had accepted the inevitable, laid his throat open to the mercy claws. But he spoke again, and this time he asked a question which surprised Furtig, for he believed Ku-La sunk in his own misery.

"What seek you?"

"Knowledge." Furtig answered with the truth. "The hidden knowledge of the Demons."

"So—also—" came the whisper. "I—found— before—I—was—taken—"

Furtig, startled, rolled over, trying to see the other in the dark. Only Gammage's clan combed the lairs for knowledge. Yet this stranger spoke with certainty.

"Records?" Furtig demanded. He could accept that Ku-La prowled perhaps hunting a superior weapon. But certainly he could know nothing of the tapes Gammage wanted.

"Demon knowledge." Ku-La's whisper was a little stronger, as if the necessity for communication actually produced strength to aid him. "They kept records in rolls of tape. Our people know this. You put them in—" His whisper died away.

But Gammage and his people were the only ones who had learned that, who studied such. Yet Ku-La spoke as one who had used such tapes. Furtig had to know more. Putting out a hand, he touched the other's shoulder, only to feel Ku-La wince with a gasp of pain.

"How do you know this?" Furtig demanded sharply.

"—live in lairs—to the east—lairs very large. We hunt knowledge—"

Another clan such as Gammage's, busy at the same task on the far side of the lairs? But it was not possible. As Ku-La had said, the lairs were large. But that they had not had contact—that hinted that Ku-La's people may have been hiding with no good intent. Had he brought out of the Rattons' claws one who was as much an enemy as a Barker or one of the evil-smelling runners in dark ways?

"Came—from a smaller lair—found knowledge there which brought us hunting here—" Ku-La continued that thread of tortured sound, bending his strength to an explanation. "We have old story—lived—with— Demons until they died—then learned—"

Could it be that elsewhere the Last Days had been different? That dying Demons had not turned upon Ku-La's tribe as they had so mercilessly here? Furtig decided that such history was possible. And if that were so, surely Ku-La's people had a head start on Demon discoveries. Yet they had come here seeking knowledge—which made Gammage's need doubly important.

Ku-La said he had found what he sought just before the Rattons had taken him! Which meant that a cache was either in Ratton territory or close enough for them to patrol there. Was that cache the one Foskatt had been aiming for?

"Where is this place of tapes?"

"There is a hall where stand many of those things like the one which broke down the wall." Ku-La's voice was steadier, even a little stronger, as if fixing his mind upon his search had drawn him a little out of his present misery. "On the wall facing the door of that—there is a space there as if one had set his hand into it. Into that you must put a light—Then it opens—" His whisper ended with a sigh. Though Furtig shook the other's shoulder there was no flinching or answer.

Was Ku-La dead? Furtig fumbled for the other's head, held his fingers over the half-open mouth. No, there was breath coming. But he did not believe he could get any more directions. This chamber—where would he find it? He had better advance in the general direction suggested by Foskatt. But in any case he could linger here no longer.

Furtig dropped his head on his crooked arm and thought of the face of Foskatt. Then in his mind he retraced his passage along the ducts, concentrating hardest on the present point. He had no assurance his message was received, but it was the best he could do. Unlatching his container of water, he pushed it under one of Ku-La's limp hands. Then he scrambled into the duct at his right to continue his journey.

As he rounded a turn, he saw again the faint slits which could only be gratings. He hurried from one to the next. The chambers he saw were piled high with boxes and containers—as if they were part of a vast storehouse in which the Demons had laid up treasures. Furtig had no idea of their contents. It would take seasons and seasons—even if Gammage realized his impossible dream and united the many tribes of the People—to explore this place.

So much of what had already been discovered was not understood, for all the prying and study of those best qualified among the In-born. If they were given time and peace—what could they learn?

The sight of all that piled below had the effect on Furtig that a clean, newly made track might have on a hunter. His fingers twitched with the desire to swing down, to claw open this or that shadowed container. But this was not what he had been sent to find. He forced himself past those tantalizing displays.

With a shock he realized that the last grating gave him a new view. He pushed close to the grill to assess what he saw. Machines—lines of those strange willing-unwilling servants lined up. And a single door at floor level. Ku-La's tale—had he found by chance the very storage place the other sought? But this could not be Foskatt's cache, unless the vague description he had caught varied in details.

In the dim light Furtig could not see any such space in the wall as Ku-La had described. He used his nose as well as his eyes and ears. The usual smell of these burrows—no taint of Ratton. If this was the chamber of Ku-La's story, there was no enemy guard. Dared he pass up the chance to prove or disprove what the stranger scout had said?

If Ku-La's people had had a longer association with the Demons, a knowledge exceeding the hard-won bits and scraps Gammage had unearthed, than any cache the other had come to find might well be superior to that listed for Furtig. He must put it to the proof!

Once more he loosened a grating, used his cord to drop to the floor below. But before he sought the end of the room, he went to the door. That barrier was shut and he wished to barricade it—but saw nothing large enough to use. He could only hope that the Rattons might betray their arrival by the noise of their coming, their rank scent.

Furtig hurried to the wall Ku-La had spoken of. And he was really not surprised to find just such a depression as had been described. It was high up; Furtig had to scratch above eye level to fit his hand into it.

What had Ku-La said? Light. What light? Furtig leaned against the wall to consider the problem. Light— the Demon weapon spat lightning—He had nothing else, and he was firmly determined to force this door if he could.

Furtig drew the weapon. Dolar had drilled him in the charge of force it would spit. The wave of fire which answered was governed by the turning of a small bar on the butt. He could set that as low as it would go—

Having done so, Furtig put the mouth of the barrel

to the depression. More than a little nervous to be using forces he did not understand, he pressed the firing button.

There was an answering glow reflected back from the cup. Then, slowly, with a dull rasping sound, as if something which had been a long time sealed was being forced, the wall split open. It did not crumble as had the wall in that other chamber when the rambler had battered it, but parted evenly, as if slashed carefully by claw tip. Furtig uttered a small purr of triumph.

But he had prudence enough not to enter a place with a door that might close and entrap him. His inbred caution warred with curiosity, and caution won to make him take what precautions he could.

Though the door remained open, Furtig turned to the machines in rows behind him. The one which had rescued them had traveled easily enough. Even if none of these were alive, could one not be pushed forward? He darted down the nearest line, trying to find one small enough to be managed. And finally, though there did not seem to be much choice as to size, he singled one out and began to pull and shove.

Then he became aware of the device that Gammage had given him, that which must locate the tapes. It was buzzing, loudly enough to sound beyond the pouch where he carried it.

Heartened by that, he redoubled his efforts and his choice moved, rolling with greater ease once he got it started, trundling forward to the door. There Furtig maneuvered it into position across the threshold so the opposed leaves, if attempt to close those did, would be held apart by its bulk. Only when it was set in place did he scramble over it.

There was a light bar within on the ceiling, so he could see before him a narrow aisle of drawered containers such as were always used for tape storage. Hooking his fingers in the pull on the nearest, he gave it a jerk. The drawer rolled open to display boxes of record tapes. Furtig was amazed by the number. If each of these—he glanced down the double row of containers—held as many as this one drawer, this was just such a storehouse as Gammage had long hoped to find.

Furtig slipped along the aisle, opening one drawer after another. But before he reached the end of that short line, he could see that the racks within were more and more sparsely filled. And the last section of drawers on the very end was entirely empty. Even so—this was a find to rejoice over.

Transportation—Furtig leaned against the far wall, looked back to the wedged door. That was a new problem. He had brought a bag, now tightly rolled in his belt, which would hold three or four double handfuls of tape cases. But how could he know which in this storehouse of wealth were those that mattered the most? There was nothing to do but make a clean sweep, transport everything here, at least into a hiding place of his own choice—which could mean somewhere along the ducts—until it could be carried back to Gammage.

Furtig went into action, filling the bag, climbing into the duct to dump its contents, returning to fill and climb again. He was beginning to tire. His effort at dragging Ku-La along the duct told when added to this. But he kept to his task, making sure he left nothing behind in any drawer he emptied.

It took ten trips, and at the end he was shaking

with fatigue. By rights he should move that machine
back, try to reseal the door, cover his tracks so that
no prowling Ratton could be guided to the treasure
trove he had to cache in the duct. But he simply
could not summon the strength to accomplish all that.
Instead he swung up for the last time, lay panting
there until he could bring into his heavy, aching arms
energy enough to reset the grill.

About him lay the tape cases in a drift which rattled
and rolled as he moved. And he knew that he dared
not leave them so near the spot where he had found
them. So he began once more, this time not only
filling his bag but pushing before him an armload of
loose tapes, taking what he could back along the duct.

When he reached the meeting of the ways where
he had left Ku-La, he heard a stirring.

"You—have-found—" Ku-La's whisper was stronger,
or did Furtig only imagine that because he hoped it
was so?

"Yes. But I must bring these here." Flinging out his
arm, Furtig sent the cases spinning, hastily emptied
his bag. He wasted no more breath on explanation
but set to retrace his way.

How many such trips he made he did not know.
Furtig only understood that he could allow himself no
long pause to rest for fear of not being able to start
again. But in the end he lay beside Ku-La with the
tide of cases piled up like a wall about them.

Something pushed against his forearm persistently.
He roused enough to shove it away, to discover that
it was the water container he had left with Ku-La.
Furtig pulled it to him, opened it, and allowed himself
two reviving mouthfuls.

Revive him those did. But now hunger awakened in turn. He hunched up as well as he could in those cramped quarters to get at his supply pouch. In turn he was heartened when Ku-La accepted some of the dried meat he pressed into his hand. If the other could eat, perhaps he was not as badly off as Furtig had earlier feared. If Ku-La could move on, help himself somewhat, their return did not seem such an insurmountable problem as Furtig had thought it.

But he did not suggest that move as yet. Having eaten sparingly and drunk even more sparingly, Furtig settled himself full length, pushing aside the welter of tape cases to stretch out in what small measure of comfort he could achieve, and took the rest he knew he could no longer do without.

How long he dozed he did not know. But he awoke, aroused by a clicking near to hand. His body tensed, his hand crept to the butt of the Demon weapon. The tapes!

"You wake?" Ku-La spoke. "I count our find—"

Furtig realized that the other must be piling the cases into some sort of order. For when he put out his hand he discovered that those he had shoved aside were gone. But—"our find"? Did Ku-La think to claim that which Furtig by his own efforts had brought out of danger? When Furtig had succeeded where the other had failed?

Save that this was no time for quarreling. Neither one would have any chance to claim anything if they did not get out of here. He was sure, in spite of the partial recovery Ku-La appeared to have made, that the other could not retrace Furtig's way in. Which meant either that Furtig must leave him here—with the majority of the tapes—or find another way out for them both.

They lay in this wider space, the junction of three ducts. Two would lead them nowhere they could go, which left the third. It was the left-hand way, which might or might not carry them deeper into Ratton territory. He said as much.

"Your way in—" began Ku-La.

"There would be a hard climb back. It was difficult to descend and I had use of both hands."

"While those gray stinkers have left me the good of only one!" Ku-La interrupted. "But you can return—"

"With a chance that the Rattons have already marked the route?" Furtig countered. "I cannot carry you—or more than a few of the tapes. Should I leave all easy prey for them?"

"The tapes being the more important. Is that not so, warrior?" Ku-La asked quietly. "Tell me, why did you risk so much to free me from the Rattons? You could not have known then that I had information about the tapes. And I am no clansman or litter brother of yours; we have shared no hunting trail. This is not the custom of your tribe, any more than it is of mine, or so I would guess."

Furtig told him the truth. "I do not know, save I could not leave any of the People, clansman or stranger, to the Rattons. Or perhaps I have listened to the Ancestor—"

"Ah, yes, your Ancestor. I have heard of his strange thoughts—that all the People, clan upon clan, must draw together in a long truce. One of his messengers spoke so to our Elders. But we could not see the wisdom in that—not then."

"There has been a change in your thinking?" Furtig was interested. Did Gammage indeed have a strong enough message to convert those with whom he had no kin tie? When his own clan would not listen to him?

"In my thinking, though I am no Elder. You did not leave me to die under Ratton fangs. Though earlier I left you and your kin brother so. And you took the knowledge I had given you and returned with what you found. Yes, one begins to see the worth in your Ancestor's suggestion. Together we have done something that neither might have succeeded in alone."

"Save that we have not yet succeeded," Furtig pointed out. "Nor shall we until we are safely back in that portion of the lairs held by the People. And with what we have found. Now we must do just that."

In the end Furtig made a blind selection from the tapes, knotting as many as he could into the bag. The rest he stacked around the duct walls. This hollow of a three-way meeting was as good a place as any to store them. Having done this, he tried his powers of concentration for the last time, tried to contact Foskatt.

There was no way of knowing whether he got through. In fact the farther he was in space and time from his contact, the more he doubted the worth of their communication. With Ku-La he ate and drank again. There was very little water left now—he was not sure it would last long enough to carry them both to some source for more. But he would not worry about that until it became a matter of real concern. Rather he must keep his mind on what lay directly before him.

Again crawling with Ku-La's one hand hooked into his belt, Furtig worked into the left-hand passage. If they moved now behind the walls of separate rooms there was no way of telling it, for there were no gratings. And distance in the dark and under such circumstances was as hard to measure as time. The duct ran straight, with no turns or side cuttings. Furtig could not help but believe they must be heading back toward the lairs used by his own kind.

He tried to tap that directional sense which had guided him so surely before. But whether he had exhausted his talent, if he had any special talent in message sending, he did not know. One thing only was certain: He had no strong urge in any direction and could only crawl unguided through the dark.

Far ahead there was a glimmer of light. Another grating? He did not greatly care, he merely wanted to reach it, the need for light as much an ache within him as hunger or thirst. As he advanced, Furtig was sure it was stronger than the weak glimmers of the other gratings.

They reached the opening, which seemed, to eyes accustomed to the black of the ducts, a blaze of light. It was a grating, but one giving on the open, even though they must be many levels into the earth. Rain was falling without, and the dampness blew through the grating to bead their fur.

Here a well had been cored through the lairs, large enough so that with the haze of the rain they could hardly see the far side. What they could make out of the walls showed them smooth, unbroken by more than gratings. Only in one place the smooth wall was blackened, broken with a hole of jagged edges.

Furtig thought of lightning and how it could rend even rocks if it struck true. Also of the lightning of the Demon weapon. Perhaps that could not have caused that hole. But suppose the Demons had similar but greater weapons, ones of such force as to knock holes through stone walls? Like giant rumblers? The old legends of how the Demons had turned upon each other in the end, rending, killing—this might mark such a battle.

On the other hand, that hole could well give them entrance into the very parts of the lairs they wanted to gain. Furtig was heartily tired of crawling through the ducts. There was something about being pent in these narrow spaces which seemed to darken his mind so that he could not think clearly any more. He wanted out, and the fresh air beyond was a restorative moving him to action.

"But this place I know!" Ku-La cried. "I have seen it—not from here, but from above—" He crowded against Furtig, pushing the other away from the grating, trying to turn his head at some impossible angle to see straight up. "No, I cannot mark it from here. But there are places above from which one can see into this hole."

Furtig was not sure he wanted Ku-La to recognize their whereabouts. It would have been far better had they found a place he knew. But he did not say that. Instead he pushed Ku-La away in turn to see more clearly; he wanted another look at the wall break. Yes, it was not too far above the floor of the well. He was sure they could reach it. And he set to work on the grating.

As he levered and pulled, he made his suggestion about going through the break.

"A good door for us," Ku-La agreed.

The grating loosened, and he wriggled through into the open. He was glad for once to have the rain wet his fur, though normally that would have been a discomfort he would have tried to avoid. He dropped easily, and water splashed about his feet. That gathered and ran in thin streams to drain through openings in the base of the walls.

Furtig signaled for Ku-La, turning his head from side to side watchfully. Above, as the other had said, there were rows of windows. And he could see, higher still, one of those bridges crossing from the wall against which he stood to a point directly opposite. Or had once crossed, for only two-thirds of it were still in existence, and those were anchored to the buildings. The middle of the span was gone.

There were no signs of life. Rain deadened scent. However, they would have to take their chances. Furtig tugged the cord which he had made fast above for the second time. Ku-La descended by its aid, the rain washing the crust of dried blood from his matted fur as he came.

Those windows bothered Furtig. He had the feeling which was so often with him in the lairs, that he was being watched. And he hated to be in the open even for so short a time. But Ku-La could not make that crossing in a couple of leaps. He hobbled, and Furtig had to set hand under his shoulder to support him or he would not have been able to make the journey at all. It seemed long, far too long, before they reached the break and somehow scrambled up and into that hole.

➤ 10 ◄

Ayana lay pent in the web, staring up at the small visa-screen on the cabin bulkhead. So she had lain through many practice landings. But this was different—this was real, not in a mock-up of the ship while safely based on Elhorn II, where one always knew it was a game, even if every pressure and possible danger would be enacted during that training.

Now that difference was a cold lump within her, a lump which had grown with every moment of time since they had snapped out of hyper to enter this system. Were the old calculations really to be trusted? Was this the home planet from which her species had lifted into space at the beginning of man's climb to the stars?

When one watched the histro-tapes, listened to the various pieced-together records, one could believe. But to actually take off into the unknown and seek that which had become a legend—

Yet she had been wildly excited when her name had appeared with the chosen. She had gone through all

*the months of testing, training of mental conditioning,
in order to lie here and watch a strange solar system
spread on the visa-screen in a cramped cabin—know
that they would flame down, if all went well, on a
world which had not been visited for centuries of
planet time.*

*She saw the shift in the protect web hung above
hers. Tan must be restlessly trying to change position
again, though the webs gave little room for such play.
Even their rigorous training had not schooled that
restlessness out of Tan. From childhood he had always
been of the explorer breed, needing to see what lay
beyond, but never satisfied with the beyond when he
reached it, already looking once more to the horizon.
That was what had made life with Tan exciting—on
Elhorn; what had drawn her after him into the project.
But what can be a virtue can also be a danger. She
knew of old that Tan must sometimes be curbed, by
someone close enough for him to respond to.*

*Ayana studied the bulging webbing—Tan safe, but
for how long? His nature had been channeled, he
had been educated as a First-in Scout. Once they had
landed, he would take off in the flitter—unless there
were direct orders against that. Now Ayana hoped
that there would be. She could not understand the
deepening depression which gathered as a fog about
her. It had begun as they had come out of hyper,
growing as she watched the visa-screen. As if those
winking points of light which were the world awaiting
them marked instead the fingers of a great dark hand
stretching forth to gather them in. Ayana shivered.
Imagination, that was her weak point, as she had
been told in the final sifting when she had almost been*

turned down for the crew. It was only because she was an apt balance for Tan, she sometimes thought unhappily, that she had been selected at all.

"Well—there they are!" There was no note of depression in Tan's voice. "So far the route equations have proved out."

Why could she not share his triumph? For it was a triumph. They had had so little to guide them in this search. The First Ship people had deliberately destroyed their past. A search of more than a hundred years had produced only a few points of reference, which the computer had woven into the information for this voyage.

Five hundred planet years had passed since the First Ships—there had been two—had landed on Elhorn. What mystery had made those in them deliberately destroy not only all references to the world from which they had lifted but some of the instruments to make those ships spaceworthy? The colonists had suffered a slow decline into a primitive existence, which they had actually welcomed, resisting with vigorous fanaticism any attempt by the next generation to discover what lay behind their migration.

There were two—three such stagnated generations. Then, with all those of the first generation gone, their stifling influence removed, again inquiry. Explorers had found a closed compartment in one ship with its learning tapes intact; though those were spotty, sometimes seemingly censored.

After that came rebuilding, rediscovery, the need to know now almost an inborn trait of the following generations. There had been a search lasting close to a hundred years, until at last nearly all the resources of Elhorn had been turned to that quest alone. Not without opposition. There had been those in each generation who had insisted that their ancestors must have had good reason to suppress the past, that to seek the source of their kind was to court new disaster. And those had been gaining followers, too. They might have prevented the present voyage had it not been for the Cloud.

Ayana's face suddenly mirrored years of parched living when she thought of the Cloud. It had been such a little thing in the beginning. Scientists had wished to get at the rare ores their detectors had located on the impenetrable South Island of Iskar, where volcanic action produced unpredictable outbursts of lethal gases. From the old records, they had created robos like those the First Ship people had used, and these had been dropped on Iskar to do the mining. But the gases apparently had eaten away the delicate robo "brains," in spite of all attempts to shield those against infiltration. Then the scientists had turned to chemical countermeasures. To their own undoing. For the equipment the "dying" robos had installed in the mines had malfunctioned. And the result was the birth and continuing growth of the Cloud.

That did not rise far in the air; it crept, horribly, with a slow relentlessness which made it seem a sentient thing and not just a mass of vapor. So it covered Iskar, where there was little to die, but later it had headed out over the sea.

The water itself had been poisoned by the passing touch of that loathsome mist. Sea life died, but died fleeing. And those refugees contaminated others well beyond. Those died also, though more slowly.

At last those who had resisted the hunt for the home world capitulated. With their limited knowledge, lacking as it was in those portions the First Ship people had destroyed, they could not deal with the monster from Iskar. And they must either find a way to strike it a death blow, or else transport all their people elsewhere.

Even as the Pathfinder had lifted, the rest of the labor force (which now meant all the able-bodied dwellers on Elhorn) had been at work rehabilitating the two colony ships. Whether those could ever be put in condition to take to space again no man knew. The Pathfinder had been constructed from a smaller scout which had been in company with the colony ships.

There were only four of them on board the Pathfinder, each a specialist in his or her field, and able to double in another. Ayana was both medic and historian; Tan, a scout and defense man; Jacel, the captain, was their com expert and navigator; Massa, the pilot and techneer. Four against the whole solar system from which the First Ships had fled in such fear that they had destroyed all references to their past.

Had there been a Cloud on the ancestral planet, too? Or worse still (if there could be worse), had men hunted other men to the death? For that, too, had happened in the past, the tapes revealed. At least on Elhorn, they had not resorted to arms to settle differences in belief.

The closer the Pathfinder came to their goal, the more Ayana feared what they might find.

For days of ship's time their flight within the ancestral solar system continued. By common consent they chose their target—the third planet from the sun. From the computer reports, that seemed to be the planet best suited to support life as they knew it.

All this time Jacel tried to raise some response to their ship's broadcast, but none came. That silence was sinister. Yet the mere lack of a reply signal could not turn them back now. So they went into a braking orbit about the world.

That it was not bare of life was apparent. Or at least it had not lacked intelligent life at one time. Vast splotches of cities spread far over the land masses. They could be picked up by viewers in daylight, and their glow at night (though sections were ominously dark) provided beacons. Still there was no answer to their signals.

"This I do not understand." Jacel sat before his instruments, but his voice came to Ayana and Tan through the cabin com. "There is evidence of a high civilization. Yet not only do they not answer our signals, but there is no communication on the planet either."

"But those lights—in the night!" Massa half-protested.

Ayana wanted to echo her. It was better to see those lights flashing out as day turned to night below, than to remark upon the glow which did not appear—the scars of darkness. Yet one looked more and more for those.

"Have you thought," Tan asked, "that the lights may be automatic, that they come on because of the dark, and not because anyone presses a button or pulls a switch? And that where they are now dark some installation has failed?"

He put openly what was in all their minds. And that was the best explanation. But Ayana did not like to hear it. If they now raced through the skies above a dead world with only that vast sprawl of structures its abiding monument for a vanished people, then what had killed them, or driven them into space? And did that menace still lurk below?

Ayana wanted to turn her head, not watch the visa-screen. But that she could not do. It had a horrible fascination which held her in thrall.

"Without a signal we cannot find a landing site—" Jacel paused. "Wait! I am picking up something—a signal of sorts!"

They were once more in a day zone. Ayana could mark the shape of an ocean below. The land masses on this world were more or less evenly divided, two in each hemisphere. And they were over one such mass as Jacel reported his signal.

"Fading—it is very weak." His voice sounded exasperated. "I shall try to tune it in again—"

"A message?" Tan asked. "Challenging who we are and what we are doing in their skies?" He spoke as if he expected that hostile reaction. But why? Unless the memory of the fears of the First Ship people touched him, even as it had her, Ayana thought.

But if that were so, if they were to be greeted as enemies—how could they hope to land? Better by far to abort—Though she was sure Tan would never consent to that.

Jacel, using the ship's resources, had another answer. The signal, he was certain, was mechanically beamed and carried no message. And as such it could have only one purpose—to guide in some visitor from space.

Hearing that, they made their decision, though not without reservations on Ayana's part, to use the beacon as a guide. As Massa pointed out, they could not continue in orbit indefinitely and they had no *other lead. But they prepared for a rough landing. The computer gave no answers, only continued to gulp in all the information their instruments supplied.*

With every protect device alerted, Ayana lay in her bunk. She shut her eyes, and would not look at the screen, glad in a cowardly fashion that it was not her duty to be in the control cabin, where she would have to watch.

The usual discomforts of landing shut out everything beyond the range of her own body, and she tensed and then relaxed. She had done this many times in practice, yet the truth differed so much from the simulation. A second or so later she blacked out.

As one waking out of a nightmare she regained consciousness. Then duty made its demands, and she fumbled with the webbing cocooning her body. It was only when she wriggled out of that protection that the silence of the ship impressed itself upon her; all the throbbing life in it was gone. They must be down, for the engines were shut off.

Not only down, but they had made a good landing, for the cabin was level. They must have ridden in the deter rockets well. So Jacel had been right to trust the beam.

Ayana stood up and felt the grip of gravity. She took a step or two, feeling oddly uncertain at first, holding to a bunk support, looking at Tan.

He lay inert, a thin trickle of blood oozing from one corner of his mouth. But even as she raised her hand to him, he opened his eyes, those wide gray eyes, and they focused on her.

"We made it!" He must have taken in at once the silence of the cabin, the fact that it was in correct

position for a good landing. His hands sped to unhook his webbing.

"You are all right—?"

"Never better! We made it!" And the way he repeated that gave her a clue to his thoughts. Perhaps for all his outward show of confidence, Tan had had doubts, strong doubts after all.

He was out of the cabin ahead of her, already climbing for the control cabin before she could follow. Voices from there announced that the two responsible for what Ayana privately believed to be a miracle— their safe landing—were already rejoicing over that.

The scene outside as shown on the visa-screen quieted them. They had indeed landed in what must have once been a spaceport, for the scars of old deter and rise rocket fire were plain to be marked as the picture slowly changed. However, there were buildings also, towering bulks such as they had never seen on Elhorn.

To their sight, though those buildings stood at a distance, there were no signs of erosion or the passing of time. But neither were there any signs of life. And Jacel, monitoring his com, shook his head.

"Nothing. No broadcast except the signal which brought us in. And it is set—"

Set by whom, why? The questions in Ayana's mind must be shared by her crew mates. If they had landed on a silent and deserted world—what had rendered it so?

Massa was consulting other instruments. "Air— nothing wrong with that. We can breathe it. The gravity is a point or two less than we have known. Otherwise, this is enough like Elhorn to suit us."

"Like Elhorn? With all that to explore!" Tan waved

a hand at the screen where more and more of the huge building complex showed as the pickup slowly turned. This must be a city, Ayana decided. Though it pointed higher into the sky with its towers and blocks than any city did—or should.

To look at it aroused a queer repugnance in her, a feeling of reluctance to approach it. As if it were some crouching animal ready to pounce, perhaps actually ingest what came too near. She wanted none of those walls and towers. Yet on the screen the constantly moving scene proved that their landing site seemed to be completely surrounded by those buildings.

She could see no green of vegetation. No growth had seemingly dared to invade this place of stone. Nor was there any other ship berthed here.

"I think," Jacel said as he leaned back in his seat, "this place is deserted—"

"Don't be too sure of that!" Tan retorted. "We could be watched right now. They might well have some reason to want us to believe no one is here. Just because you flashed out the old code, or what we believe is the old code, does not mean that they could understand it. How long has it been since the First Ships lifted? We have been on Elhorn five hundred planet years, but we have no idea how long was their voyage out, or ours back. A lot can change even in a single generation."

He pointed out the obvious, but Ayana wished he would not. With every word he spoke those distant windows seemed more and more like cold eyes spying on them. And in all that mass of buildings there could be many hiding places for those who had no wish to be found.

"We cannot just stay here in the ship," Jacel said. "Either we explore here—or we lift, try for a landing somewhere else."

Ayana saw her head shake mirrored by the others. Now that they were down, the best thing to do was abide by their choice—explore.

Fiercely she fought her fears under control. Even if the people were dead there would be records. And those records could hold some secret which might halt the Cloud or otherwise aid those who had struggled to send them here. They had a duty that was not to be balked by shadows and uneasy fears. Some rebel emotion, though, replied to that argument; this fear she felt was not small, and she must work hard to subdue it.

They ran out the ramp. Tan opened the arms locker, and they all wore blasters at their belts as they went out. Massa remained on guard at the hatch, ready to activate the alarms at any sign of danger. There was a wind, but the sun was warm. Ayana could detect no odor in the breeze against her face. It was like any wind, and this might be a fall morning on her own home world.

"A long time—" Jacel had trotted over to the nearest burn scar, was down on one knee by that scorched fringe. "This was done a long time ago." He held a radiation detect, and its answering bleat was low.

Tan stood with his hands on his hips, turning slowly as if he himself was a visa-recorder. "They were builders." And there was excitement in his voice as he added: "What a world to claim! An empty world waiting for us!"

"Do not be too sure." Jacel joined him. "I have

a feeling—" He laughed as one startled and a little dismayed by his own thoughts. "I feel we are being watched."

Tan's answering laugh had none of the other's apologetic undertones. He threw out his arms wide and high. "Ghosts—shadows—let them watch us if they will. I say mankind has come again to claim his home! And—let·us get busy out there"—he waved to the buildings—"and find out what awaits us."

But training remained to tame his exuberance a little. He did not indeed urge them to instant invasion of the watching, waiting city (if city it was). He was content to wait for their agreement that that must be done. Instead he got busy in the storage compartments, transporting to the open the parts of the flitter which must be assembled for a flight of discovery.

It was well into late afternoon by the signs before the framework of the small flyer was together. Tan was still working on it when Jacel appeared, stringing behind him a length of cord, while stacked in his arms were small boxes. Tan, perched on the nose of the flyer, hailed him.

"What are you doing?"

"Seeing that we—or the flitter—have no unheralded visitors. Nights can be dark." Jacel set down his load. Without being asked, Ayana came to help him place the detects, string cord between them to complete a circle about the flitter.

This was one of the best warning devices they carried. Nothing could cross that circle of cord once it was set, for it created a repelling field of force. Not only that, but any attempt to approach would ring alarms in the ship.

"A trap for ghosts," Tan said. But he did not protest as Jacel carefully triggered each box.

Tan finished and left the flitter, and Jacel made the final setting. They were safe within the ship once the ramp was in. For there was no possible way of attacking those holed up in a spacer; the ship was a fort in itself.

However, Tan seemed reluctant to follow the others up the ramp, to seal up for the night. He turned to look at the towers.

"Tomorrow!" He made a promise of that one word, spoken loud enough for Ayana to hear. Though whether he meant it for her or only himself she did not try to learn.

Tomorrow, yes—there would be no holding Tan back then. He would circle out, looping wider and wider with every turn, relaying back all the information the instruments on the flitter could pick up. Then they would learn whether the city was truly dead or not, for among those devices was one which registered the presence of life force. They were not altogether helpless—

Now why had she thought that? As if they were indeed under siege and had only the worst to fear? Ayana ran her tongue across her lips. She had been passed as emotionally stable, enough so (and the tests had been as severe as those preparing them could devise) to be selected for the voyage. But the minute she had entered this solar system, it was as if she had been attacked by forces which tampered with her emotions, threatened that stability in ways she could not understand. She was a medic—a trained scientist—yet she feared windows! Now she once more fought those fears—pushed them back—strove to conquer them.

They ate, of ship's rations which tonight seemed even less satisfying and tasteless. Would they find fruit, or perhaps other food they could stomach here? She would be a party on the second or third trip—to be sure no ghost of disease lingered. She would have to go muffled and clumsy in a protect suit, but that she had practiced on Elhorn.

"Tan—Ayana." Massa's voice over the com and the excitement in it made Ayana reach for the blaster on her discarded belt. "Look at the screen!"

Windows were alight! The dark ringing the ship was not complete. Apparently Massa had set the pickup on the move again to give them the changing view. There was one lighted tower and then another. Not all were alight. Ayana managed to be objective after her first startled reaction. There were blocks of lights, then again scattered single ones. Some buildings were altogether dark. Such uneven lighting hinted of inhabitants. There were people there—there had to be!

"Tan—do you see?" Ayana's question was a kind of plea against his plans for tomorrow. He must not take off alone, cross that grim, watching place, in the light flitter. That had a shield, of course, every protect device they could give it. But above that giant, and she was sure hostile, pile—

Those lights, surely Tan would accept them as evidence of life. They could lift ship, find one of those all-dark cities they had marked from space. That was only sensible. But she knew she would not have a chance to argue that when Tan answered:

"Doesn't mean a thing. Do not worry, Big Eyes. Those are probably automatic and some circuits have long gone. Anyway, I have the force shield."

Even his use of the private name he had for her (which she cherished because of the sweet intimacy it stood for)—even that hurt. It was as if he deliberately used it to scoff at her concern. Ayana closed her eyes to those lights, tried to find sleep and perhaps dream of the safety of Elhorn before this wild venture became her life.

➤ 11 ◄

The sudden clamor outside this new corridor was one
Furtig had heard before, which set fur erect along his
spine, flattened his ears to his skull, parted his lips
to hiss. He caught an echo of that hiss from Ku-La.
Yet in a second or two both realized that this was
not the hunting cry of a Barker pack.

No, it held pain and fear rather than the hot triumph of the hunter upon his quarry. Furtig, belly
down on the floor of the corridor, wriggled forward
to peer through the transparent outer wall.

There was the Barker, threshing wildly about, one
foot—no, a foot and a hand caught in something. He
was in such a frenzy that he snapped with his well-
fanged jaws, striving to cut what held him. Then his
head was caught! His flailing body fell, or was jerked,
to the ground. Seconds later he was so trapped in the
substance which had entangled him that he could not
move save in spasmodic jerks, each of which worsened
his plight. His baying came in muffled snorts.

They came running from concealment where even

Furtig's sharp sight had not detected them. Rattons—a gray-brown wave of them. They piled on the Barker, seeming to have no fear of what had felled him, and began to drag the captive away.

Toward this building! Furtig hissed again. He had not smelled Ratton, seen Ratton, heard Ratton, since they had come through that break in the wall into these corridors. But if the Rattons were towing their catch into this structure, it was time to be gone.

He crept back to Ku-La, reporting what he had witnessed.

"A stick-in trap. They coat the ground with something you cannot see or scent, but it entangles you speedily," the other said.

"Yet they went to the Barker, handled him without getting stuck—"

"True. We do not know how they are able to do that. Perhaps they put something on themselves to repel the trap. We only know—to our sorrow—how it works on us!"

"A Barker in the lairs—" Furtig picked up the bag of tapes, was ready to help Ku-La on. "A scout?"

"Perhaps. Or they may also seek knowledge." Ku-La gave an involuntary cry as he pulled himself up. He was limping very badly, keeping going by will alone, Furtig knew.

His admiration for the other's determination and fight against pain had grown. No longer did he wonder why he had endangered his mission to rescue Ku-La; he accepted him as a comrade like Foskatt.

"If they bring the Barker here," Furtig began warningly. It seemed cruel to keep urging Ku-La on, but Furtig had lately picked up the homing signal in his mind, knew their goal, and also that they dared waste no time in these dangerous corridors.

"True. Though Rattons seem to have little liking for going aloft," Ku-La commented, drawing small breaths between words. "They keep mainly to the lower ways."

They rounded a curve in the wall. Furtig stayed close to the inner wall; that long expanse of almost invisible surface on the outer made him uneasy. Today that feeling was worse as the wind and rain beat hard in gusts which vibrated in the walls about them.

But—as they rounded that curve, looked out upon a new expanse of open, Furtig came to a halt—Light—a moving light!

It rose from the ground, soaring high as if a flying thing carried a huge hand lamp. Now it danced back and forth erratically in the sky, swooping out and away. And through the curtain of the rain Furtig could not follow it far.

Ku-La made a sharp sound. "A sky-ship—a sky-ship of the Demons!"

Furtig did not want to accept that. In fact at that moment he discovered he had never really believed in Demon return. But there was such conviction in Ku-La's identification that belief was now forced on him.

The return of the Demons! Even in the caves of the People such a foreboding had been used as a horrible warning for the young. But as one grew older, one no longer could be frightened so. Only enough remained of the early chill of such tales to make one's blood run faster at such a time as this.

One ship—a scout? Just as the People sent one warrior, two, three, ahead to test the strength of the enemy, the lay of the land, how it might be used for offense or defense before a clan moved into hunt?

Such a scout could be cut off. And, with small clans, the loss of a warrior was warning enough. They fell back, sought another trail. No tribe was large enough to take the loss of seasoned warriors as less than a major calamity.

Only, in the old tales the Demons had been countless. Cutting off a single scout would not discourage a migrating tribe with many warriors. Gammage might have an answer; he was the only one among the People now who would.

"We must hurry—" Furtig said, though he still watched for that light marking the Demon ship. He leaped back toward the inner wall. No light, yet something had almost brushed the rain-wet outer wall—something far larger than any flying thing he had ever seen. Luckily there were no wall lights here, nothing except the wan daylight. Perhaps they were lucky, and the flying thing in its swift passage had not seen them. For Furtig had the dire feeling that it might possess the power to smash through the transparent wall, scoop them out, were such action desired.

"Move!" He shoved Ku-La with his free hand. The other needed no urging; he was already hobbling at the best pace he had shown during their long, painful journey. As if the sight of that Demon thing had spurred him to transcend the wounds he bore.

They reached a second curve in the corridor, and this time Furtig gave a sigh of relief. For that transparent wall which made him feel so vulnerable vanished, there were solid barriers on either side.

That relief was very short, for they came soon

to one of those bridges in the air. Furtig crouched, peering into the outer storm, his hands cupped over his eyes. What made his disappointment the greater was that they were now close to their goal. For he recognized the tower at the other end of the bridge as the building in which he and Foskatt had tested the communication box. They need only cross this span and they would be in their, or Furtig's home territory.

Only, to cross, they must go along that narrow and slippery way, under not only the beating of the wind and rain, but perhaps also the threat of the flying thing. He thought he could do it—the People were surefooted. But Ku-La—

The other might be reading his thought. "What lies there?" His throaty voice was near a growl.

"The lair where my people hold."

"Safety of a kind then. Well, we can do no less than try to reach it."

"You are willing to try?" Surely the other could see his danger. But if he chose to go, then Furtig would do what he could to aid him.

He pulled out that cord which had served them so well, was preparing to loop them together belt to belt. But the other pushed his hands aside.

"No! I shall take the way four-footed. And do not link us—better one fall than both, the second without cause."

"Go you first then," Furtig replied. He did not know what he might be able to do if the other, unlinked, did slip. But he felt that if he could keep Ku-La before his eyes during that crossing he might be able to help in some fashion. And four-footed was surely the best way for them both.

Not only would it make them more sure-footed, but it would also make them less distinguishable to the flying thing. If they were unlucky enough to have that return.

The rain hit them like a blow, and Ku-La moved under its pounding very slowly. While Furtig wanted nothing so much as to be free to leap over that creeping shape before him and run with all possible speed to the promised safety of the far doorway. Yet he crawled behind Ku-La, the bag of record tapes slung about him, the water soaking his fur and trickling from his whiskers. He did not even raise his head far enough to see the doorway; rather he concentrated on Ku-La.

Twice the other halted, went flat as if his last strength had oozed away with the water pouring on him. But each time, just as Furtig reached forth a hand to try to rouse him, he levered up to struggle on.

They had passed the halfway point, though neither of them was aware of that in the agony of that slow advance, when the sound came. It was warning enough to flatten them both to the bridge, striving to give no sign of life as the thing drew closer.

It did not scream as one of the preying flying things, nor give voice in any way Furtig recognized. This sound was a continuous *beat-beat*. First to the left as if it hung in open space viewing them, then overhead. Furtig's nerve almost crumbled then. He could somehow see in his mind giant claws reaching out—coming closer—ready to sink into his body, bear him away.

So intent was he on that fearful mental picture that he was not even aware that the *beat-beat* was growing fainter, not until it had vanished. He lay on the bridge, unharmed, able to move. And the thing was gone! Had—had it taken Ku-La then, without his knowing it in the depths of his fear?

But when Furtig raised his head the other was there, stirring to life, creeping—

If they had time now before the thing returned—! For somehow Furtig could not believe that it was going to let them go so easily. There was a menace in it which he had sensed. And that sense he trusted, for it was one of the built-in protections of his kind and had saved lives many times over. The flying thing was to be feared, perhaps as much, if not more, than anything he had ever in his life faced before.

Tan ran a finger approvingly along the edge of the recorder. Got a good taping there. Tan's luck again. He smiled. Tan's luck was something which once or twice had made a real impression on the trainees back on Elhorn. He had managed so many times, usually through no reason he was aware of, to be at just the right place at the right moment, or to make the right move, even when he had no idea whether it was right or wrong.

So—with all those faint life-readings he had picked up in this pile but nothing in the open where he could get a visual record, it was his luck to catch that thing—or things (in that poor visibility they had looked like blobs as far as he was concerned)—right out in the open. They might have posed to order so he could get a good tape.

Blobs—certainly they did not look like men. He had sighted them edging out on the bridge and they had wriggled along there, almost as if they were crossing on their bellies. Nothing about them to suggest they were of his species at all. Tan tried to picture men crawling on hands and knees. Would the blobs resemble those? Could be. Except they were smaller than men—children?

But what would children be doing out alone in such a storm as this, crawling from one building to the next? No, easier to believe that they were something else, not human at all.

Tan was no longer smiling. After all, they had never discovered what had sent the First Ship people to Elhorn. It had been a very strong motive, not only to force them to take the perilous trip across space, but to leave them so intent thereafter on suppressing all they could of the world of their origin and the reason for colonizing another.

Tan had picked up some dim life-readings here, but not, oddly enough, in the buildings which had shown the greatest wealth of lights at night. No—they were widely scattered. And the readings varied. Enough that Ayana ought to be able to make something out of the variance. Such would not show up so plainly just because the pickup carried over unequal distances. It was more as if the life forms themselves varied. At least he had a reading and a picture of the blobs to turn in and that would give them a beginning reference.

And—there was not a single one of these life-readings which touched the proper coordinate for man on the measuring scale. That was what had made him buzz lower and lower, hang between the towers in a reck-less fashion, trying to pick up as many registrations on the tapes as he could.

Men had built this place. Tan knew enough from his

race's own fragmented records to recognize the form of architecture of his ancestors. But if there were no readings for "man" here—what did live within these walls?

The enemy of which they had no records? Only surmises presented by their imaginations? If the former, then the enemy was those blobs, and the quicker they were identified the better. Tan turned the flitter, swept out and away from the structures, heading for the ship with the small scraps of knowledge his first scouting flight had gained.

There was no *beat-beat* now—none at all. Ku-La scrambled ahead with a burst of speed Furtig hoped would not hurl him off that narrow way. But—in the doorway ahead was movement!

Rattons? Barkers? Furtig had the Demon weapon. The past hours had conditioned him to expect the worst, even in the People's lairs. Then he made out a furred head—They were coming forward to aid Ku-La—his own kind at last!

Gammage was at ease on the wide bed place. His tail curled across his thighs, and only the tip of it, twitching now and then, betrayed his excitement at Furtig's report.

The tapes had been carried off by the In-born trained to evaluate them. And a picked group, led by Foskatt, had set out to salvage the rest of Furtig's haul from where he had left it in the ducts.

Ku-La was in the room of healing, and Furtig was finding it difficult to keep his eyes open, his mind alert to answer the Ancestor's questions. But he discovered to his amazement that Gammage was not startled by the flying thing.

That a Demon sky-ship had landed was already known to the lair People. Its coming had been foretold by certain watchers who were not of flesh and blood, but servants of metal. When those gave the alert, the People had first been baffled, then made guesses as to the cause for alarm. And, hiding out, scouts had witnessed the actual landing of the ship.

Every device which could be put to defense or used to gain knowledge of the invaders had been trained on that ship. Without, it was hoped, having yet aroused the suspicions of the old masters of the lairs.

"They are indeed Demons," Gammage said. "Drink this, clan son, it will warm you. It is made of leaves and is refreshing to our spirits."

He waited while Furtig sipped from the bowl Liliha brought him. She did not leave, but settled on the other end of Gammage's divan as one who had a rightful part in this conference. Furtig was aware she watched him unblinkingly. He wondered if she did so to weigh within her own mind the truth of his tale.

The odor of the hot liquid was enticing, so much so that just to sniff its vapor raised his spirits, gave him courage, and renewed his energy. The taste was as good as the scent. The feeling of warmth that spread through him made him even more drowsy than he had been. But two full swallows were all that he took, holding the cup from him lest his pleasure in its contents cloak his mind to what must be firmly faced.

"We viewed them through those glasses which bring the far close," Gammage continued. "They brought many things from their ship and put together a flying thing. By that time it was night, and they went again into the ship and closed it, as if they believed they might be in danger. Four of them only, though there may be more inside we did not see.

"With the morning, in spite of the storm, one came forth and entered the flying thing. He raised it into the air and flew back and forth, in and out, among the buildings. He did not try to land, but hovered above. As if the Demon sought something. But we cannot guess what he sought, nor the manner of his seeking. With Demons—who can know?"

"He found us on the bridge," Furtig returned. "But he did not attack, only stayed above us for a space and then flew away."

"Returning," Liliha said, "to the ship. It could be that when he hung above you he marked who—or what—you were."

Gammage chewed reflectively on a claw tip. "What you found, with the aid of Ku-La, is a treasure of knowledge. But whether we shall be given time to use it is another matter. If these Demons plan to reclaim the lairs I am not sure we can defeat their purpose."

"You can withdraw—to the caves—as our forefathers did when the Demons hunted them before," Furtig suggested.

"That is the last resort. The lairs are very large and, as you proved, clan son, there are ways we smaller people can travel in secret. The Demons cannot force their greater bodies into such passages."

"Perhaps we shall be both Demon-hunted and Ratton-attacked in the end." Furtig saw the gloomiest of futures.

"There are also the Barkers—" Gammage chewed again on his claw.

For the moment Furtig was content enough to sit

and let his fur dry in the warmth of the chamber, sniff at the odor of his good drink, and now and then sip it. But he longed for sleep; even if the Demons were to tramp these corridors soon, a warrior had to sleep.

He fought his eyes' closing by drinking the last of the liquid. Gammage spoke again:

"The Barkers are not ones to take kindly to the trapping of their scout. Unlike our people, they are happiest in the pack rubbing shoulders to the next. And they will move as a pack to avenge their kind."

What the Ancestor said was no more than all knew. You killed or took a Barker prisoner, and you had to face his fellows in force. It was one of the things that made the Barkers so feared.

"They hunt by scent." Still the Ancestor recited common knowledge. "Therefore they will trail in here, and find the trap of the Rattons. The Rattons will take to inner ways, and in doing so, they may escape the Barkers. But—if the Barkers invade they can well pick up our scent—

"Ku-La, when he is healed, will go to his people and invite them to join us. As he has told me, those know about the Demons, and the lairs—of how we must labor to save what we have learned. If we take to the wilds, it will need many backs and hands to help carry what we must. Therefore, as Ku-La goes to his tribe, so must you and Foskatt go to the caves. There you must tell them of the coming evil and that they must send their warriors—or bring hither all the People—"

"Do you think they will listen to me, Ancestor? I am not an Elder, I am one who failed in the Trials, and went forth from the caves. Will they heed my

words? You know our clans and that they are slow
to believe in new things."

"You speak as a youngling, clan son. From here
you will carry certain things to impress the Elders.
And you do not go alone—"

"Yes, Foskatt, too." But privately Furtig thought
Foskatt, for all his longer time in the lairs, would
have little more weight than he had himself.

Gammage had been a long time away from the
caves, he had forgotten the hold of custom on those
living there.

"Besides Foskatt," Gammage said, "Liliha goes,
also, by her own choice. And she, as well as you,
shall take weapons such as those of the caves have no
knowledge of. These are gifts, and you shall promise
more if your people come to us.

"This," he continued, "will be easily done—"

Furtig did not agree with that statement in the
least, but he had no chance to protest, as the Ancestor
swept on—

"The Barker must be found. If he still lives, he
must be freed and returned to his People. That will
give us for the first time a small chance of holding a
truce talk with them. Otherwise they will storm into the
lairs, perhaps causing a disaster at the time when we
must unite against Demons, not war among ourselves.
Now we have a common cause with even Barkers."

So they were back to Gammage's wish, that all the
peoples, even those hereditary enemies, make a common cause against the greater menace. Listening to
him, sometimes one could almost believe that would
work. But—perhaps he would even suggest sending
a truce flag to the Rattons—!

Apparently Gammage was not prepared to go that far. He was nodding a little, his tail tip beating back and forth.

"To the Barkers we shall suggest a truce. The Rattons—no—we cannot deal with them in any way! They are as accursed as the Demons and always have been. We must warn whom we can to stand together. Liliha, see to the clan son. I think he sleeps now, even though his eyes are open!"

Furtig heard that as a distant murmur. There was a touch on his arm. Somehow he blundered to his feet and wavered off, that light touch steering him this way and that, until he had come to his own bed place and stretched out there.

Demon—Ratton—Barker—sleep won out over all.

➤ 12 ◄

"Animals!" But even as Ayana spoke she knew that was not true. Yes, those bodies were furred. And they had tails. But neither could it be denied that they wore belts around their waists, and attached to the belt of one was a laser! The thing was armed with a weapon much like the most potent in the ship's locker.

She studied the scene on the record reader into which Tan had fed his tape. The light was admittedly poor, but the longer she looked the more new details she could see. Animal, no, but neither was it like her norm for "man."

However it had a haunting familiarity. And it carried a lumpy burden—the rear one of the two, that is—on its back. Animals were used so. What of the gorks on Elhorn—ungainly, half-feathered, half-scaled, of avian descent but lacking their ancestors' wings? For an instant or two she remembered gorks with a homesick nostalgia.

No, the bundle did not mean that the creatures on the bridge were servants of men—not as the gorks served. Not when one of them also wore a laser. Still—she was teased by a wisp of memory.

"Animal—you are sure?" Jacel roused her from that search.

"No, it is armed and wearing the belt—how can we be sure?"

"It is matched with this life-reading." Massa consulted the dial. "And there are similar life-readings here, here, and here." The computer had produced a sketch map earlier and Massa's pointer tapped that. "Now here, and here are two other readings of a different type, one differing from the other—three kinds in all." She made checks now on the map surface with yellow for the first, red for the second, blue for the last.

Yellow marked the building towards which the two on the bridge headed, red lay behind them.

"Those blue—they are near the outer rim." Tan surveyed the results with satisfaction. He had brought back enough to keep the computer busy. Catching those two in the open had been the crowning bit of luck—Tan's luck.

"The creature to the fore,"—Ayana moved closer, "it has been hurt." Her medic-trained eyes were not deceived by the effects of rain and wet fur. Was she watching part of a drama such as one had on a story tape—perhaps the rescue of a wounded comrade from the enemy?

"Fighting?" Tan sounded excited. "Two species at war?"

She looked up from the screen, startled by that note in his voice. His eyes were shining. It took a certain temperament to produce a scout. Tan had tested high in all the attributes the commanders believed necessary.

But there had followed rigid training. And the Tan who had survived that training, winning over all others to gain his place with this crew, was not exactly the same Tan to whom she had been drawn.

Ayana knew that her own place in the ship depended not only on her ability to do her own job, but also on the fact that she was a complement to Tan, supplying what he lacked. It was the same with Jacel and Massa. They had to complement one another or they would not have been put together to form a crew, necessarily living closely during the voyage; their personalities were so related as to assure the least possible friction.

But now there was something in Tan Ayana shrank from, refused to face. The Tan who had come out of the grueling training had a hardness which she secretly feared. He could look upon that wounded body dragging painfully along, and what he thought of was the struggle which had caused those hurts. It was as if he actually wanted to watch such a battle. And that Tan—no, she would not believe that that Tan was the ruler of the mind and body she loved.

"But there is not"—Massa, frowning, paid no attention to Tan's comment "a single life-reading for our own kind! Yet this is a city built by man. We have landed on a site such as our fathers made on Elhorn, save that they did not ring it about there with a city—a city so vast that Tan's record"—she shook her head—"is more than we expected—"

"Expected?" Tan challenged that. "We can expect anything here. This is the world which sent the First Ships into space, where secrets, all the secrets we need, lie waiting!"

"And from which," Jacel pointed out dryly, "our

own kind seems to have gone. We had better keep that in mind when we go prying about for secrets, lest some of those we find are other than we care to own or discover. Do not forget that this city has inhabitants—such as these—" He pointed to the reader. *"And do not forget either, Tan, that those men of mighty secrets, our parents of the First Ships, fled in such fear that they tried to keep hidden the very existence of this world."*

Tan looked impatient. *"We have protection that those animals do not know of—"*

"Animals who carry lasers?" Jacel was not to be shaken. *"And if this is indeed a storehouse of waiting secrets, perhaps some of them are already in the paws—or hands—of those who intend to keep them. We walk softly, slowly, and with all care now. Or it may be, in spite of caution, we cease to walk at all."*

He did not put any undue emphasis on those words. Yet they carried the force of an order. Ayana hoped that the conditioning they had all accepted—that the will of Jacel was to hold in any final decision—would continue to control Tan. Let him work off his restlessness, his energy, in his sky exploration of the city.

It would seem that her hopes held the next day. The storm died before midnight, and sunrise brought a fair day. The light caught the windows in the buildings, some of which did not seem windows at all but clear bands running in levels around the towers. And those blazed as the sun struck them fairly.

Tan took off in the flitter, this time to trace the outer boundaries of the city. Again he carried equipment to feed back to their computer all the data he gained.

The others did not lift ramp at once, but set out

sensors to pick up any approach at ground level. Jacel supervised that, being very careful about the linkage. When he had finished he stood up.

"Nothing can pass that. A blade of grass blown by the wind would cause an alarm," he said with conviction.

Ayana had climbed part way up the ramp. She shaded her eyes against the steadily warming blaze of the sun, tried to view the flitter. But Tan must have streaked straight away, wasting no time hovering as he had yesterday.

That furred creature, the hurt one—it must have long since reached the tower. She wished she could remember why it seemed so familiar. The records of the First Ships, because of that destruction, often withheld just the details one needed most.

Oddly enough it came to her back in her own cabin, and from the strangest source. She had been fed by that feeling of nostalgia to open her small packet of allowed personal items. They were, perhaps to a stranger, a queer collection. There was a flower preserved between two-inch-wide squares of permaplast, its violet-blue as richly vivid as it had been when she had encased it. And a water-worn pebble that came from the stream outside her home at Veeve Station. She had kept it because the crystalline half was so oddly joined to the black stone. And then there was Putti—

Ayana stared now at Putti wide-eyed. There had always been Puttis—round and soft, made for children. They were traditional and common. She had kept hers because it was the last thing her mother had made before she died of the one illness on Elhorn they had found no remedy for. Puttis were four-legged and tailed. Their heads were round, with shining eyes made of buttons or beads, upstanding pointed ears, whiskers above the small mouth. Puttis were loved, played with, adored in the child world; their origin was those brought by children on the First Ships.

She had seen one of those original Puttis, also preserved in permaplast. And that one had been covered with fur.

Putti! She could not be right, to compare the soft toy with that muscular furred creature on the bridge. But Putti could have been made by someone trying to represent just such a creature in softer materials than flesh, blood, and bone. She was about to start up, to hunt Jacel and Massa with news of her discovery, when second thoughts argued against that. The resemblance, now that she studied Putti closely, grew less and less. She might make the connection in her own mind, but that was not proof. Putti, a toy—and a weapon-bearing primitive (if not an animal) skulking through buildings long deserted by her kind—No, it was foolish to expect the others to accept that suspicion.

Furtig held the platter of meat on his knee and tried to show proper manners by not stuffing his mouth or chewing too loudly. He was hungry, but there was Liliha, smoothing her tail as she rested on a thick cushion, now and then fastidiously flicking some small suggestion of dust from her fur. He could hear, just, her very muted throat purr, as if she were lost in some pleasant dream. But he did not doubt she was aware of every move he made. So he curbed his appetite and tried to copy the restraint of the In-born.

"The flyer"—she broke her self-absorption—"is

in the air again. It does not hang above us but has headed toward the west. Dolar and two scouts saw it rise. There was a Demon in it."

"It is not like the servants here then, able to go on its own?" Furtig wanted to keep her talking. Just to have Liliha sitting there while he ate, relaxed in the thought that he had won to safety through such adventures as most warriors never dreamed of, and that he had rested well and was ready to follow the outer trails again, was pleasing.

"So it would seem. They made it of pieces they brought in the sky-ship."

Furtig marveled at her patience. He should have remembered that; Gammage had spoken of it the night before. But at that time Furtig had not been thinking too clearly. Now he glanced up hastily, but Liliha was not eyeing him with scorn.

"If they made it," she continued, "then within these lairs may lie that which can also be used for the same purpose. Gammage has set those who watched the making into search for such."

Privately Furtig did not doubt that, given the time and the means, the Ancestor and his followers would be able to duplicate the flyer. But then to find someone to fly in it—that was a different matter. Though he could imagine Gammage ready to make the attempt if offered the chance. He, himself, preferred to do his traveling—and any fighting—on the solid and dependable ground. But there were advantages to such craft. They could take a scout higher than any spy tree. Just as the Demon was now viewing the lairs from above.

On the other hand, unless the Demon had some unheard-of way of looking through solid roofs and walls, he would see only the lairs and not what or who moved in them under cover. Only in the open country could such servants be used to advantage.

Furtig swallowed the last mouthful of meat. Now he raised the bowl and lapped as mannerly as he could at the residue of good juices gathered in the bottom. The lair people lived well. They had fish, found in small inner lakes (made it would seem for no other purpose than to hold them in readiness to be eaten). And there were other places where birds and rabbits were preserved in runs, fed and kept safe until they were needed.

The cave people might well think of that. Suppose they kept alive some of the creatures they hunted or netted, fed them in pens. Then when game became scarce and the weather ill for hunters, there would be food at hand. Yes, there were more things than Demon knowledge to be learned here in the lairs.

He ran his tongue along the bowl rim to gather up the last drop, then licked upper and lower lips clean.

"What of the Barker?" he asked.

He still believed that Gammage's plan of trying to make truce with Barkers would not work. But he was also wary of guessing the outcome of any of the Ancestor's plans. He had witnessed too much of what had been accomplished here for that.

"Dolar has sent a party with two of the rumblers. The Rattons fear those greatly, for they run forward, crunching all in their path, and cannot be turned aside in any way the Rattons have yet discovered. With those to break a path for our warriors we hope to free the Barker. In the meantime—Foskatt has found the other tapes, and they are being brought

back. Ku-La is out of the healing place. Soon he will
go to talk to his people."

"As I must to the Elders of the caves." Furtig
stood up. He was no longer tired, nor was his fur
matted by crawling through the dust of the ducts and
then through the pelting of the storm. It was sleek
and smooth. He fastened on his belt neatly, seeing
that in the newly improvised loop there was still the
lightning-bolt weapon of the Demons. Apparently
that was yet his.

Such a weapon would impress the Elders. If he
remembered rightly Gammage's words during that
last meeting, he would be given other weapons to
influence their decision. The sooner he took the trail
to that purpose then, the better. He said so as he
finished checking his belt.

"Well enough," Liliha agreed. Her guidance would
take them through the lairs to the best point from
which to strike out for the caves.

Furtig had slept a long time, almost a full day.
It was close on evening and shadows were painting
larger and larger pools for concealment as, at last, the
three of them threaded a way through silent corridors,
past echoing rooms which might not have known life
and use since the Demons died or fled. As a guide
Liliha went first, wearing a pack between her slim
shoulders and around her waist the same belt of tools
and weapons as the warriors wore. Then came Furtig
and Foskatt, ready to play rear guard if needed.

They must move their swiftest while under the
protection of the lair roofs, Furtig thought. For he did
not forget the flyer. Why the Demon had not killed
them on the bridge was a mystery to him. And he

did not want death to strike out of the sky now. It was difficult enough to fight at ground level.

If Demons could see in the dark, then even the coming of night would not aid them. To the end of the lairs they could keep under cover, descending to the underground ways when there was need. But Furtig did not forget that wide expanse of open between the lairs and the beginning of the growth that provided normal cover for his kind. He hoped the night would be cloudy when they reached that point.

Liliha brought them to a window from which they could see that open space. They were at the edge of the lairs. Furtig's sense of direction was in operation. They were to the north of that place where he had crossed before, but not too much so.

He studied the strip narrowly. His own fur was dark, not far different in shade from the withered grass. And Foskatt had the same natural adaptation to the country. It was different for Liliha. Not only was her fur lighter, but it was so thin a coating of fluff that she might well be sighted from above.

"Look you, woods warriors," she said as he commented on that. She slipped off her pack and shook out something she had taken from it. Now she held not a small square but a mass of something—

Furtig shook his head and tried to concentrate on what she held. But it was no use—his keen sight failed him. He could not look at it directly! To do so made him queasy. He wanted to strike out, tear that disturbing substance from her.

But she was winding it about her. And where that stuff covered her body, he could no longer look. Finally only her head remained free of the distortion.

"Another Demon secret, and one but lately discovered. Gammage has but two of these, cut from a single one. When I wear this no one can look at me. Unless he wishes to have his eyes turn this way, that way, and his head whirl about. Now, do not worry about me, look to yourselves, warriors, and cross quickly. The flyer makes itself known by noise. If you hear it coming, take what cover the land offers. I shall meet you where the trees grow. Good traveling to you."

Furtig could not look at her at all now. She had pulled a flap of the distorting stuff up over her head and become hidden. He had to turn away and knew she slipped out the window only by the faint sounds made by her going.

"The Demons," remarked Foskatt, "seem to have an answer for any problem. Let us hope that such answers can, in turn, be used against them. She is well gone. It is indeed a kind of hiding I am glad we do not have to deal with often. To the trail then, clan brother!"

The window was wide enough to let them slip through together. Furtig crouched on the ground almost happily. It was good to feel fresh soil and not pavement, the ways of the Demons. He did not look ahead yet, having no wish to see some eye-twisting shimmer in the moonlight covering Liliha's going. His hunter's training took over, and he fell back into the patterns he had learned as a youngling.

It was difficult to keep on listening for the beat in the sky, the possible return of the flyer. Once within the screen of the brush beyond the open, Furtig rose to his full height and gave a purring sigh of relief.

"For so far," Foskatt echoed his feeling, "we have done well. But—"

Furtig swung around. He had picked up a scent that was not Liliha's. No, this was strong and rank. He was downwind of a Tusker, probably more than one. And that surprised him, for Tuskers had no interest in the lairs, very little curiosity about their past, and were seldom to be found hereabouts.

There was still a truce between the People and the Tuskers. And they shared the same territories, since the Tuskers fed upon roots and vegetation. Though the Tuskers were meat, they had no appeal for the People, they were far too formidable to be prey.

Furtig could hear now that low grunting which was Tusker speech. None of the People could imitate it, any more than Tusker throat and tongue could shape the proper words of a warrior. But they understood sign language and could answer it.

A warning? Did the Tuskers know of the flyer? It might be well to suggest that they keep under cover.

Furtig uttered a low wailing cry to announce his coming. And without waiting to see if Foskatt followed, swung into the heavy, disagreeable scent which would lead him to the grubbing ones.

When he reached them, they were in battle formation, their big heads, weighed down by the great curved tusks which named them, low to the ground. The older warriors stood still, watching with their small red eyes. One or two of the younger ones on the back fringes of the party pawed the soil, kicking it up in warning.

They were not a full family party as Furtig had expected. There were no females or younglings behind that outer defense of one great Elder and such of his male offspring as had not yet gone to start their own families. Furtig knew that Elder—the seam of an old scar across his nose marked him. Unlike the People the Tuskers had kept to four feet, never learning to walk on two. Also they used no weapons except those nature provided. But mind to mind they were no less than warriors of the caves or the lairs.

Furtig saw that that they were deeply angered and would have to be approached with care. For the temper of such as Broken Nose was uncertain when he was in such a mood. Furtig advanced no closer, but sat down, curling his tail over his feet in a peace sign.

The younger Tuskers snorted. One pawed again, wrinkling lips to show fangs. Furtig paid them no attention. It was Broken Nose who ruled here. Having waited for a small time to show that he had not only come in peace but for good reason, he held out his hands and began to try to tell the complicated story of the Demons' landing, of the flyer, in a series of signs.

One of the younglings grunted and his neighbor shouldered him roughly into silence. Encouraged, Furtig ran through his signs slowly, began to tell the same tale again. This was no exchange of general news about the countryside; he must improvise signs to explain things totally new to both their peoples.

And having told it twice, he could only wait to see if he had been clever enough to get his message into a form Broken Nose could understand. For a very long moment he waited and his heart sank. The boar made no move. It could be Furtig had failed. He was about to begin again when Broken Nose grunted.

One of the younger of his band moved forward a little. He squatted clumsily on his haunches, balancing so he could raise one hoofed foot from the ground to gesture or use to draw in the leaf mold.

It was a complicated business that exchange of information. But at last Furtig thought he had the story, and his fur stiffened and he hissed.

The Tuskers had witnessed the landing of the Demon ship, though its final settling to the ground had been hidden by the lairs. The unusual flashing of fire had alarmed Broken Nose. He was old and wily enough to know that suspicion and safety went hand in hand. So he had sent his females and younglings into what he believed good hiding in a rock-walled place where there was but one entrance, which would be well defended by two nonbreeding females, both formidable opponents. Then he, with his warriors, had set out to discover the meaning of the strange fire.

Having prowled along the edge of the flat lands beyond the lairs, they had decided there was no danger and had withdrawn. But they had been starting out of their stronghold among the rocks only this afternoon when the flyer had appeared.

There was a sudden giddiness, a strange feeling in their heads. Even Broken Nose had fallen as one gored. From the belly of the flyer had come what the Tusker could only describe as a long root. This had somehow caught up two of the smallest younglings, jerked them aloft. Then the flyer had gone away.

It was Broken Nose's firm intention to track down the attacker and wreak full vengeance—though he was clever enough not to charge in, but to scout the enemy position first. And the fact that he had seen the flyer disappear into the lairs had shaken him. For that was country he did not know, and many dangers might lurk there.

➤ 13 ◄

"Hunters—at least of Tuskers—" Foskatt spoke for the first time. The soft growl in Furtig's throat grew louder. Not that he had any kin ties with the young of the Tuskers. But if today it had been those of Broken Nose who disappeared into the flyer, tomorrow that might appear at the caves and lift some youngling Furtig knew.

That there was any hope of freeing the captives he doubted. And Furtig thought the old Tusker knew that, knew also that his proposed expedition against the lairs would be hopeless.

Alone, yes. But what if Gammage's urging could not only bring in the People, but the Tuskers as well? Furtig rubbed his hands across his furred chest, tried to think out telling signs for communication.

Furtig was startled by a sharp grunt from one of the young Tuskers. A moment later the familiar scent of Liliha filled his nostrils. She came to sit down beside him, no longer muffled in that distorting material. And her coming gave him an idea of how to approach the Tusker Elder. Swiftly he began to sign, trying to put all the meaning he could into that flexing of fingers, waving of hands, drawing on the ground. The moon was full tonight, and this small clearing was well lighted.

The Tuskers appeared to follow the explanation that this female was one who lived in the lairs, one who sought the secrets of the Demons in order to defeat them with their own weapons. Having finished, Furtig spoke to Liliha without turning his head:

"Show them something to prove the powers of the lairs."

There on the ground where he had drawn suddenly shone a round of yellow light. The Tuskers grunted. Furtig could hear the youngsters stamp nervously, though Broken Nose betrayed no sign of surprise. As Elder he must so assert his superiority.

"This"—Furtig moved his hands into that light—"is one of the secrets of the lairs. We have others, many others. So that this time the Demons will not find us defenseless. There is one ship of them only, and we have counted but four Demons."

"Scouts may run before the tribe," pawed out the young boar. "There may be many more coming."

"True. But now we are warned. There are many hiding places in the lairs." Furtig was getting a little excited. It might be he was going to win allies for Gammage even before he reached the caves and had to face the skepticism of his own Elders.

"And no dangers?"

"There are Rattons there, on the lower levels."

This time Broken Nose himself grunted. Rattons could be understood better than Demons. If the

Tuskers had not seen Rattons, they had heard of them
and their devilish traps. Then Foskatt spoke softly:

"We have little time to argue with the Tuskers.
This is a matter of our own people."

He was right. They had delivered a warning to the
Tuskers, who must now make their own decision to
flee beyond the range of the flyer or to stand and
fight. Furtig began the last signs—

"We go to our people. But watch for the flyer—stay
under cover."

Again Broken Nose grunted. This was an order to
his own followers, for they turned and trotted into
the bushes, only the old boar and his interpreter
lingering. The latter signed:

"We stay to watch."

Furtig was glad of their choice. Those eyes in the
huge tusked head, swung low before him, seemed small.
But he knew their keen vision. There was no more
deadly foe to be faced than this clan when its anger
was roused and it prepared for battle. There could be
no strangers leaving the lairs along here that the Tuskers would not mark. And, Furtig thought, even armed
though they might be with strange weapons, if the
Demons came on foot, they had better come warily. For
all their bulk and seeming clumsiness, the Tuskers were
able to lurk undetected in hiding. They had vanquished
Barkers many times in red defeat, using the wind itself
to mask their scent.

*Ayana gazed at the plate before her. The meat's
rich juices formed a natural gravy. The others were
eating eagerly, with the greed of those who have
been on E rations for a long time. The meat had*

tested harmless, resembling the best one could find on Elhorn. Why then did it nauseate her to look at it? She lifted a piece to her lips, found she could not bite into it. Why?

"A whole herd," Tan said between mouthfuls. "We shall have food in plenty close to hand."

Ayana continued to look at the meat. It was well cooked, and, while it had been cooking, the savor had made her mouth water. She had hardly been able to wait, any more than the others, until it was ready. She had been as eager as they to taste the first real food they had seen since they lifted.

"Luck, pure luck," Tan continued, "running into these on my first cast into the open country. They have not been hunted for a long time. Easy enough to pick up a couple."

Ayana stood up. She had been fighting the thought valiantly with all her strength of will. But it broke now through her defense, and she could not control her words.

"How do we know that—this is an animal?"

She was a fool, of course. But there were those furred things on the bridge. Without the trappings, the weapon, they might be called animals. Yet she was sure they were not. These things they had cooked had not had the same appearance, that was true. But they knew too little, far too little of this world. She could not stomach meat which might be—be the flesh of intelligent beings. There, she had faced the thought which had struggled darkly in her mind. With a little cry she clapped her hands over her mouth, pushed past Jacel, and hurried, not only from the cabin but down through the ship until she reached the ramp hatch.

But that was closed; they were sealed in. And it seemed to her that she must have fresh air, that the fumes of the cooked meat, which she had thought so appetizing earlier, were now a sickening vapor.

Ayana battered at the hatch fastening, the door rolled open, and she could fill her lungs with the air of night. Then hands fell in a harsh, punishing grip on her shoulders, jerking her back into the ship's shell.

"What are you trying to do? Set yourself up as a perfect target for anything out there?" Tan was angry. She had heard that note in his voice only a few times in her life.

He pushed her to one side forcibly, turned to reseal the hatch. Ayana rubbed her arm, blinking fiercely. Tan was not going to see betraying tears in her eyes.

When he had the seal tight, he swung around, his eyes hot and hard, watching her.

"Now—what did you mean by that scene?" he demanded as if there had never been, or could be, any good feeling between them.

And his hostility awakened her own spirit.

"Just what I said. We know too little of the situation here. You thought of those beings on the recorder tape as animals. But they are not, and deep in your mind, you know that. Now—you bring others back—for food!" Her revulsion returned. She had to cover her mouth for a moment. "We do not know what they are!"

"You need a mind-clear treatment." His anger was chilling, no longer hot and impulsive but worse. He was entering one of those remote moods when he froze anyone who tried to communicate. "You saw what I brought back. It was all animal. Perhaps"—he came a little closer, stood looking down at her with that cold

menace—"*perhaps you do need a mind-clear. You did not test out as entirely level-stable—*"

"*How do you know that?*" Ayana demanded.

Tan laughed, but there was no lightness of spirit in that sound.

"*I had my ways of learning what I needed to know. It is always well to be aware of the weaknesses of one's fellows. Yes, I know your L report, my dear Ayana. And do you believe that I cannot put that knowledge to the best use?*"

He caught her shoulders again and shook her, as if to impress her with his strength of both body and will. It was as if that ruthless handling shook from her mind a shield she had clung to for years. Tan was—Tan was—She stared at him, beaten for the moment, not by his will, but by her own realization of what Tan really was.

"*We will have no more stupid imaginings.*" He did not wait for her to answer; perhaps he believed she was fully cowed. "*Eat or not—if you wish to starve that is your decision. But you will keep your mouth shut on such ideas.*"

Jacel, Massa, were not fools, nor, Ayana believed, could they be dominated by Tan. If what she had said made them consider—But for the present, until she had time to think, she must let him believe that he had won. Though he appeared to have no suspicion that he had not. There was confidence in the way he pulled her around, shoved her at the ladder, with the unspoken but implied order to go aloft.

The worst was that Ayana must continue to share their small cabin. The horror that grew in her was even greater than the desolation she had known moments

*earlier. Tan would enforce such a relationship, she knew.
There was only one escape. She was the medic—and
the cramped medic-lab cabin was hers alone. She could
shelter there until she had had time to think things out.*

*She climbed, her thoughts racing. If Tan believed he
had broken any resistance in her—One level more—
the medic cabin. She had hardly believed she could
escape him so easily. But she made a quick dash,
thumb-locked the door behind her. She fully expected
him to bat out his rage against its surface. But there
was only utter and complete silence.*

*Ayana backed away until she came up against the
patient's bunk. She faced the door, taut, listening.
When there came no assault, she relaxed on the edge
of the bunk.*

*The palms of her hands were sweating, she felt
weak, sick. The confrontation of the past few moments
had frightened her as she had never been frightened
before in her life. Tan knew her L report. He could
turn that to his own advantage. Every weakness, every
way of reaching her had been charted on that! He
could use such knowledge to influence the others to
distrust her. Her outburst at the table had given him
a base on which to build false claims. She had played
directly into his hands—She was—*

*Ayana began to fight back. He had thrown her so
far off base that he had gained the advantage for a
while. It was time she forgot what had happened and
began to consider the immediate present. She had
been warned; perhaps Tan had made his first mistake
in revealing that he thought he could dominate her.*

*Think, use her brain; she had a good one, L report
or not. Ayana had a good and useful mind. Now*

was the time to put it to work, not allow herself to become enmeshed by emotion, let alone fear, the most weakening of all.

She must not depend on either Jacel or Massa, but stand alone. For if Tan could prove to be an entirely different person from the one she thought she knew, loved, then whom could she trust? Herself—and her skills. Ayana began to look about the cabin and what it contained. Herself and her skills—perhaps she would find that enough.

Though she did not rise, her head was up, her shoulders no longer hunched as if she expected at any moment to feel the sting of a lash laid across them. She was Ayana and she fought to remain that—herself, not something owned by Tan.

Bright as the moon had been in the clearing, it was no guide to paths under the growth cover. But Furtig slipped along easily, treading the way in memory as well as if he walked one of the well-paved ways of the Demons. These were hunting lands where those of the caves often came.

The night had voices, birds whose hunting also depended upon the cover of the dark hours, insects, smaller life, which stilled instantly as the scent of the travelers reached them.

Furtig breathed deeply, planted each foot with pleasure in the fact that it met soil and not the hard surface of a corridor. He was of the caves after all. And with every whisper of sound, the rich scents the wind brought him, he rejoiced.

Liliha, for all her In-born life, did not lag, but with gliding grace matched the pace the two warriors set.

Perhaps she looked from right to left and back again more often than they, for to her this was all new. But she appeared to find more interest than cause for alarm in what lay about.

They halted at a spring Furtig remembered well, drank their fill, ate of the supplies they had carried with them from the lairs. But always they listened, not for the usual night sounds, but for the beat of the Demon flyer within weapon reach overhead.

"If there are only four of them," Furtig said, "then they can be defeated. Even if they are scouts—if they did not return, their clan would take warning."

"It depends," Foskatt pointed out, "on why they scout. If it is merely to seek new ground, and they do not return, yes, perhaps that would be the end for their kin."

"We cannot," Liliha said with the assurance of the In-born, to whom the study of Demons was a way of life, "judge anything that the Demons do by what we would do in their place. They do not think as we."

"If they think straightly at all," Foskatt growled. "Remember the old tales—in the final days after the Demons had loosed their own doom, they were so twisted in their ways that they hunted and preyed upon each other, dealing death to their kin as well as to our kind in turn. And it would seem that they have begun such ways once more. At least they have taken the Tusker younglings without cause—for one purpose—"

"Again you are not sure," Liliha countered. "It may be they have taken the younglings to study them, to see what manner of people are now in possession of the world they ruled so evilly in the old days."

"I do not think so," Furtig said. He was unable to prove that Foskatt was right in his reading of the Demons' motives. But somehow he was as sure of it as if he had indeed witnessed the outcome of the stealing of Broken Nose's young.

"Why did they not capture Ku-La and me in the same fashion?" he continued. Ever since he had heard of that seizure from the air which the flyer had practiced, this had puzzled him. It would have been very easy to capture the two of them from that open bridge. Of course, had the Demon tried it, Furtig had held the lightning weapon. Was that why they had escaped? Had the Demon seen and recognized from aloft the lightning thrower? If so—then Gammage's plan to arm as many of the People as they could had great merit.

It was as if Liliha now read his thoughts. "You were a warrior, armed—not a helpless and frightened youngling. It may be that the Demon wanted no trouble with captives so he chose the least dangerous that could be found. How much farther are these caves of yours?" she ended briskly.

"If we do not have to turn from the straight trail, we shall be there shortly after sunrise."

They kept on under trees, using brush as a canopy where trees thinned or failed. They crossed any open space with a rush, always listening for ominous sounds from the air. Dawn found them working their way into the higher lands of the caves. Furtig heard the yowl of the first sentry, alerting the next. That cry would pass from one to the other until it reached the ears of the Elders. He did not know if he had been recognized for himself, or merely as one of the People.

But the fact that the three came openly was in their favor. Sentries and guards would loosely encircle them as they went but would not try to stop them. However, as the three breasted the next-to-the-last slope before they reached the cliff of the caves, they were fronted by one who rose out of the dried grass to await them. Her gray fur was silken, shining in the sun. And though she was small, she held herself proudly erect.

"Eu-La!" The sight of her brought back the warm memory of how she had sent him forth on this venture armed not only with the fighting claws she had found, but also with her belief in him.

"Cave brother," she said gravely, as gravely as one who had mothered younglings, so dignified was she. But her eyes slid from him to Liliha and her lips parted on a hiss.

"You bring a strange Chooser—!" She spat the words as if they were an ill saying.

"Not so!" He should have known. Just as a warrior would flatten ears and twitch tail at the sight of a non-kinsman, so would female meet strange female. "This is Liliha, an In-born of the lairs. She has not chosen, nor will she, save among her own kin—that is lair law."

Eu-La was openly suspicious, but she looked again to Liliha, studying her carefully.

"She is not like the cave Choosers. That is true."

"And it is also true, as your kinsman has said," Liliha uttered in the throaty, purring voice of friendship, "that I have not come to choose among you, but to speak of other things, things of danger, to your Elder Chooser."

She moved closer, and, as if Eu-La were suddenly convinced, they each extended a pink tongue, touched it to the cheek of the other, in the touch-of-friend.

"Open is the cave of Eu-La to Liliha of the lairs," Eu-La said. Then she looked to Foskatt, who had fallen a little behind. "But this is also a stranger."

"Not quite so, cave kin. I was once of the caves before I went seeking Gammage. I am Foskatt, but perhaps you have not heard my name, for I went forth seasons ago."

"Foskatt," Eu-La repeated. "Ah, you are of the cave of Kay-Lin. The Elder Chooser there has spoken your name."

He was startled. "And who is that Elder Chooser?"

"She is Fa-Ling."

"Fa-Ling! Who was litter sister of my mother! Then indeed I still have close kin in the caves!"

"But you, Furtig, have you learned all Gammage's Secrets that you return?" There was a teasing purr in Eu-La's voice.

"Not all, sister. But a few—yes." His hand went to the lightning thrower at his belt. "But more than any talk of secrets, we bring news for the Elders."

"Two sets of Elders now," she told him. "There have been changes at the caves. The western People have come to join us. They have taken over the lower caves. A new tribe of Barkers moved into their lands and they lost five warriors and an Elder in battle. There is much fear now that the Barkers move against us next. And it is a large pack."

Furtig listened closely. Perhaps now the Elders might agree to Gammage's plan. If they believed that they could not hold the caves, even uniting two tribes, they might be pushed into trekking to the lairs.

Save—the Demons and what had happened to the younglings of the Tuskers. Perhaps one could suggest that the cave clans take to flight, yes. But away from both Barkers and lairs, not into the buildings where Rattons and Demons alike waited. Bad or good, Furtig could not judge. He could only deliver the message and warning he carried.

Resolutely Furtig continued on, Eu-La matching him step to step. Now and then she glanced at him measuringly, as if so trying to read his thoughts. But she asked no questions, seemed pleased enough that he had returned.

Her acceptance of Liliha had been quick. Furtig hoped that was a sign that the other females would do the same. If the In-born could continue to make it clear that she was no threat to their mate-choice, he did not see why they would be hostile. Compared to Eu-La—or Fas-Tan—her scantily furred body might not please, might seem to be ugly. Though being used now to the In-born Furtig did not consider it so. But he hoped, for the sake of their mission, that the others would.

If Liliha had any vanity she had not displayed it. And perhaps now she was quick enough to see that the uglier and stranger she made herself seem, the more acceptable she would be. Ugly, strange—the two things Liliha could never truly be!

Ayana moved in the medic cabin. Her body was stiff; she had held herself so tense, her muscles had cramped. At least she had a plan, but its success depended upon a great many factors. And most of those could only be resolved by time. She had no idea how long she had crouched here, considering what Tan might do, and then what she could do to oppose him.

Yes, time and patience. She must hold on to patience as if it were a safety line. Yet patience had never been a strong part of her.

She rubbed her hands down her cheeks; her face was cold, she shivered slightly. Nervous chill. Suddenly she wished for a mirror, to look into it and see the new Ayana, how much she had been changed by this time of facing black truths and learning that she might live and die by uncertain choices. Just as Tan would never again look to her as when he wore that mask he must always have assumed before her.

As she arose she swayed, clutched for a hand-hold. Not only was she stiff, but movement brought vertigo, as if the whole world were unstable. But Ayana reached a cabinet in the wall, brought out a tube of tablets. One of those she held to dissolve under her tongue. She did not mind its bitter taste.

Now she worked swiftly, stripping the shelves of certain things, until a small pile of vials and tubes lay on the bunk. Possession of those gave her weapons and defenses. But she must find somewhere to conceal them.

> 14 <

"Thus it is." Furtig faced the Elders, and not only them but all those in the caves, who had crowded in crouching rows behind. He could read no emotion in their eyes, which, when the light of Gammage's lamps touched them, were like disks of glowing fires, orange, red, and green. At least the messengers had been given cave hospitality—not warned off.

Before him lay the weapons they had brought. And he had demonstrated each. There were two lightning throwers, another producing a thin stream which made ice congeal about the target, even though this was not the cold season.

The fourth, which Liliha had carried and which she alone knew how to operate, was the strangest of all. For a warrior might escape by luck or chance the other two. However, from this tube spun small threads at Liliha's twirling. Those floated as might a windborne spider's web. That web, once launched, was drawn instantly to the warrior at whom Liliha had aimed it, in this case Foskatt.

456

Once it had touched his shoulder, as if that touch was a signal, it straightaway wrapped itself about his body so he could not move. Nor could he break that hold, though the cords of the web were very fine and thin. Liliha had to cut it in two places, and then the whole thing withered and fell in small black particles to the ground.

The Elders, in spite of this display, kept impassive faces. But from the others came growls and small hisses of wonder and alarm that such things existed. Liliha was frank: these tanglers were few, some did not work at all. But the lairs held endless caches of other wonders.

"But you say"—it was Ha-Hang, one of the Elders of the western tribe, who spoke—"there are others in the lairs. You have spoken of Rattons in force, and Demons, at least as a scouting party. If the Demons have indeed returned, it is best to let them have the lairs. Those of our kind saved their lives before by taking to the wilds when the Demons hunted."

For the first time Foskatt spoke. "Only just, Elder. Remember the tales? It was only because the Demons sickened and died, fought among themselves, that our mother kin and a few mates escaped. It took many seasons thereafter of hiding and bearing litters, in which too many younglings died, before the clans could do more than run and hide.

"These Demons are neither sick nor fighting among themselves. If they come in strength, how long will it be before they hunt us again?"

Furtig did not wait for any to answer that question; he carried on the attack. "Also, Elders, in those days we had no Gammage, no seekers of Demon secrets, to aid us. Those who were our ancestors had no weapons and little knowledge. Compared to us they were as fangless, as clawless, as a newborn youngling. Perhaps these Demons are scouts, but among us how is the move to a new hunting ground made? We send scouts and if they return with ill news, or do not return, then what is the decision? We go not in that direction but seek another.

"These Demons' ancestors must have been those who fled the sickness and the fighting of their kind, even as we fled the lairs. Therefore their legends of the place are sinister; they will be ready to believe that evil awaits them here. And if their scouts do not return—"

It was the best argument he could offer, one which fit in with their own beliefs and customs.

"Demons and Rattons," Fal-Kan said. "And Gammage wishes all, strangers and caves alike, to gather to make war. Perhaps he also speaks of a truce with Barkers?" His voice was a growl, and he was echoed by those about him.

Liliha spoke, and, because she was a Chooser, even Fal-Kan dared not hiss her down. She held out her hand with its strangely long fingers, pointed to where the Elder Chooser of Fal-Kan's cave sat on a cushion of grass and feathers, holding the newest youngling to her furry breast.

"Do you wish the little one to become Demon meat?"

Now the growl arose sharply, ears flattened, and tails lashed. Some of the youngest warriors rose, their claws ready for battle.

"The Tuskers believed they were safe. Would any

of you dare to take a Tusker youngling from his mother's side?"

That picture startled them into silence. All knew there was no fiercer fighter in the whole wilds than the Tusker female when her young was threatened.

"Yet," Liliha continued, "a Demon flying through the air did so. Can you now say that you will be safe in the wilds when this Demon can fly at will, attack from above, perhaps kill with such weapons as these?" She gestured to the display. "In the lairs we have hidden ways to travel, so small the Demons cannot enter. Our only chance is to turn on them, while they are still so few, the very deaths they used in the old days to destroy our kind.

"You war with the Barkers, but not the Tuskers— why is that so?"

It was not an Elder who answered when she paused but Furtig, hoping to impress at least the younger warriors of that company—those not so set in the ways of doing as always.

"Why do we fight the Barkers? Because we are both eaters of meat and there is a limit to hunting lands. The Tuskers we do not fight because they eat what is of no use to us. But there is food in the lairs, much of it, and no need for hunting. And if you saw before you a Barker and a Demon and had a single chance to kill—which would you choose? That is what Gammage now says—that between Barkers and Demons he chooses the Demons as the greater enemy. As for the Rattons, yes, they are a spreading evil within the lairs, and one must be on constant guard against them.

"But also they promise an even worse fate if they are not put down. For Gammage has proof they seek out the secrets of the Demons also. Do you want Rattons perhaps riding sky things and capturing warriors, and Choosers, and younglings with such as these?"

With his foot he edged forward the tangler so that they could understand his meaning. This time the growl of protest was louder. War with the Barkers was open and fierce, yet there was a grudging respect for the enemy on both sides. The Rattons were different; the very thought of them brought a disgusting taste to the mouth. There were far off, strange legends of individual Barkers and People living together when they were both Demon slaves in the lairs. But Rattons had always been prey.

Ha-Hang spoke first. "You say Barkers are less dangerous than Demons. We have lost warriors to Barkers, none to Demons. And what is a Tusker youngling to us?"

He had a gap on one side of his jaw where he had lost a fighting fang, and both ears were notched with old bite scars. It was plain he was a fighting Elder rather than a planning one.

"Truth spoken!" applauded Fal-Kan.

They were losing, Furtig knew. And perhaps the Elders were right to be cautious. He himself, until he had heard the Tuskers' story of the flyer, had been of two minds about the matter. But those moments when he had lain on the bridge with the Demon hovering over him had given him such a deepset fear of the flyers that he wished he could make it plain to these here what an attack from the air might mean.

Yes, they could hide in the caves. But what if the Demon took up patrol so they could not come forth again? What if the flyer swept low along the very edge of the cliffs, attacking the cave mouths? Furtig had a hearty respect now for Gammage's warnings against Demon knowledge. One could expect them to do anything!

"This affair concerns not only the caves and their defense," the Chooser of Fal-Kan's cave, she who was of the Ancestor's blood, said throatily. "It also concerns our young. And this matter of the Tuskers' young whose mothers could not defend—"

"We live in the caves, the Tuskers in the open," growled Fal-Kan. And his warriors added a rumble of approval.

"Younglings cannot live in caves all their lives," the Chooser continued. "I would listen to this Chooser from the lairs; let her tell us of the younglings there and how they are cared for. What knowledge have they gained beside that of knowing better how to fight, which is always the first thought in the mind of any warrior?" Fal-Kan dared not protest now, nor interrupt.

So Liliha spoke, not of battles or the need for fighting, but of life within the lairs as the Choosers would see it. She spoke much about the ways of healing which had been discovered, how Choosers about to bear young went to places of healing, and how thereafter the young were perfect in form and quick and bright of mind. She spoke of the new foods which ensured even in the times of poor hunting that there would be no hunger, and told of the many things a Chooser might do to make her own life of greater ease and interest.

Some of what she said Furtig had seen with his own eyes, but much of it was as a Chooser would explain it to a Chooser, and this talk in a mixed assembly was new. At first the Elders stirred, perhaps affronted by the breaking of custom, yet not able to deny it when the Choosers themselves, who were even sterner guardians of custom, accepted it. Then Furtig could see even the males were listening with full interest.

She talked well, did Liliha. Foremost in the line of Those-Who-Would-Come-to-Choose sat Eu-La, her eyes fast on the almost hairless face of the female from the lairs. Furtig looked from his clanswoman to Liliha and back again. Then he caught a glimpse of Foskatt.

Perhaps the other had heard Liliha's information many times over, for there was an abstraction about him. He was leaning forward a little, staring at—Eu-La! And there was a bemusement on his face which Furtig knew for what it was. Just so had he seen the Unchosen look at Fas-Tan when she passed with a slow swing of her tail, her eyes beyond them as if, as males yet Unchosen, they had no place in her life.

Eu-La—but she was hardly more than a youngling! A season at least before she would stand with the Choosers. Startled, Furtig studied her. She was no longer a youngling. He had seen that when she had met them outside the caves, but it had not really impressed him.

Eu-La a Chooser? There was a small rumble of growl deep in his throat as he thought of her perhaps in the open with a Demon flyer above. Furtig's fingers stretched and crooked involuntarily, as if he wore his fighting claws.

But he had no time to consider such things now, for Liliha had finished and the Elder of the Choosers spoke:

"There is much to be thought on, kin sisters. Not yet, Elders, warriors, Unchosen, are the cave people ready to say that this or that will be done."

Never in his life had Furtig heard a Chooser speak so before. But perhaps the Elders had, for not one of them protested her decision. And the gathering broke up, the Choosers threading into the caves, Liliha following the Chooser who had spoken.

Furtig and Foskatt gathered the sample weapons into their carrying bag again. The warriors padded out into the dark, making no sound as they moved. And the guardian of the lamp had come to stand beside it as if impatient for Furtig and Foskatt to follow.

"What do you think?" Furtig asked in a whisper. "Has Liliha made the right impression?"

"Ask me not the way of a female mind," returned Foskatt. He was tightening the cords about the bundle. "But it is true that when it comes to the general safety and good of younglings it is the Choosers who decide. And if they believe that the lairs promise more than the caves, then these people will go to Gammage."

Had Tan thought about the advantage this cabin gave her? Ayana sat up on the bunk in the medic-lab. She had no idea how long she had been asleep, but she awoke with a mind free of that fear and despair which had held her. Was it the fact that she had been selected, even conditioned, to be the other half of Tan that had made her so helpless?

But, if they had selected, conditioned, her so, that preparation had not endured. She would think for herself, be herself—and not Tan's mate, Tan's other part, from now on.

Looking back at the years on Elhorn, even the days of the voyage, Ayana could not understand the person she had been. It was as if she had slept and was now awake. And Tan—certainly Tan had changed too! It could not be only the alteration in herself which had caused the break between them.

She had known him to be impatient of restraint, curious to the point of recklessness. But now all his faults were intensified; never before had he been ruthless or cruel. It was as if this world, the long-sought home of their kind, had acted on him—on her—

And if that was so—what of Jacel, Massa? Were they, too, other people? If they were now four others, their old, carefully cultivated close relationship broken, how could they work as a unit, do their duty here?

Ayana looked at the small kit she had put together before she had slept, and she shivered. What had been in her mind to seek out those particular drugs and want to hide them—or use them? She had been more emotionally disturbed than she could believe possible, in spite of all her training.

If she, a medic, one supposedly dedicated to the service of life, could, in some wild moment of terror, contemplate such an array of armament, what would the others do? She might do well now to destroy all which lay there, so that if such wild thoughts came to mind again there would be nothing—

Save that which lay there could help as well as harm. The drugs were specially selected for this voyage and they could not be replaced. No, not destruction; however—concealment.

No one knew this cabin, its fittings, better than she did herself. Ayana began a careful search for a hiding place, finding it at last, and strapping the packet on the underside of the bunk.

That done, Ayana faced her ordeal. She must leave the safety of this cabin, go out into the ship. Somehow she must be able to pass off what had happened as a temporary emotional storm, and present to all eyes, including Tan's, the appearance of firm self-control.

As she forced herself to her own cabin, she met no one. There was no sound in the ship. Twice she paused to listen. Without the vibration, the life which had coursed through its walls while they were spaced, this whole complex of cabins had a curious hollow and empty feeling.

It—it was as if she were encased in a dead thing! Ayana caught her lip between her teeth, hit upon it hard that that small pain might be a warning. Emotions rising, fear—What was wrong with her?

She would have no armor against Tan's charges, against the others, until she could face this objectively. Was it herself—or this world? Was there something about this planet that upset her, forced her out of her pattern of living? It was better to believe that than to think that there was a flaw so deep in her that she was breaking because of it.

No one in the cabin. But Tan's protect suit was gone. He must have taken off again. And where—when—?

Ayana climbed to the control cabin. No one there— had they all gone and left her? Alone in a dead ship, on a world which their ancestors had fled after some disaster so great that it must be erased from all records?

She almost fell down the steps in her hurry to seek the cabin of Jacel and Massa. But now she smelled food—the mess cabin!

Massa sat there alone. Between her hands was a mug of hot nutrient. Of the two men there was no sign.

"Massa—"

She looked up and Ayana was startled out of asking the question she had ready. Massa was older than Ayana by a planet year or two. She had never been a talkative person, but there had been about her such an air of competence and serene certainty that her presence was soothing. Perhaps that was one of the factors the home authorities had considered when they made the final selection of the crew. She had always been detached, held people at arm's length. What she was in private to Jacel must have satisfied him. However, Ayana had held the other girl in awe, had not seen in her any ally against Tan.

But this was not Massa's usual serene and untroubled face. She looked as if she had not slept for a long time, and her eyes were red and swollen as if she had been crying. The way she stared back at Ayana— hostile! That very hostility brought an end to the wall between them. Had Massa, also, discovered Jacel to be another person?

"Where is Tan—Jacel?" *Ayana slipped by to the heating unit, poured herself a mug of nutrient, and seated herself to face Massa, determined now not to be driven off by a forbidding look. In fact, the signs of the disturbance in the other girl acted on her in an oddly calming way.*

"You may well. ask! Tan—he is like a wild man! What did you do to him?"

"What has Tan done?"

"He has persuaded Jacel to go in—on foot, not in the flyer. On foot! Into what may be a trap. He—he *is unmotivated.*" She spat forth the worst she could find to say about a supposedly trained colleague.

"On foot!" Ayana nearly choked on the mouthful she had taken. Two men in that huge expanse of ruined buildings! They could easily be lost, trapped—

"On foot!" Massa repeated. "They have been gone"— she consulted the timekeeper on the cabin wall above them—"two complete dial circles."

"But the coms! Why are you not monitoring the coms?"

"The hook-up is in." Massa laid her hand on the wall com. "They have not reported for a half-circle. I have the repeat demand on automatic. If they answer we can hear them at once."

"We can trace their way in then, through that." Ayana nodded to the com.

"Yes. But dare we try to use it so? I was trying to decide." Massa set her elbows on the table, leaned her head forward into her hands. "Trying to decide," she repeated dully. "If we leave the ship and go hunting and are caught by those creeping horrors—"

"Creeping horrors?"

"Tan went out early this morning. He returned with recordings. The picture was blurred, but it showed small life forms, in an open place between buildings. They signaled him with one of the old recognition codes—though it did not quite make sense by our records. There was no place near that point where he could land the flyer. That's why they went on foot. But I say that those things—they were not people!"

"But to go out like that, it is against everything we have been taught, against all the rules of safety."

Massa shrugged. "It seems that home rules do not

apply any more as far as Tan is concerned. And—he came and talked at Jacel—not to him but at him! It was almost evil the way he worked on Jacel, made him believe he was not a real man unless he would go to meet those signaling things. They, neither one of them, would listen to me when I tried to urge some sense. It was as if they were different people from those I had always known. And sometimes, Ayana, I feel different, too. What is this world doing to us?"

There was nothing left of her serene confidence. Rather the eyes now looking into Ayana's were those of someone lost and wandering in a strange and frightening place. So—she was not alone! Massa felt it also, that this world was somehow altering them to fit a new pattern, one which was for the worse, compared to that they had known.

"If we only knew," Ayana said slowly, "the reason why the First Ship people left here. That reason—it may be that we have to face it again now. And we have no defense, not even guesses. Was it invasion of furred creatures like those on the bridge, or like these others who now signal in our own old codes? Disease? It could be anything."

"I only know that Jacel has changed, and Tan is a stranger, and I no longer understand myself at times. You are a trained medic, Ayana. Could this air here, which our ship's instruments tell us is good, be some kind of subtle poison? Or is it something from those rows of dead buildings, standing there like bones set on end to mark old graves which must not, for some terrible reason, be forgotten—something reaching out to send us mad?"

Her voice rose higher and higher, her hands began

to twitch. Ayana put down her mug, caught those hands to hold them quiet.

"Massa! No, do not imagine things—"

"Why not? What have we left us but what we imagine? I did not imagine that Jacel has taken leave of his senses and gone out to hunt evil shadows in those buildings. He is gone, Tan is gone, and both for no sane reason. You cannot say I have imagined that!"

"No, you have not." By will Ayana kept her own voice level and steady. "But are you of any help now? What if—"

She had no time to see if that argument had any effect on Massa. For at that moment there was a clicking from the com, and they both looked to it, tense, reading in that rattle of sound the message.

"Need aid—Ayana—medic—"

"Jacel!" Massa jerked from Ayana's hold, was on her feet. "He is hurt."

"No. That was Jacel's sending. Did you not recognize it? And if he is sending, he cannot be the one in need."

Clicks might not have any voice tone, but they had practiced so long together that they were able to distinguish the sender by rate of speed.

And it would only fit the pattern that Tan, driven by whatever beset him on this world, had gotten into difficulty—bad—or Jacel would not have sent for her.

"Keep on that direction beam." Now that she was being pressed into action, Ayana knew what to do. "We may need a beacon call back."

"I am going too—"

"No. They need a medic, and we must have someone in the ship. Your place is here, Massa."

For a long moment it looked as if she would argue

that. Then her shoulders slumped, and Ayana knew she had won.

"I will take a belt com, go in on their out-wave. Set that for me, Massa, while I go to get a suit and my kit."

"And if this is somehow a trap?"

"We have to take that chance. I must go." *Ayana faced the bare truth squarely.*

➤ 15 ◄

It was mid-morning with no clouds or sign of storm. The sun was warm, too warm across the glare of fused scars where ships had taken off and landed—how long ago? Beyond, the gray-white cliffs of the buildings. Ayana wearing her protect suit, her belt heavy with explorer's devices and aids, the medic kit at her back, tramped on, the com beep at her belt as a compass.

As long as those she sought wore similar devices she would eventually find them. How long would that take? Her impulse was to run, her self-command kept her to a ground-covering stride which would not invite disaster. There had been no more messages. But she had left Massa at the com in the control cabin ready for any such call. Massa would relay to her any message, but somehow she was sure that none would come.

Now she approached the buildings. Windows regarded her slyly. The sensation of being spied upon was like a crawling touch on her skin. She had to fight her fears to keep on in the direction the com marked for her. Though at a distance the blocks of the buildings seemed to ring in solidly the open landing site, yet, as Ayana advanced, she saw that this was not true. There was a space at a side angle, where one could pass between two towers.

The opening was a narrow street at a sharp angle in relation to the port, so that when Ayana was only a step or so down it, she could no longer look back to the ship. But the com urged her ahead—this was the way.

There were drifts of sand and earth at the beginning of the street, but farther down, where the wind could not reach so readily, the pavement was bare. On both sides there were no windows or doors in the first stories of the buildings, leaving them blankly solid like the walls of a fortification. Though well above there were windows. It was not until Ayana reached the first crossway that there was a change. Here were doors, windows, at street level. The doors were closed and she tried none of them. Her beeping guide turned her into another cross street which headed yet farther into the city. They had believed that they had built cities on Elhorn during the last two hundred years. But what they had done there was the piling up of children's blocks compared to this! And what had brought it all to nothing?

There were no signs of such destruction as a natural catastrophe or war might have left. Just silence—but not emptiness! No, with every step she took, Ayana was aware of hidden life. She could not see it, nor hear it, and she did not have a persona detect (that had gone with Tan), but she knew something was there. So her hand swung close to her stunner, and she looked continuously from side to side, sure that soon—from some doorway—

Another crossway, again she was to go right according to the com. Something—Ayana stopped short, the stunner now drawn; something had scuttled away up ahead. She was sure imagination had not tricked her. She had actually seen that flicker of motion at a door. All her instincts warned her to retreat, but the beep of the com held steady. Somewhere ahead Jacel, or Tan, or both of them had their coms on call, and that would not happen unless need was greater than caution. She had no choice after all.

But Ayana kept to the middle of the street, well away from those buildings. The open would give her what small advantage there might be. Now she reached the doorway where she had seen the movement. The door there was open, but, as far as she could detect, nothing crouched within. She did not explore. But as she passed it, she went stiff and tense; to have that behind her was bad.

The second cross street brought her out into a place which was in direct contrast to the rest of the city. Here was a sprawl of growing things, a huge, autumn-killed tangle choked in a frame of corroded metal. Ayana, facing that mass, thought she could trace in some of the upright and horizontal crossbeams the frame of a building. But if it had ever been more than just the skeleton of such, the vines and other growth had taken over and destroyed all but the bones.

Much of the riotous vegetation was dry and dead. But from that black, withered mass new shoots rose. Not of an honest rich green, but of a green that was oddly grayed, as if it were indeed only the ghost of the plants that had put forth new shoots and runners. It was into the center of that sickly mass that the *beep directed her. Though how she could enter such a tangle—*

Ayana walked along the outer fringe of the growth, seeking by will, not by inclination, some possible opening. Shortly she came upon a path hacked, broken, burnt. Though why those she sought had forced their way into that unwholesome mass she could not guess.

What bothered her most was the sight of a couple of the ghost-gray vines, perhaps as thick as two fingers together, looped directly across the hacked way. They looked as if they had had days to re-establish themselves, although they could only have had hours.

Slipping her hands into the suit gloves, making sure her flesh was well covered, Ayana reached out and jerked at the stalks. They broke easily, showing hollow stems from which spurted thin streams of reddish liquid. But the noisome smell of rot made her gag.

Broken, the vines visibly shriveled, wilted back against the mass from which they had trailed. Ayana forced herself into the path.

Her boots sank a little at each step into a muck which gave off putrid puffs. Soon, unable to take that continued assault on her nostrils, she stopped to draw up her face mask. What this place had been she could not guess. But the eroded partitions showing here and there were pillars which must have once supported a roof.

The hacked way was several times barred by vines she had to snap. There was no difficulty doing that; they offered no resistance. Except that Ayana had such a horror of touching them, even with gloved hands, that she had to force herself to the act each time.

So she reached the center of this horror garden, if

garden it had been. There was a wide, square opening in the ground. Oddly enough, none of the vegetation crowded near that hole, or door. For it was not a chance opening. Around it was a band of stone over which none of the vines hung.

. The signal was—down. But how? Ayana shone her hand lamp into the hole. Flashing here and there showed her a room, or perhaps a section of corridor. And the floor was not too far below. If she hung by her hands, with her suit inflated for a landing, she could make it. Again it would seem she had no choice.

Ayana landed. When she got to her feet, swinging the lamp around, she saw that this was a small chamber with a door in only one wall—that way—

What had Tan—Jacel—been hunting which had brought them here? To her it had more and more the smell of a trap. But it had been Jacel who had beamed that help call, and he would not have urged either Massa or her into danger. Or, could one depend on Jacel's reactions anymore?

In the underground ways the beep was even louder, more persistent than it had been above. By all indications she was close to what she sought. There was no turning back—

Ayana held the lamp in one hand, her stunner ready in the other as she went on. Then she stiffened, stood very still, listening.

Sound ahead, but not a call of her kind, or the tread of one walking in protect boots, but rather a swishing noise. She longed to call out, to be reassured by a human voice that one of those she hunted was there. But fear kept her dumb. It needed all her willpower to force her ahead.

A crosswise passage—At her belt the beep was a continuous note. She was close to its source. To her right, along that sideway . . .

"Ayana!"

Jacel! Her lips, her mouth were so dried she could not produce more than a hoarse croak in return. But she began to run, turned right. And there was light ahead.

Furtig sat by the stream from the spring. The morning was going to be fair. He sniffed the air, good smells. He had not realized how few good smells there were in the lairs. Oh, there were those places where things grew, but those seemed different, even if they were plants. It was as if they had never been the same as those of the wilds, or else that far back, like the People, they had been somehow changed. He feasted eye and nose now on what was familiar and right, and had not been wrought upon by any Demon knowledge.

It was a promising morning—outwardly. But of what it promised for his mission here there was no hint. None of the Elders, or even the younger warriors, had spoken after the withdrawal of the Choosers. Furtig thought that a bad sign. His people were normally curious. If they did not ask questions about the weapons or the lairs, such silence seemed hostile.

"A good day—" Foskatt came down the slope. He had spent the night in the outer part of the cave of his own family line. Now he squatted on his heels by the water, running the fingers of one hand back and forth across the scar of his healed wound as if that still itched a little.

"Any talk?" he asked.

"Not so. It was as if I had come from a hunt only, and an unsuccessful one at that," Furtig growled.

"With me the same. But do not forget that Liliha argued well for us. If she convinced the Choosers—"

Furtig gave a hiss of irritation, though he knew that Foskatt spoke the truth. It was the Choosers who ruled when it came to the point of safety for the full clan.

"Ssss—warriors who greet the dawn!" Both their heads turned swiftly.

Eu-La stood, her hands on her slender hips, her tail switching gently, evoking an answering whisper from the dry grasses it brushed. She was smaller than Liliha, but her body was well rounded. Yes, she was close to the season when it would be her turn to sit high on the Choosing ledge and watch warriors contend for her favor.

"We are not the only ones early astir," Furtig answered. "What brings the cave sister from her sleeping nest?"

"Dreams—dreams and wishes—" Suddenly she flung wide her arms, holding high her hands to the sky. "Long have I dreamed, and wished, and now it seems that I shall walk into the full of my dreams, have my wishes—"

"Those being?" Foskatt's question rumbled hoarsely.

"That I go to Gammage, that I learn more than can be learned in these caves—that I can use these, my hands, for greater things than I do here!" Now she held her hands before her face, flexing her fingers. These were not as long as Liliha's, but neither were they as closely stubbed as those of many of her sisters. "If the clans decide to go or not, still I travel with you, cave brother." She looked to Furtig. "I have spoken to Liliha and she has agreed. It is my right as much as any warrior's to go to Gammage!"

"True," Furtig had to agree. She was correct. If she longed for what the lairs had to offer, then she could profit by what she could learn there.

Perhaps this was another way out. Perhaps even if the Elders held back those of the clans who were bound by custom, there would be those, among the younger ones, who would go to Gammage and so swell even by a few the force within the lairs.

It was as if Eu-La could read his thought at that moment, for after she jumped lightly down beside them and leaned forward, about to lap daintily from the free-flowing water, she glanced up to add: "But I think that the Elders of the Choosers will have made up their minds soon. There was talk in the second cave last night. When it comes to the safety of younglings, then they listen well. And Liliha answered many more questions in the dark hours. Do not believe you have failed until you are told so."

She dabbled in the water, flicking droplets here and there like a youngling playing. But Furtig, watching her, was reminded again of Fas-Tan, who acted as one alone even when she knew well that warriors watched her longingly. Again he saw on Foskatt's face that same intent look he had seen the night before.

For a moment a growl rumbled deep in Furtig's throat. Eu-La he had known for a long time. It was she who had encouraged him before he went to Gammage. Eu-La was very precious. But if Eu-La were at this moment a Chooser and looked at him, Furtig, would he rejoice?

The turn of his thoughts surprised him almost as much as Foskatt's reaction to Eu-La had done. Eu-La choosing him? He liked her much, but not, he realized, as Foskatt did. He would fight for her in one way, to protect her against harm. But he would not strive to win her Choosing favor. That was not how he thought of Eu-La.

When he thought of a Chooser—Sternly Furtig tried to order those straying thoughts. There was no more chance of that than there had been in the other days of winning Fas-Tan's favor. Not all warriors won even the passing interest of a Chooser. And they lived and did as they had to—though many became far rovers without clans.

He was lucky. Within the lairs there was much to be done. If he could not equal the In-born with their learning and their mastery of the Demon machines, there was always exploring and fighting the Rattons. Yes, he was lucky to have so much, and ought not, even in his thoughts, reach for that which he could never win. Foskatt—Eu-La—if it came to that it might be very well.

But these were days to think not of Choosing and the beginnings of new clans and families, but of what was going to happen to those already in existence.

Eu-La proved right. In the end the Choosers' decision was that the move to the lairs was better than a life in the wilds, where younglings might be taken as had those of the Tuskers. Their answer to the threat of Rattons and Demons was that four Demons with their own weapons turned against them were not formidable. As for Rattons—from the earliest legends of the People such had been their natural prey. Therefore Gammage might expect these clans to come to him before the moon overhead vanished into the Nights of Dark.

But Eu-La wished to return with the messengers. So four rather than three set out again by night to return to the lairs.

There was no sign of the flyer, though they never felt safe from it. And when they met again the Tusker patrols, they learned it had not been seen.

The Tuskers had another message. One of their scouts had witnessed at the far end of their territory a strange thing. A truce flag had been set up. And, left by it with food and water to hand, a Barker who seemed to be recovering from ill treatment. Those who left him were a party of People from the lairs. He had been claimed by his own kind before nightfall, and the Barkers had not torn away the flag.

Rather they were now gathering, with more of their scouts arriving all the time. And there were signs they planned to camp nearby in the woods.

"So we freed that Barker from the Rattons," Furtig said. "But that may have been by far the easier part. To get the People and the Barkers under a common truce flag is a thing unheard of."

"Yet," pointed out Liliha, "the Barkers did not tear down the flag. It still stands. Thus they have not yet refused to talk. They summon their own clans to speak together, even as we have gone to argue with those of the caves. But whether—"

"We cannot trust Barkers!" Furtig broke in. "Even if the Demons are all the legends say they were, we cannot trust Barkers."

"Barkers lived with the Demons," Eu-La said.

"That is where they first learned evil ways." She was repeating the old legend of their own kind,

"But so did our people once," Liliha reminded her. "The First Ancestors fled from the lairs only when the Demons turned against them in their last madness and cruelty. But you are right in this—Gammage must have a powerful argument to make the Barkers listen. Saving one of them from the Rattons is not enough. But it is a beginning."

Furtig thought of the truce flag. Even though the Barkers had not thrown it contemptuously to earth, refusing contact, it would take great courage for any warrior of the People to go to it unarmed, trusting in the good will of his enemies. Who would Gammage choose—or who would volunteer to do that? And how would he who went know that it was the proper time? Would the Barkers advance a flag of their own in answer?

Furtig was suddenly more eager than ever to get back to the lairs, to know what had happened since they had left. Had the Demons been reinforced? But a quick question to the Tuskers reassured them as to that—no second sky-ship had come down.

Broken Nose and his people would keep guard here, and, being informed of the coming of the cave clans, they would provide an alarm system to let those travel in such safety as could be devised.

Ahead lay the lairs and what might await them there. They slipped into the open with all the stealth and craft they possessed.

Ayana stripped off the sterile gloves, and crumpled them into a small ball, since they could not be used

again. Jacel lay with beads of pain sweat still plain on his face. His eyes were closed, and she knew that the pain reliever had taken effect. Also the wound was not so bad as she had first feared. If they could now get him to the ship and under a renewer, in a day's time he would have no more to show for that gash than a well-closed seam.

But she was more than a little puzzled. There was a med-kit at Jacel's own belt. Tan wore another. And such a gash as this was easily handled by the materials they carried. Why had they sent out that panicked call for her?

She had asked no questions until now, being intent on the patient. Tan, standing against the wall, had volunteered nothing. Nor had Jacel. In fact, he had appeared to be affected out of all proportion to the seriousness of the wound itself. Perhaps—Ayana glanced around the bare chamber—there had been some poisonous substance feared—but instant anti-spray would have handled such.

Now that she had time to think—Ayana did not look at Tan squarely, but as if she did not want him to see she noticed him. But Tan was not watching her; he was staring on through the other door in the room, seemingly so absorbed that he must see or hear something—or be waiting for something to happen.

"What is it?" Her words sounded too loud, even echoed a little.

Now he turned his head. And in his eyes Ayana saw that queer gleam which frightened her. She shivered. Cold as this place was, the protect suit should have kept her warm; but Tan now had the ability to chill her through when he looked like that.

"You will have another patient, a very important one. We have had wonderful luck, Ayana, we have made contact—"

"Contact with whom—or what?" she demanded when he paused.

"With those who live here. Do you know, Ayana, this is a storehouse of information. They have shown us tapes, machines—What we learned from the First Ships is nothing, nothing at all to what we can learn here. If we have time—"

"What do you mean?"

"Well, our friends are not the only ones trying to get this information. There are others—and they may be closer. There was a war here in the old days. And do you know what kind of a war?" He came away from the wall to stand over her.

Ayana rose quickly, not liking to have him towering above her so.

"A war between men and animals—animals, mind you! Things with fur and claws and fangs that dared to think they were equal with man—dared!" He was breathing fast, his face flushed. "But there were others. Men in their last days here were few, they had to have friends, helpers—and they found them. Then, when man was gone those others were left, left to defend everything man had fought for, all the knowledge he had won through his own efforts, defended against the animals. They are still fighting that battle, but now it is our fight, too!

"They need you, Ayana. There is a place of medical information—think of it—a storage of all the wealth of knowledge of man's time on this world! They have been trying to hold that against the enemy. They

*need our help so badly. One of their leaders, a genius
among them, one who has been able to untangle many
of the old records, was badly injured in fighting the
animals. He has been taken to this center, and now
they need your aid.*

*"Think of it, Ayana—such devices of healing as were
just hinted at in our records! You can see them, learn
to use them—you can help this leader. It is such a
chance as only luck could have given us."*

*He was in one of his exultant moods, but to a
degree she had never seen before.*

"Tan's luck—" she said before she thought.

*He nodded vigorously. "Tan's luck! And it is going
to help us—help us win a whole world for man again!
But they're coming—listen!"*

*She could hear Jacel's heavy breathing, and then
something else, a light pattering. There was a gleam of
light beyond the door, and those Tan expected arrived.
Ayana gasped and shrank back.*

*These were not the furred creatures of the bridge
which she had half-expected, but something she instinctively found repulsive.*

*They scuttled on their hind feet, but they had
naked tails at the ends of their spines. And they were
small, the largest standing a little above her knee at
its full height. Fur grew on them in ragged patches,
with naked skin between. On some, the smaller, that
fur was a dirty gray; on the two largest it was white.
Their heads had the long, narrow muzzles of animals
showing sharp teeth. Against the domes of their skulls
their ears were pointed.*

*Ayana hated them on sight. She watched with frozen
horror as Tan advanced to greet the tallest white-furred*

one, which seemed to be their leader, squatting down so that his head came closer to that of the creature.

Around its neck hung a small box. It reached with one paw—hand?—and touched that. Then it uttered a series of squeaks, but from the box came distorted but still recognizable words.

"Chief—waits. Hurry, hurry—"

"She is here." Tan nodded toward Ayana. "She is ready."

"No!" Ayana cried. Not for all the knowledge, all the treasure of this world heaped up before her, would she go with these small horrors deeper into their burrows.

Tan, on his feet, came at her, and she could not get away. She could not even slip along the wall out of his reach.

"Little fool!" He caught her arm in so painful a grip that she gasped. "Do you go with them on your own two feet, or do I inject you with a sleep-shot and let them carry you? No stupidity is going to wreck my plans now, do you understand?"

And she knew that he would do just that. If she went, perhaps with an outward show of willingness, she could at least see the road they took, might even be able to escape. If he drugged her and they took her—no, she had no choice.

"Try no tricks with them, they are no animals." Tan showed his teeth almost as if they were the fangs of the waiting squad. "Jacel discovered that. Now get going—"

He gave her a push, and she stumbled toward the door. Around her the creatures closed in.

➤ 16 ◄

Ayana stood looking about, first in bewilderment and then with a growing excitement which drew her attention from those chittering things which had brought her here—and even from Tan, who had followed behind and with whom she had not spoken since this nightmare began. For he had actually picked up and carried the chief horror—that half-bald, half-white-furred leader, exchanging speech with him. The girl had pushed ahead to avoid that monstrous companionship. For monstrous her emotions told her it was!

But this place! She had studied in detail every scrap of information having to do with medical knowledge that they had found in the looted tape banks of the First Ships. Ayana had had access in addition to all the combined learning, surmise, and speculation of those who had had more than a hundred years before her to study the same records.

So now she turned slowly about, surveying a vast and much better lighted chamber, cut by many partitions rising to her shoulder height or beyond, into booths

*and cubicles. This was indeed a medical center such
as her teachers had hardly dared dream existed on the
parent world.*

*Some of the machines she recognized from old
diagrams—diagnostic, operative, healing—For a moment,
in her amazement and excitement, Ayana forgot her
company and went forward confidently, pausing here
and there before an installation she did know, passing
for now those she could not understand. Why—with
these—if they still worked—one could cure a nation!*

*Ayana put out her hand, ran fingertips along the
outer transparent wall of a healing cell. If they worked!
But how long had it been since they had been put to
use? She might be able to work out the procedure for
activating those she did know, always providing they
were intact. But if their machinery was at fault, she
had no way of knowing what a tech would do to put
that right again.*

*She passed down one aisle between those partitions
and came into an open space. There before her—*

*That table—the smell—the pools of—blood! Ayana
recoiled as she faced it. Amid the sterile disuse of the
rest of the place, this was like a blow in the face,
to bring her to the realization of how she had come
here. The tangle of blood-stained instruments thrown
in an ugly pile on one end of the table hinted more
of cruel butchery than of any desire to heal. What
had they done here—these small monsters with whom
Tan seemed to have made some evil pact?*

*"Well?" Tan's voice from behind made her start.
"What do you think of this? Did I not tell you there was
more to be found than you could guess? Now—Oudu
wants to know if you can use it to cure his chief."*

She looked away from that blood-stained table with a shudder, tried to close her mind to it. And she was able to find voice enough to croak:

"Some of this was on the tapes. The rest"—Ayana shook her head—"is new. And we do not know whether the power works."

"Oudu will know." He looked at that thing he carried, as if, Ayana thought, it was human!

"Some work—" The dry rustle of the words overlay the shrill chittering as the box on the creature's chest translated. "There is material to try with—"

"Material?" Ayana could not force herself to look directly at Oudu, nor address it—him. "What does he mean?"

"I believe they have been experimenting for themselves. They have taken prisoners from time to time, the animals roaming in here. They use them, just as our ancestors used to do. That's why those were here in the first place—they were lab animals."

"We—we were helpers of the Great Ones!" came that other voice. "Workers here. The others, they were used to try the machines upon—as we do now. But many escaped, many lie in wait—kill—destroy. They destroy the records, the knowledge. Soon all will be gone if we do not stop them."

"See?" Tan demanded. "We have to stop such destruction—or we'll lose everything."

"Do not waste time." Oudu cut in. "Shimog dies. Let this knowing female use her knowledge to make Shimog live again."

Ayana swallowed. "I have to see—see—"

"Naturally. They have him down here." Tan passed that ghastly table as if it did not exist, and she followed, glad to leave it. But she knew now that she played a game, and it would not be Tan's. No alliance with these things—she could not do it. Not for all the knowledge here!

Not even, asked something within her, if it means the success or failure of your mission? The life or death of those on Elhorn? But Elhorn was far away, and here—here was now, before her. She could only follow Tan's lead for a time, waiting for a chance, a plan, to wrest herself free of this nightmare.

They came to a cubicle at the end of the line, and there was a gathering of the creatures, several on guard at the door, two by the cot within. Lying on the cot was one even larger than Oudu and even more scantily furred.

It—he—was swollen of paunch. And the skin, where it showed, was dark, scaled with sores. Breath came and went in slow, heavy panting, as if the effort to breathe was almost too great. Its attendants drew back as Ayana forced herself on her knees close to the creature.

She could not find any pity, even when the thing turned its head a fraction and looked at her. For the consciousness within those eyes was coldly evil. Ayana recognized intelligence of a type so alien to all she believed in that it was like meeting black and deadly hatred formed into a repulsive body.

There was no way of telling how or why Shimog suffered. She could only guess that it was from some disease. But that might be native to this planet, or to the creature's own foul species. Certainly she had never seen such symptoms before.

"What can you do?" Tan demanded impatiently.

*What? She had no idea. Except one. She had seen
something out there she had recognized—a renewal
chamber. If this Shimog was in the least responsive to
what would act for humans, that might be the best hope.*

*"The renewal chamber. If the installation works—
that might help."*

*"A machine?" Oudu demanded. "You can run this
machine?"*

*"I have seen directions for such," she answered,
careful not to make any promises to these small dev-
ils. "I would have to try it, to make sure that it was
running properly, before we used it on your chief."*

*"To do so then you must have an animal?" came
the swift demand.*

"But it will only work on one hurt—or ill."

"We have what is needed."

*Oudu did not add to that, but he might have given
some inaudible order, for most of those who had come
with them scurried away.*

Troubled, Ayana arose. "I must see the renewer—"

*Free of that cubicle with its fetid odor, its aura of dark
hate, she ran back to the glass-walled booth with the
soft flooring. It was large enough to accommodate some
twenty beings of Shimog's size, perhaps five humans.*

*She did not open the door, but went to the controls.
Since she could not set for any particular disease, well,
it would be full treatment. Yes, here were the symbols
she had seen on the tapes. And a single finger press
brought an answering spark of life—it worked! At
least the power was still on. And—*

Ayana whirled—those sounds!

*Toward her—she wanted to be sick. Those they were
dragging, crying, babbling. No—this was a deadly*

nightmare! Then her head rang as Tan slapped her hard across the face.

"Those are only animals, experimental animals, do you understand? Sure, the Rattons don't play pretty with their enemies but neither do the animals with Rattons!"

Ayana caught her tongue between her teeth, bit on it. Tan—was this Tan? Not her Tan but the one who had come alive since they had landed on this cursed world. For cursed it had to be!

The nightmare crew pulled, rolled those torn and mangled bodies into the renewal chamber, slammed the door.

"Get to it!" Tan's hands on her shoulders brought her about before the controls. "Prove it, one way or the other."

She could not think straight—but she must. Those poor wrecks, perhaps she could give them merciful unconsciousness, death. Ayana sent the machine into humming life. She did not look into the chamber as she jerked the lever up to full power, hoping that would kill mercifully, quickly. Now she was disciplining her thoughts into some kind of coherent order.

She would never join Tan in his alliance with these Rattons—not ever! There was a point past which no thought of gain could carry one. And Ayana was there.

Therefore, if she was to get out of this venture alive, she would have to move before the Rattons realized that she was not their ally.

Tan had taken her stunner, but she had something else in her kit which could be a weapon. If she could get that in hand—

"This will take time." She kept her voice level. "And Shimog—a sedative might help."

"Give it to him then."

Still not looking into the chamber, Ayana went back to the ailing leader. She brought out openly what she needed, charged it. Luckily Tan knew no more than the necessary medic first aid. Correct dosage of this meant nothing to him.

"I will give your leader"—she would not look to Oudu—"sleep that he may rest until the machine is proven."

"Not so!" Oudu's harsh protest shook her, though she hoped not to open betrayal. "Prove no harm—Mog!"

One of the guard came forward.

"Prove on Mog."

"Very well." She held the injector to the Ratton's forearm, pressed the plunger.

He blinked, gave a little sigh, and crumpled to the floor. Oudu bent over him for a moment.

"Truth. Mog sleeps. Let Shimog also sleep."

Ayana bent to that task. The easiest part of her plan was over. She screwed at the cap of the injector as if closing it. But instead she opened it to full. Now she held a weapon of a sort, one meant to handle perhaps even more than one difficult patient at a time, ones who could not be closely approached.

What she had used on Mog and Shimog had been but a small portion of the dosage with which she had charged this. The trouble now was the difference in height between her enemies—Tan so much the taller.

Because of his superior height and strength, she decided he must go first. Ayana arose, still watching Shimog, as if she wished to be sure of his condition. Then she turned swiftly, the injector ready.

Straight into Tan's face went that subduing spray.

She had no time to see its efficacy as she went on to aim at the Rattons.

"You—you!" Tan's hands came at her. His fingers actually closed on her arm, then loosened as he went down. Around him the Rattons, bewildered by her attack, also wilted.

Ayana caught up her kit. She did not know how long they would be unconscious. By the time they recovered, she must be well away from here—perhaps even back to the ship, if that were possible. But before she left she had one more duty, to make sure those poor things in the chamber were safely dead, their suffering over.

Down one aisle, up the next, then she was at the chamber where the motor purred on. She looked in—

It was not possible!

With both hands flat against the glass Ayana watched something out of a wild dream. Lost, mangled limbs, mutilated bodies—they could not regrow—heal—in this fashion! She had turned the power to full force. Had she, in hopes for a swift death for the wreckage the Rattons had dragged there, done just the opposite—given them not only life, but healed such hurts as she had thought no living thing could long survive?

If—if this was happening as her eyes reported—then she could not go and leave them. Once the Rattons recovered, knew she was gone, then the vengeance they would take on these—! She would have condemned them to far worse torment.

But the changes, the healing, although already spectacular, would have to be complete, and how long dared she wait?

Ayana opened her kit. She had one more charge of

the sedative, but it was less than the full one she had just used. Her only chance would be to keep watch on those she had left with Shimog. What if others came? Shimog was their leader. Would there not be visitors, a changing of guard?

Tan's weapons—the blaster—her stunner!

Ayana ran back. She rolled Tan over, plundered his belt of everything which could serve as a weapon. Then, as she passed that terribly stained table, she swept off the instruments, the things which had been used to maim and not repair.

Back before the chamber she piled up her strange assortment of armament. How long would she have to wait? Waiting was harder to face, she discovered, than open attack.

In the time which followed she prowled back and forth between the cubicle and the renewal chamber.

On her second visit to the cubicle she heard a scuttling and stood ready with the stunner.

Moments later five more Rattons were laid out with their fellows. But how long before someone took alarm and sent a larger force, perhaps one even a blaster could not rout? There was no hurrying the healing, but every time she checked the process, Ayana was amazed at what was happening. What wonders her ancestors had been able to do! But if they could produce such miracles of life, then what had brought about the death of this city, the flight of the First Ship?

The Rattons boasted that they had been the companion-aides of the men who had once lived and worked here. She knew that degeneration could cause awesome changes in both physical and mental states. But she did not believe that man and

Ratton—Ratton? There was a familiar sound to that name—she frowned and began to search memory.

Those others, too, the animals—Once more she went to study them. There was still the teasing resemblance to Putti—If she could only remember!

"Ratton—" She repeated that name aloud. "Ratton—rat!"

Rat! A tape picture came to vivid life in her mind. Rat—a creature used in lab experiments! But those had been small! What had happened to bring a four-footed, small rat to the size of the erect-standing, intelligent Ratton? Had this been the result of experiments? But rats had been tools used by men, never his aides—unless something had gone wrong. If they could only learn the truth!

"Rat!" Ayana said again. The word was ugly, as ugly as the things it named. She looked once more to her patients. They lay as if asleep, but they breathed easily, mended steadily—if perhaps too slowly for all their future safety.

They were akin to the creatures Tan had recorded on the bridge. Then they had gone armed. It was apparent that they walked erect and were not animals. About them that elusive memory—Putti—but not really the soft-bodied plaything of childhood. More pictures on learning tapes? Ayana tried systematically to recall what she could of those. If the Rattons had been rats—then these must also have had another beginning.

Like a flash on a visa-screen, bright and sharply clear, she remembered at last.

Not Putti but cat!

"Cat!" Ayana called that name as if to awaken the sleepers.

Cats! So the Rattons had lied. For the cat on the ancient tapes had been truly a companion of man. So much so that his children had lovingly cherished their *Puttis* when they could not have the real creature to solace their wandering days.

Though these, in turn, were not cats of the past. Ayana could trace the likenesses, perhaps most in the heads with the stiffly whiskered faces, in the upstanding, pointed ears, and in the tails.

But one of the sleepers was again different—another species. She studied him now. There were no whiskers, though he was tailed. But the tail did not lie in as limber a way. His "face" had a longer muzzle, and his ears, larger, were in flaps.

The others were cats, or they had come from cats. But what was this one? Again Ayana returned to memory pictures. And she found what she sought—canine—dog! Again an old companion of man.

Cat-people, dog-people, still here in man's home carrying on war with Rattons. But where were the men? How long since they had disappeared? And why had they gone? Were the Rattons responsible? Ayana could hardly believe that. Even though those horrors might be able to muster whole armies, they could not have cleared out their masters, masters who were equipped with the weapons she knew existed here—the kind she had seen the cat-person wearing.

One of the patients stirred, opened his eyes. Large and green, they stared straight into hers. His ears flattened to his skull, he drew himself up against the wall of the chamber, his clawed hands coming up in menace.

He must believe she was one with the Rattons! But now they had a common cause. How could she *explain? Unless by understanding where he was, what was happening, he would know—*

The look in those green eyes, cold and measuring, daunted Ayana. She edged away from the window, decided it was time to check again on the sleepers. But this time went more slowly. If the cat-people, the dog-person, should turn on her, too—She could use the weapons, but if she did she would never learn the truth, perhaps never herself escape from this place in which the inhabitants apparently hunted each other with ferocious zeal.

Ayana stood looking down at Tan. When she left he would remain. So she must give him a chance. He was no longer one with her, if he had ever really been so, but he was one of her kind. And she believed that these filthy new allies of his would turn on him viciously when they discovered what had happened. She should return the stunner to him, give the rest of the sleepers an extra spray so they would still be under when his sedation wore off. In the meantime, she would try to prevent any more arrivals.

The door at the end of the hall had no locks that Ayana could understand. But she closed it and then piled there all the loose and heavy objects she could turn into a barricade.

When she had finished she stumbled back to the renewal chamber so tired she could barely urge one foot before the other. She had Extend pills, enough to renew her energy for the final dash out of here. But she would not waste those by premature use. There were E rations, one tube, in her belt loops. She turned the cap to heat and waited until she could twist that off and squeeze the semi-liquid contents into her mouth.

Having eaten, she went to look in the chamber. Time was passing far too fast, she might be pushed to a move soon.

Those inside were all conscious. The one cat-person who had first revived was standing. As she watched, he reached down to draw another up, a female, the scars of her wounds still rawly red but closed.

There was another male, and the dog-person, who, Ayana saw, had moved away from the other three, fitting his back into a corner as if he expected to be attacked.

There came a sudden sharp sound, enough to bring a weapon into Ayana's hand, set her looking about wildly. Then she realized that the light on the control board had gone out, the hum of the machine was subsiding. Apparently the chamber had turned itself off. Perhaps some indication that the work was done.

Now that the time had come to release the captives, Ayana found herself hesitant. The manifest anger in the male's expression—But they were weak, helpless, and she was armed—

With the stunner ready in her right hand, she spun the lock with her left. The door opened.

They were gathered just within as if ready to bolt for freedom, the three cat-people to the fore, the dog-person behind. Ayana heard hisses—a rumble of growl. She did not want to use the stunner, it might plunge them all straight back into captivity.

"No—" But they could not understand her, of course. However she babbled on as if they could. "Friend— friend!"

Their ears were flat to their skulls, their fangs exposed, their hands up with claws extended. If they came at her she would have no recourse but to shoot.

"*Friend—*"

A louder growl in answer. Ayana moved aside, retreated slowly, step by step, leaving a clear path between them and the door through which Tan and the Rattons had earlier brought her. Though she still held the stunner at ready, she waved them on in a gesture she hoped they would understand.

They moved slowly, stiffly, but gave no sign of pain. They moved with their heads turned toward her, their eyes watching. Then they reached the door and were gone, though for a moment or two she could still hear the shuffle of their feet.

Ayana breathed a sigh of relief. Her waiting was done. Now she must make good her own escape. She went for the last time to the huddle of the Ratton party, giving the Rattons a dose of stunner ray and then laid the weapon in Tan's lax hand.

He groaned and she jerked back as if he had made to seize her. He must be close to waking. She must get away fast—Ayana turned and ran, stopping only by the renewer to catch up her kit, following the path of the released captives.

She was afraid to use her torch. Luckily there seemed to be a very dim light here, enough to show the way. She must concentrate on the route she had tried to memorize when they brought her in. But first the Extend pills. Her chest hurt as she breathed after that last spurt of speed. Ayana groped within the kit. Two ought to be enough. She mouthed the tablets.

They were bitter and she had trouble swallowing them dry. But she hurried on even before they worked, so she was in another passage when that aching fatigue lifted. Ayana felt not only completely rested, but alert of mind, able to do anything. The euphoria which was a side effect of such a large dose of Extend gripped her and she forced herself to remember that this feeling of superb well-being was only illusionary.

This passage—had they come this way? But they must have—The trouble was that one of these ways looked exactly like another. Where had they left Jacel? She had tried to establish landmarks on the way in but had found few. And there were several places of forking corridors. She must remember—she must!

She had no warning. Out of some shadowed way she had not even glanced into, they sprang. Furred arms closed about her thighs as one attacker struck with force enough to crash her to the ground.

➤ 17 ◄

Furtig studied their captive. So—this was a Demon!
Though a female, not a warrior. But still a Demon
and as such to be feared. He heard a soft hiss of
breath. Eu-La, somewhat accustomed now to the
wonders of the legendary lairs, had moved beside
him and with her Liliha. While behind them came
two of the In-born males carrying a box with a coil
of wire laid on its cover.

The Demon was awake. When they had taken her
captive, she had fallen heavily and struck her head,
so they had taken her easily enough before she could
reach for weapons. And now here came Jir-Haz, to
whom they owed the capture itself.

"You can do this?" Furtig asked Liliha. "Speak to
the Demon in her own tongue?"

"We hope to do this thing. By listening to Demon
voices on their tapes we can understand their words.
But we cannot make those same noises ourselves. But
perhaps with this"—she laid a proprietary hand upon

the box—"we can twist our speech enough for her to
understand our questions."

But the Demon spoke first. She had been looking
from one to the other of them, first in what Furtig
relished as open fear (thus proving that the warriors
of the People could strike fear even into Demons)
and now with something close to appeal. For she
spoke to Liliha, at first so fast and in such a gabble
of sound, Furtig could make little of it.

However, Liliha, her ears attuned from very young
years to the teaching machines, did sort out enough
of those uncouth noises to make sense.

"She wishes to know where she is—and who we
are." Then, the In-born having set one end of the
wire into the box, Liliha took up a disk fastened to
the other and held it close to her mouth, speaking
slowly and carefully into it.

"This is the lair of Gammage. We are the People."

It was weird, for they could hear Liliha's words.
But also there was a secondary gabble, like a blurred
echo following.

The Demon's face was so strange, so unlike that of
a rational being that one could hardly hope to learn
anything from her expression. But Furtig dared to
imagine she was surprised.

"Speak slowly," Liliha was continuing. "We can
understand Demon speech, but our tongues cannot
twist to answer it."

He saw the Demon's tongue tip on her lower lip.
She could not move; they had bound her after peeling
off her coverings. For it seemed that the Demons had
no fur but wore loose outer skins to be stripped off.

"You—are—cats—" Even he could understand those queerly accented words.

"Cats? No, People," Liliha corrected her. "Why come you here?"

"What—are—you—to—do—with—me?" The Demon looked beyond Liliha to Jir-Haz. "He—was—in—the—healing—chamber. I—let—him—go—"

"Who knows a Demon's purpose?" Jir-Haz demanded of them all. "Yes, I was healed, as was Tiz-Zon, and A-San and the Barker. After we were near to death, she had the Rattons put us there. That they might return us to life and then once more rend us for their pleasure! Is that not so, Demon?" He leaned closer to hiss at her.

"I—could—have—killed—" the Demon said. "But—I—let—him—go."

"That is the truth?" Liliha asked Jir-Haz.

His tail lashed. "We told our story to the Elders. Yes, she let us go. Doubtless that the Rattons might have the sport of once more hunting us! Why else would a Demon heal our bodies and then release us?"

Liliha spoke into the disk. "Jir-Haz says that you did this for the Rattons, that they might once more torment our people. Such was what the Demons did in the old days."

"The Rattons—" The Demon's face was flushed. She tried to loose her hands, struggled against the ties. "I—was—with—the—Rattons—against—my—will—"

"There was another Demon, a male," Jir-Haz cut in. "He was not with her when she came to look in upon us during the healing. Nor was he there when she loosed us. Ask her concerning him!"

Liliha relayed the question. The Demon lay still as if she knew the folly of battling those bonds.

"I—left—him—with Shimog. I—put them all—to sleep so I might—escape and your—people also—"

"Why?" Liliha asked, almost, Furtig thought, as if she could believe what must be a false answer. For why should a Demon turn against one of her own kind to aid the People? No, she was false and would betray them if they believed her.

"Because—I saw Shimog and—what—they had done to—your people. I am a healer of—hurts not one to give them!"

"All Demons are false!" burst out Jir-Haz. "The other Demon, the Rattons, stayed out of sight that she might play friend and later point out our trail."

But Furtig had been thinking, and Jir-Haz's last accusation bothered him.

"When you captured this one," he asked, "was she not alone? Were there any Rattons or the other Demon with her?"

"Yes," Liliha added. "If she was alone, why was that so, supposing that she hunted you? Your story is that you had sent A-San ahead, and the Barker had gone his own way. She had three trails to follow, which did she seek?"

Jir-Haz's tail twitched. "None," he said slowly. "The Demon was taking a fourth way, going from our part of the lairs. And it is true she was alone. Also, after we had taken her we waited for a space, but none followed."

"So, we can believe that this Demon was not hunting you. She was alone when she watched you in the healing chamber, she was alone when she opened the door of that and bid you go. These are all the truth?"

"It is so," Jir-Haz acknowledged.

"Then what you yourself saw and report being so much the truth, must we not begin to believe that this Demon was not engaged in any hunt devised by Rattons, and that perhaps she too speaks the truth?"

"But she is a Demon!" Jir-Haz protested.

For the first time Eu-La broke silence. She had gone to stand close beside the bed on which they had laid the Demon.

"She does not look like one who kills. See—" Eu-La leaned over to set claw-tip to the Demon's middle. "She is all softness, easily torn. And, though like all Demons she is large, yet I do not believe that our warriors need look upon her as an ever-ready enemy. If she loosed Jir-Haz and the others from the Rattons, perhaps she had some reason. Why not ask her? She said she heals not harms, ask her how she does this and why. And how she came among the Rattons—"

"Also, to some purpose," Furtig cut in "ask her why she came to the lairs and if more Demons are on the way." Of course the answer to that might not be true, but it would do no harm to ask it.

He wished Gammage was here. Of them all, certainly the Ancestor was best-suited to deal with a Demon and weigh truth against not-truth. But the lair leader had departed to a truce flag meeting with the Barkers—since that hard-voiced people had sent a message and a flag to stand beside the first, thus agreeing to the meet. The second Barker, whom this Demon had freed, was he another scout of the same pack? And if so was he now making his way back to his people? What influence would his report have on the negotiations?

Slowly the Demon answered their questions. Yes, she had come from the sky—she was one of four—

All that they knew. So they were learning nothing. But when they questioned her about the Rattons—then they could not check her story. She had come from the ship at a call for help from one of her companions. She had found him injured and had treated him. Then the other, the Ratton friend (if anyone could friend that scum) had ordered her to treat a Ratton leader, had threatened her if she did not.

The longer Furtig listened to her halting, slowly spoken words, the easier it was to understand them. And somehow they sounded true. In spite of Jir-Haz, his own inborn distrust of Demons, everything, he could not say this was false. When she spoke of Shimog, the very tone of her voice (now that he was more familiar with it) bore out her aversion to the Ratton leader. But it was Liliha who brought home with a question the strange point in the whole tale.

"So they told you that Rattons were the comrades of Demons? But we have not learned it so. In fact, it is recorded that until the final days when the Demons went mad, Rattons were enemies to all. My people, the Barkers—we once lived in friendly company with Demons. Then the evil which the Demons themselves wrought seized upon them. They turned against all other living creatures, hunted them—"

"This evil." There was such urgency in the Demon's voice as made them all stare. "What manner of evil? I tell you—we came searching for the reason we left this world, why my people long ago lifted to the stars and then hid all mention of the past from us. Tell me, if you know, why did they go? What happened to them here, to you—to this place?"

She looked from side to side as if begging one or another to answer. Such was the power of the emotion which flowed from her that Furtig believed in her wholly—that she had come seeking just what she said. Liliha did not answer at once. She spoke to Furtig:

"Cut her loose!"

His hand slipped into fighting claws in obedience. Then he hesitated. Jir-Haz growled warningly. It would seem that he still clung to his suspicions.

"Loose her," Liliha repeated. "What do you fear?" she asked Jir-Haz. "Look, she has no weapons, not even claws. Do you believe she can overcome us all?"

Furtig went forward and, seeing his hand so armed, the Demon shrank back with a cry, trying to free herself before he could reach her. Liliha spoke swiftly.

"He will not harm you, he comes to loose you."

She quieted then, and he cut swiftly through the cords.

"What would you do with me?"

"We can show you better than we can tell. Come."

So they brought the Demon to the room of learning, and there Liliha started the tape readers, those records which had given them the information concerning the last days of the Demons. Though these were faulty and lacking in many details, as if those who had made them had lost the skill to do so properly. Afterward Liliha explained even more of the traditions of the People and of what Gammage and the In-born had learned. But that took some time. And Furtig was not long a part of it. He had other duties, and it was true that the Demon female did not need such guarding—she was weaponless and surrounded by Choosers who were certainly as keen-eyed as any warrior.

There was still the matter of the Demon male and the Rattons. How deep into Ratton territory they dared send their own scouts was a question to bother even Dolar. But before night their numbers began to be augmented by an inflow of People. Not Furtig's as yet, but Ku-La's forces.

What these brought with them, as well as their weapons and supplies, was information, some bits held from the days of the Demons, some gathered by investigation in those parts of the northeastern lairs where Gammage's explorers had never done any real searching. Once their Choosers and younglings were established in the safe heart of Gammage's territory, their warriors spread out to join the In-born and the handful of newcomers such as Furtig.

Reports came in now from questing scouts. The Demon who had been injured had crawled out of the tunnels, gone back to the grounded ship, which was always under observation. The ship itself was sealed, no hatch open. It was as if the two within it held it as a fort against attack. On the other hand the fourth Demon, he who had joined the Rattons, had also been sighted.

A young warrior of Ku-La's people, very small and slim and so able to take ways closed to those of larger frame, had managed to squirm through a side duct and look into a very busy place in the Ratton burrows. There were machines there like the rumblers, and these the Rattons were swarming over, working on, under the leadership of the Demon. It was apparent that the machines were being readied and that could only be to attack.

Armed with this report Dolar, with Furtig in tow, went to the chamber where the Demon female was with Liliha. She had shared food with them, and at her request they had given her back those looser skins she wore. As the warriors entered she was sitting with Liliha exchanging talk, the translating machine on a divan between them.

"Ask her," Dolar said abruptly, "what the Demon does with the machines and the Rattons. We believe that they prepare an attack, and we must know how these machines will work."

Liliha relayed the question. But when the Demon answered, she spoke directly to Dolar.

"There are many kinds of machines. Can you tell me, or show me, the form of these?"

He clanged his fighting claws together. A machine was a machine. How could you find words to describe it? Then he rounded on the In-born who was his at-tail messenger.

"Bring the seeing box."

The warrior had not gone empty-handed into the narrow ways, but had taken with him one of the discoveries of his own people, a box which made a permanent record of what he saw. When this case was set before the Demon she appeared to know it for what it was, instantly pressing the right button. Across the room, on the wall, appeared a picture, small enough for Furtig's two hands to cover, yet clear in details.

For a long moment the Demon studied the picture and then she spoke:

"I do not know what all these machines may be.

See, there are at least three different kinds. But there—that one upon which the Ratton stands—that shoots forth fire. It is like the weapon your people took from me but much more powerful, for the fire spreads wider. I believe that these are machines of war." Her voice died away, and yet she continued to look at the picture as if there was something there to hold her full attention.

"Machines of war, fearsome ones," Dolar repeated as if to himself. "Let those come seeking us and perhaps the Rattons will win."

The Demon female spoke again. "You have showed me much. Also—there is something—if I can only make it plain to you—" She twined her hands together, finger punishing finger in that tight grip, as if she might wring the words she wanted to say out of her own flesh. "I am one who heals. I have been taught to do so since I was very young. We did not know why our ancestors—our long-ago Elders—left these lairs. And we have a trouble on our home world which is bad—therefore we were sent to seek out our old homeland, and aid.

"But when our ship landed here—we—we changed. No more were we as we had always been. We became strangers one to the other—" She looked at none of them as she spoke thus, but ever at the wall pictures. "We seemed to become—no, perhaps I cannot say it. But you have showed me that there was once a madness here, an evil thing which possessed my kind. I think that the shadow of that lingers still, so that we are becoming enemies, one to the other. If this is true, that illness must be healed, and we must go. And it may be too late." She covered her face with her hands, sat shivering so that Furtig could see the shudders of her body. Liliha put out her hands, laid them upon the Demon's shaking shoulders. Then, as he never thought to see, she drew the Demon to her as she might in comforting a sister Chooser, and held her so.

Ayana pulled away, though the comfort of that soft warmth the cat-woman offered was such that she longed to cling to it. She wiped her wet cheeks with the backs of her hands. All that she had learned was a weight on her spirit. But it was, as these people made much of saying, the truth. No wonder her kind had fled this place. This sickness of spirit was as strong as once had been the sickness of body which had either produced it or been the end-product of it. She need only look at that picture of Tan, at his intense, absorbed face as he readied machines to wipe out life, and know how deeply they had been stricken.

These lairs, as they called them, lairs of darkness in spite of all the light within, lairs of knowledge which could kill as well as cure. Knowledge, could one pick and choose among knowledge? A thing which might cure in one form could be used to kill in another. As a medic, who should know better than she? Had she not even sought out death dealers herself on board ship, gathered them together?

But what Tan intended—that must not be! And there was something else, a warning she must give of another kind. She had seen this Gammage only briefly when they had first brought her in. His urging for union among intelligent species—yes, that was a step forward. But his thirst for alien knowledge—his *tinkering with the scraps and remnants they played with here—no! That was tampering with that which might end him and his people as surely as the Rattons and Tan, equipped with war machines, could do.*

However, the immediate threat—resolutely Ayana pushed aside what might happen tomorrow, concentrated on today. Suppose Tan and his nightmare army of allies did activate those machines of crawling death? Weapons used by men who had built and inhabited this complex would be very sophisticated. And Tan would release what he could not control.

These cat-people looked to her for an answer. And she did not have one. Jacel—Massa—could help, but would either of them do so? She had no idea of what had happened between Jacel and Tan before she had reached them. But that comment of Tan's about Jacel's discovery that the Rattons could be dangerous if crossed lingered now in her mind. There must have been ill-will between the two men, some argument. Could she build on that? It seemed to Ayana a very thin hope, but it was all she had now.

"There are many machines, and I have no knowledge of them." *She made her explanation as simple as possible.* *"But those in the ship still can help. I see no other way—"*

She had been long enough with the cat-people now to be able to read expressions a little, and she saw that suggestion was not welcome, especially to the large male with the scarred ears. But she could not help them. Only Jacel and Massa knew the machines. And how much time did they have?

The growling, spitting speech of the People among themselves was prolonged. Finally the males went out together, leaving her once more with the females she had learned to call Liliha and Eu-La.

"You are a Chooser?" *Liliha asked, and Ayana saw both the cat-women watching her closely, as if her answer was important.*

"What is a Chooser?"

They appeared startled. Then Liliha explained. "There is a time when one wishes younglings. One's body is ready to hold such. As mine—" *She slid her hand over her slim belly.* "But not yet is Eu-La so." *She pointed to her companion's slighter figure.* "When this time comes the warriors display their strength so that we Choosers may look upon them, judge their skills, select one to father a youngling. You have so chosen?"

Ayana looked down at her own hands. Not to get a child had she chosen (or rather had had the choosing done for her) but rather that a certain needed series of traits could complement and perhaps fill out another's character. Had she been subtly conditioned to accept Tan so readily? Now she suspected that. He had become a stranger so fast, as if the sickness which clung here had broken through that shell of acceptance.

"I did not choose, he was chosen for me." *She felt an odd shame at making that confession.*

"This then is the custom of the Demons, that a Chooser may not choose for herself?" *Liliha asked after a long moment of silence.*

"Because there were but four of us in the ship, and we must each know certain things, yes, we were chosen by others."

"Ill doing." *Liliha's voice was a hiss.* "For when a Chooser chooses in truth, she knows the worth of *a warrior and he does not later become an enemy. I sorrow for you that this was so, that now you must eat bitterness and ashes." Her hand rested over Ayana's. "It is well you do not have a youngling within you."*

"That is true," replied Ayana.

She was not left alone, nor was she still outwardly a prisoner. Oddly enough, she had no desire to leave. Liliha, Eu-La, the other cat-women who drifted in their soundless way in and out, brought food, or simply came to sit and look at her (though she never found their curiosity rude or disturbing) were somehow comforting, though she could not have told why. Several brought babies, purred them to sleep or played with them. But after a space Ayana began to worry.

The memory of Tan and the Rattons, busy with the war machines, was never erased from her mind, though she did sleep at last. And she drifted off to a purring song Liliha seemingly sang to herself as the cat-woman brushed the shining length of her tail. There was only the gray light of early dawn coming through the windows when they roused her. Liliha was there, and, by the door, the cat-man she had seen with the scarred older warrior, the young one who had been present before when they had questioned her. He was making the small, almost yowling sounds of their excited speech, and Liliha used the translator.

"The Ancestor would speak with you—it is very urgent."

The male crossed the room with lithe strides, holding the translator. Ayana noted that his strange claw weapons hung from his belt, that belt which was his only clothing. For, though the cat-people appeared to vary in the amount of natural fur on their bodies, nearly hairless like Liliha in some cases, or as deeply furred as this male, they wore no coverings.

They went along the corridors, down two ramps, and then climbed another for some distance, until they reached a room where there was a gathering of warriors, a sprinkling of females. All were grouped about one male. He was a little stooped, his muzzle fur frosted, his arms and legs thin and shrunken. About his bowed shoulders was a cloak of shimmering stuff, which set him apart from the others, though his very air was enough to do that. She recollected having seen him much earlier, in that time she had been a bound prisoner.

This was Gammage who was their leader, or ruler, whose dream it was to reclaim the Demon knowledge for his people. He stared straight at Ayana as she entered. In one hand he held a translator disk, the box resting before him on the floor.

"They tell me," he began abruptly, "that you believe those in the ship have more knowledge of these war machines."

"That is so." Cat—man—mixture—there was something very impressive about this Elder. Ayana could understand how he had managed to gather together seekers after knowledge and inspire them through the years.

"Will they support the Rattons, or will they aid us?" He came directly to the point.

"I do not know, I can only ask," she said simply, as directly as he had asked.

Gammage made his decision. "Then that you shall do."

➤ 18 ◄

Furtig crouched in the shadow of the doorway, one of the party that had escorted the female Demon out of the lairs. She stood out there alone now, in full sight of those in her ship. And the People had given her back the device to signal her companions. Furtig held one of the lightning throwers. He could send the crackling lash to cut down the Demon at the first suspicion of betrayal.

Liliha, though she was armed—so close to him now that when she moved the thin ruff of fur on the outside of her rounded arm brushed his—made no move to draw her weapon. She had insisted that the Demon was to be trusted, that she wanted indeed to halt the Rattons and her own male. Though it was hard for the warriors to accept such a turning against one's own kind.

It would seem that this was a Chooser thing, allied in a way to whatever moved them when they made mate choice. Liliha had sworn before the Elders, and it was very plain she believed what she said, that this Demon, though she had chosen the male now preparing to send fiery death against them, had not done that by her own willing and that she wanted no youngling of his.

Strange were the ways of Demons, strange even were the People's ways now. For their party had not only been augmented by Ku-La's warriors, but, in addition, by those from the caves, who had finally arrived. And—in an opposite doorway—were Barkers!

Never had Furtig believed he would be allied in any way with those. Yet Gammage and the two scouts rescued from the Rattons had convinced the Barkers to send in a small pack, perhaps as observers only. Still they were warriors, and no real fight would leave them lurking in the shadows.

A strange sound from the field—the bridge into the sky-ship was now dropping from the open hatch in its side. The Demon need only to run up that to be safe. Furtig was not sure any of them could use the strange weapons quickly enough to cut her down.

Liliha held to her ear one of the coms—as the Demon called them. Through that she could hear what the Demon said to her own kind. And she was not running, not moving at all. For some very long moments nothing happened. No one appeared in the hatch. All through those dragging minutes Furtig fully expected some awesome weapon to come into action, to their finish.

However, it would seem Liliha was right about the female Demon keeping to her word. At length a figure appeared on the ship's bridge, advancing slowly. It was muffled in clumsy wrappings so it hardly looked like a living thing, more like one of the unreliable lair servants.

It tramped down the ramp, strode ponderously toward the waiting Demon. While it was still some paces away, its thick-fingered hands, almost as clumsy as Furtig's own when he tried to use some delicate lair tool, thumbed something at throat level. The head covering rose and flopped back on its shoulders.

"That is the other female," Liliha reported. "The one Ayana calls Massa—"

Furtig supposed that among themselves the Demons had names as did the People, the Barkers, even the Rattons. But he had never thought of the enemy as living normal, peaceful lives—only as the evil creatures of the old tales.

Dolar was beyond Liliha. "What do they say?" he rasped.

"The one from the ship asks questions—Where has Ayana been, what happens here. Now Ayana tells her there is much danger, they must talk. She asks about the other Demon—Jacel. Massa is angry. She says that he is ill, that Ayana must come and see to his illness. She asks where is Tan—there is anger in that. Now she says that Tan is the one who allowed the Rattons to wound her mate. That he must be wrong in his head—"

"Twist-minded like the Demons of old," cut in Dolar. "Mad—then dead. We must see to it that this time we are not also caught in that death! What say they now?"

"Ayana tells Massa that there is great danger, that Tan will bring death unless he is stopped. Massa says let Tan do as he will here, let them get on the ship and raise it into the sky, return to their own world—"

How easy that would be! Furtig growled, heard a similar sound from Dolar. Easy enough for these

Demons to lift, leaving the evil one to finish here. And how could any of the People stop him? Oh, they might be able to blast these two females now. Then the one left in the ship—if he were sick perhaps he was also twist-minded—might join the one in the lairs in loosing the weapons the ship carried—

"Ayana says 'no,'" Liliha's voice quickened with excitement. "She says that the one called Tan must be stopped. That they can never learn what they came for—"

"And what is that?" demanded one of the warriors crouched behind them.

"They came here—Ayana spoke with Gammage of it this morning," Furtig answered, as Liliha was plainly intent on the com to her ear, "hunting two things—the reason their Ancestors quit this world, and an answer to an evil now destroying their new home among the stars. Gammage has promised that when we have beaten the Rattons she may seek such knowledge."

"When we beat the Rattons—say rather if we beat the Rattons!" commented someone else. Furtig saw that speaker was Fal-Kan.

"Be that as it may, there is knowledge here that they seek," Furtig answered with not quite the deference due an Elder. "Gammage made a bargain with this Demon. But she must persuade those in the ship to honor it."

"The one called Massa"—Liliha signaled for silence—"says she will do nothing until Ayana aids the sickness of her mate. If he is helped, then she will think of this."

"If the Demon goes inside the ship we shall have no way to watch her!" Dolar instantly objected.

"She will not go alone." Liliha arose. "I go with her."

Into the private lair of the Demons? Furtig moved. He had already slipped his left hand into his fighting claws. And in the other he had the lightning thrower.

"Not alone!" He thought his tone was not his usual one, but no one seemed to notice. Dolar twitched tail in assent.

Liliha handed the second com to the tough old Elder. "Set it so." She fitted it into his ear. "I do not know whether it will reach into the ship for you to hear. We can only hope it does."

Without glancing at Furtig, she stepped gracefully out of the doorway, her tail curled upward a little as if she went with pleasure. Pride brought him level with her, trying to assume the same appearance of unconcern.

The Demon Massa saw them first, gave a cry, and Ayana turned her head. Liliha, having no interpreter box, pointed to her, the ship, and used hand language.

Ayana nodded her head. Furtig, with the other interpreter, caught fragments of speech. She spoke much faster than she did with the People, and so was difficult to understand.

"We will go to Jacel."

Massa turned, all those extra layers of loose skin making her move slowly. Ayana walked behind her, Liliha and Furtig keeping pace. So they climbed the ramp to the ship.

Furtig's nostrils expanded, took in the many odors, most of them new, some disagreeable. There were strange pole steps one must climb. He set the lightning thrower between his jaws, for he must use all four limbs here. He hated the closed-in feeling of a trap which the cramped interior gave him.

Yet he stared carefully about him, intent on making good use of this chance to see the marvels of the Demons, wishing he could understand it all better.

In the small side chamber where the other male Demon lay in a niche within the wall, there was room for only the two females. But Furtig and Liliha could watch through the doorway. The Demon's face was flushed, his head turned restlessly from side to side, his eyes were half-open. But, though they rested on Furtig, there was no sign that the Demon really saw the warrior.

Ayana was busy. She used a box from which wires ran to pads she held against the Demon's head, against his chest, watching the top of the machine where there sounded a steady clicking. Then she took up two small rods, opened them to slide in even thinner tubes in which liquid moved as she turned them. The ends of the outer rods she pressed to the bare skin of the Demon, on his arm, on his chest, at one point on his throat.

Before she had finished, his head no longer rolled, but lay quiet, his eyes closed. Then she spoke to Massa, slowly, as if she wanted the People to hear and understand.

"He will sleep, and wake all right. It is an infection from his wound, but not serious. This place is poisonous in more ways than one, Massa."

Massa had settled down beside the sleeping male, her hand over his, watching his face intently.

"Tan—Tan did this to him," she said. "What happened to Tan?"

"The same thing which destroyed those who remained here." Ayana put away the instruments. "Madness. And now Tan is about to destroy even more. You will have to help stop him, Massa, help us—"

"Us? Us, Ayana? You are helping these—these animals?" The Demon Massa looked to Furtig and Liliha, and there was fear in her eyes.

"Not animals, Massa—people—the People. This is Liliha, Furtig." She motioned from one to the other. "They have their lives and more than their lives at stake here. Our ancestors made them—"

"Robos?"

Ayana shook her head at that queer word. "No. Remember the old learning tapes, Massa? Remember 'cat' and 'dog' and 'rat'—and Putti, a dear friend?"

Furtig saw a little of the fear fade from the other's eyes, a wonderment take its place.

"But those were animals!"

"Were once. Just as we were once also. I do not know what really happened here, besides the spread of a madness which wrecked a whole species and altered others past recognition. But whatever our ancestors loosed, or tried to do deliberately, out of it grew the People who were cats, the Barkers who were dogs, and the Rattons—rats. And it is the latter Tan deals with—the filthy, merciless, torturing latter! He uses their aid to start old war machines, planning to wreck this world. Our ancestors left the company of those who began this grim wastage; we must stop it now."

"I do not know how you have learned all this." Massa raised the hand of the sleeping Demon and held it to her cheek. "But Tan—he turned those evil Rattons on Jacel. I owe him for that!"

Beside Furtig, Liliha stirred. She spoke in a small whisper. "This one did not have a mate chosen for her, or if she did, then her choice was the same. She will join us, I think, because she hates the ones who harmed him."

Thus when they came forth from the ship again they were not three but four. And all of them carried boxes and containers Ayana and Massa had chosen from supplies. They transported these to that place where Gammage had gathered his battle leaders. Not only were Elders of the Barkers there, keeping to themselves, watching the People from eye corners (as the People surveyed them in return), but also Broken Nose brought in the pick of his warriors and they stood snuffling and grunting in one corner, their heavy-tusked leader in the circle about Gammage.

While the Ancestor made hand and speech talk, deft-fingered In-born moved small blocks here and there on the floor.

"The passages run so." Gammage gestured to the collection of blocks. "Walls stand thus. They can bring out the war machines only here, and here. We have scouts at each exit to warn of their coming—"

"But will we have time for such a message to reach us?" The Barker Elder's hand signs were awkward by the People's standard but effective enough to be understood.

"Yes—he will do it." Gammage pointed to Furtig.

"He is here—the scouts are there—" The gestures of the Barker were impatient.

"He can see—in his head—"

Furtig only hoped that Gammage was right, that his ability to contact the scouts would work. Foskatt was one, having with him the box to step up their communication. A second warrior, a small, very agile follower from Ku-La's tribe, had tested out well in box-Furtig contact too. It was the best they could do, for Foskatt could not cover both exits at once.

The Barker chief stared at Furtig. If he did not believe Gammage, at least he did not say so. Perhaps he had been shown enough inside the lairs to lead him to accept any wild statement.

"Only two ways for them to come," Gammage continued vocally for his own people and the Demon females. "And it is near to those that they must be stopped. We have taken all the servant machines and set them at the beginning of each way, ready to put into action. Though those will only cause a little delay. And with such fire shooters"—he looked now to Ayana—"as you say those are, perhaps the delay will be a very short one."

"Massa?" Ayana spoke the name of her sister Demon like a question.

The other was studying a picture projected on the wall, the one showing the details of what Tan and the Rattons were doing. "Those are storage-powered." Her words made little sense to Furtig. "If the power could be shorted, or stepped up by feed radiation—"

"They would blow themselves up!" Ayana joined her. "Could we do that?"

"With a strong enough transmitter hook-up. But to do it underground—The backlash would be so powerful—there is no way of measuring what might happen."

"Yet if they bring those out—use them—"

Massa looked from Ayana to the mixed company of allies. "To whom here do we owe a debt? And remember, Tan would be lost, too."

Ayana turned her head also, looked from Liliha to Furtig, to Gammage, old Broken Nose, the people of Ku-La, those of the lair, the caves, the Barkers. It was as if she studied them all to make sure she knew them.

"Tan has already made his choice," she said slowly. "The debt is owed to all these. It is an old debt. Those of our blood started them on the road which they now travel. Our blood did ill here, and if we do not halt Tan, it shall do worse. Since we were responsible, these must have their chance. There is our old madness—and here is new life beginning. If we allow this war to break loose, we shall have to face a second failure for our kind. We must do what we can here and now."

"You then accept the full consequences of what will happen?" Massa spoke solemnly like one giving a challenge to battle.

"I accept."

"So be it."

Under the guidance of Massa, who went through the storerooms of the In-born (pausing sometimes with exclamations of one finding treasures until she was hurried on by Ayana), the lair defenders drew out many things they did not understand, placed those on carts which could be driven down into the lower levels.

They finally chose a single point, where the attackers must pass if they would reach the key entrance to Gammage's territory, and there they erected the barricade. Massa crawled in and out laying wires, placing boxes, those she had brought from the ship, others from the stores.

Furtig saw none of this. Against his will he sat

in Gammage's headquarters, trying to keep his mind receptive to scout reports. Squatting on their heels before him were two younglings selected for their swift running, ready to carry warning to those who set up the final line of defense.

Meanwhile, out of this section of the lairs in which Gammage's people had so long sheltered, that tribe and the more recently joined kinsmen were moving not only their families and personal belongings, but load after load of the highly useful discoveries. For Massa had warned that when attack came, and if the counteraction she planned worked, there might even be an end to the buildings themselves.

Warriors, shaking with weariness, started appearing from below, stopped to pick up and stagger on with some last loads of discoveries. At last came the final party of all, Gammage, Dolar, the two Demons, three of the People, and two Barkers.

"We go—" Gammage staggered. He looked very thin and frail and old, as if all his years had fallen on him at once. Dolar was supporting him as he went. "The Demon says this is a distance weapon, released by what she has in her hand—"

Furtig did not rise. "I cannot receive the alarm from below at any greater distance than this." As he said that a hollow emptiness was in him as if he hungered—but not for food, rather for the hope of life. He had tested the limits of the mind-send—and had accepted the fact that he could not retreat with the rest, any more than could Foskatt or the young scout of Ku-La's band, who were at their posts below.

"But—" Ayana paused after that one word.

Slowly Dolar made an assenting tail sweep.

"How long"—Furtig hoped his voice was reasonably steady, the proper tone for a warrior about to lead into battle—"must you know before you use this machine of yours?" He was using the interpreter and spoke directly to the Demon.

Ayana pulled at her wrist, loosening a band holding a round thing with black markings. One of those markings moved steadily.

"When this mark moves from here to here—that long do we have between alarm and when we use the weapon."

She slipped the band off, gestured for Furtig to take it.

Furtig turned now to Gammage. "How long before the Demon war machines can reach the place of the trap after they are sighted coming forth?"

The Ancestor bit at claw tip and then went to look at the blocks which stood for the level ways. "If the war machines go no faster than rumblers, and if those we have put in place do hold them back for a space—" He broke off as Liliha came running lightly across the chamber. In her hands was a wide dish of metal and in its center a cone. Furtig recognized it as what the In-born used to measure time. Gammage took it and spanned the cone with two claws.

"Light this at your first warning. Let it burn as far as I have marked it—then give us your signal."

So at both ends there was a small length of time— time for Foskatt and the scout below—time for himself.

"These go with you." Furtig pointed to his messengers. He caught up the covering on the divan, ripped it apart, and went to a window.

"See, when the scouts' signal comes that they move

out below, and this burns to the line—I shall fire this with the lightning thrower. It will blaze in the window, and you, seeing it, can set off your weapon."

He hoped it would work. At least the arrangement gave him a small chance. The others left, taking the last of the bundles with them. If Massa was right—how much of the lairs would be lost? But better lose all than their lives and have the Demon and Rattons rule.

Furtig went back to the divan and sat down. Now he must concentrate on the messages. His skin itched as if small bugs crawled over his body. He licked his lips, found that now and then his hands jerked. With all his might he strove to control his body, to think only of Foskatt and the other scout—think—and wait.

It had been two days since the Demons had agreed to aid them. What had the Rattons and the other Demon been doing all that time? Putting machines to work—? All the pictures the hidden scout had taken were essentially the same. Apparently some machines had been discarded—others chosen—

How much longer—a night, another day? The longer the better as far as the rest of the People and their allies were concerned. They would be on the move away, back from this whole section of lair which was now a trap. Only the Demons and the war leaders would stay with the power broadcaster.

Periodically Furtig contacted the scouts. Each time the report was the same—no sign of any attack. Night came. Furtig ate and drank, walked up and down to keep mind and body alert.

He had returned to the divan when the long-awaited signal came—from Foskatt.

Instantly Furtig ordered the other scout to withdraw,

then touched the cone on the plate with a drop of liquid. There was a burst of blue flame, followed by a steady burning. Furtig drew the lightning weapon, hurried to the doorway, his attention divided between the cone and the bundle of stuff in the window.

Longer than he had thought! Had he mistaken the markings Gammage had made on the cone? He held the dish—no, there was the line clear to be seen. Now he looked at that other measure which Ayana had given him, ready to depend upon it when the dish light marked the time.

Now!

Furtig hurled the dish from him, aimed at the bundle in the window, pressed the firing button. A long shaft of lightning crossed the chamber. His aim had been good, striking full upon the bundle. There was flame there which certainly the watchers in the next building could not mistake.

He was already through the door, running at top pace down the corridor, coming out on one of the bridges lacing building to building. And he kept on, intent only on trying to put distance between him and the place he had just quitted. Another corridor, one of those shafts for descent. Not daring to wonder if it worked, Furtig leaped into it as he might into a pool of water.

Then he floated down, his heart pounding. The tremor came. And that almost caused his death, for the soft pressure which supported him failed. It was only that it strengthened again for a moment that saved him, gave him a chance to catch at a level opening.

He was swinging by his hands and somehow scrambled up and through. There came another tremor.

The building about him shook. Furtig ran, wanting only to gain the open. The rest of his flight was a nightmare. He kept picturing the whole of the lairs about to crash down on him.

Only when he reached the open did he turn to look back. There was a change. It took him several half-dazed moments to realize that the outline of at least one tower against the sky was now missing. All the buildings were now dark, no lights showing.

Liliha, Gammage, the Demons, the party who had remained to set off the trap—

Furtig, his panic gone, turned around. He dared not trust the interior of the lairs now. In fact the conviction was growing in him that, knowledge or no knowledge, he was through with the lairs. But he must know if the others had escaped. And Foskatt—underground—

He could not search the lairs—Why had he not thought straight? Furtig hunkered down on the ground, began to use his own talent.

Liliha! It was like looking into her face and she—she felt his questioning—understood! Foskatt—Furtig began again—but perhaps they were too far separated. He hoped that was the answer when he could not raise the other.

Morning came and they stood on the edge of the site where the sky-ship pointed up and out. Foskatt and the other scout were still missing. They were all there but one—and without that one—

"He was very old." Ayana's eyes held a tiredness in them as if she needed to rest a long, long time. "And he was weaker than he let you know. He must have been. When the explosion came"—she raised her hand

and let it fall with a small guttering gesture as if she tried their sign language—"then he went."

Gammage, the Ancestor, the one who had always been—a living legend. A world without Gammage? But now Ayana spoke again.

"In a way he was wrong. He wanted you to be stronger, more intelligent with every generation. He wanted you to, as he thought, be like us. So he sought out our knowledge for you. He did it, wanting the best for his people. But in a way he gave them the worst. He wanted you to have all we once had—but that was not the answer. You know what happened here to us. Our knowledge killed, or drove us out.

"You have your own ways, learn through them. It will be slower, longer, harder, but do it. Do not try to change what lies about you; learn to live within its pattern, be a true part of it. I do not know if you understand me. But do not follow us into the same errors.

"One thing Gammage did for you which is right and which you must save more than you save anything you have taken from the lairs: He taught you that against a common enemy you can speak with Barkers under a truce flag, gather and unite tribes and clans. Remember that above all else, for if he had only done that much, Gammage would be the greatest of your race.

"But do not try to live as we. Learn by your own mistakes, not ours. This world is now yours."

"And the Demons?" Dolar growled into the interpreter. He moved very slowly, as if with Gammage's death some of the other's great age had also settled upon him.

"We shall not come again. This is no longer our world. We have found in the lairs the knowledge which will perhaps save us on our new home. And our people will accept that, after hearing what we have to say. Or if they do not accept—" She looked over their heads to the lairs. "Be sure in my promise—we shall not come again!"

Even, she thought, if we have to—to make sure that the ship does not return to Elhorn. This promise must be kept. She did not look back to the People as she drew herself wearily up the ramp. If matters had been different, if the old madness had not gripped them—if Tan—resolutely she closed her mind to that. But if the madness had not struck in the beginning perhaps the People would not have existed either. Did ill balance good somehow? Now she was too tired, too drained to think.

Those on the field scattered back to the lairs. There were warriors questing about the ruins, hunting signs of Rattons, but so far none had been sighted. They had, though, brought back a dazed Foskatt, who had been struck on the head and was now closely tended by Eu-La. The other scout was still being sought.

Furtig and Liliha stood together, watching fire sprout around the sky-ship. They hid their eyes then against the glare as it rose, pointing out. The Demon had promised—no return.

But the other things she had said—that Gammage had been wrong, that they must find their own kind of knowledge—How much of that was truth? They would have time now to discover.

"They have gone," Liliha said. "To the stars—where

someday, warrior, we shall follow. But before then, there is much to be done—even if we are no longer Gammage's people."

He would follow her willingly, even back into the lairs. Furtig had a feeling that henceforth wherever Liliha light footedly trod he would follow. No—not follow—for she was waiting for him to walk beside her. He purred softly, and his tail tip curved up in warm content.

The following is an excerpt from:

TO SAIL A DARKLING SEA

JOHN RINGO

Available from Baen Books
February 2014
hardcover

CHAPTER 1

∽◦❧〰❧◦∼

Robert "Rusty" Fulmer Bennett III wasn't a guy
to just sit around if he could help out. But he
also wasn't, still, in the best of shape.

When he'd boarded the cruise ship *Voyage
Under Stars* with his buddy, Ted, he'd weighed
337 lbs, nekkid. By the time the rescue teams
from Wolf Squadron found him, Ted had long
before zombied and Rusty weighed 117 lbs and
was naked, covered in bed sores and mostly
unconscious on his filth covered bunk. Since he
was still 6' 7", and, honestly, big boned, 117 was
pretty bad. The one nurse Wolf had found so far,
no doctors, said it was a miracle he'd survived.

So he still wasn't in the best shape of his life
when he sat down in the "Wolf Squadron Human
Resources" office. In the four weeks since he'd
been found he'd put on about twenty pounds
but that wasn't much. And he could barely work
out at all. He wasn't sure that he could hack it

as a "clearance specialist" but he was all up for killing zombies.

He filled in his name on the clipboard and took a seat. Then he opened up a packet of sushi and started to munch.

"Still putting on weight, huh?" the guy next to him asked.

"I never thought I'd like sushi," Bennett said, offering some of the rolls. "Anything is, like, *the best food in the world*, now. Except hummus. If I never eat hummus again I'll be so glad."

"Gotta try fish eyeballs," the guy said, taking one and nodding. "Mmmm... tuna is sooo much better raw than dolphin. Brad Stevens."

"Rusty Bennett," Rusty said. "Actually, it's Robert Fulmer Bennett Third. But everybody calls me Rusty. Like, you ate a *dolphin*?"

"Not the Flipper, ark, ark, kind," Stevens said. "It's a kind of fish. But, hey, when that's what you've got." He shrugged. "I'd have eaten a, you know, dolphin, dolphin if I could have caught one. There were a couple of times I'd have eaten the *asshole* of a dolphin..."

"I'd have eaten the asshole of an asshole," Rusty said.

"You're like a string-bean pole," Stevens said. "How much did you lose?"

"Two hundred pounds," Rusty said. "I was kinda big when we got locked down."

"Oh," Stevens said, wincing. "In one of the cabins on the *Voyage*?"

"Yep," Rusty said. "One of the reasons I want to go do something is every time I walk in the damned cabin I'm afraid the door's going to close behind me and never open again."

"I thought I'd lost weight. I can't believe they cleared you for work."

"I just walked down here," Rusty said, shrugging. "The worst they can do is say no..."

"Stevens...?"

"You're still in very poor shape, Mister Bennett," the lady said. Like most he'd seen, she was pregnant.

"I really want to help out," Rusty said. "And I've got to get out of that fu... forking cabin, ma'am. I keep having nightmares that the door won't open."

"I took this job on the *Grace* because it's the biggest boat I could get on," the lady said, smiling. "Try having nightmares that you're back in a tropical storm in a life raft and you're suffering from morning sickness and starving."

"Yes, ma'am," Rusty said. "I'm good with my hands. But I'm not a mechanic or anything. I can shoot. I've been shooting my whole life. And I want to fight zombies, ma'am."

"You'd never make the medical requirements for clearance personnel," the lady said. "They carry tons of gear when they clear."

"I heard there's some thirteen-year-old girl that does it, ma'am," Rusty argued. "If she can..."

"Don't compare Shewolf to your normal thirteen-year-old girl," the woman said, laughing. "You haven't seen the video have you?"

"No, ma'am," Rusty said. "I haven't gotten out, much."

"If you go up to the lounge, you can probably find somebody who can show it to you," the lady said. "Shewolf *led* the boarding of the *Voyage*. She wasn't supposed to, but it happened. The *Dallas* had used a machine gun to clear some of the zombies but while she was going up more showed up. She went over the side, anyway. There was a Marine in a little bit better shape than you, not much but a little, who was supposed to go right after her and got bogged down climbing. One of the reasons they want people in the best possible shape for clearance. At that point, most of the copies... You know that song, 'I get knocked down, but I get up again...?'"

"Sort of?" Rusty said. "Kinda before my time."

"Go watch the video," the lady said, looking at her screen. "Since you know she made it, it's a hoot. But... I mean you can go try to track down Nurse Schoenfeld and get her to clear you. But I'd suggest something lighter. At least for now. And I'd guess you don't like enclosed spaces..."

"I don't mind if I know I can open the door, ma'am," Rusty said.

"Being on a small boat is physically wearing,"

the lady said, "but they need people for light clearance. Clearing life rafts and small craft. Not many people want to do it because you get beat up on those little boats. But..."

"Ma'am," Rusty said. "Being out in the air on a small boat... That'd be like heaven, ma'am."

"How strong of a stomach do you have?" the lady asked.

"I... pretty strong?" Rusty said.

"You're on the assignment board," the lady said, making a definitive tap on her keyboard. "Since you don't have a defined skill that anyone is looking for right now, you've got a week to find something. After that, you get put on boat cleaning or you can go into the hold with the lame and lazy. People who don't want to help out."

"Cleaning?" Rusty said.

"Cleaning up a boat after zombies have trashed it."

"I don't want to have to clean out a new boat," Sophia said, mulishly. "I've seen these boats. And I've cleaned them up. Rather get knocked around on a thirty-five."

Sophia "Seawolf" Smith was one of the founding members of the Wolf Squadron. As such, despite being fifteen, she was a shareholder and not a minor one, as well as being a member of the Captain's Board as skipper of the thirty-five-foot *Worthy Endeavor*. The boat had gotten beaten up by nearly six months at sea, not to mention the zombies that took it over, but it was still *her* boat.

"You won't," Fred said. "*You*, especially, won't."

Fred Burnell was the "Vessel Preparation and Assignments Officer" on the *Grace Tan*. The massive supply ship had an open center and rear deck. On it were, now, four "cabin cruiser" yachts on props in various stages of repair and refitting. Since all of them worked when they were brought alongside it was mostly a matter of cleaning them out.

"Things change," Burnell said. "We've got crews cleaning them up, now. But we're retiring the thirty-fives. They're just too small and don't have enough range."

"So, what am I looking at?" Sophia said.

"You don't remember me, do you?" Burnell said, smiling slightly.

"No," Sophia said, frowning. "Sorry. Should I?"

"No," Burnell said. "I guess seen one castaway, seen 'em all. The *Endeavor* plucked me off a life raft. So let's just say I owe you one even if you don't know it. There's a very nice 65' Hatteras Custom sitting out there. Not too beat up by zombies. The only ones on it were below, and we're changing out all the below materials. Good engines, low hours..."

"I appreciate it," Sophia said. "Sorry for snapping your head off."

"Not a problem," Burnell said. "Can't tell you

how happy I was when you blew that foghorn. Oh, you'll need two light clearance personnel and deck hands. Bigger boat."

"I guess I need to go do some scrounging," Sophia said. "What happens in the meantime?"

"Support for the clearance of the *Iwo Jima*," Burnell said. "I think you know how that works?"

"Hopefully better than the *Voyage*," Sophia said.

"Okay, okay, *seriously*?" Faith "Shewolf" Smith said. The thirteen-year-old had gotten her height from her father and it had kicked in young. Nearly six feet, slender and with some of the look of a female body-builder, her fine blonde hair was currently hanging limp and damp on her neck in the heat.

"You say that a lot," Sergeant Thomas Fontana replied.

The thirty-two-year-old black Special Forces sergeant had become fond of his . . . well he couldn't call her "protégé" since she'd taught *him* the ins and outs of close-quarters battle with infecteds. Partner was the right term but it was hard to apply to a thirteen-year-old girl, no matter how well she fought zombies.

"The middle of this ship is *missing*," Faith said, pointing pointedly. "There is a great big gaping hole in the *middle of this ship. Below* the waterline!"

The foursome were looking, in amazement in

Faith's case, at the USS *Iwo Jima*, an Amphibious Assault Carrier the size of a WWII "Fleet" carrier. The combination aircraft carrier, troop ship and floating dock, while not as big as the *Voyage Under Stars* was really, really big. Especially from the waterline looking into its cavernous well-deck.

"It's not missing," Fontana said. "It can't be missing if they never put anything there."

"That's the well-deck, Faith," her father said. Steven John Smith was six foot one, with sandy blond hair and a thin, wiry, frame. Although he was the putative commander of Wolf Squadron, so designated by the US Navy no less, he did clearance as well. They still had only four hard clearance personnel and he was good at it. Besides it burnished the reputation and this "squadron" was all about force of personality. "Obviously, it's where they pull landing craft in and out."

"That doesn't make it not nuts," Faith said. "I know nuts when I see nuts. Letting water into a ship? That's nuts."

"The good news is the well-deck *is* open," Smith said. "You don't have to climb a boarding ladder up to the flight deck."

"They dropped the stern gate when we abandoned ship, sir," Lance Corporal Joshua "Hooch" Hocieniec said.

Hocieniec completed the foursome that had only recently completed clearing the cruise liner *Voyage Under Stars*, listed as the world's second largest "super cruise liner." Larger than any passenger liner in history, it was best described as a floating Disneyland and just about as damned large. While the *Iwo* was big, as large as a WWII aircraft carrier and with much the same look, it wasn't the *Voyage*, thank God. The only larger ships on the ocean than the *Voyage* were supertankers, which had relatively small areas for zombies to inhabit and a supercarrier. God help them, the Hole was sort of hinting they'd like one of *those* cleared. Steve had flatly told them "Not until we've got *a lot* more Marines."

Hocieniec was the only survivor of the *Iwo* they'd picked up so far. There were sure to be more out there but all the life rafts from the amphibious assault ship found so far contained only the dead. And the few people picked up from the *Voyage* who might be potential reinforcements were still in too bad a condition to assist. With any luck there would be some Marines alive on the boat. They'd found that people were awfully inventive, given the slightest chance, at staying alive.

"And, look," Faith said, "a welcoming party."

Zombies, not so inventive. But very tenacious. It seemed like all zombies needed was fresh water. Which would seem in short supply at sea except their concept of "fresh" was about the same as a dog's. And if one died from the water quality, well, the survivors would just eat him or her.

Which was why there were at least thirty zombies waiting for them on the deck of a hover craft inside the ship. Which was more or less exactly where they were going to have to go. Fortunately, the stern gate was down and conditions were calm. Very calm.

The *Iwo Jima* had been, deliberately, "parked" in the Horse Latitudes zone of the Sargasso Sea. The Sargasso—the only sea not bounded by land—was surrounded by, but not affected by, the various currents of the North Atlantic. The Horse Latitudes were, in turn, a zone where there was always little to no wind and only very rare storms. They were the bane of early explorers of the Atlantic for the constant calm. They were called "the Horse Latitudes" because those were the latitudes where you had to eat the horses.

The combination, along with the somewhat entrapping sargassum weed that gave the region its name, meant that the assault ship was going to *stay* there. Except for the minor waves transmitted from distant storms, the area was pretty much flat calm, a nice change from the storm they'd left behind in Bermuda.

Since they'd gotten in contact with the Hole in Omaha, center for the Strategic Armaments Control, Wolf Squadron had found out that *most* Navy surface ships as well as many major commercial vessels had been similarly "parked" for the duration. The opinion of the "powers that be" prior to the Fall was that that way they'd be more or less impossible, or at least difficult, to find and they wouldn't be blown away by hurricanes or other storms. The commercial ships had apparently gone into the normally untraveled zone to avoid the Plague and have a place where they could maintain minimal power. As far as anyone knew, none of them had been uninfected.

On the horizon there was a supertanker full of Liberian crude. The normally empty zone was, relatively, chock with *big* ships full of H7D3 infected.

"You know," Faith said, musingly, "if we get this running we're going to have to rename it the *Galactica*, right?"

"Ouch," Fontana said. "Geek points galore."

"What?" Hooch said.

"Wait," Faith said. "Does that make the infected . . . wait for it . . . *Zylons*?"

"Ow!" Fontana said, snorting.

"With due respect, Staff Sergeant . . ." Hocieniec said. "What the *hell* are you talking about?"

"Shall I shoot the Zylons with my Barbie Gun?" Faith said, hefting a USCG M4.

Faith did not like the M4. Calling it a Barbie Gun was an indictment not a compliment. She also didn't like Barbie Dolls if for no other reason than her having a passing resemblance to the doll. Her main problem with the M4 came down to its round, the NATO 5.56mm.

It was hoary legend in the military that the 5.56 had been developed to wound the enemy so as to create a greater logistics burden on the enemy. The truth was that it was a light round with a high velocity, giving the M-16, the original of the M4, the ability to, ostensibly, fire accurately on fully automatic. The round also was light, permitting more of them to be carried by an infantry soldier as well as more moved logistically. And it, yes, did not "overkill" as had the previous .308 of the M14 much less the brute force .30-06 of World War II. It did *just enough* damage in the opinion of the technologist oriented defense department weenies and generals of the Vietnam era.

Faith's opinion could be summed up in one line, taken from a webcomic she'd enjoyed before the Plague: "There is no overkill. There is only 'Open fire' and 'Reloading.'" The first weapon she'd used for zombie clearance was a variant of the AK47 called a "Saiga" that fired 12-gauge shotgun shells. A zombie hit by a 12-gauge was not getting back up. When she ran out in a magazine and didn't have time to reload, she would switch to her H&K .45 USP. Zombies hit by .45 ACP also rarely stood back up. When they had run low on 12-gauge she had switched to her custom built AK firing the original 7.62X39 round, again a decent zombie killer.

When, desperate and with one of the largest cruise liners in the world still to clear, they had started using M4s and 5.56mm salvaged from a Coast Guard cutter, her normally sunny disposition had taken a downward turn. She disliked that she had to shoot zombies four or five times to get them to lie down and be good.

"Or we could use a, you know, machine gun," Fontana said.

"Ah," Faith said. "There's only like thirty of them. Back the *Toy* up to this tub and let's just shoot them off one by one."

"I thought you liked machine guns?" Fontana said.

"The whole belt fed is so last week," Faith said. "I still think it's a design flaw that you have to let up on the trigger."

"We're working on some you don't," Steve said.

"How?" Fontana said. "I mean, the only way to do that is coolant and . . ."

"Coolant," Steve said, nodding. "I've got the shop over on the *Grace* working on a water-cooled Browning."

"Doing the sleeve is going to be a bitch, sir," Hocieniec pointed out. "And that whole pump thing is . . ."

"Tech has changed remarkably since World War One, Hooch," Steve said, drily. "Think coiled copper tube and an electric pump. But that's for later. Shoot them off with aimed fire or break out the 240? As usual, I'm more worried about bouncers than anything. If we use the 240, even with these light rolls, we're going to have lots of bouncers."

"We could ask the *Dallas* to come up on it for us again," Faith said.

"That . . . Is not a bad idea," Steve said. The subs' hulls were made of thick, high-tensile steel, which was largely invulnerable to small arms fire.. "*Dallas*? You monitoring as usual?"

"*Wolf,* Dallas."

"Got a zombie entry problem again," Steve said. "You up for some kinetic clearance?"

"*We're out of seven six two, Wolf. Stand by…*"

"Standing by," Steve said.

"They floated theirs off for us," Fontana said. "Remember?"

"If it was during clearing the *Voyage*, the answer is 'It's all a blur,'" Steve said.

"*Wolf, bringing up the* Boise. *Be about twenty. You might want to clear your boats.*"

"Roger," Steve said. "Squadron Ops, you monitoring?"

"*Roger, Commodore. We'll send out the word.*"

"Get them well back and to the side," Steve said. "Five miles by preference. Stacey!"

"Moving!" Stacey Smith called. She put the *Tina's Toy* under full power and pulled away from the assault ship.

"Okay," Fontana said. "The *Dallas* has been in contact all along. Then the *Charlotte* tows the Coast Guard cutter down. Now it turns out the *Boise*'s out there. How many fricking fast attacks are around us?"

"Your continued buildup of nuclear vessels in this region proves that you have access to vaccine!"

General Marshall Sergei Kazimov was the

acting commander of Russian Strategic Forces or, as he frequently referred to it, Soviet Strategic Forces. He had bluntly stated that he was Chairman of the Soviet Union. Also that if the "renegade Anglo-Sphere forces" did not immediately "vaccinate all his crews" he would "turn all of America's cities to ash."

Every time he used the term "nuclear vessels," Frank Galloway, National Constitutional Continuity Coordinator, tried not to break into a hysterical giggle. The general had no capacity at all to pronounce the "v."

"Mister Smith has stated, and our *very few* naval personnel who have gone through vaccination and quarantine have confirmed, that there are less than forty units of primer and booster in Smith's control," Galloway stated, again. It was always this way negotiating with the Russians. You just repeated the truth until they either gave in or the truth changed. "Our nuclear wes... vessels in the area are purely for what support they can provide to Wolf Squadron's clearance operations..."

"You lie!" Sergei shouted. "Wolf lies!"

"I wish he did," Galloway said, sighing. "I wish that he could immediately begin production of the vaccine. But until he has more clearance personnel and can clear a land base with the right facilities, that's impossible..."

"You will provide us with the vaccine or I will blow you to *hell!*"

"And we shall retaliate," Galloway said, trying not to sigh this time. "With what we have left. Which is, Sergei, far, *far* more than *you* have. You *will* be dead, I *might* be dead, there will be some radioactive wastelands that used to be infected-filled cities and what's the point? Oh, yes, there is the point that right now, Wolf is the only chance we have to get the world back in shape . . . !"

"Thanks, *Boise*," Steve commed.

"You're welcome, Wolf Squadron," the *Boise's* commander replied. *"Please consider us for all your future kinetic clearance needs."*

The team had rigged up while the *Boise* was potting zombies at long range with their MG240 and they now approached the wash deck of the assault carrier in a center-console inflatable.

Rigged up has a special meaning when zombie fighting. Troops in combat just thought they rigged up. Then there was "extreme hazard close-quarters biological clearance."

Each of the foursome were wearing multiple layers of clothes, including fire-fighting bunker gear, respirators, helmets and so many weapons and clearance tools it would have been ludicrous if they hadn't proven, at least once, that all of it was necessary. Not a single square inch of skin was uncovered or was in any way, shape or form "biteable." It was hot, it was heavy and it was cumbersome. It was especially hot in the Horse Latitudes, which were well inside the tropical zone.

It also meant that, as Faith and Hooch had proven, you could be absolutely dogpiled by zombies and still keep fighting. Faith, in particular, added a knife whenever she found a good one.

"Everyone remember where we parked," Faith said, stepping off the inflatable.

"Everyone remember to *drink*," Fontana said. "And how come you get to make the first landing, again?"

"I'm the cute one," Faith said. "You coming or not?"

"Faith, we've got to explain some language to you," Fontana said.

"Oops, live one," Faith said, as a zombie came loping down the catwalk above. She fired, missed and fired again. The second round hit but the zombie just stumbled then resumed running in their direction.

"Fucking *Barbie* gun...!"

—end excerpt—

from *To Sail a Darkling Sea*
available in hardcover,
February 2014, from Baen Books

Andre Norton

"The sky's no limit to Andre Norton's imagination…a superb storyteller." —The New York Times

---

Time Traders　　　　　0-671-31829-2 ★ $7.99 PB
"This is nothing less than class swashbuckling adventure—the very definition of space opera." —*Starlog*

Time Traders II　　　　　0-671-31968-X ★ $19.00
Previously published in parts as *The Defiant Agents* and *Key Out of Time*.

Janus　　　　　0-7434-7180-6 ★ $6.99 PB
Two novels. On the jungle world of Janus, one man seeks to find his alien heritage and joins a battle against aliens despoiling his world.

Darkness & Dawn　　　　　0-7434-8831-8 ★ $7.99 PB
Two novels: *Daybreak: 2250* and *No Night Without Stars*.

Gods & Androids　　　　　0-7434-8817-2 ★ $24.00 HC
Two novels: *Androids at Arms* and *Wraiths of Time*.

Dark Companion　　　　　1-4165-2119-4 ★ $7.99 PB
Two complete novels of very different heroes fighting to protect the helpless in worlds wondrous, terrifying, and utterly alien.

Star Soldiers　　　　　0-7434-3554-0 ★ $6.99 PB
Two novels: *Star Guard* and *Star Rangers*.

Moonsinger　　　　　1-4165-5517-X ★ $7.99 PB
Two novels: *Moon of Three Rings* and *Exiles of the Stars*.

From the Sea to the Stars　　　　　1-4165-2122-4 ★ $15.00 TPB
Two novels: *Star Gate* and *Sea Siege*.

Star Flight　　　　　1-4165-5506-4 ★ $7.99 PB
Two novels: *The Stars Are Ours* and *Star Born*.　.

Crosstime　　　　　1-4165-5529-3 ★ $23.00 HC
Two novels: *The Crossroads of Time* and *Quest Crosstime*.

Deadly Dreams　　　　　978-1-4391-3444-3 ★ $7.99 PB
Two novels: *Knave of Dreams* and *Perilous Dreams*.
